Pacific Passages

Pacific Passages

An Anthology of Surf Writings

Edited by
Patrick Moser

UNIVERSITY OF HAWAI'I PRESS
Honolulu

© 2008 University of Hawai'i Press
All rights reserved
Printed in the United States of America
13 12 11 10 09 08   6 5 4 3 2 1

Library of Congress Cataloging-in-Publication Data
Pacific passages : an anthology of surf writing / edited, with
an Introduction and notes by Patrick Moser.
   p. cm.
Includes bibliographical references.
ISBN 978-0-8248-3155-4 (pbk. : alk. paper)
1. Surfing.   2. Surfing—Literary collections.
I. Moser, Patrick (Patrick J.), 1963–
GV840.S8P23   2008
797.32—dc22
                    2008005589

University of Hawai'i Press books are printed on acid-free
paper and meet the guidelines for permanence and
durability of the Council on Library Resources.

Designed and composited by Santos Barbasa Jr.

Printed by Versa Press

*This book is dedicated
to my longtime
surfing companions:
Steven Moser,
Carver, Greg Schneider,
and Jeff Tappan*

Contents

Part VI. What Is Surfing?   281

Acknowledgments

My deep appreciation to the writers who appear in this anthology, especially those who generously donated their work. Thanks also to the Bishop Museum, the University of Hawai'i Press, the *Honolulu Star-Bulletin*, and *Surfer* magazine.

I am greatly indebted to Nanea Armstrong, who freely gave her time to review and edit aspects related to Hawaiian language and culture, especially the material in Part I. My gratitude as well to the helpful and knowledgeable staff at the Bishop Museum Library and Archives: Patty Lei Belcher, Betty Kam, BJ Short, and DeSoto Brown. To the staff in the Olin Library at Drury University—Myrna Berry, Bill Garvin, Craig Smith, Steve Stoan, Tracy Sullivan, and especially Katherine Bohnenkemper and her student workers in Interlibrary Loan—for obtaining and processing hundreds of surfing-related books, videos, magazines, and articles for my courses on surf culture and for this anthology. My thanks also to Rita Fabin and her staff in Carbon Copy, to Charles Taylor and Drury University for their support of this project by providing travel funds to the Bishop Museum to conduct research. The Hawai'i Council for the Humanities provided much needed financial support for author permission fees.

To Georges Van Den Abbeele, friend and mentor, for his encouragement and his work with the Pacific Regional Humanities Center. The Humanities Center, in concert with Greenwood Press, published *The Pacific Region*, which includes an early version of the introduction that appears in this anthology.

Thanks to Carl W. Bell at Baylor University for sending me a copy of the original Jack London essay that appeared in *Lady's Home Companion*. To Kay Chubbuck for her helpful insights on Isabella Bird. To Gary Lynch for providing information on Tom Blake, and to Craig Lockwood for information on Tommy Zahn. To my friends and colleagues in the

Hawaiian Islands for their expertise in various aspects of surf history: Mark Fragale, Sandy K. Hall, and Tim DeLaVega. To Fenton Johnson at the University of Arizona for his astute suggestions on the introductions.

I am grateful to the Honors Program and my colleagues at Drury University for their support in allowing me to develop and teach a highly unusual course on the history and culture of surfing from which this anthology developed. My thanks also to my students who helped in the selection process. A big "thank you" to Aaron Scott for the long hours he spent formatting the anthology for the Honors course and for the proposal to the University of Hawai'i Press.

I benefited from the holdings of several libraries, including the Huntington, the University of Hawai'i at Manoa, the Bibliothèque Nationale in Paris, the British Museum in London, and the Los Angeles Public Library.

I am grateful to my editor at University of Hawai'i Press, Masako Ikeda, to David and Maria denBoer, to the Editorial Board at the University of Hawai'i Press, and to the helpful reviewers.

Finally, to my wife, Linda Trinh Moser, for her endless faith and support, and to my sons, Miles and Ryan, for their stoke.

Introduction

Surfriding has not changed much over the centuries. A surfer paddles a board out to the waves and rides back toward shore. Then does it again. Surfboards have become shorter and lighter, the addition of fins has improved maneuvering, but the basic procedure—with the exception of recent innovations in tow-in surfing—has remained the same for possibly a thousand years or more.

What have changed substantially over the centuries are the images—in the broad sense of representations—that have introduced this Oceanic sport to primarily Western audiences. First documented in the journals of Captain Cook's mariners, later in sketches that accompanied travel narratives to the Pacific, ultimately in photographs and film, surfriding has undergone transformations as diverse and complex as the cultures in whose records it appears. These surfriding images typically reveal more about the culture *imagining* (or imaging) than the culture *imagined* (or imaged).

One of the first written accounts of surfriding offers an example of this process. David Samwell, surgeon's mate aboard Captain James Cook's *Discovery*, made the following observation when the ship pulled into Kealakekua Bay in January 1779: "Thus these People find one of their Chief amusements in that which to us presented nothing but Horror & Destruction." Samwell categorized surfriding as an "amusement" because Europeans did not imagine that such activity could find a place within a larger spiritual belief system (as surfriding in fact did in Polynesia). His "Horror & Destruction" betrays land-based cultural values formed within a European tradition that associated the ocean—even water in general—with disease and death.[1] Witness the following words from pilgrim William Bradford's *Of Plymouth Plantation* (1620–1647) derived from this same tradition. Describing his group's first landing in the New World in 1620, Bradford wrote: "Being thus arrived in a good harbor, and brought safe to land, they fell upon their knees and blessed the God of Heaven, who had brought them over the vast and furious ocean, and delivered them from all the perils and miseries thereof, again to set their feet on the firm and stable earth, their proper element."[2]

Recognizing that Europeans considered land their "proper element" provides an initial context for understanding the stunning cultural differences perceived by Captain Cook's mariners. Surgeon's Mate William Ellis noted: "We never saw a people so active in the water, which almost seems their natural element." Surfriding in particular highlighted these differences as Hawaiians—described on this same trip as "almost amphibious"—were seen riding waves that Europe's hardiest seamen, in the words of David Samwell, "could look upon as no other than certain death." Fear and horror, astonishment and admiration: these were the contradictory responses associated with the first Western descriptions of surfriding.

And yet contradiction is to be expected. "The literature of encounter," note the editors of the South Seas anthology *Exploration & Exchange*, is "richly paradoxical."[3] Amid the most extreme observations of cultural difference, human affinity maintains its influence: "God of creation," wrote Corporal of Marines John Ledyard, commenting on the thousands of Hawaiians who streamed into Kealakekua Bay to greet Cook's ships, "these are thy doings, these are our brethern and sisters, the works of thy hands, and thou are not without a witness even here where for ages and perhaps since the beginning it has been hid from us, and though the circumstance may be beyond our comprehension let it not lessen the belief of the fact."[4] Ledyard's certainty of kinship with the Hawaiians contrasts strongly with the images proliferated by the next significant group of Westerners to impact surfriding: New England Protestant missionaries.

"Can these be human beings!" observed Hiram Bingham as members of the first missionary expedition to Hawai'i looked upon natives some forty years after John Ledyard.[5] Bingham's mission of making the "almost naked savages" worthy of Heaven involved transforming the image of surfriding and other native traditions that did not square with the religious and cultural values of the New Englanders. Although Bingham wrote an account of surfriding that showed his fascination with a surfboard "wrought exceedingly smooth, and ingeniously adapted to the purpose of gliding rapidly in the water," he nevertheless placed surfriding among those evils that degraded moral values and jeopardized souls. Bingham recorded the following incident where missionary-trained Hawaiian

Thomas Hopu became a *porte-parole* for Calvinist morality to the high chiefess Ka'ahumanu:

> *Kaahumanu*, though informed, at the same time, that the morrow was the Sabbath, and invited to attend public worship, went, the next morning, with *Taumuarii* [Kaumualii] to *Watiti* (Witete) [Waikīkī] and drew a great multitude after, to spend the Sabbath there playing in the surf. In the afternoon Messrs. Bingham and Thurston, and Hopoo [Thomas Hopu], followed them, and at evening proposed to preach to them, in case they desired to hear the word of God. They consented, and the Lord's prayer was expounded to them. *Kaahumanu* asked Hopoo what he meant by saying to one of her servants, in the morning, that if he did not keep the Sabbath, he would be burned. Hopoo had said to one of them, as they were going to their sports, that men who do not observe the Sabbath of the Lord, will go "*i ke ahi a roa*" (to the endless burning).[6]

By such means did the missionaries exert their influence to transform the image of surfriding, in this case for the Hawaiians themselves. By 1829 Bingham could look back upon the changes that had occurred during his first nine years on O'ahu and boast: "the slate, the pen, and the needle, have, in many instances, been substituted for the surf-board, the bottle, and the *hula*."[7]

The observations of Englishman William Ellis, one of the most knowledgeable missionaries in the Pacific (he had spent six years in the Society Islands before arriving in Hawai'i in 1822), also show the strong impact of the Protestants. Ellis commented that the decline of native traditions in Tahiti was "on no account, matter of regret." He added: "When we consider the debasing tendency of many, and the inutility of others, we shall rather rejoice that much of the time of the adults is passed in more rational and beneficial pursuits." Later, during a visit to the island of Hawai'i, Ellis passed an unusually quiet Sunday—"No athletic sports were seen on the beach; no noise of playful children, shouting as they gambol'd in the surf"—and he concluded: "It could not but be viewed as the dawn of a bright sabbatic day for the dark shores of Hawaii."[8]

The missionaries largely succeeded in transforming the image of surfriding for many native Hawaiians (Ka'ahumanu, de facto ruler of the Islands, converted to Christianity in 1825). Ellis's Western audience would have been a disappointment to him: his lengthy description of surfriding in *Narrative of a Tour through Hawaii* (1826) became the most popular reference for nineteenth-century travelers seeking to witness, even try for themselves, this exciting native sport. Ellis's vivid tableau ends with these stirring words: "but to see fifty or one hundred persons riding on an immense billow, half immersed in spray and foam, for a distance of several hundred yards together, is one of the most novel and interesting sports a foreigner can witness in the islands."

South Seas beachcomber and novelist Herman Melville was one of the first to draw upon Ellis's account and spin the image of surfriding away from Protestant mores and into the realm of adventure. Outside of Polynesian lore, Melville's novel *Mardi* (1849) was the first to fictionalize surfriding and tap into the inherent drama this novel sport held for Western readers. Subsequent travel writers proliferated images of the sport that became inseparable from the island experience itself. The same year *Mardi* appeared, Henry Augustus Wise offered a vignette of "island beauties" surfriding: the water was "their native element for grace and witchery," Wise wrote, "whilst cleaving the yielding fluid with rounded limbs and streaming tresses." Mark Twain and Charles Warren Stoddard added further exotic touches to surfriding's image. Twain described "naked natives, of both sexes and all ages, amusing themselves with the national pastime of surf-bathing." Stoddard painted the surf adventures of Kahēle, who "leaped to his feet and swam in the air, another Mercury, tiptoeing a heaven-kissing hill, buoyant as vapour, and with a suggestion of invisible wings about him." These and other writers portrayed the Islands as a tropical balm for the soul, a place of romance where one lived among strong and sensuous natives who followed no laws save those of nature. In more practical terms, Hawai'i was well on its way to wearing the crown of Pacific tourism, with surfriding one of its more precious jewels. Playing its role in an enduring social irony, surfriding—along with volcanoes, canoe rides, hula dances, eating *poi,* and visits to Captain Cook's last stand at Kealakekua Bay—became a draw for Westerners anxious to experience the remnants of a society that, along with most other Pacific Island cultures in the nineteenth century, their own society had put on the road to extinction.

Hawaiian myths, legends, and histories appear in print during this period, part of the complex missionary legacy that attempted both to banish traditional Hawaiian beliefs and record them for posterity. Under the guidance of Sheldon Dibble and the Lahainaluna School on Maui, native students Samuel Mānaiakalani Kamakau, David Malo, and S. N. Hale'ole sought out native informants beginning in the 1830s and recorded the stories and beliefs that formed part of traditional Hawaiian society. Their collective efforts were published in Dibble's *Ka Moolelo Hawaii* (1838) and also appeared in Hawaiian-language newspapers. Relying upon Kamakau and other native informants, Abraham Fornander completed his influential *An Account of the Polynesian Race: Its Origins and Migrations* (1879) and the *Fornander Collection of Hawaiian Antiquities and Folk-Lore* (1916–1920). In 1888 King David Kalākaua and Rollin M. Daggett published their collaboration, *The Legends and Myths of Hawaii: The Fables and Folk-Lore of a Strange People*. Within these and other works surfriding took its place in a broader Polynesian culture that was communal, hierarchical, animistic—and filtered either through the language and perspective of Westerners (like Fornander and Daggett), or through their religious and educational systems (like the Lahainaluna School). We have no written history of surfriding that is wholly "Polynesian" or "Hawaiian"; rather, we read traditions that have been recorded in Western languages, or if recorded in Hawaiian, then related by native Hawaiians trained in Western schools, nearly exclusively those established by missionaries. With that caveat, the myths and legends in this anthology present a native society in which surfriding was enjoyed by the entire community and the gods, celebrated in story, practiced for competition, and governed by sacred rituals. These images have added depth and breadth to surfriding, casting it back into a distant Pacific past where it served as catalyst for the actions of lovers, chiefs, divinities, and an entire world of beings who shifted between human and divine.

Perhaps the most prevalent image of surfriding to endure throughout the latter part of the nineteenth century held that, as Mark Twain commented in 1872, "none but natives ever master the art of surf-bathing thoroughly." We know that Westerners had tried surfriding at least as early as 1846, when scientist Chester S. Lyman visited Waikīkī and had "the pleasure of taking a surf ride towards the beach in the native style." Toward the end of the century, in 1890, Henry Carrington Bolton was "initiated in the mysteries of surf-riding" on the island of Ni'ihau. Bolton claimed that "for persons accustomed to bathing in the surf, the process is far less difficult than usually represented." Visitors to this same island had apparently been enjoying surfriding with the island's owners, the Sinclairs, ever since the 1860s, when the family had taken up the sport. And yet the belief that surfriding remained exclusively a native Hawaiian practice was generally accepted until Jack London arrived in the Islands and helped usher surfriding into the modern era of Westernized sports.

The heavy wooden board London paddled out at Waikīkī in the summer of 1907, the manner in which those around him rode waves that day (it is not clear whether London himself ever succeeded), certainly the "bull-mouthed breakers" themselves—none of these had changed substantially for the better part of a millennium. But as Hawai'i's political and social structures had Westernized during the nineteenth century, so followed suit its "national pastime" in the twentieth. London's article, "Riding the South Seas Surf" (1907), transformed the image of surfriding to coincide with Western individualism and a man-conquers-nature ethos that remain central to the sport's image today. London's dramatic narrative is the epitome of the anti-industrialism and anti-Victorianism among Americans that Jackson Lears analyzes in *No Place of Grace: Antimodernism and the Transformation of American Culture, 1880–1920.* London was among those who abandoned repressive Victorian values of the previous century and began to glorify "primitive" cultures and "the cult of the strenuous life" championed by President Theodore Roosevelt (1901–1909), which included an enthusiasm for sports. London wrote:

> It is all very well, sitting here in the cool shade of the beach; but you are a man, one of the kingly species, and what that Kanaka can do you can do yourself. Go to. Strip off your clothes, that are a nuisance in this mellow clime. Get in and wrestle with the sea; wing your heels with the skill and power that reside in you; bit the sea's breakers, master them, and ride upon their backs as a king should.

Pumping himself up for a surf session, London also glorified the Hawaiian as a "black Mercury"—"a man, a natural king, a member of the kingly species that has mastered matter and the brutes and lorded it over creation"— and in doing so transformed the native into a Western-style mythic hero whose "heels are winged, and in them is the swiftness of the sea." Regal, male, heroic: London sounded the trumpet of Westernization for surfriding, promoting the sport as a means of establishing a hyper-masculine dominance over nature. With London's seal of approval, the popularity of surfriding grew steadily in Hawai'i and Southern California over the next half century, a period that saw sports and outdoor activities like surfriding become a way not only to demonstrate one's masculinity but to build personal character and promote citizenship. The image of surfriding could not have been healthier when it ran head-on into California youth culture.

The most popular images of surfing today trace their origins back to the sport's sudden launch into mainstream culture in the late 1950s and early 1960s. By that time all of the elements that fueled the launch were in place: a large youth population in Southern California relatively well-off thanks to postwar prosperity, a fast-growing car culture that allowed easy access to surf spots along the coast, an established film industry close at hand, and a small but growing number of surf shops ready to provide the latest surfboard designs. Jack London's hyper-masculine mastery over the ocean and its waves gave way to the more frivolous world of Southern California teenagers; their dress, music, dances, language, cars, and general attitude all became irrevocably a part of surfing's image through popular novels, films, and music. The *Gidget* phenomenon, and songs by the Beach Boys and Jan and Dean, were the most iconic expressions of the sport's latest transformation.

Although low-budget surf films had been showing since the early 1950s, *Gidget* (1959) was the first film to capture surfing for a mainstream audience. Technicolor images of Southern California beaches, warm waves, and a carefree lifestyle struck a chord with audiences that has continued to amplify ever since. Kahuna, the main surf character in the film, signals a number of important trends taking place in surfing at the time. His Hawaiian name and beach shack on the shores of Southern California trace the historical link between the two surf cultures, with the latter gaining prominence after World War II. Kahuna portrays himself as a "beach bum" who lives to surf and "follow the sun"; he is antiestablishment, individualistic, strongly sexualized, and has an aura of danger about him, though he remains generally a positive figure. These basic qualities—some new, some familiar to surfing—essentially define the popular image of surfers today.

The Beach Boys had an equally strong impact on the popularity of surfing because they succeeded in associating the sport with the same idealized images used by nineteenth-century writers: romance, travel, adventure—open to all at the nearest beach. Fellow singers Jan and Dean and surf musician Dick Dale, along with a string of blockbuster *Beach Party* films that followed *Gidget*, reinforced Southern California as one big beach where young people rode waves, danced, and maneuvered more or less successfully through sexual escapades. As Hawai'i lent its exotic ambiance to nineteenth-century narratives, so Southern California in the latter half of the twentieth century became an inseparable part of surfing's new image. Mainstream advertisers soon appeared in newly formed magazines like *Surfer* (founded by John Severson in 1960) and began sponsoring surf contests to associate their products with fun in the sun. Surfing, for decades the recreation of a modest number of island enthusiasts along California's coastal fringe, suddenly transformed into a lifestyle that could be packaged and sold to middle America.

The proliferation of surfing in mainstream media created a unique figure in the history of the sport: the "surfer." *Gidget*'s Kahuna is the archetype, based on historical figures like Tom Blake, who transplanted the Hawaiian beachboy ideal to Southern California in the late 1920s and 1930s. What *The Wild One*'s Johnny Strabler (Marlon Brando) did for motorcycle riders in the 1950s, *Gidget*'s Kahuna (Cliff Robertson) accomplished for surfers in the 1960s. Hunter S. Thompson's *Hell's Angels* outlined the phenomenon: *The Wild One* "told the story that was only beginning to happen and which was inevitably influenced by the film. It gave outlaws a lasting, romance-glazed image of themselves, a coherent reflection that only a very few had been able to find in a mirror, and it quickly became the bike rider's answer to *The Sun Also Rises*."[9]

Before Kahuna, the idea of dedicating one's life to riding waves existed for at most a small group of people. Before Kahuna, surfing was an activity people did, it wasn't who they were or how they defined themselves. Among Hawaiians, surfing belonged to part of a larger experience and relationship with the ocean. And though Polynesian traditions record the exploits of many expert surfers, the sport would not have defined them socially in the sense that one could be designated an *ali'i* (chief) or *kahuna* (priest, craftsman, teacher) or *maka'āinana* (commoner). The concept of a person's identity being entirely constituted by riding waves is a Hollywood construction. In *Gidget*, Kahuna plays a role that he himself admits is fabricated, confirmed by his destruction of the beach shack at the end of the film and his return to society as an airplane pilot. Even Kahuna was not a "surfer" (or "surf bum" in his words). And yet the image, once created, has proliferated in the popular imagination.

And this image has changed over the decades. In the late 1950s and early 1960s, the surfer image established by Cliff Robertson in *Gidget* (1959) and Frankie Avalon in *Beach Party* (1963) followed the dark, leading-man looks of Elvis Presley and Marlon Brando. In the 1970s and 1980s, following surfing's integration with the drugs, long hair, and mysticism of West Coast counterculture, the surfer image shifted to figures like Jeff Spicoli (Sean Penn) in *Fast Times at Ridgemont High* (1982) and Bodhi (Patrick Swayze) in *Point Break* (1991). Despite differences in their physical appearance from Kahuna, the sandy-brained doper (Spicoli) and the bank-robbing adrenaline junkie (Bodhi) share an important quality with their big-screen predecessor: they all live to ride waves.

The past several decades have seen a number of layers added to the image of both surfing and surfers, some of them in direct response to Hollywood fictions. In the mid-1970s, a contingent of Australians, South Africans, and Hawaiians created the first international circuit of surf contests, promoting a new "professional" side of surfing that they hoped would provide a respectable image for the sport. Their efforts have largely succeeded—though in terms of the professional image more so abroad than in the United States—with a small percentage of surfers today earning six-figure salaries in sponsorship and prize money. The Surfrider Foundation, established in 1984, ushered in a new era of surfers acting en masse as environmentalists and social activists. In the early 1990s, surfing became linked to "extreme" sports: big-wave riders using personal water craft and towropes to pull their partners into enormous waves previously considered unridable. Tow-in surfing has altered fundamental conditions and images of surfing so radically—transforming an individual sport into a team endeavor and substituting human paddling with a gasoline-powered engine—that some surfers question whether tow-in surfing qualifies as surfing at all.

Surfing's image received another jolt in the early 1990s, when William Finnegan published "Playing Doc's Games" in the *New Yorker*, a two-part article describing surf life in San Francisco and Finnegan's embattled relationship with surfing. Finnegan's superb writing and the *New Yorker*'s cultural cachet combined to boost the sport's prominence and provide inspiration to writers as they reformulated their ocean experiences into the language of literature. Thomas Farber's *On Water* (1994) and Daniel Duane's *Caught Inside: A Surfer's Year on the California Coast* (1996) continued to plumb surfing's depths while evoking themes similar to those of Finnegan: sounding the ultimate value of a pursuit considered "non-productive" by society even as its mastery requires an enormous investment of time and energy. The superficial image of surfing established in the late 1950s is clashing evermore with the pursuit that many writers have come to articulate as a formative part of their identities.

So surfing has a history, transmitted through images that have a history themselves and that change over time. Tracking these images through Polynesian and Western cultures allows us insight into the values and ideals of these cultures, how each culture transforms surfing based on those values and ideals, and how surfing—while transforming cultures itself—has shown an amazing ability throughout the centuries to survive, adapt, and prosper.

Surfriding and Surfing

As images of surfing have a history, so too the terms used to describe the sport. *Surfriding* has been selected for the title of Part I and throughout the early chapters of the anthology for several reasons. Mostly archaic, the term is nevertheless useful in characterizing the general act of riding waves with a board in any position: prone, kneeling, standing, or any combination of these. Many early narratives like those from Cook's third voyage do not specify the natives actually standing on their boards (what we would call surfing today). The mariners used a variety of expressions to explain what they saw—*diversion, amusement, playing in the surf*—which could encompass any manner of riding waves. The first description that notes natives standing on surfboards occurs in James Morrison's narrative on Tahitians, witnessed sometime in the years 1788–1789. This does not mean that Hawaiians were not standing on their boards when Cook visited, only that the Westerners did not specify as much. This is the case in many descriptions throughout the nineteenth century as well, and thus *surfriding* seems to be the more appropriate term for that era.

Surfriding and *surfrider* also hold the honor of being the terms in longest continual use to describe the act of riding waves and those who ride them. The former appears for the first time apparently in Edward T. Perkins's *Na Motu: or, Reef-Rovings in the South Seas* (1854). Describing his experience in the waves on Maui with a group of "about twenty girls, of various ages, and a dozen boys," Perkins wrote: "the art of surf-riding is not so simple as it would seem."[10] Because the verb *to surf* had not yet come into usage in the sense of "to ride waves," Perkins wrote that he "sported" in the waves" for about fifteen minutes until he wiped out: "a roller caught me as it broke, and wrenching the board from my hands, whirled me along in every conceivable attitude; and on recovering from the shock, I was compelled to abandon my aquatic sports for the remainder of the day." Perkins was not actually surfing in the sense we would use the word today (again, standing on a board), but rather body boarding or boogie boarding. And so *surfriding* is indeed the appropriate term in this case. Other terms in use during this period that have subsequently died out are *surf swimming, surf playing,* and *surf-bathing.* (This last term was used by Mark Twain.) *Surf-riding* still appears in contemporary book titles such as O. B. Patterson's *Surf-Riding: Its Thrills and Techniques* (1960), Arthur H. Klein's *Surf-Riding* (1972), and Wayne Warwick's *A Guide to Surfriding in New Zealand* (1978).

The word *surf-rider* first appears apparently in Reverend Henry T. Cheever's *Life in the Sandwich Islands: or, The Heart of the Pacific, as it Was and Is* (1851). "In this consists the strength of muscle and sleight-of-hand," observed Cheever, "to keep the head and shoulders just ahead and clear of the great crested wall that is every moment impending over one, and threatening to bury the bold surf-rider in its watery ruin." The term did not catch on—other period descriptions included *surf swimmer* or *surf-board swimmer*, and *surf-bather*—until Kalākaua and Daggett published "Kelea, The Surf-Rider of Maui" in 1888, and then both *surf-rider* and *surf-riding* became the most prevalent terms. But again, the descriptions in this period are not always clear whether the surfriders are in fact standing on the surfboard. (On a side note, the earliest usage of *surf-board* appears in the diary of Ebenezer Townsend, who landed in the Hawaiian Islands aboard a sealing ship in August 1798: "They sometimes make use of surf-boards," wrote Townsend. "The surf-board is about their own length and floats them lighter."[11]) *Surfrider* is still used today in such names as the Surfrider Foundation (1984) and Matt Warshaw's *Surfriders: In Search of the Perfect Wave* (1997).

Surfing and *surfer* appear only in the twentieth century and—when the terms are used by themselves—indicate the act of standing on a surfboard, or one who stands on a surfboard. Any other positions on a board today either have different names (*kneeboarding, kneeboarder; boogie boarding, boogie boarder*) or are somehow qualified: *windsurfer, kitesurfer, tow-in surfer*. *Surfing* appears apparently for the first time in a *Hawaiian Gazette* article (December 8, 1905) as a translation for the Hawaiian *heʻe nalu*. A sled and small surfboard (used for surfing) thought to be nearly three hundred years old and belonging to a Hawaiian chiefess named Kaneamuna were found in a cave at Hoʻokena, Hawaiʻi. Alexander Hume Ford appears to be the first to use the term *surfer* in a letter requesting support for the proposed Outrigger Canoe Club (letter dated April 7, 1908). The letter stated: "The main object of the club being to give an added and permanent attraction to Hawaii and make Waikiki always the Home of the Surfer, with perhaps an annual Surfboard and Outrigger Canoe Carnival which will do much to spread abroad the attractions of Hawaii, the only islands in the world where men and boys ride upright upon the crests of the waves."[12] The association of "Surfer" with riding "upright on the crests of the waves" established the term as one used exclusively for those who stand on surfboards. In his later article for *Paradise of the Pacific*, "Aquatic Sports" (1908), Ford used both *surfer* and *surf-rider* (as well as *surfing*) and the names became commonly interchangeable through the 1950s. In his *California Surfriders* (1946), Doc Ball selected the terms *surfer, surfrider, surfboarder*, as well as *surfing* and *surfboarding*. Tommy Zahn used *surfboarding* in his 1954 article (see Part III) to describe what we would call paddleboarding today. Because *surfer* and *surfing* have become the dominant terms since the 1960s, and because the majority of texts in the concluding chapters refer explicitly to standing on surfboards, the terms *surfer* and *surfing* are used in reference to these texts rather than the outdated and more encompassing terms *surfrider* and *surfriding*.

Order, Dating, and Selection of Texts

Although all of the texts in Part I were written after the first Western accounts of surfriding in Part II, the Polynesian myths, legends, chants, and proverbs open the anthology because they form part of an oral tradition that predates the Western texts. Surfriding developed most fully in Polynesia, and so it is appropriate that Polynesian texts hold this place of honor.

The texts in Part II appear chronologically from when the authors actually witnessed surfriding (when this has not been possible to determine, the year of publication is used). Part of this anthology's purpose is to track surfriding's ebb and flow through the centuries; knowing when (and if possible where) surfriding actually occurred helps to establish this continuum. The period between Hiram Bingham's departure from Hawai'i in 1840 and the revival at Waikīkī in the early twentieth century has been an especially obscure chapter in surf history. The handful of selections from these decades helps to illuminate surfriding's continued existence and thus belie such often-quoted misrepresentations of the sport as the following by G. W. Bates: "Of the numerous national games and amusements formerly practiced by the Hawaiians, surf-bathing is about the only one which has not become extinct. Lahaina is the only place on the group where it is maintained with any degree of enthusiasm, and even there it is rapidly passing out of existence" (*Sandwich Island Notes*, 1854). Down but not out, surfriding maintained its presence in the outlying regions where most Western visitors did not venture.

The remaining parts follow a roughly chronological order (with dates corresponding to year of publication) and present texts that capture the most significant trends in surf culture over the past century. Due to space limitations, many writings had to be omitted from the final version; the most important of these are referenced in the annotated bibliography.

Two main criteria determined the selection of texts: historical importance and quality of writing. Although native Polynesian views appear throughout, the majority of texts present surfriding from a Western perspective. Some accounts will complement one another; others will offer contrasting views and opinions. Such positioning allows this anthology to serve as a starting point for further inquiry into the many historical and cultural images that have surrounded surfriding. Finally, because of the enormous amount of material published about surfing since the 1960s, the choice of texts—save seminal works like *Gidget* or *The Pump House Gang*—to represent this most recent era becomes largely subjective.

Nevertheless, one could hardly hope to find a more authoritative or articulate group of voices in the latter chapters. Once again, embedded in the final selection is the hope of inspiring continued conversations about a social activity that has been the catalyst for so much reflection and debate over the centuries.

Hawaiian Spelling

Diacritical marks have been added to Hawaiian words and Hawaiian names in the editor's introductions to reflect contemporary usage. Works published before this usage became current have been reproduced in their original form.

Part I

Surfriding in Polynesian Culture

Myths, Legends, Chants, and Proverbs

Polynesian mythology encompasses legends of the most sacred divinities, stories of the highest chiefs, and the everyday folk wisdom of the common people. In song, in dance, in stories of lovers lost and found, surfriding weaves its way through these traditions and plays its own distinctive role in the life of the Pacific.

Kelea, and the version of Lāʻie-i-ka-wai presented here, highlight surfriding's most pervasive role in Polynesian mythology: a catalyst for love and desire. Riding waves provides an ideal opportunity for native men and women to intermingle in the surf and demonstrate their beauty and skill to one another. As we will discover, it also provides opportunities for deception. Upon seeing the interloper Hala-aniani "poised with great skill" on the crest of a wave, for example, Lāʻie-i-ka-wai yields to his "seductive fascination." Such scenes are repeated time and again in Hawaiian lore, from the story of the two Kauaʻi princesses, Hoʻoipo and Hinaʻūʻū, who "immediately fell in love with Moʻikeha" as he was surfriding, to the tale of the princess Kolea-moku whose desire suddenly piques when she sees that the prince, Kiha-a-Piʻilani, is a "fine looking man, and that he was an expert surf-rider."[1] According to Hawaiian historian Samuel M. Kamakau, chiefs and commoners enjoyed surfriding so much not only because it showed "which man or which woman was skilled," but also "which man or woman was the best looking."[2]

The two tales by William Westervelt demonstrate that seduction in the surf extends to Hawaiian *ʻaumakua* (guardian gods) and *kupua* (part-human, part-divine beings). Depending on their fickle moods, divinities can either protect natives in the waves or lure them away. The broader tradition records the adventures of the young Kauaʻi chief Puna-ʻai-koaʻe ("Puna tropic-bird eater") who sees the *moʻo* goddess Kiha-wahine disguised as a beautiful woman and falls in love with her at Waikīkī. Assuring Puna-ʻai-koaʻe she knows the location of better waves, Kiha-wahine paddles him all the way to Molokaʻi, where they live happily in her cave until he—like Kelea—once again hears the call of the surf.[3] For Puna-ʻai-koaʻe, Kelea, the Kauiʻi prince Ka-hiki-lani (in Clarice B. Taylor's "Faithless Lover Is Turned to Stone") and countless others, desire for the opposite sex directly competes with the equally strong desire to ride waves.

Mele inoa, or name chants, are the most common songs to include reference to surfriding. They honor the skill of chiefs and kings, they evoke the beauty and drama of the waves themselves, and, in the many repetitions of specific locales and generational ancestors, they emphasize the enormous importance of place and parentage in Polynesian culture. Mary Kawena Pukui's translation of the "Name Chant for Naihe" is the closest surfriding comes to having an epic poem, a six-part *mele inoa* that both glorifies Kane and the many surf breaks he visits, and honors the island progenitors Wākea and Papa from whom all Hawaiians trace their lineage.

Several of the selections in this part of the book were originally gathered from native informants and published in the latter half of the nineteenth century, a time when the Hawaiian race was threatened with extinction and a certain urgency compelled native and non-native historians to gather as much information as possible on traditional beliefs. Others represent more contemporary expressions of a thriving oral tradition: myth and song that celebrate surfriding and draw upon its inherent adventure and possibilities for intrigue. As surfriding continues to grow in popularity around the world, these stories ancient and modern reinforce its deep roots in the island cultures where surfriding was born and nurtured.

CHAPTER 1

"Kelea-nui-noho-'ana-'api'api" (1865)

Samuel Mānaiakalani Kamakau

1815–1876

Samuel Mānaiakalani Kamakau is one of several native historians whose invaluable writings have preserved much Hawaiian history during a period of dramatic change. Learned in the traditional Hawaiian culture into which he was born and the new Western education that arrived with the missionaries in 1820, Kamakau began actively to record native history beginning in the 1830s under the guidance of the missionary Sheldon Dibble at Lahainaluna School on Maui. His publications, predominantly appearing in Hawaiian-language newspapers, include *Ruling Chiefs of Hawaii* (1961), *Ka Po'e Kahiko: The People of Old* (1964), *The Works of the People of Old: Nā Hana a ka Po'e Kahiko* (1976), and *Tales and Traditions of the People of Old: Nā Mo'olelo a ka Po'e Kahiko* (1991). Along with his work as historian, Kamakau taught at Lahainaluna and served several terms in the Hawaiian legislature.

The story of Kelea is among the most well known, and most often repeated, Hawaiian legends connected with surfriding. It first appears in English in Abraham Fornander's *An Account of the Polynesian Race* (1878), the outline of which is based upon the present version by Kamakau. The story surfaces ten years later in *The Legends and Myths of Hawai'i: The Fables and Folk-lore of a Strange People* by King David Kalākaua and Rollin M. Daggett, then again in 1900 in Charles M. Skinner's *Myths & Legends of Our New Possessions & Protectorate* and in Alexander Twombley's novel *Kelea: The Surf-Rider: A Romance of Pagan Hawaii*. Cora Wells Thorpe picks up the legend once more in *In the Path of the Tradewinds* (1924), as does the *Hawaiian Almanac and Annual* (1931). Part of the reason for the legend's popularity is Kelea herself, a strong and beautiful figure whose skill in the surf is only matched by her willfulness on land.

KELEA-NUI-NOHO-'ANA-'API'API was a beautiful chiefess with clear skin and sparkling eyes. Her hair fluttered like the wings of the *ka'upu* bird, and so she was called Kelea-nui-noho-ʻana-ʻapiʻapi, Great-Kelea-Who-Flutters. She was the sister of Kawaukaohele [Kawaokaohele], the *mōʻī* of Maui.* Surfing was her greatest pleasure. She lived at Hamakua-poko and Kekaha and at Wailuku, surf riding with all the chiefs.

When Lō Lale was the chief of Līhuʻe on Oʻahu, he sent some chiefs on a search for a wife for himself. The canoe expedition in search of a wife set out from Waiʻalua, circled Molokaʻi without finding a wife, circled Lanaʻi without finding a wife, and set out to circle Maui in search of a wife. When the chiefs reached Hana, they heard of Kelea, the beautiful chiefess who was the sister of Kawaokaohele. She was living at Hamakua-poko because of the surf riding there, reveling in the curling breakers of the midmorning when the sea was smooth and even. She enjoyed surfing so much that at night she dwelt upon the morrow's surfing and awakened to the murmuring of the sea to take up her board. The early morning, too, was delightful because of its coolness, and so she might go at dawn.

When the wife seekers heard these words about Kelea, they decided to obtain her as wife for their master and quickly got ready to leave Hana. The *kamaʻaina*** residents tried to make them stay a little longer, but they would not listen. When they drew close to Hamakuapoko, they saw many people ashore, and when Kelea saw them her countenance faded at being seen by these strangers, and her heart throbbed. But she heeded their voices inviting her to board the canoe and showed herself to be the unsurpassed one of east Maui. The men said, "O Chiefess, ride ashore on the canoe." She agreed—perhaps because of the glance of one of them. They were all "soaring *ʻiwa* birds," constantly moving on the shifting billows of the ocean, bronzed and reddened of cheek by high seas. The chiefess did not know that this was a "wife-snatching" canoe, *he waʻa kaʻili wahine.*

The first time, they rode a wave ashore, and a second time, they rode a wave ashore, but the third time, there was a dashing away to vanish at sea, "*ua hiki mai o Pupuhi ma*" ["blown away" has arrived]. Those who searched for them found nothing; they searched on Hawaiʻi, Oʻahu, and Kauaʻi without finding a thing.

When Kelea was landed at Waiʻalua, she was quickly taken up to Lihuʻe and became the wife of the Lo chief of Lihuʻe, Lo Lale. They had three children, Kaholi-a-Lale, Luli-wahine, and Luli-kane. They were among the ancestral chiefs of Oʻahu as you shall see later.

---

* *mōʻī:* a king or principal chief.
** *kamaʻāina:* a longtime resident (lit. "child of the land").

After living with her husband in the uplands of Lihuʻe for ten years, Kelea asked him to let her go down to the seashore of ʻEwa to go sightseeing. He agreed to her request and said, "You may go. Living on our inland land is dejecting—there is only the scent of *kupukupu* ferns and *nene* plants here."

Aloha koʻu hoa i ka puʻali,	Farewell, my companion of this restricted place,
I ka wai o Pohakea	Of the water of Pohakea
He luna o Kanehoa.	Above Kanehoa.
He lai ʻino o Maunauna . . .	The brow of Maunauna is stormy . . .
O Lihuʻe ke hele ia!	She leaves Lihuʻe!
Honi aku i ke ala o ka mauʻu,	Sniff the scent of the grasses,
I ke ala o ke kupukupu,	The fragrance of the kupukupu ferns,
E lino ʻia ʻana e ka Waikoloa,	That are twisted about by the Waikola wind,
E ka makani he Waiʻopua la,	By the Waiʻopua wind,
Kuʻu pua!	My flower!
Me he pula la i kuʻu maka,	As though a mote were in my eye,
Ka ʻoni i ka haku ʻonohi;	The pupil is disturbed;
Ka wailiʻu i kuʻu maka e.	Salty tears fill my eyes.
E auwe! Auwe!	I grieve! I grieve!

Kelea went down to the plain of Ke-ahu-moa, to the rushing waters of Waipahu, to the "hand-holding" sands of ʻEwa-uli. Beautiful was the view of the channels of Puʻuloa. When she and her traveling companions reached Halawa, she inquired of them, "What is the place before us like? Is it as nice as the places we have passed through in coming this far?" Her companions answered, "Yes, even more so. It is dense with *kou* and coconut trees, and it is also a place where one may watch the chiefs enjoying surfing." When Kelea heard the word "surfing," desire rose in her, for surfing had been her favorite pastime. She said to her companions, "Let us continue our sightseeing and go to see the place that you two speak of." They answered, "If it is your wish that we go, then that is what we shall do. You are the one whose sightseeing journey this is, and we two are merely to accompany you. That was the command of your husband to us."

They went along until they entered the coconut grove of Kawe-hewehe in Waikiki. The *kamaʻaina* of the place saw this beautiful woman and welcomed her and shook down coconuts for the three to eat. They asked, "Where are you from? And where are you going?" "We have come from ʻEwa from the upland of Lihuʻe because we wanted to go sightseeing. This is the most pleasant place we have seen." The *kamaʻaina* said, "This is a place for enjoyment. Over there is the kou grove of

Kahaloa where one may view the surfing of the chiefs and of the *ali'i nui** Kalamakua."

Joyful at the thought of surfing, Kelea said to her companions, "Let us go on." They entered the *kou* grove of Kahaloa and watched the chiefs surfing in. Kelea inquired of the *kama'aina*, "Is it possible to obtain a surfboard for the asking?" "*Ka!* Are you skilled at surfing?" "Who would not be if one had a board?" retorted Kelea. When the *kama'aina* heard these words, they were astonished; those of Lihu'e were accustomed to slicing *mo'okilau* ferns and *popolo* stalks, but of surf riding these people knew nothing. The *kama'aina* thought that Kelea had been born at Lihu'e; they did not know she came from Maui.

The *kama'aina* said that a surfboard could readily be obtained. So she asked them for a board, and perhaps because she was so beautiful a woman, someone gave her one. When she received it, she went to the edge of the sea and rubbed off the red dirt of 'Ewa from her feet so as to look fresh. When she had finished, she dipped into the sea, then jumped upon her board and paddled off like an expert. Those who were watching saw that she managed her board like one trained, moving along easily and noiselessly without the least heeling over.

When Kelea reached the place where the surf broke, she left that place to the *kama'aina* and paddled on out to wait for a wave to rise. As she floated there, the first wave rose up but she did not take it, nor did she take the second or third wave, but when the fourth wave swelled up, she caught it and rode it to shore. As she caught the wave, she showed herself unsurpassed in skill and grace. The chiefs and people who were watching burst out in cheering—the cheering rising and falling, rising and falling.

While Kelea was surfing, the chief Kalamakua was working in his fields. When he heard those loud shouts he was startled and asked his men, "What is that shouting reverberating from the seashore?" "It is probably because of a skilled woman surfer," they answered. The chief remembered the chiefess of Maui, Kelea. He left off his work and went to stand on the shore to watch. As Kelea rode in on a wave, the *mo'i* ran to the edge of the sea and stood there. When the chiefess reached the sand, he took hold of her board and asked, "Are you Kelea?" "Yes," she answered. She stood up, naked. The *mo'i* removed his *kihei* shoulder covering and wrapped it around her as a *pa'u*** and took her to a *kapu* place. That was the beginning of her life as the *ali'i wahine mo'i* and she married (*ho'ao mare*) the *mo'i* Kalamakua.

---

* *ali'i nui:* high chief.
** *pā'ū:* a woman's skirt.

CHAPTER 2

"The Story of Laie-i-ka-wai" (1888)

King David Kalākaua
1836–1891

Roland M. Daggett[4]
1831–1901

The following excerpt derives from a popular romance that follows the adventures of twin sisters—Lāʻie-i-ka-wai ("Lāʻie in the water") and Lāʻie-lohelohe ("the drooping pandanus vine")—who must be separated and hidden at birth to protect them from a father who has vowed to let no daughters live until his wife bears him a son. The sisters, ultimately unsuccessful at securing royal husbands who are faithful to them, eventually end their days being worshipped as goddesses. Martha Beckwith categorizes the story of Lāʻie-i-ka-wai as "romantic fiction," a genre whose protagonist is invariably a woman in search of a man of the right rank with whom to bear a son. The magical realm of Pali-uli ("green cliff") described in the story is the most famous of the floating islands that appear in Hawaiian mythology, an "earthly paradise of the gods" that floats in the clouds above the islands.[5]

THE KING AND QUEEN OF KAUAI both dying a short time after the events just before recorded, they left the sovereignty of the island to their son, Ke-kalukalu-o-ke-wa. They also left in his charge a magical bamboo (ohe) called Kanikawi, and enjoined upon him a promise to seek out and marry Laie-i-ka-wai of whom many reports had reached Kauai.

The new king ordered an immense fleet of canoes for his trip to Hawaii, and sailed in the month of *Mahoemua*, or August. At Makaha-naloa he saw the rainbow over Keaau, and sailed thither. Waka foresaw his coming and advised Laie-i-ka-wai to marry him and become the queen of the whole island.

After waiting four days Laie-i-ka-wai and her *kahu*,* the hunch-

---

* *kahu:* guardian; nurse.

back, went down to Keaau, and watched the king and his two favorite companions sporting in the surf. They knew the king by his not carrying his own surf-board when he landed. She returned to Paliuli and informed Waka that she would accept him for a husband.

Waka then arranged that Ke-kalukalu-o-ke-wa should go at sunrise the next morning and play in the surf alone; that a dense fog should settle down, under cover of which Laie-i-ka-wai would join him in the surf; that when the fog raised the two would be seen by all riding in together on the same roller, and then they were to touch noses. A fog would again envelop them, and then birds would bear the pair to Paliuli. She was forbidden to speak to any one after leaving the house.

Now, it appears that Hala-aniani, a young man of Puna, noted for his debaucheries, had often seen Laie-i-ka-wai at Keaau, and ardently longed to possess her. Learning that she was about to marry the king of Kauai, he implored his sister, Malio, to exert her magical powers on his behalf. She consented, and by her direction they both went to sleep, and when they awoke related to each other their dreams. She dreamed that she saw a bird building a nest and leaving it in the possession of another, which was a sure omen in favor of Hala-aniani. Malio declared that her magical powers would prevail over those of Waka, and gave her brother minute instructions, which he strictly observed, as will appear.

They went to the beach and saw Ke-kalukalu-o-ke-wa swimming alone in the surf. Soon the fog of Waka settled down on the land. A clap of thunder was heard as Laie-i-ka-wai reached the surf. A second peal resounded, invoked by Malio. The fog lifted, and three persons instead of two were seen in the surf. This was noted with surprise on shore.

When the first roller came the king said, "Let us go ashore," and he rode in on the breaker with Laie-i-ka-wai, while Hala-aniani remained behind. At that moment the king and his companion touched noses. Three times they rode in on the waves, while Hala-aniani, as directed by his sister, remained outside among the rollers.

The fourth time Laie-i-ka-wai asked the king why he desired to repeat the sport so often. "Because," said he, "I am not used to the short surf; I prefer to ride on the long rollers." The fifth was to be the last time for the Kauai king and his promised bride.

As soon as the two started for the shore Hala-aniani seized Laie-i-ka-wai by the feet and held her back, so that the surf-board slipped from her grasp, and Ke-kalukalu-o-ke-wa was borne to the shore without her. She complained of the loss of her surf-board, and it was restored to her.

Hala-aniani persuaded her to swim farther out to sea with him, telling her not to look back, as he would let her know when they reached *his* surf. After swimming for some time she remonstrated, but he induced her to continue on with him. At last he told her to look back.

"Why," said she, in amazement, "the land is out of sight, and Ku-mukahi, the sea-god, has come to stir the waves!"

"This is the surf of which I told you," he replied; "we will wait and go in on the third roller. Do not in any case let go of your surf-board."

Then he prayed to his patron deity, and the breakers began to rise. As the third came thundering on, he exclaimed, "*Pae kaua!*" ["Let us ride to shore!"] and, mounting the roller, they started for the shore. Laie-i-ka-wai was in the overhanging arch of the wave, and, looking up, saw Hala-aniani poised with great skill on the crest. At that moment she began to yield to the seductive fascination of Hala-aniani.

As they came in, Waka supposed her companion to be Ke-kalu-kalu-o-ke-wa, and she sent down the birds in the fog; and when it cleared away Laie-i-ka-wai and Hala-aniani were occupants of the feather-house at Paliuli, where their union was consummated.

Waka wondered why her granddaughter did not come to her that night or the next day, as had been promised, and the day following she went to the house to learn if anything serious had happened. Laie-i-ka-wai and her husband were sleeping soundly. Waka was enraged, for the man was not the one she had selected.

Waking her granddaughter and pointing to the man, she exclaimed, "Who is this?"

"Ke-kalukalu-o-ke-wa," was the answer.

"No," returned Waka; "this is Hala-aniani, the brother of Malio!"

Angered at the deception, Waka declared that she would deprive Laie-i-ka-wai of her powers and privileges, and desired never to behold her face again.

CHAPTER 3

"A Surfing Legend" (1913)

William Westervelt
1849–1939

Reverend William Westervelt first came to Hawaiʻi from Chicago in 1889 to study mission work. He settled in the Islands permanently ten years later and studied Hawaiian language, history, and mythology. Numerous collections resulted from his research, including *Legends of Old Honolulu* (1915), *Legends of Gods and Ghosts* (1915), and *Hawaiian Historical Legends* (1923).

The following legend presents a typical form of human transfiguration that occurs in Hawaiian tradition with heroes who are part human, part divine. These supernatural figures are known as *kupua*. Their god nature, writes Martha Beckwith, "is likely to be derived from some animal ancestor whose spirit enters the child at birth."[6] *Kupua* often display special skills that allow them to overcome adversaries in various physical contests or the popular Hawaiian tradition of riddling matches. The story of the chiefess Māmala describes specifically her talents riding the largest waves of Honolulu. Following her *kupua* nature, Māmala takes on the particular form of the *moʻo*, or water spirits, who were worshipped in the Islands. According to Samuel M. Kamakau, these spirits could appear in a number of different forms, including sharks or lizards colored pitch-black who had "extremely long and terrifying bodies." People worshipped them, Kamakau explains, because "they were the guardians who brought the blessing of abundance of fish, and of health to the body, and who warded off illness and preserved the welfare of the family and their friends."[7]

The story of Māmala is a reminder of how human and divine figures regularly intermingle in the traditional Hawaiian belief system, and how gods and goddesses become associated with particular island locales. Māmala Bay on the south side of Oʻahu, and Waikīkī in particular, are ancient surfriding spots that have much lore connected with riding their waves. And as with the following tale, riding waves often goes hand in hand with finding and losing lovers.

HONOLULU WAS RICH IN old Hawaiian legends. The most interesting were those connected with the typical Hawaiian sport, surf-riding, the most religious, those connected with the founding of the local *heiau*, or temples.

One of the old surf legends was that of Mamala, the surfrider. Kou ["kou tree"] was the ancient name of Honolulu—the place for games and sports among the chiefs of long ago. A little to the east of Kou and inside the present filled land for the United States quarantine and coal station was a pond with a beautiful grove of coconut trees belonging to a chief, Honoka'upu ["the albatross bay"], and afterwards known by his name. Straight out toward the ocean was the narrow entrance to the harbor, through which rolled the finest surf waves of the Honolulu part of the island of Oahu. The surf bore the name "Ke-kai-o-Mamala," "the sea of Mamala." When the surf rose high it was called "Ka-nuku-o-Mamala," "the nose of Mamala." So the sea and entrance to the harbor were known by the name Mamala, and the shore gave the name Kou to the bay.

Mamala was a chiefess of Kupua character. This meant that she was a *mo'o* or gigantic lizard or crocodile, as well as a beautiful woman, and could assume whichever shape she most desired. One of the legends says that she was a shark and woman, and had for her husband the shark-man, Ouha, afterward a shark god having his home in the ocean near Koko Head. Mamala and Ouha drank awa together and played *kōnane** on the smooth konane stone at Kou.

Mamala was a wonderful surf-rider. Very skillfully she danced on the roughest waves. The surf in which she most delighted rose far out in the rough sea, where the winds blew strong and white-caps were on waves which rolled in rough disorder into the bay of Kou. The people on the beach, watching her, filled the air with resounding applause as they clapped their hands over her extraordinary athletic feats.

The chief, Hono-kau-pu, chose to take Mamala as his wife, so she left Ouha and lived with her new husband. Ouha was very angry and tried at first to injure Hono and Mamala but he was driven away. He fled to the lake Ka-'ihi-Kapu ["the tabu sacredness"] towards Waikiki. There he appeared as a man with a basketful of shrimps and fresh fish, which he offered to the women of that place, saying "Here is life (i.e. a living thing) for the children." He opened his basket, but the shrimps and the fish leaped out and escaped into the water.

The women ridiculed the god-man. The ancient legendary characters of all Polynesia as well as of Hawaii could not endure anything that

---

* *kōnane:* a game like checkers played with pebbles.

brought shame or disgrace upon them in the eyes of others. Ouha fled from the taunts of the women, casting off his human form, and dissolving his connection with humanity. Thus he became the great god-shark of the coast between Waikiki and Koko Head.

The surf-rider was remembered in the beautiful mele or chant coming from ancient times and called the mele of Hono-kau-pu.

The surf rises at Koʻolau,
Blowing the waves into mist,
Into little drops,
Spray falling along the hidden harbor.
There is my dear husband Ouha,
There is the shaking sea, the running sea of Kou,
The crab-like moving sea of Kou.
Prepare the ʻawa to drink, the crab to eat.
The small konane board is at Honokaʻupu.
My friend on the highest point of the surf.
This is a good surf for us.
My love has gone away.
Smooth is the floor of Kou,
Fine is the breeze from the mountains.
I wait for you to return,
The games are prepared,
Pa-poko, pa-loa, pa-lele,
Leap away to Tahiti
By the path to Nuu-mea-lani (home of the gods),
Will that lover (Ouha) return?
I belong to Honokaʻupu,
From the top of the tossing surf waves.
The eyes of the day and the night are forgotten.
Kou has the large konane board.
This is the day, and tonight
The eyes meet at Kou.

CHAPTER 4

"A Shark Punished at Waikiki" (1915)

William Westervelt
1849–1939

According to Samuel M. Kamakau, the story of Ka-ehu occurred in 1834. The shark's full name is Ka-ehu-iki-manō-o-Puʻu-loa ("the little yellow shark of Pearl Harbor"). Kamakau states that "because sharks save men in times of peril, protect them when other sharks try to devour them, and are useful in other ways in saving lives at sea and on the deep ocean, some people were made into shark ʻaumakua, or guardian gods." This process involved offering a deceased relative's body (or his or her bones wrapped in *tapa* cloth) to a priest who would accept various payment in the form of pigs, *tapa* cloth, and ʻawa (a narcotic drink used in ceremonies) and would ensure the transfiguration from human to shark form over the course of a few days. As proof of the transfiguration, the shark would take on the physical attributes of the deceased relative (or the markings of the *tapa* in which the bones were wrapped) and would then be considered a family pet and honored through daily food offerings.[8]

The story of Ka-ehu and the man-eating shark Pehu highlights the close-knit relationship between islanders and their shark ʻaumakua. "We must kill this man-eating shark who is destroying our people," Ka-ehu tells his shark friends. "This will be a part of our pay to them for honoring us at Puʻu-loa (Pearl Harbor)." Worshipping shark ʻaumakua was especially important for native fishermen—and the surfriders in this tale—who spent a great deal of their time in and around the ocean.

AMONG THE LEGENDARY CHARACTERS of the early Hawaiians was Ka-ehu—the little yellow shark of Pearl Harbor. He had been given magic power and great wisdom by his ancestor Ka-moho-alii the shark-god, brother of the fire-goddess Pele.

Part of his life had been spent with his parents, who guarded the sea precipices of the Coast of Puna in the southern part of the island Hawaii. While at Pearl Harbor he became homesick for the beauty of Puna, so he chanted:

O my land of rustling lehua trees!
Rain is treading on your budding flowers,
It carries them to the sea.
They meet the fish in the sea.
This is the day when love meets love,
My longings are stirring within me
For the spirit friends of my land.
They call me back to my home,
I must return.

Ka-ehu called his shark friends and started along the Oahu shores on his way to Hawaii. At Waikiki they met Pehu, a shark visitor from Maui, who lived in the sea belonging to Hono-ka-hau. Pehu was a man-eating shark and was swimming back and forth at Kalehua-wiki.* He was waiting for some surf-rider to go out far enough to be caught.

Ka-ehu asked him what he was doing there. He replied, "I am catching a crab for my breakfast."

Ka-ehu said, "We will help you catch your crab."

He told Pehu to go near the coral reef while he and his large retinue of sharks would go seaward. When a number of surf-riders were far out he and his sharks would appear and drive them shoreward in a tumultuous rush; then Pehu could easily catch the crab. This pleased the shark from Maui, so he went close to the reef and hid himself in its shadows.

Ka-ehu said to his friends: "We must kill this man-eating shark who is destroying our people. This will be a part of our way to pay them for honoring us at Puu-loa (Pearl Harbor). We will all go and push Pehu into the shallow water."

A number of surf-riders poised on the waves, and Pehu called for the other sharks to come, but Ka-ehu told him to wait for a better chance. Soon two men started on a wave from the distant dark blue sea where the high surf begins.

Ka-ehu gave a signal for an attack. He told his friends to rush in under the great wave and as it passed over the waiting Pehu, crowd the men and their surf-boards to one side and push the leaping Pehu so that he would be upset. Then while he was floundering in the surf they must hurl him over the reef.

As Pehu leaped to catch one of the coming surf-riders he was astonished to see the man shoved to one side, then as he rose almost straight

---

* The reference here is to Kalehua-wehe, an ancient surfing area in Waikīkī (see Pukui, *Place Names,* 76).

up in the water he was caught by the other sharks and tossed over and over until he plunged head first into a deep hole in the coral. There he thrashed his great tail about, but only forced himself farther in so that he could not escape.

The surf-riders were greatly frightened when they saw the company of sharks swimming swiftly outside the coral reef—but they were not afraid of Pehu. They went out to the hole and killed him and cut his body in pieces. Inside the body they found hair and bones, showing that this shark had been destroying some of their people.

They took the pieces of the body of that great fish to Pele-ula, where they made a great oven and burned the pieces.

Ka-ehu passed on toward Hawaii as a knight-errant, meeting many adventures and punishing evil-minded residents of the great sea.

CHAPTER 5

"Faithless Lover Is Turned to Stone" (1958)
Clarice B. Taylor

Birds are among the most prevalent animals in Hawaiian mythology. According to Martha Beckwith, gods may be man-eating birds who take on human form, or they may appear as birds themselves to serve their family descendants. Beckwith notes that birds were also worshipped by canoe makers: "When a canoe was to be built, a priest would go to the forest, select a tree, and pray to the gods of the woods to bless it, then wait for an elepaio bird to alight on the trunk. If it merely ran up and down, the trunk was sound; but where it stopped to pick at the bark, that spot was sure to be found rotten and the builder would run the risk in making use of the trunk."[9] Since the *kahunas* who crafted surfboards followed similar rituals as the canoe builders, it is not difficult to imagine that they worshipped birds in much the same way.[10] *The Story of Laie-i-ka-wai* demonstrated how mythical birds transported Lā'ie-i-ka-wai and her lover, Hala-aniani, to the feather-house at Pali-uli. The following tale describes a Bird Maiden who uses her bird messengers both to secure a lover and to survey his fidelity.

The story of the Kaui'i prince Ka-hiki-lani ("the arrival [of] chief") is also of interest for its illustration of the strong link between Hawaiian myth and landscape. Many native tales derive primarily as explanations for specific, local features of geography (like the "George Washington" stone mentioned here). Finally, the story of Ka-hiki-lani is well known in surf culture because the prince's fate is sealed at the famed break of *Pau-malū*,* or Sunset Beach, on the North Shore of O'ahu. A challenging field of play for both ancient and contemporary surfers, Sunset Beach continues to create legends as modern-day incarnations of Ka-hiki-lani come to test their skill at one of the world's most dangerous and exciting waves.

---

* *Pau-malū:* "taken secretly." In *Place Names of Hawai'i*, Pukui notes, "a shark bit off the legs of a woman who caught more squid than was permitted" (182).

As you travel along the Ka-mehameha ["the lonely one"] Highway on the western side of Oahu Island, you pass Waialee and come to a barren ridge above Pau-malu Bay. There you will see a tourist bureau marker, George Washington Stone. Some people see the head of George Washington on the mountain side facing the sea, but that is not the ancient tradition.

The head is that of a Kauai Prince named Ka-hiki-lani who had heard of the wonderful and difficult surfing to be had at Pau-malu Bay. Ka-hiki-lani came to Oahu determined to learn the art of riding the Pau-malu surf. He practiced day after day and was constantly watched by a maid of supernatural bird powers who lived in a nearby cave.

The bird fell in love with the Prince and sent her bird messengers to place a *lehua** lei about his neck and bring him to her. By circling about the Prince, the birds guided him to the Bird Maiden's cave. The Prince was enchanted with the maid and spent months with her until the return of the surfing season. The call of the surf was too much for him; he left the maiden after promising her that he would never kiss another woman.

His vow was broken almost immediately. A woman passing by saw him surfing, placed an *ilima** lei about his neck and kissed him. Ka-hiki-lani thought nothing of the act, but the bird messengers of the Bird Maiden were watching him. They flew away to tell their mistress that Ka-hiki-lani was faithless.

The Bird Maiden ran to the beach with a *lehua* lei in her hand. She snatched the *ilima* lei from his neck and replaced it with the *lehua*.

Ka-hiki-lani ran after her. As he got halfway up the mountain side he was turned to stone. He sits there today with a rock *lehua* about his neck, a warning to all faithless lovers.

---

* *lehua*: "The flower of the *'ohi'a* tree . . . The plant has many forms, from tall trees to low shrubs . . . The flowers are red, rarely salmon, pink, yellow, or white" (*Hawaiian Dictionary*). Elizabeth Tartar notes that the *lehua* "is also the sacred flower of the goddess Hi'iaka, younger sister of Pele" (*Chant*, 23).

* *'ilima*: "Small to large native shrubs . . . bearing yellow, orange, greenish, or dull-red flowers; some kinds strung for leis. The flowers last only a day and are so delicate that about 500 are needed for one lei" (*Hawaiian Dictionary*). It is worth noting that both the *'ilima* and *lehua* were flowers used to decorate the *kuahu* altar in the hula temples (*hālau hula*) built to honor the hula-goddess Laka (see Barrère, *Hula: Historical Perspectives*, 57–58).

* Pukui notes that Ka-hiki-lani was turned to stone because his wife had called upon her *'aumakua*, or family god (*Place Names*, 64).

CHAPTER 6

"Name Chant for Naihe" (1973)

Translated by Mary Kawena Pukui
1895–1986

Alfons L. Korn

Polynesian *mele* (songs, chants) are the first surf songs known to exist. In *Nineteenth Century Hawaiian Chant*, Elizabeth Tatar writes that *mele* are "expressions of religious devotion and personal emotion, as well as formal documentation of genealogy and history." She adds: "As a type of poetry, *mele* were always chanted in certain named styles." Some of these styles included prayer chants, genealogical chants, animal chants, chants in praise of genitals, and chants for expressing love. The chants that follow all belong to the style of *mele inoa,* or name chants. In addition to praising the individual in general terms, the *mele inoa* contain references to ancestors and parents (often naming the family clan) and to particular places and events relevant to the actual occasion of naming the individual.[11]

The following *mele inoa* is presented in two parts (there are six parts to the entire *mele*): the first is a well-known fragment from Part One translated by Mary K. Pukui and Alfons L. Korn. (Elizabeth Tatar indicates in *Nineteenth Century Hawaiian Chant* that the chant was first published in 1886 as part of the jubilee birthday celebration in honor of King David Kalākaua [45].) Pukui and Korn introduce Naihe as "an accomplished orator and athlete of Kona, island of Hawai'i, who flourished during the first thirty years of the nineteenth century." He was a warrior for Kamehameha I and the husband of the famous chiefess Ka-pi'o-lani.[12] In her original introduction to Naihe's name chant, Pukui explains:

Naihe was an expert surf rider and this made some of his fellow chiefs jealous. At their suggestion, a surf riding contest was held in Hilo, in which all the chiefs participated. Naihe came from Kau with two of his attendants, one an old woman, a chanter. The journey was slow and the contest had begun when he arrived. The old woman went to sleep when Naihe joined the chiefs. Not until Naihe was already in the water was he told of the rule that no one was to come ashore unless his chanter stood on the shore to chant his surf chant. This was a plot to keep Naihe in the water, in order to be rid of him. All the chiefs had their chanters with them except Naihe. A Puna chief had compassion on Naihe and secretly sent his servant to waken the sleeping woman. When she heard of her master's plight, she hurried to the beach and, with tears streaming down her cheeks, chanted his surf chant.[13]

The second part presents Part Three of the *mele inoa* in its entirety.[14] This section makes specific reference to the tradition of Wākea and his wife, Papa, ancestors from whom all Hawaiian genealogies derive. Genealogies are extremely important in Hawaiian social life since, according to Martha Beckwith, "no one can claim admittance to the *Papa ali'i* or ranking body of high chiefs with all its privileges and prerogatives who cannot trace his ancestry back to Ulu or Nanaulu, sons of Ki'i and Hinakoula."[15] Both genealogical lines, Beckwith adds, derive from Papa and Wākea.

Part I

The big wave, the billow rolling from Kona,
Ka nalu nui a kū ka nalu mai Kona

makes a loincloth fit for a champion among chiefs.
Ka malo a ka māhiehie

Far-reaching roller, my loincloth speeds with the waves.
Ka 'onaulu loa a lele ka'u malo

Waves in parade, foam-crested waves of the loin-covering sea,
O kaka'i malo o Hoaka

make the *malo** of the man, the high chief.
O ka malo kai, malo o ke ali'i,

Stand, gird fast the loincloth!
E kū, e hume a pa'a i ka malo

Let the sun ride on ahead guiding the board named Halepō
O ka 'ika'i ka lā i ka papa 'o Hale-pō

until Halepō glides on the swell.
A pae 'o Halepō i ka nalu

Let Halepō mount the surf rolling in from Kahiki,
Hō'e'e ka nalu mai Kahiki

waves worthy of Wākea's people,
He nalu Wākea, nalu ho'ohu'a

waves that build, break, dash against our shore.
Haki 'opu'u ka nalu, haki kuapā

---

* *malo:* loincloth.

Now sea-spray of surfing looms into sight.	*Ea mai ka maka kai heʻe nalu*
Craggy wave upon wave strikes the island	*kai heʻe kākala o ka moku*
pounded by a giant surf	*Kai kā o ka nalu nui*
lashing spume against a leafy altar, Hiki-au's temple.	*Ka huʻa o ka nalu o Hiki-au*
At high noontime this is the surf to ride!	*Kai heʻe nalu i ke awakea*

Beware coral, horned coral on the shoreside.	*Kū ka puna, ke koʻa i uka*
This channel is treacherous as the harbor of Kakuhihewa.	*Ka mākāhā o ka nalu o Kakuhihewa*
A surfboard smashes on the reef,	*Ua ʻō ia noha ka papa*
Maui splits, trembles, sinks into slime.	*Nohā Māui nauweuwe Nauweuwe, nakelekele.*

Many a surfman's skin is slippery,	*Nakele ka ʻili o ka i heʻe kai*
but the champion of chiefs skims into shore undrenched	*Lalilali ʻole ka ʻili o ke akamai*
by the feathery flying sea-spray of surfriders.	*Kāhilihili ke kai o ka heʻe nalu*

Now you have seen great surfs at Puna and Hilo!	*ʻIkea o ka nalu nui o Puna, o Hilo!*

Part III

Kane surfed on the waves of Oahu	*Na Kane i hee nalu Oahu*
And all around Maui, (island) of Piilani,	*He puni Maui no Piilani*
He surfed through the white foam, the raging waves,	*Ua hee a papa kea i papa enaena*
The top of his surfboard in triumph rose on the crest	*Ua lilo lanakila ke poo o ka papa*
(As waves) crashed against Kauiki.*	*Ua nahaha Kauiki*
The oncoming waves are blocked by that land.	*Ka moku o ka nalu e paa ai*
From Maui on he went to Hawaii,	*Ai Hawaii ia Maui,*
On to Mauwele, his land,	*Ai Mauwele i kona moku,*
To Kuakua, the woman	*Ai Kuakua, ka wahine,*
Of the island of Papa	*I ka mokupuni o Papa*

---

* *Ka-ʻuiki:* "the glimmer"; Head, point, and lighthouse, Hana, Maui, home of the demi-god Maui, and birthplace of Ka-ʻahu-manu (*Place Names*, 92).

(There they) competed in the surf,	*Hoopapa kaihee nalu,*
The long, low-sweeping surf.	*O i nalu i hoohale*
The chief surfed to that shore of enthralling beauty,	*Hee ka lani i ka hiwakalana*
His skin white with wave (foam).	*Ili kamakea i kona nalu*
Back he swam to the deep sea.	*Aulono i ke kai hohonu*
(Graceful) as a woman surfed the chief	*Hee wahine ka lani*
Toward the *ohia*s* along the shore	*Kauka ohia la*
Through the froth of the wave.	*Ia ka hu'a o ka nalu*
Lono was the chief of Kauai,	*O Lono alii o Kauai*
The first born son of Mauokalani,	*O alii haipo ia Mauokalani*
A tender leaf bud of the lineage of Kawelo,*	*O ka muo o kau maka Kawelo*
An offspring of the highest born.	*Ka pua ka lakona,*
In Kona, at Ahuena* was his surfboard,	*I Kona i Ahuena ka papa*
At Holualoa* was the surf to ride on,	*I Holualoa ka nalu e hee ai*
The shiny surfboard was laid down at Kahakiki;	*I Kahakiki papa o ka hinu*
The woman went there, she mounted the board,	*Hele ae ka wahine, a ee i ka papa*
[She rode] the rough waves of Mana-alii.	*Ai kuku, Oi o Manaalii ka nalu*
At Kapuololani	*I Ka Puololani*
Was Kauhi [of the family] of Kihapiilani.*	*O Kauhi o Kihapiilani*
Multitude of lightnings flashed in the sky,	*Manomano uwila Lapuila i ka lani*
The forked lightnings flashed in the sky,	*Wakwaka uwila Lapauila i ka lani*
They reverberated in the heavens; the voice	*Kani aaina i ka lani, Haka-ka*
Of the chiefly thunder roared above.	*Ka leo o ka hekili alii,*
Meehonua, son of Kamalalawalu was the man,	*O ka Meehonua a Kamalalawalu kekane*
His was the inshore surf of Manini,	*O kona kai kukio Manini,*
The turbulent [surf] of the woman Manini,	*Owali ka wahine Manini*
Turbulent laid Manini in the sun;	*Owali manini ka la*

---

    * *'ohia:* a tree [Pukui's note on manuscript].

    * *Kawelo:* legendary Kaua'i chief; for legends of Kawelo, see *Hawaiian Mythology,* 404–414.

    * *Ahu-'ena:* "red-hot heap"; *Heiau* [temple] for human sacrifices restored by Kamehameha I, adjoining his residence at Ka-maka-honu, Kai-lua, North Kona, Hawai'i (*Place Names,* 6).

    * *Holua-loa:* "long sled course" (*Place Names,* 48).

    * *Kihapi'ilani:* legendary chief of Maui; for story of Kihapi'ilani learning to surf on O'ahu, see *Hawaiian Mythology,* 388.

Manini the fish was bleached there,	*Manini na Ia keokumu kea*
Like the bleached tapa cloths of the women.	*Mehe kapa okumu kea la no kawahine*
To him belonged the surfboard	*Ia ia ka papa*
On which to ride the waves,	*Oi ee pu mai iluna o ka nalu*
He whose wave it was, reached the shore.	*A ili a pae ke kane nona ua nalu*
The wild duckling flew, casting a shadow on the full moon.	*O ke kupu koloa keaka lele Mahealani*
As though to inquire of me, it flew on,	*Oi ui o'u la lele i wa*
It moved to the wise and learned Kahakumaka	*Ka onia ula lae puni a o Kahakumaka*
Kakaunioa [and] Kamakaihiwa.	*O Kakaunioa o Kamakaihiwa*
The skin was dampened by the rapid movement	*O ka Ili kapule o ka ia ka oni*
Of the living man.	*A ke kanaka ola*
The waves moved about,	*No ka oni ka nalu*
They moved sideways and washed ashore at Kahaluu.*	*Hooholo i ka lala a pae i Kahaluu*
[He] bathed in the water at Waikuaaala.	*Auau i ka wai i Waikuaaala*
The natives were at home at Ohia-kalele,	*I ka kupa na hale i Ohia-kalele,*
There was the board for the man to mount on,	*Ilaila ka papa kau kanaka*
It was I's board, he who was Kapo's parent.	*Ka papa a I, a makua Kapo*
He came in, so that the chiefs might go to surf	*Hele mai, i hehee na lii i ka nalu*
To [other] islands; they gathered on the shore	*Kaholomoku o lakou kai ke kahakai*
To heap the sand into mounds,	*I hoopuepue ai pue i ke one*
To bathe in the sea,	*I hoauau ia i ke kai*
To lie upon [this beach],	*I mamae* luna*
To wear wreaths of coconut blossoms,	*I hoolei ia ai i kalei pua niu*
Of mao blossoms, of laeloa blossoms,	*Pua mao pua ka laeloa,*
Of ilima blossoms growing thickly along the trails,	*Me ka pua ilima papa o ke alanui*
Strung together with the blossoms of the nohu,	*I pauku ia me ka pua o ka nohu,*
With the blossoms of the noni and those of the akulikuli.	*Me ka pua noni opai o kamo pua akulikuli*

---

* *Kaha-luʻu:* "diving place"; beach and surfing area (*Place Names,* 62).

* The possibility of "momoe" is noted in parentheses by the translator on the manuscript.

They rose to lift up their chief.	*I ka lele i hapai alii,*
The sea was chiefly, it was shiny with the boards,	*Alii ka moana ua ala ika hinu,*
The boards whose points showed [above the surf].	*I ka papa i makaioio*
Let your surf roll, O Kahaluu,	*Popoi kai e Kahaluu*
The sea grows rough, the billows rise,	*Inoino ka moana uluulu ku uluku*
The waves wallow in troughs and rear above.	*Hawaawaa ka ale nienie ka nalu*
This is a surf riding chant for [our] chief.	*He inoa nalu noia nei,*
The waves break, they swell at sea,	*O Haki nalu pupue mai kai*
From the sea rushes the waves,	*Mai kai a nanae kau o ka nalu,*
They spread out on the shore,	*I hohola he ae no ka nalu*
On the windward side, by the grey cliffs of Koholalele,*	*Koolau kaika pali hinahina i Koholalele*
The sprays rise over the sea,	*Lelekahuna a ke kai*
Sprinkling salt water into the eyes.	*Oalia i maka*
Then I shall glance [ashore],	*Alaila au kilohi aku*
The sea foam has whitened the pandanus of Kamakea,	*Pau huakai ka hala o Kamakea*
All of the waves lie unevenly,	*Maioio ka nalu o ka pau loa,*
The eyes of the teaser look out of the corners;	*Liolio ka maka o ke ka hana wale*
All these I see over the waves.	*A pau ka au ike i ka nalu,*
The sands are rolled into innumerable mounds,	*Ku hewa o ke Ahua*
The sea rolls in in great swells,	*Ke poi 'la kekanui*
The earth reddened waves break in sideways,	*Kalamaula Hakilala ka nalu*
They withdraw in circling pools	*Kahi o ka poai*
Like rainbows on the sea floor.	*Mehe anuenue la ka papa,*
The footprints	*Kamawa a ka wawae*
Of man are seen round about,	*O ke kanaka lewa o ka poai,*
They are erased by the first waves of the rainy season,	*Ke helula ia ka nalu mua a kau o Hooilo*
They are washed out by the waves.	*Ke ooki aku la i ka nalu*
When the light [of the sun] bursts forth	*Makui o Pohakea*
The boards of the women are taken out	*Lilo ka papa o na Wahine*

---

* *Kohalā-lele:* "leaping whale" (*Place Names,* 115).

To the rapid onslaught of the sea of Aawa.*	*I ka iliki ia eke kai o Aawa*
Put away [the boards] in the houses of the parents,	*Hahao a aku i hale o ka makua*
The boards of the chiefs of Kaumelilani,	*Ka papa o ke alii o Kaumelilani*
Of Keaka, of Kaumelilani,	*O Keaka o Kaumelilani*
Of Kahili [chief] of Maui,	*O kahili o Maui*
Of Ku who goes about, who shows his light	*O Ku hele nui lele malama*
In the sky, of Kahili, of Lelekoni,	*O ka lani, O kahili o Lelekoni*
Of Haakoa of the gentle face, of Ku-kainaina,	*Ohaakoa i maka wali o Kukainaina*
Of Umalei, the husband,	*O Umalei ke kane,*
Of Umauma the wife,	*O Umauma la ka wahine*
Of the followers of Kane-epu-lono,	*O ka nui Kaneepulono*
The chief, of whose wave we speak.	*Ke alii nona ua nalu kena-ahea-*
This is his name chant.	*—He inoa—*
A storm raged in Kahiki,* the rain clouds were emptied,	*Ua ino Kahiki ua malolo ka opua*
The wind drove and broke the clouds, the sea arose;	*Ua pauli ke ao makani kaikoo*
That was the source of Wakea's waves.	*Ke kumu noia o ka nalu o Wakea*
Wakea dwelt with Papa his wife,	*Noho ia Wakea o Papa la ka wahine*
They lived closely together, they slept together,	*Laua i pipili laua i momoe*
Wakea slept with Papa.	*Momoe Wakea ma laua o Papa*
Hawaii was born to be peopled by men,	*Hanau Hawaii kupu laha kanaka*
Hoohoku was born a girl.	*Hanau Hoohoku he kaikamahine*
He, [Wakea] dwelt with Hoohokukalani,*	*Noho ia Hoohokukalani,*
His daughter and wife.	*E ke kaikamahine wahine au e wakea*
I am I's offspring, he who had many followers.	*Na I hoi au na ka hai kanaka*
Pakaalana is the temple of Kaao the god,	*O Pakaalana ka unu o Kaao ke Akua*

---

* 'A'awa: "wrasse fishes"; ancient surfing area, West Maui (*Place Names*, 5).

* *Kahiki*: foreign lands; often more particularly, the Society Islands, including Tahiti.

* Ho'ohōkū-ka-lani: ("The heavenly one who made stars") (*Hawaiian Mythology*, 294).

I have reached it, [I] who am able to sprinkle its waters.
From the men of old
Came Kalakaua;
Born was Kamaka Kaumaka
Of the eyes of Haloa,
The chief whose waves obey his will.
Give me the waves that I may ride upon them
Lest I be ashamed
When I reach the shore.

Pa no iau i ka Pipiwai e

He hai Kanaka kahiko
O Kalakaua mai laila mai,
Hanau o Kamaka Kaumaka
Ka maka o Haloa
Kealii nona ua nalu kena
Homai he nalu—ehee aku au

O hilahila au auanei
Ke pae—iuka—

CHAPTER 7

"'Auhea 'O Ka Lani' (Where Is the Royal Chief?)" (1957)

Nona Beamer

Nona Beamer indicates in her preface to *Nā Mele Hula* that nearly all of the chants and hula she has compiled were handed down to her as part of the oral tradition from previous generations. "Starting in the fourteenth century with our ancestor King Liloa," she writes, "and the fifteenth century with Queen Ahiakumai Ki'eki'e, until the modern times of Kamehameha I, our family has honored these chants and dances, and we still recite these poems today."[16]

As described by Pukui, hula were both sacred and secular dances which, in traditional Hawaiian culture, were of secondary importance to the words of the chant they accompanied; in modern times this role has reversed, with the dance generally taking prominence.[17] In the sense that the dances were practiced by old and young, chiefs and commoners (including competitions), and its historical trajectory followed a period of decline and revival in the nineteenth and twentieth centuries, the hula has shared many characteristics with surfriding. The following *mele inoa*, as described by Beamer, comes from the Puna district of Hawai'i and celebrates the surfing exploits of William Charles Lunalilo, king of Hawai'i (ruled 1873–1874).

Chant type: Mele Inoa (name)
Chant style: Kānaenae (prayerful)
Hula type: Hula Noho Kānaenae (prayerful), Hula 'Ulī'ulī (gourd rattle), Hula 'Ili'ili (pebbles)*

---

* *Hula 'Ili'ili*: "In the hula *iliili* pebbles (*iliili*) are held in the hand and struck together as gestures follow the words of the chant" (Barrère, *Hula: Historical Perspectives*, 93).

Where is the royal chief?	'Auhea 'o ka lani la
There surfing	Aia i ka he'e nalu
Surfing on the long wave	He'e ana i ka lala la
Returning on the short wave	Ho'i ana i ka muku
On the Hō'eu* wave	A ka nalu o Hō'eu la
We both return	Eu ho'i a'e kāua
And land at the sea of Kaimū*	A pae a'e Kaimū la
Where the natives gather	Ho'omū nā kānaka
We bathe in the fresh water	'Au'au i ka wai la
The pond of Wai'ākolea*	A 'o Wai'ākolea
We dive and surface*	Lu'u aku a ea mai la
A prayerful chant for the chief	Kānaenae o ka lani
Tell the refrain	Ha'ina mai kapuana la
In the name of Lunalilo	No Lunalilo nō he inoa
"In the name of Lunalilo"	"HE INOA NŌ LUNALILO"

---

* *Hō'eu*: "very high, referring to royalty."

* *Kai-mū* ("gathering [at the] sea [to watch surfing]"): land in Hawai'i "noted for its surf and its black sand beach. . . . The surfing site was formerly called Hō'eu and Ka-poho, but now is called Kai-mū" (*Place Names*, 69).

* *Wai'ākolea*: "water of the *'ākolea* fern."

* *Lu'u* ("Lu'u aku a ea mai la"): style of diving with leaf in mouth.

CHAPTER 8

"Ka Hui Nalu Mele: The Surf Club Song" (1989)

Rerioterai Tava

Moses K. Keale Sr.

The island of Niʻihau holds a long tradition of surfriding and includes many local stories and chants. Rerioterai Tava and Moses Keale relate one particular story of a surfer named Puʻuone, "whose boast was '*E keiki mai au no Kawahamana*,' or 'I am the child (champion) of Kawahamana.' It seems that his wife had left him for someone else. In his frustration, he went surfing. While he was surfing, the ocean suddenly became very rough; he had to paddle all around Niihau looking for a place to come ashore, aware that the people were watching him paddle about. He finally came to Kawahamana. The surfer was exhausted, but he wished to impress his wife so she would return to him. When he finally did catch a wave, he rode it all the way to shore, landing at Hapalua, which is close to Tahiu. He was cold and tired and when he reached the beach, his friends had a fire going to warm him. Because he was so brave, his wife returned to him."[18]

The following chant was written to commemorate the annual surfing festivals and competitions that took place between royalty each October at Kamoana.

He mele he inoa no ka hui nalu haulani make kai o Kamoamoa.	A song, a name for the surfing meet, and the restless seas of Kamoana.
Alawa ae oe ani kamakani moae kaulana no Kawaihoa.	Softly blows the breeze as you glance, the celebrated *moae* winds of Kawaihoa.
E aha ia ana kau aheahe me haaheo i kaili ka.	What, is this the time to be quiet? Cherish with pride the surface of the sea.
Aloha kahi nalu o Kamoamoa ike ani peahi mehe ipo ala.	Beloved is the wave of Kamoana, as it waves and beckons as if a loved one.

E kono mai ana la i kahi manao	It is inviting your desires to come
e pili meke kai hoeha ili.	and be with the sea that hurts your skin.
Ilihia i ka nani ke ike aku	Thrilled by the splendor that you see,
na pua hiehie a Kahelelani.	the regal children of Kahelelani.
Lia au i kala meka makemake	You have a yearning to be free,
kahi nalu hai mai o Kamoamoa.	but the waves of Kamoana will break you.
Hoohihi kamanao poina ole	Intertwined in my memory, I can't forget
ika papa hee nalu o ka muliwai.	the backwash that steals my surfboard.
Kohu kapa ahuula no Kamoamoa	Kamoana surf is likened to the red cloak,
hooheno ika ehu ehu o ke kai.	caressing power and the majesty of the sea.
Kai no paha oe ua i ke aku	The surf dances before you and you have
ia Lehua mokupuni ika ehu kai.	seen as the salt spray drifts upon Lehua.
He home noho ia na ke koolau	The home where the koolau wind resides,
poina ole ai kahi manao.	my longing for cannot be quenched.
Kohu lio kakela no Kamoana	Performing well on the horse of the ocean,
he pakika he pahee i ka ili kai.	gliding and sliding over the sea's surface.
Ua ana ia a ili wai like	You constantly struggle for breath,
na hana noeau a ka makua.	unlike the skillful deeds of our forefathers.
Oka milo hae no kau aloha	The furious curl is what is loved,
olai oke kai hanupanupa	gliding smoothly over the surface of the sea.
He manao no kou ae ike lihi	Desire compels me to surf the edge
ike kai popolo o ke ahiahi	of the dark evening sea.
Akahi alana mai ka manao	I have this one floating thought,
e ike ika nalu ao Ohia.	to behold the waves of Ohia.
Alia hoi oe eka makemake	I have to wait, thought I desire,
e ui lani nei paa ole iho.	it's beautiful but I can't catch it.
Ulu wehi wale ai o Kamoamoa.	Festively adorned is Kamoana,
i ka puni kauoha a na kupuna.	so deemed by the ancestors.

Nana i kono mai kahi manao *e ike ia kaleponi he aina hau.*	Kamoana has invited the idea of seeing California, land of ice.
Mea ole na ale o Kamoana *ka ilio hae o ka pakipika.*	The billows of the sea are insignificant like the bark of a vicious dog of the Pacific.
Ke kiina iho ia ake akamai *a loaa mai au pahi koe pua.*	At the eyes' glance the expert knows, if you don't, the knife that scrapes will get you.
Nana inoi i nowelo aku *pau pono na ale o Kamoana.*	He has asked to search for wisdom, on all the waves of the sea.
Kilohi aku oe la oka nani *molina wai Rula anapanapa.*	Gaze and behold the beauty of the gold glittering colored border.
Hea ia kou inoa o ka hui nalu *o ka hae Hawaii kou makia.*	Recited is your name, of the surfing club, the banner of Hawaii your purpose.
Haina kapuana ua lohe ia *kahi nalu hooheno o Kamoamoa.*	The song is ended, my story is told of the affection for the surf of Kamoana.

CHAPTER 9

Hawaiian Proverbs & Poetical Sayings (1983)

Translated by Mary Kawena Pukui
1895–1986

Author, teacher, Hawaiian translator, and researcher, Mary Kawena Pukui was the coauthor with Samuel Elbert of the seminal *Hawaiian Dictionary* (1957) and with Elbert and Esther T. Mookini of *Place Names of Hawaiʻi* (1966). The preface to *Hawaiian Proverbs & Poetical Sayings* states: "Since the sayings carry the immediacy of the spoken word, considered to be the highest form of cultural expression in old Hawaiʻi, they bring us closer to the everyday thoughts and lives of the Hawaiians who created them. Taken together, the sayings offer a basis for an understanding of the essence and origins of traditional Hawaiian values."[19] Along with the myths, legends, and chants, these sayings reinforce the broad role that surfriding plays in Hawaiian culture, from stories of divinities and rulers to the everyday expressions that evoke the humor, skill, and wisdom of the Hawaiian people.

285

E ho ʻi ka uʻi o Mānoa, ua ahiahi.
Let the youth of Mānoa go home, for it is evening.

Refers to the youth of Mānoa who used to ride the surf at Kalehuawehe in Waikīkī. The surfboards were shared among several people who would take turns using them. Those who finished first often suggested going home early, even though it might not be evening, to avoid carrying the boards to the *hālau* where they were stored. Later the expression was used for anyone who went off to avoid work.

403

Hāʻawi papa heʻe nalu.
A surfboard giving.

To give a thing and later ask for its return. A surfboard is usually lent, not given outright.

504

Hāwāwā ka heʻe nalu haki ka papa.
When the surf rider is unskilled, the board is broken.

An unskilled worker bungles instead of being a help. There is also a sexual connotation: When a man is unskilled, the woman is dissatisfied.

649

He kāʻeʻaʻeʻa pulu ʻole no ka heʻe nalu.
An expert on the surfboard who does not get wet.

Praise of an outstanding surfer.

1013

Hō aʻe ka ʻike heʻenalu i ka hokua o ka ʻale.
Show [your] knowledge of surfing on the back of the wave.

Talking about one's knowledge and skill is not enough; let it be proven.

1402

Kaikoʻo ke awa, popoʻi ka nalu, ʻaʻohe ʻike ʻia ka poʻe nana i heʻe ka nalu.
The harbor is rough, the surf rolls, and the rider of the surf cannot be seen.

A stormy circumstance with uncertain results.

2356

O ʻAwili ka nalu, he nalu kapu kai na ke akua.
ʻAwili is the surf, a surf reserved for the ceremonial bath of the goddess.

Refers to Pele. There were three noted surfs at Kalapana, Puna: Kalehua, for children and those just learning to surf; Hoʻeu, for experienced surfers; and ʻAwili, which none dared to ride. When the surf of ʻAwili was rolling dangerously high, all surfing and canoeing ceased, for that was a sign that the gods were riding.

2433

O ka papa heʻe nalu kēia, paheʻe i ka nalu haʻi o Makaiwa.
This is the surfboard that will glide on the rolling surf of Makaiwa.

A woman's boast. Her beautiful body is like the surfboard on which her mate "glides over the rolling surf."

Part II

Explorers, Missionaries, and Travelers
(1769–1896)

Explorers

Surfriding—in the form of Tahitians bodyboarding the stern of an old canoe—fell among the exotic sights Westerners first witnessed on Captain James Cook's maiden voyage to the Pacific (1768–1771). Accounts from Cook's third voyage to the Pacific (1776–1780) added information on variations of the sport: canoe surfing, and the first published descriptions of Hawaiians riding waves on surfboards. The detailed entries from this latter group—from Charles Clerke's observations of tandem paddling to David Samwell's description of a group of Hawaiian children surfriding—testify to the great novelty of surfriding for a group of men unsurpassed in their knowledge and respect for the ocean (at least in the West). Later accounts from William Bligh's infamous voyage of the *Bounty* offer additional valuable information about surfriding from Tahiti: the equal skill of men and women in the surf, and the first description of islanders standing on surfboards. Peter Puget's journal entry, from George Vancouver's voyage to the Pacific (1791–1794), shows a similar expertise among women in the Hawaiian Islands. Reading these journal entries as a group offers a unique look at this critical juncture in the history of surfriding: the same fascination these explorers felt when they first observed natives riding waves continues to inspire millions of surfriders today.

Prefacing the journals is an excerpt from John Papa 'Ī'ī's *Fragments of Hawaiian History*. 'Ī'ī's descriptions of surfriding provide a helpful context for the first accounts of the sport by Western explorers. The traditions, equipment, and popular surf locales he details under Kamehameha I would have been the same as those encountered by the crews of Captain Cook. Because these visitors generally remained only a very brief time, their conception of surfriding—like that of Polynesian culture in general—was necessarily narrow. 'Ī'ī gives us a much more culturally integrated view of the sport, from the beach, as it were. We learn, among many other things, that surfriding was a skill practiced and refined by the highest-ranking members of the ruling class, including Kamehameha I and his favorite wife, Ka'ahumanu. Beyond the simple "amusement" as recorded by Westerners, 'Ī'ī warns, "There are rules to be observed when riding on a surf."

Missionaries

Catholic and Protestant missionaries followed on the heels of explorers to the Pacific. Two Spanish missionaries arrived in Tahiti in 1774, although they requested leave the following year. In 1797, the London Missionary Society established its first Protestant mission in Tahiti; in 1820, American Congregationalists from New England established their first mission on the island of O'ahu. The popularity of recreational activities like surfriding greatly decreased during the years when the missionaries were most influential in Hawai'i, from the time of their arrival in 1820 until the departure of their most prominent leader, Hiram Bingham, in 1840. Along with their bibles and school supplies, the missionary families brought an austere view of life that held little room for the many pastimes that had become integral to island culture. Ironic, then, that the writings of missionary William Ellis became the most influential narrative of surfriding for the rest of the century.

Criticism of missionary activities, particularly their suppression of sports like surfriding, began to appear in travel writings in the 1830s and 1840s; two of those texts, by W. S. W. Ruschenberger and Charles Wilkes, appear in this part of the book followed by Hiram Bingham's response in *A Residence of Twenty-one Years in the Sandwich Islands.* Although Christianity was not alone in diminishing native pastimes during the nineteenth century—depopulation through disease undoubtedly had the biggest impact—the missionaries have remained a traditional target of criticism within the surf community.

Travelers

Americans and Europeans began a steady stream of travel to Hawai'i in the second half of the nineteenth century. Rather than exploration or conversion, these voyagers sought the pleasure of travel, improved health, or often material for articles and books. Herman Melville, Mark Twain, and Isabella Bird spun surfriding into adventure novels and romantic travel narratives. Along with hula dancing, eating *poi*, scaling volcanoes, and visits to Captain Cook's last stand at Kealakekua Bay, surfriding became known as the "national pastime" travelers read about in books and expected to see during their visits.

This is also the period when surfriding was often reported as "rapidly passing out of existence."[1] The experience of travel writer Samuel S. Hill offered a provocative alternative: surfriding had decreased in popularity in the European-controlled urban areas (where most travelers remained), but natives maintained the practice as part of traditional culture in the outlying regions. Coming upon the village of Keauhua on the island of Hawai'i in 1849, Hill learned that "all the men, women, and children . . . were sporting with their surf-boards in the water." His encounter with the effects of poverty, disease, and depopulation also provided a useful counterweight to the romantic depictions of island life so prominent in travelogues of the period. And yet, amid the grim realities of daily existence, Hill found that surfriding remained a traditional outlet of pleasure as an entire community enjoyed the arrival of a new swell.

A more rudimentary side of surfriding appeared later in the century from scholars like Henry Carrington Bolton who were interested in describing why waves broke, how riders maintained their motion on the wave, and how surfriding, for those accustomed to the water, was "far less difficult than usually represented." Contrasting this scientific perspective is the final text of the section, "Hawaiian Surf-Riding," a description by an anonymous native Hawaiian of the rites and rituals surrounding surfriding in the traditional Polynesian religion. Little more than a decade after the publication of this text, the valuable cultural information presented by its author would be completely obscured by the reinvention of surfriding as a Western-style recreation.

CHAPTER 10

"Activities in Court Circles," from *Fragments of Hawaiian History: Kuokoa* (1866–1870)

John Papa ʻĪʻī

1800–1870

John Papa ʻĪʻī's account of Hawaiian court life during the reign of Kamehameha I (1758?–1819) offers a rare glimpse of daily life under the ancient kapu system that was abolished in 1819, one year before the arrival of New England missionaries whose religion and influence permanently altered the course of Hawaiian history, including the life of ʻĪʻī himself. After serving in the household of Liholiho—the future Kamehameha II (ruled 1819–1824)—ʻĪʻī was sent by the king to study under Hiram Bingham, the self-appointed leader of the newly arrived missionaries, "so that the king could observe the effects of the new Christian teaching."[2] He subsequently worked as Bingham's assistant, then as a teacher himself in Bingham's school. ʻĪʻī eventually became one of the kingdom's leading citizens as Hawaiʻi developed into a constitutional monarchy, appointed by Kamehameha III (ruled 1824–1854) to several political positions, including the House of Nobles and associate justice of the Supreme Court of Hawaiʻi.

Fragments of Hawaiian History reveals, in the many names of surf spots and their subtle differences from one another, the enormous popularity of surfriding and the extensive ocean knowledge the natives possessed. We learn about the different kinds of surfboards, their strengths and liabilities depending on surf conditions, how surfriding encouraged gambling among natives, and how Kamehameha I and his favorite wife Kaʻahumanu were experts at aquatic variations of surfriding like *lele waʻa,* or "canoe leaping." ʻĪʻī's memories of his youth reveal how a new swell brings together in the surf all levels of a highly stratified society, how children and chiefs regularly engaged in a sport whose technique, traditions, and communal nature had been developing for the better part of a millennium before Captain James Cook's *Resolution* and *Discovery* sighted the island chain in January 1778.

Activities in Court Circles

Rules for canoe paddling were customarily observed in ancient times, and Kamehameha had been trained until he was skilled at it. In paddling either on the right or on the left he moved his paddle from the outside inward. He was also taught canoe surfing, in which both he and Kaahumanu were most skilled, board surfing and so forth.

In Puaa, North Kona, is a famous surf called Kooka, where a coral head stands just outside a point of lava rocks. When the surf dashed over the coral head, the people swam out with their surfboards and floated with them. If a person owned a long narrow canoe, he performed what was called *lele wa'a*, or canoe leaping, in which the surfer leaped off the canoe with his board and rode the crest of the wave ashore. The canoe slid back of the wave because the force of the shove given it with the feet. When the surfer drew close to the place where the surf rose, a wave would pull itself up high and roll in. Any timid person who got too close to it was overwhelmed and could not reach the landing place. The opening through which the surfer entered was like a sea pool, with a rocky hill above and rows of lava rocks on both sides, and deep in the center. This was a difficult feat and one not often seen, but for Kaahumanu and the king it was easy. When they reached the place where the surf rose high, they went along with the crest of a wave and slipped into the sea pool before the wave rolled over. Only the light spray of the surf touched them before they reached the pool. The spectators shouted and remarked to each other how clever the two were. This art was held in esteem at that time, and so the surfing places were constantly filled with men and women.

The surf of Huiha at Honuaula in Kailua proper, directly above the place where ships anchored and just seaward of Keikipuipui, was rough when it rose. A person who had just learned to surf was afraid of it, but those who were skilled regarded it as fun. The landing place for this surf was a circle of sand. The water swirled gently as it went out from the shallows, and it was there that the surfers came in to reach the sand circle.

Huiha and Kiope were covered with surf riders when the sea was rough and the surf went all the way up to them. There were two small points on the north side of the sandy landing place, covered with the coarse *'aki'aki* grass, and to the north, a point of pahoehoe. Just a little north of this point were two coral heads which were used to gage the surf. On the inner side of the pahoehoe and on the north of Keikipuipui, was a surfing place for children and for timid men and women.

If the king rode in, he went ashore gracefully on the surf of Huiha; but when it was rough he went right on in to Kiope. Sometimes he could hardly reach Kiope because of the narrow entrance. The surf dashed over the point of pahoehoe and washed unobstructed and gently into Kiope. Here the mark that was observed for the rising of this surf was the point of Kaliliki. If the sea sprays rose upward two or three times, that was the number of the waves. If the sea sprays of Kaliliki went upward with force, a high surf was indicated and the timid kept away. The skilled went close to the source of the surf and remained there. As to the king, he was frequently seen leaping from a canoe on this surf. Expert surf riders unused to this surf were tossed about by it and found it was wise to sit still and watch the native sons, who were familiar with it, crouch in the flying sprays. A swimmer daring enough to try to land would be killed.

Many surfs were used in this popular sport. There is a surf on the south side of Huiha. Kiikau is the inner surf; Naohulelua, the outer one. Both run toward the south going shoreward. The surf of Kamakaia at Auhaukeae runs shoreward toward the north. When the sea is rough the surfs there meet with those of Naohulelua.

The surf of Kamoa at Keolonahihi and Puu runs toward the north side of Puu, directly beyond the spring there. The surf of Kaulu in Keauhou is a long one, and similar to the surf of Kamoa. The surf of Kapahukapu is at Napoopoo. There is also a surf at Keei and another on the east side of Kalae in Kau named Kapuuone. Two others are the surfs of Paiahaa at Kaalualu and Kawa at Hilea.

Kanukuokamanu in Waiakea, Hilo, also has a surf; Punahoa has one; and Piihonua has one, named Huia. There is also the surf of Paula at Puueo. The surf of Kapoai is a long one, said to run a distance equal to that of fifteen *ahupuaʻa*, beginning at the Honolii stream. Papaikou has a surf that rolls toward the mouth of the stream. There is also a surf at Laupahoehoe, said to be the surf that Umi and Paiea used.[3] Waipio, in Hamakua, has a surf that runs toward the sand.

The surf of Maliu in Halelua, Kohala, rises on the east side of Kauhola Point and is 3 to 4 chains long, or longer. Kekakau surfed there, and it is said that he was most skilled in surfing. He was a kamaaina of the place, and it was he who led Kaahumanu to the surf of Maliu. Perhaps that was when the chiefs were farming in Kauhola. No one remembers the year, but it is said that Kauhola was cultivated before the two battles of Laupahoehoe.

As the story goes, Kaahumanu and Kekakau swam or went by canoe to the spot where the surf rose. Before they left, Kekakau talked with the king about the nature of the surf and showed Kaahumanu the places to land, which would be signaled by the waving of a white tapa. If the tapa was moved to the right or to the left, she was to go to the side indicated before the sea rose up high and overwhelmed her. If the tapa was spread out, or perhaps wadded into a ball, the signal meant to go in on the middle of the wave. Kekakau told the chiefess to observe the signals on shore while they rode shoreward from the place where the surf rose to the place where the wave rose up high until they landed. Before they started the earth ovens had been lighted for roasting dogs, and by the time they reached shore, the dogs were cooked.

The surf of Kumoho, which is at Naohaku on the left side of Maliu, was not ridden when the sea was rough. The surf of Puakea did not look large, resembling a sea pool, yet it was famous. The surf of Kapuailima is in Kawaihae, and Kahaleula is in Mahaiula. Honokohau has a surf, and there are others in the various districts of the island of Hawaii. . . .

Here are three kinds of surfboards. The *ʻolo* is thick in the middle and grows thinner toward the edges. It is a good board for a wave that swells and rushes shoreward but not for a wave that rises up high and curls over. If it is not moved sideways when the wave rises high, it is tossed upward as it moves shoreward. There are rules to be observed when riding on a surf.

The *kikoʻo* reaches a length of 12 to 18 feet and is good for a surf that breaks roughly. This board is good for surfing, but it is hard to handle. Other surfers are afraid of it because of its length and its great speed on a high wave that is about to curl over. It can ride on all the risings of the waves in its way until they subside and the board reaches shore.

The *alaia* board, which is 9 feet long, is thin and wide in front, tapering toward the back. On a rough wave, this board vibrates against the rider's abdomen, chest, or hands when they rest flat on it, or when fingers are gripped into a fist at the time of landing. Because it tends to go downward and cut through a wave it does not rise up with the wave as it begins to curl over. Going into a wave is one way to stop its gliding, and going onto the curl is another. Skilled surfers use it frequently, but the unskilled are afraid of this board, choosing rather to sit on a canoe or to surf on even smaller boards.

Body surfers use their shoulders like surfboards. When the surf rises before breaking, it is time to slip onto the wave by kicking hard and working the arms. The contraction in the back of a surfer causes him to be lifted by the wave and carried ashore. The right shoulder becomes the board bearing him to the right, or the left shoulder becomes the board bearing him to the left. Liholiho was most skilled in this sport.

There are many ways to show skill in canoe surfing. The king was especially noted for it, and so was his pupil, Gideon Laanui. They were often seen together gliding on the surf outside of Haleumiumiiole at Kawaihae and at Kapuni, outside of Kiikiiakoi. They would allow waves to go by until they saw one they wished to glide on, then ride it to the spot where they chose to land. There are ways of selecting waves which will go all the way to shore, and the king and his pupil were unusually skillful at this. Such things were actually taught.

It was said that a person skilled in canoe paddling and estimating waves could overcome obstacles if the wind was from the right direction, and the ability of the participants became something on which to gamble. This custom remains to this day, and it may be so in the future.

EXPLORERS

An Account of the Voyages Undertaken by the Order of His Present Majesty for Making Discoveries in the Southern Hemisphere (1773)

Sir Joseph Banks
1743–1820

Captain James Cook arrived in Tahiti in 1769 on his first voyage to the Pacific (1768–1771) to establish a temporary observatory to record the transit of Venus across the sun and to search for a fabled southern continent.[4] Sir Joseph Banks, a botanist by training and later president of Britain's Royal Society, was returning from an unlucky visit he had made with Cook and other crew members to a local Tahitian chief (the men had had most of their clothing and other personal effects stolen during the night) when he recorded the following description of natives riding waves using the stern of an old canoe.

Matavai Bay, Tahiti
May 28, 1769

Having given up all hope of recovering our clothes, which indeed were never afterwards heard of, we spent all the morning in soliciting the hogs which we had been promised; but in this we had no better success: we therefore, in no very good humour, set out for the boat about twelve o'clock, with only that which we had redeemed from the butcher and the cook the night before. As we were returning to the boat, however, we were entertained with a sight that in some measure compensated for our fatigue and disappointment. In our way we came to one of the few places where access to the island is not guarded by a reef, and, consequently, a high surf breaks upon the shore; a more dreadful one indeed I had seldom seen; it was impossible for any European boat to have lived in it; and if the best swimmer in Europe had, by any accident, been exposed to its fury, I am confident that he would not have been able to preserve himself from drowning, especially as the shore was covered with pebbles and large stones; yet, in the midst of these breakers, were ten or twelve Indians swimming for their amusement: whenever a surf broke near them, they dived under it, and, to all appearance with infinite facility, rose again on the other side. This diversion was greatly improved by the stern of an old canoe, which they happened to find upon the spot; they took this before them, and swam out with it as far as the outermost beach, then two or three of them getting into it, and turning the square end to the breaking wave, were driven in towards the shore with incredible rapidity, sometimes almost to the beach; but generally the wave broke over them before they got half way, in which case they dived, and rose on the other side with the canoe in their hands: they then swam out with it again, and were again driven back, just as our holiday youth climb the hill in Greenwich park for the pleasure of rolling down it. At this wonderful scene we stood gazing for more than half an hour, during which time none of the swimmers attempted to come on shore, but seemed to enjoy their sport in the highest degree; we then proceeded in our journey, and late in the evening got back to the fort.

CHAPTER 12

A Voyage to the Pacific Ocean (1784)

William Anderson
1750–1778

William Anderson served as surgeon's mate on Cook's second voyage to the South Pacific (1772–1774), and was named surgeon on the *Resolution* during Cook's third voyage (1776–1780). He authored large portions of the final account, so much that Cook's modern-day editor, J. C. Beaglehole, mentions that he "might almost go on to the title-page as a third author."[5] He composed some thirty pages in volume 2 of the official account on Tahiti, including the following well-known description of a Tahitian "canoe surfing." Anderson's observation captures a certain timeless quality about the act of riding waves: not only is the Tahitian completely absorbed by the motion of gliding along a wave, but the act is entirely sufficient to itself; whereas other islanders collect around the novelty of Western tents and ships, the canoeist rejects such trappings and chooses to paddle back "in search of another swell."

Matavai Bay, Tahiti
August 24–September 28, 1777

Neither are they strangers to the soothing effects produced by particular sorts of motion; which, in some cases, seem to allay any perturbation of mind, with as much success as music. Of this, I met with a remarkable instance. For on walking, one day, about Matavai Point, where our tents were erected, I saw a man paddling, in a small canoe, so quickly, and looking about with such eagerness, on each side, as to command all my attention. At first, I imagined that he had stolen something from one of the ships, and was pursued; but, on waiting patiently, saw him repeat his amusement. He went out from the shore, till he was near the place where the swell begins to take its rise; and watching its first motion very attentively, paddled before it, with great quickness, till he found that it overtook him, and had acquired sufficient force to carry his canoe before it, without passing underneath. He then sat motionless, and was carried along, at the same swift rate as the wave, till it landed him upon the beach. Then he started out, emptied his canoe, and went in search of another swell. I could not help concluding, that this man felt the most supreme pleasure, while he was driven on, so fast and so smoothly, by the sea; especially as, though the tents and ships were so near, he did not seem, in the least, to envy, or even to take any notice of, the crows of his countrymen collected to view them as objects which were rare and curious. During my stay; two or three of the natives came up, when there was an appearance of a favourable swell, as he sometimes missed it, by his back being turned, and looking about for it. By them I understood, that this exercise, which is called *ehorooe*, was frequent amongst them; and they have probably more amusements of this sort, which afford them at least as much pleasure as skating, which is the only one of ours, with whose effect I could compare it.

CHAPTER 13

The Journals of Captain James Cook on his Voyages of Discovery (1967)

Charles Clerke

1743–1779

Charles Clerke holds the honor apparently of recording the earliest use of surfboards in Hawai'i. Cook's ships had chanced across O'ahu on January 18, 1778, but were unable to land. Winds pushed them west off the island of Kaua'i, then Ni'ihau, where the explorers traded with natives (and transmitted venereal disease) to replenish their supplies of food and water before sailing to the coast of North America in search of a northwest passage. Clerke's journal entry dates from this first brief encounter with the Hawaiians. Blocked by arctic ice, Cook returned in November of the same year to the Islands, eventually sailing into Kealakekua Bay on January 17, 1779. Clerke assumed command of the *Resolution* after the death of Cook on February 14, though his tenure was brief: he died at sea from tuberculosis on August 22, 1779, and was succeeded by Lieutenant John Gore, who took charge of the expedition.

Waimea, Kaua'i /Kamalino, Ni'ihau
January 19–February 2, 1778

These People handle their Boats with great dexterity, and both Men and Women are so perfectly masters of themselves in the Water, that it appears their natural Element; they have another convenience for conveying themselves upon the Water, which we never met with before; this is by means of a thin piece of Board about 2 feet broad & 6 or 8 long, exactly in the Shape of one of our bone paper cutters; upon this they get astride with their legs, then laying their breasts along upon it, they paddle with their Hands and steer with their Feet, and gain such Way thro' the Water, that they would fairly go round the best going Boats we had in the two Ships, in spight of every Exertion of the Crew, in the space of a very few minutes. There were frequently 2 and sometimes 3 upon one of these peices of board, which must be devilishly overballasted; still by their Management, they apparently made very good Weather of it.

CHAPTER 14

An Authentic Narrative of a Voyage Performed by Captain Cook and Captain Clerke in His Majesty's Ships Resolution and Discovery (1782)

William Ellis
d. 1785

William Ellis served as surgeon's second mate aboard the *Discovery* and later the *Resolution*. Because he published his account of the voyage in 1782, two years before the official version appeared, the following excerpt represents the earliest published description of Hawaiian natives riding surfboards. Since the word *surfboard* did not yet exist, Ellis decided to call them *sharkboards*. His concluding comment that water seemed the "natural element" of Hawaiians became a regular trope among travelers to the Pacific, many of whom characterized the natives as "amphibious."[6]

Waimea, Kaua'i
January, 1778

Their canoes or boats are the neatest we ever saw, and composed of two different coloured woods, the bottom being dark, the upper part light, and furnished with an out-rigger. Besides these, they have another mode of conveying themselves in the water, upon very light flat pieces of boards, which we called sharkboards, from the similitude the anterior part bore to the head of that fish. Upon these they will venture into the heaviest surfs, and paddling with their hands and feet, get on at a great rate. Indeed, we never saw people so active in the water, which almost seems their natural element.

CHAPTER 15

The Journals of Captain James Cook on his Voyages of Discovery (1967)

David Samwell

c. 1751–1799

After spending most of 1779 off the coast of North America looking for a northwest passage, Cook's two ships returned to winter in the islands (Kaua'i and Ni'ihau) that they had crossed earlier that year. They arrived to the southeast of those islands, sighting Maui in late November, then the most southern island, Hawai'i, where the ships found harbor at Kealakekua Bay. Samwell was surgeon's mate first aboard the *Resolution*, then the *Discovery* after the death of William Anderson in 1778. His journal entry describes a scene that emphasizes the stark contrast between Western and Polynesian cultures and their relationship with the ocean: what Samwell recorded as an activity that would be "nothing but Horror & Destruction" for the mariners was mere child's play to the young Hawaiians riding their surfboards.

Kealakekua Bay, Hawai'i
January 22, 1779

As two or three of us were walking along shore to day we saw a number of boys & young Girls playing in the Surf, which broke very high on the Beach as there was a great swell rolling into the Bay. In the first place they provide themselves with a thin board about six or seven foot long & about 2 broad, on these they swim off shore to meet the Surf, as soon as they see one coming they get themselves in readiness & turn their sides to it, they suffer themselves to be involved in it & then manage so as to get just before it or rather on the Slant or declivity of the Surf, & thus they lie with their Hands lower than their Heels laying hold of the fore part of the board which receives the force of the water on its under side, & by that means keeps before the wave which drives it along with an incredible Swiftness to the shore. The Motion is so rapid for near the Space of a stones throw that they seem to fly on the water, the flight of a bird being hardly quicker than theirs. On their putting off shore if they meet with the Surf too near in to afford them a tolerable long Space to run before it they dive under it with the greatest Ease & proceed further out to sea. Sometimes they fail in trying to get before the surf, as it requires great dexterity & address, and after struggling awhile in such a tremendous wave that we should have judged it impossible for any human being to live in it, they rise on the other side laughing and shaking their Locks & push on to meet the next Surf when they generally succeed, hardly ever being foiled in more than one attempt. Thus these People find one of their Chief amusements in that which to us presented nothing but Horror & Destruction, and we saw with astonishment young boys & Girls about 9 or ten years of age playing amid such tempestuous Waves that the hardiest of our seamen would have trembled to face, as to be involved in them among the Rocks, on which they broke with a tremendous Noise, they could look upon as no other than certain death.

CHAPTER 16

Captain Cook's Final Voyage: The Journal of Midshipman George Gilbert (1982)

George Gilbert
c. 1759–?

Midshipman aboard the *Discovery*, George Gilbert offers the most detailed description of a surfboard among the explorers. Like Ellis's "sharkboards" and Clerke's "bone paper cutters," the outline of the board
described by Gilbert—"nearly in the form of a blade of an oar"—is consistent with John Papa ʻĪʻī's description of an *alaia*, "thin and wide in
front, tapering toward the back." Gilbert's concluding remarks, together
with the preciseness of his measurements, demonstrate his keen interest
in the boards, and make one wonder if some of Cook's men might not
have tried paddling the crafts themselves.[7]

Kealakekua Bay, Hawaiʻi
February, 1779

Several of those Indians who have not got Canoes have a method of swimming upon a piece of wood nearly in the form of a blade of an oar, which
is about six feet in length, sixteen inches in breadth at one end and about
9 at the other, and is four or five inches thick, in the middle, tapering
down to an inch at the sides. They lay themselves upon it length ways,
with their breast about the centre; and it being sufficient to buoy them up
they paddle along with their hands and feet at a moderate rate, having the
broad end foremost; and that it may not meet with any resistance from
the water, they keep it just above the surface by weighing down upon the
other, which they have underneath them, between their legs. These pieces
of wood are so nicely balanced that the most expert of our people at swimming could not keep upon them half a minuit without rolling off.

CHAPTER 17

The Journals of Captain James Cook on his Voyages of Discovery (1967)

James King
1750–1784

James King, second lieutenant on the *Resolution*, then commander of the *Discovery* after the death of Clerke, captained a five hundred-ship convoy to the West Indies immediately after the completion of Cook's voyage in 1780. He composed the greater part of his journals from Cook's voyage after having returned to England from this latter trip. Despite his comment that surfriding was "only intended as an amusement, not as a tryal of Skill," King's vivid details support John Papa 'Ī'ī's description of how expert surfriders practiced maneuvering their boards through dangerous outcroppings of rocks.

Kealakekua Bay, Hawai'i[8]
January 18–February 14, 1779

But a diversion the most common is upon the Water, where there is a very great Sea, & surf breaking upon the Shore. The Men sometimes 20 or 30 go without the Swell of the Surf, & lay themselves flat up an oval piece of plank about their Size and breadth, they keep their legs close on the top of it, & their Arms are us'd to guide the plank, they wait the time for the greatest Swell that sets on Shore, & altogether push forward with their Arms to keep on its top, it sends them in with a most astonishing Velocity, & the great art is to guide the plank so as always to keep in a proper direction on the top of the Swell, & as it alters its direct[ion]. If the Swell drives him close to the rocks before he is overtaken by its break, he is much prais'd. On first seeing this very dangerous diversion I did not conceive it possible but that some of them must be dashed to mummy against the sharp rocks, but just before they reach the shore, if they are very near, they quit their plank, & dive under till the Surf is broke, when the piece of plank is sent many yards by the force of the Surf from the breach. The greatest number are generally overtaken by the break of the swell, the force of which they avoid, diving & swimming under the water out of its impulse. By such like exercises, these men may be said to be almost amphibious. The Women could swim off to the Ship, & continue half a day in the Water, & afterwards return. The above diversion is only intended as an amusement, not as a tryal of Skill, & in a gentle swell that sets on must I conceive be very pleasant, at least they seem to feel a great pleasure in the motion which this Exercise gives.

CHAPTER 18

A Voyage to the Pacific Ocean (1784)

John Douglas, ed.
1721–1807

John Douglas, bishop of Salisbury, edited the official account of Captain Cook's second voyage to the South Pacific and was charged with editing Cook's final voyage. Such editions were normally the result of a compilation: Douglas would have gathered all journals from the voyage and produced the final version, integrating various observations and generally smoothing out the rough language of the mariners. Because of the many differences between this final version and the preceding journal entry of James King—including specific details that Douglas could hardly have credibly invented—one is led to the probability that King either provided Douglas with more information as the two worked on the final version, or Douglas based this passage not on King's words, as has long been thought, but on a text that has not yet come to light. Authorship aside, the following version became the most influential account of Hawaiian surfriding for the next fifty years. Surfriding was introduced to the West as a "perilous and extraordinary" exercise in which Hawaiians perform "difficult and dangerous manœuvres"—a description that remains accurate today.

Kealakekua Bay, Hawai'i
January 18–February 14, 1779

Swimming is not only a necessary art, in which both their men and women are more expert than any people we had hitherto seen, but a favourite diversion amongst them. One particular mode, in which they sometimes amused themselves with this exercise, in Karakakooa [Kealakekua] Bay, appeared to us most perilous and extraordinary, and well deserving a distinct relation.

The surf, which breaks on the coast round the bay, extends to the distance of about one hundred and fifty yards from the shore, within which space, the surges of the sea, accumulating from the shallowness of the water, are dashed against the beach with prodigious violence. Whenever, from stormy weather, or any extraordinary swell at sea, the impetuosity of the surf is increased to its upmost height, they choose that time for this amusement, which is performed in the following manner: Twenty or thirty of the natives, taking each a long narrow board, rounded at the ends, set out together from the shore. The first wave they meet, they plunge under, and suffering it to roll over them, rise again beyond it, and make the best of their way, by swimming, out into the sea. The second wave is encountered in the same manner with the first; the great difficulty consisting in seizing the proper moment of diving under it, which, if missed, the person is caught by the surf, and driven back again with great violence; and all his dexterity is then required to prevent himself from being dashed against the rocks. As soon as they have gained, by these repeated efforts, the smooth water beyond the surf, they lay themselves at length on their board, and prepare for their return. As the surf consists of a number of waves, of which every third is remarked to be always much larger then the others, and to flow higher on the shore, the rest breaking in the intermediate space, their first object is to place themselves on the summit of the largest surge, by which they are driven along with amazing rapidity toward the shore. If by mistake they should place themselves on one of the smaller waves, which breaks before they reach the land, or should not be able to keep their plank in a proper direction on the top of the swell, they are left exposed to the fury of the next, and, to avoid it, are obliged again to dive, and regain the place from which they set out. Those who succeed in their object of reaching the shore, have still the greatest danger to encounter. The coast being guarded by a chain of rocks, with, here and there, a small opening between them, they are obliged to steer their board through one of these, or, in case of failure, to quit it, before they reach the rocks, and, plunging under the wave, make the best of their way back again. This is reckoned very disgraceful, and is also attended with the loss of the board, which I have often seen, with great terror, dashed to pieces, at the very moment the islander quitted it. The boldness and address, with which we saw them perform these difficult and dangerous manœuvres, was altogether astonishing, and is scarcely to be credited.

CHAPTER 19

The Log of the Bounty (1937)

William Bligh
1754–1817

William Bligh had been sailing master aboard the *Resolution* during Cook's third voyage and subsequently led an expedition to Tahiti in 1787 to transport breadfruit tree saplings from the South Pacific to the Caribbean. Bligh reached Tahiti aboard the *Bounty* on October 26, 1788, and remained almost six months, during which time he recorded the following observation of natives surfriding on "paddles." The *Bounty* left Tahiti with the supply of breadfruit on April 4, 1789; Fletcher Christian's mutiny occurred on April 28. After a historic open-boat trip with eighteen members of his crew, Bligh eventually made it back to England and was promoted to commander. He returned to Tahiti in 1792 to complete his original mission.

Matavai Bay, Tahiti
November 28, 1788

The heavy surf which has run on the shore for a few days past has given great amusement to many of the Natives, but is such as one would suppose would drown any European. The general plan of this diversion is for a number of them to advance with their paddles to where the Sea begins to break and placing the broad part under the Belly holding the other end with their Arms extended at full length, they turn themselves to the surge and balancing themselves on the Paddles are carried to the shore with the greatest rapidity. As several seas follow each other they have those to encounter on their return, which they do by diving under them with great ease and cleverness.

The delight they take in this amusement is beyond anything, and is of the most essential good for them, for even in their largest and best Cannoes they are so subject to accidents of being overturned that their lives depend on their swimming and habituing themselves to remain long in the Water. They also practise with small Cannoes in these high surfs, and it is seldom that any of them get overturned or filled.

CHAPTER 20

The Journal of James Morrison, Boatswain's Mate of the Bounty (1935)

James Morrison
1761–1807

James Morrison offers the first known description of Pacific islanders—in this case, Tahitians—standing on their surfboards. His account also echoes the communal nature of surfriding, and the equal skill of men and women, that appear in many Hawaiian legends. Morrison composed his narrative in jail in 1792 after having been returned to England for taking part in the mutiny on the *Bounty*. He was found guilty by a court martial and sentenced to death, though he later received a full pardon. Although Morrison's account was not published until 1935, his journal was made available to other voyagers headed to the South Pacific and subsequently appeared in such works as James Wilson's *A Missionary Voyage to the Southern Pacific Ocean, 1796–1798* (1799), and *History of the Otaheitean Islands* (1800).[9]

Matavai Bay, Tahiti

1788–89

When the Westerly Winds prevail they have a heavy surf Constantly running to a prodigious height on the Shore & this Affords excellent diversion and the part they Choose for their Sport is where the Surf breaks with the Most Violence—when they go to this diversion they get peices of Board of any length with which they swim out to the back of the surf, when they Watch the rise of a surf somtimes a Mile from the shore & laying their Breast on the board, keep themselves poised on the Surf so as to come in on the top of it, with amazing rapidity watching the time that it breaks, when they turn with great Activity and diving under the surge swim out again towing their plank with them—at this diversion both Sexes are Excellent, and some are so expert [as] to stand on their board till the Surf breaks—the Children also take their sport in the smaller surfs and as Most learn to swim as soon as walk few or no accidents happen from Drowning.

They resort to this sport in great Numbers and keep at it for several Hours and as they often encounter each other in their passage out and in they require the greatest Skill in swimming to keep from running foul of each other—which they somtimes cannot avoid in which case both are Violently dashd on shore where they are thrown neck & heels and often find very Coarse landing, which however they take little Notice of and recovering themselves regain their boards & return to their sport.

The Chiefs are in general best at this as well as all other Diversions, nor are their Weomen behind hand at it. Eddea is one of the Best among the Society Islands & able to hold it with the Best of the Men Swimmers.[10]

This Diversion took place during the time the Bounty lay in Maatavye Bay when the Surf from the Dolphin Bank ran so high as to break over her, and we were forced to secure the Hatches expecting the Ship to go on shore evry Minute.

After they have been at this sport they always wash in Fresh Water, as they always do when they have been out in their Canoes or have been wet with salt water.

They have also a diversion in Canoes, which they steer on the top of the Surf with Great dexterity, and can either turn them out before it breaks or land safe tho it Breaks ever so high.

CHAPTER 21

A Voyage of Discovery to the Northern Pacific Ocean and Round the World, 1791–1795 (1984)

Peter Puget
1765–1822

Peter Puget served as lieutenant aboard the *Discovery* when it sailed for the South Pacific in 1791 under George Vancouver. After completing survey missions and resuming a search for a northwest passage along the American coast (Vancouver named present-day Puget Sound after his lieutenant), the expedition returned to the Hawaiian Islands, during which time Puget observed an impromptu surf session. Keeaumoku was an important ally of Kamehameha I, who ceded the island of Hawai'i to Great Britain during this same visit. Namahana was the mother of Ka'ahumanu, an expert surfrider and the powerful chiefess whom Hiram Bingham later converted to Christianity. The following entry shows the high level of skill in the waves shared by mother and daughter.

Kealakekua Bay, Hawai'i
January 27, 1794

From [Keeaumoku's] village we walked through some pleasant cultivated Grounds to a Small Stony Beach where the natives were amusing themselves in the Surf on Swimming Boards. Nammahana [Namahana], the wife of Tayomodu [Keeaumoku], who is reckoned one of the most expert at that Diversion immediately Stript naked and she certainly notwithstanding her Corpulency performed her part with wonderful Dexterity. The first Sea or Surf that brought her in towards the Beach was immensely high, on its Top she came, floating on a Broad Board till the Break[er] had nearly reached the Rocks, she then suddenly turned, went under that & the one following and so on till she had regained her Situation at the back of the whole. Then she waited for a large Swell and once more performed her part with great Expertness; Numbers of Men Women and Boys were in her Company and I was in Momentary Expectation of seeing some dashed to pieces.

MISSIONARIES

CHAPTER 22

"Mission at the Sandwich Islands" (1822)
Hiram Bingham
1789–1869

Hiram Bingham's account of his visit to Kaua'i in 1821 represents the first description of Hawaiian surfriding by a missionary, and the most detailed since the journals of Cook's third voyage. Bingham, the most influential of the first Protestant missionaries who arrived in Hawai'i in 1820, oversaw the conversion of key Hawaiian rulers—and subsequently their subjects—to Christianity. A controversial figure because of both his strict religious policies and difficult personality, Bingham describes a scene in the following journal entry that allows us to see both the impact of Westernization on Hawaiian culture (in the "imported goods" provided by Kaumualii, the king of Kaua'i) and the remnants of the tabu system abolished two years prior (the king prohibits the common people "from entering the enclosure, where Kaneo, and her ladies and servants were lodged"). One of the effects of Hawaiian royalty importing goods was the forced labor of commoners to supply products like sandalwood for exportation; such labor was one of the reasons for the decline of surfriding in the nineteenth century.

Kaua'i
July 9, 1821

ARRIVAL OF KANEO[11]

Soon after noon, Kaneo, with her attendants, landed just in front of the mission house, where the king and queen, with their attendants, met her, embraced, and joined noses, with loud crying, many tears, and other expressions of emotion. After some minutes, all sat down together on the sand for a considerable time, till the first bursts of feeling had subsided, when the king conducted his guests to the house, which he had prepared for their reception, by removing a quantity of imported goods lately purchased, and spreading his best mats, both in the house, and the court in front. Having ordered the slaughter of hogs, dogs, &c. for the purpose, he prepared a full repast for the company. At evening, he resigned his own dwelling house to his guests, and retiring to another, sent out a crier to prohibit the common people from entering the enclosure, where Kaneo, and her ladies and servants were lodged, and set a guard also at the gate.

July 10

The king's company, that is, his wife Tapoolee and particular friends, Kaneo and her attendants, spent much of the day in decorating themselves with a kind of temporary ornaments, which they call "Laualla beads;" and in a favorite amusement of playing in the surf, of which a pretty good description is given in "Trumbull's Voyages."[12] All engage in it, without distinction of rank, age, or sex; and the whole nation is distinguished by their fondness for the water, and the dexterity and facility with which they manage themselves in that element.

The surf-board and the manner it is used.

The surf-board, or the instrument used in playing in the surf, is of various dimensions, from three feet in length, and eight inches in breadth, to fourteen feet in length and twenty inches in breadth. It is made of light wood, thin at the edges and ends, but of considerable thickness in the middle, wrought exceedingly smooth, and ingeniously adapted to the purpose of gliding rapidly in the water. The islander, placing himself horizontally on the board, and using his arms as oars, paddles out into the sea, meeting the successive surges, as they roll along towards the shore. If they are high, he dives under them, if they are low, or smooth, glides over them with ease, till he is ready to return, or till he gains the smooth sea beyond where the surf breaks. Then choosing one of the highest surges, adjusting his board as it approaches him, directing his head towards the shore, he rides on the fore front of the surge, with great velocity, as his board darts along swifter than a weaver's shuttle, while the whitening surf foams and roars around his head, till it dies on the beach, and leaves him to return or retire at pleasure. Often, several of them run at the same time, as in a race, and not infrequently on a wager. The board moves as down an inclined plain, and the art lies principally in keeping it in proper position, giving it occasionally an accelerating stroke with the hands, so that it shall not lose the propelling force of the wave, and thus fall behind it; or retarding it with the foot, when liable to shoot forward too fast. Sometimes the irregularity or violence of the water tears their board from under them, and dashes it on the rocks; or threatening to carry them into danger, obliges them to abandon it, and save themselves by diving and swimming.

I informed the king, as he sat on the beach witnessing the sport, of the design of building a church, or a house for the public worship of the true God, at Woahoo [Oʻahu]. He expressed his approbation, and also his intention to send his brig to Taheite.[13]

CHAPTER 23

Narrative of a Tour through Hawaii (1826)[14]

William Ellis
1794–1872

William Ellis, one of the most experienced missionaries in the South Pacific, had spent six years in the Society Islands before arriving in 1822
on O'ahu, where his fluency in Tahitian allowed him to preach to the
native Hawaiians in a shared Polynesian language. His subsequent visit
to the island of Hawai'i became the most influential account of the Islands—and of surfriding—throughout the nineteenth century. Ellis had
a keen eye for detail and natural beauty, and though his depiction of surfriding repeated certain clichés—natives as "a race of amphibious beings"
engaged in activities that "would be fatal to an European"—his facility
with the language allowed him to present much new information: Western readers discovered for the first time, for example, the Hawaiian name
of a surfboard—"*papa hé náru*" (*papa he'e nalu*); and Ellis's description
of how natives cared for these boards revealed their significant value in
Hawaiian culture. Ironically, the general exuberance of Ellis's prose, despite his formal disapproval of adults engaging in such activities, inspired
the imaginations of countless travelers seeking to witness, even try for
themselves, this exciting native sport. The following excerpt opens with
Hawaiian men "shipping sandalwood," a much sought-after island commodity whose production represented another activity that drew natives
away from traditional activities like surfriding.

Waimanu, Hawai'i
Summer, 1823

We found Arapai, the chief, and a number of his men, busy on the beach
shipping sandalwood on board a sloop belonging to the governor, then
lying at anchor in a small bay off the mouth of the valley. He received us
kindly, and directed two of his men to conduct us to his house, which
was on the opposite side. The valley, though not so spacious or cultivated
as Waipio, was equally verdant and picturesque; we could not but notice

the unusual beauty of its natural scenery. The glittering cascades and water-falls, that rolled down the deep sides of the surrounding mountains, seemed more numerous and beautiful than those at Waipio.

As we crossed the head of the bay, we saw a number of young persons swimming in the surf, which rolled with some violence on the rocky beach. To a spectator nothing can appear more daring, and sometimes alarming, than to see a number of persons splashing about among the waves of the sea as they dash on the shore; yet this is the most popular and delightful of the native sports.

There are perhaps no people more accustomed to the water than the islanders of the Pacific; they seem almost a race of amphibious beings. Familiar with the sea from their birth, they lose all dread of it, and seem nearly as much at home in the water as on dry land. There are few children who are not taken into the sea by their mothers the second or third day after their birth, and many who can swim as soon as they can walk. The heat of the climate is, no doubt, one source of the gratification they find in this amusement, which is so universal, that it is scarcely possible to pass along the shore where there are many habitations near, and not see a number of children playing in the sea. Here they remain for hours together, and yet I never knew of but one child being drowned during the number of years I have resided in the islands. They have a variety of games, and gambol as fearlessly in the water as the children of a school do in their play-ground. Sometimes they erect a stage eight or ten feet high on the edge of some deep place, and lay a pole in an oblique direction over the edge of it, perhaps twenty feet above the water; along this they pursue each other to the outermost end, when they jump into the sea. Throwing themselves from the lower yards, or bowsprit, of a ship, is also a favourite sport, but the most general and frequent game is swimming in the surf. The higher the sea and the larger the waves, in their opinion the better the sport.

On these occasions they use a board, which they call *papa hé náru*, (wave sliding board,) generally five or six feet long, and rather more than a foot wide, sometimes flat, but more frequently slightly convex on both sides.[15] It is usually made of the wood of the *erythrina*, stained quite black, and preserved with great care. After using, it is placed in the sun till perfectly dry, when it is rubbed over with cocoa-nut oil, frequently wrapped in cloth, and suspended in some part of their dwelling-house. Sometimes they choose a place where the deep water reaches to the beach, but generally prefer a part where the rocks are ten or twenty feet under water, and extend to a distance from the shore, as the surf breaks more violently over these. When playing in these places, each individual takes his board, and, pushing it before him, swims perhaps a quarter of a mile or more out to sea. They do not attempt to go over the billows which roll towards the shore, but watch their approach, and dive under water, allowing the billow to pass over their heads. When they reach the outside of the rocks, where the waves first break, they adjust themselves on one end of the board, lying flat on their faces, and watch the approach of the largest billow; they then poise themselves on its highest edge, and, paddling as it were with their hands and feet, ride on the crest of the wave, in the midst of the spray and foam, till within a yard or two of the rocks or the shore; and when the observers would expect to see them dashed to pieces, they steer with great address between the rocks, or slide off their board in a moment, grasp it by the middle, and dive under water, while the wave rolls on, and breaks among the rocks with a roaring noise, the effect of which is greatly heightened by the shouts and laughter of the natives in the water. Those who are expert frequently change their position on the board, sometimes sitting and sometimes standing erect in the midst of the foam. The greatest address is necessary in order to keep on the edge of the wave: for if they get too forward, they are sure to be overturned; and if they fall back, they are buried beneath the succeeding billow.

Occasionally they take a very light canoe; but this, though directed in the same manner as the board, is much more difficult to manage. Sometimes the greater part of the inhabitants of a village go out to this sport, when the wind blows fresh towards the shore, and spend the greater part of the day in the water. All ranks and ages appear equally fond of it. We have seen Karaimoku [Kalanimoku] and Kakioeva [Kaikioewa], some of the highest chiefs in the island, both between fifty and sixty years of age, and large corpulent men, balancing themselves on their narrow board, or splashing about in the foam, with as much satisfaction as youths of sixteen. They frequently play at the mouth of a large river, where the strong current running into the sea, and the rolling of the waves towards the shore, produce a degree of agitation between the water of the river and the sea, that would be fatal to an European, however expert he might be; yet in this they delight: and when the king or queen, or any high chiefs, are playing, none of the common people are allowed to approach these places, lest they should spoil their sport.

The chiefs pride themselves much on excelling in some of the games of their country; hence Taumuarii [Kaumualii], the late king of Tauai [Kaua'i], was celebrated as the most expert swimmer in the surf, known in the islands. The only circumstance that ever mars their pleasure in this diversion is the approach of a shark. When this happens, though they sometimes fly in every direction, they frequently unite, set up a loud shout, and make so much splashing in the water, as to frighten him away.

Their fear of them, however, is very great; and after a party returns from this amusement, almost the first question they are asked is, "Were there any sharks?" The fondness of the natives for the water must strike any person visiting their islands: long before he goes on shore, he will see them swimming around his ship; and few ships leave without being accompanied part of the way out of the harbour by the natives, sporting in the water; but to see fifty or a hundred persons riding on an immense billow, half immersed in spray and foam, for a distance of several hundred yards together, is one of the most novel and interesting sports a foreigner can witness in the islands.

CHAPTER 24

Polynesian Researches (1829)

William Ellis
1794–1872

William Ellis republished his Hawaiian material in *Polynesian Researches*,
adding observations from his years in the Society Islands that also included a description of Tahitian surfriding. This supplementary material
echoes certain portions of his Hawaiian description of the sport; at the
same time it offers a valuable comparison of the state of surfriding in the
two locales by someone who had witnessed both. The appended description of a shark attack at Lahaina, Maui, reminds us of the practical dangers of surfriding—even today—and the persistence of the native belief
system a number of years after the abolition of the tabu system in 1819.
The selection concludes with remarks on the disappearance of native customs, an example of the perspective for which missionary practices have
long been criticized.

Fare, Huahine

1817–22

Like the inhabitants of most of the islands of the Pacific, the Tahitians
are fond of the water, and lose all dread of it before they are old enough
to know the danger to which we should consider them exposed. They
are among the best divers that are known, and spend much of their time
in the sea, not only when engaged in acts of labour, but when following
their amusements. One of their favourite sports, is the *faahee*, or swimming in the surf, when the waves are high, and billows break in foam
and spray among the reefs. Individuals of all ranks and ages, and both
sexes, follow this pastime with the greatest avidity. They usually selected
the openings in the reefs, or entrances of some of the bays, for their
sport; where the long heavy billows of the ocean rolled in unbroken
majesty upon the reef or the shore. They used a small board, which they
called *papa faahee*—swam from the beach to a considerable distance,
sometimes nearly a mile, watched the swell of the wave, and when it

reached them, resting their bosom on the short flat pointed board, they mounted on its summit, and, amid the foam and spray, rode on the crest of the wave to the shore: sometimes they halted among the coral rocks, over which the waves broke in splendid confusion. When they approached the shore, they slid off the board, which they grasped with the hand, and either fell behind the wave, or plunged toward the deep, and allowed it to pass over their heads. Sometimes they were thrown with violence upon the beach, or among the rocks on the edges of the reef. So much at home, however, do they feel in the water, that it is seldom any accident occurs.

I have often seen, along the border of the reef forming the boundary line to the harbour of Fare, in Huahine, from fifty to a hundred persons, of all ages, sporting like so many porpoises in the surf, that has been rolling with foam and violence towards the land, sometimes mounted on the top of the wave, and almost enveloped in spray, at other times plunging beneath the mass of water that has swept in mountains over them, cheering and animating each other; and, by the noise and shouting they made, rendering the roaring of the sea, and the dashing of the surf, comparatively imperceptible. Their surf-boards are inferior to those of the Sandwich Islanders, and I do not think swimming in the sea as an amusement, whatever it might have been formerly, is now practised so much by the natives in the south, as by those in the northern Pacific. Both were exposed in this sport to one common cause of interruption; and this was, the intrusion of the shark among them. The cry of a *mao* among the former, and a *manó* among the latter, is one of the most terrific they ever hear; and I am not surprised that such should be the effect of the approach of one of these voracious monsters. The great shouting and clamour which they make, is principally designed to frighten away such as may approach. Notwithstanding this, they are often disturbed, and sometimes meet their death from these formidable enemies.

A most affecting instance of this kind occurred very recently in the Sandwich Islands, of which the following account is given by Mr. Richards, and published in the American Missionary Herald:

"At nine o'clock in the morning of June 14th, 1826, while sitting at my writing-desk, I heard a simultaneous scream from multitudes of people, *Pau i ka mano! Pau i ka mano!* (Destroyed by a shark! Destroyed by a shark!) The beach was instantly lined by hundreds of persons, and a few of the most resolute threw a large canoe into the water, and alike regardless of the shark, sprang to the relief of their companion. It was too late. The shark had already seized his prey. The affecting sight was only a few yards from my door, and while I stood watching, a large wave almost filled the canoe, and at the same instant a part of the mangled body was seen at the bow of the canoe, and the shark swimming towards it at her stern. When the swell had rolled by, the water was too shallow for the shark to swim. The remains, therefore, were taken into the canoe, and brought ashore. The water was so much stained by the blood, that we discovered a red tinge in all the foaming billows, as they approached the beach.

"The unhappy sufferer was an active lad about fourteen years old, who left my door only about half an hour previous to the fatal accident. I saw his mother, in the extremity of her anguish, plunge into the water, and swim towards the bloody spot, entirely forgetful of the power of her former god.

"A number of people, perhaps a hundred, were at this time playing in the surf, which was higher than usual. Those who were nearest to the victim heard him shriek, perceived him to strike with his right hand, and at the same instant saw a shark seize his arm. Then followed the cry which I heard, which echoed from one end of Lahaina to the other. All who were playing in the water made the utmost speed to the shore, and those who were standing on the beach saw the surf-board of the unhappy sufferer floating on the water, without any one to guide it. When the canoe reached the spot, they saw nothing but the blood with which the water was stained for a considerable distance, and by which they traced the remains, whither they had been carried by the shark, or driven by the swell. The body was cut in two, by the shark, just above the hips; and the lower part, together with the right arm, were gone.

"Many of the people connect this death with their old system of religion; for they have still a superstitious veneration for the shark, and this veneration is increased rather than diminished by such occurrences as these.

"It is only about four months since a man was killed in the same manner at Waihee, on the eastern part of this island. It is said, however, that there are much fewer deaths by the shark than formerly. This, perhaps, may be owing to their not being so much fed by the people, and therefore they do not frequent the shores so much."

. . . These are only some of the principal games, or amusements, of the natives; others might be added, but these are sufficient to shew that they were not destitute of sources of entertainment, either in their juvenile or more advanced periods of life. With the exception of one or two, they have all, however, been discontinued, especially among the adults; and the number of those followed by the children is greatly diminished. This is, on no account, matter of regret. When we consider the debasing tendency of many, and the inutility of others, we shall rather rejoice that much of the time of the adults is passed in more rational and beneficial pursuits. Few, if any of them, are so sedentary in their habits, as to need these amusements as a means of exercise; and they are not accustomed to apply so closely to any of their avocations, as to require them merely for relaxation.

CHAPTER 25

Narrative of a Voyage Round the World (1838)

W. S. W. Ruschenberger
1807–1895

A career U.S. naval officer and author, W. S. W. Ruschenberger was serving as Fleet surgeon in the East Indies and China when he published his account of the Islands, which included the following brief criticism of missionary influence on activities like surfriding. Ruschenberger approached his criticism from a mental and physical health perspective: he argued that suppressing such activities had serious adverse health effects on the natives. His assertion that the missionaries "impress upon the minds of the chiefs and others, the idea that all who practice [these sports], secure to themselves the displeasure of offended heaven" seems to be corroborated by Hiram Bingham's account in *The Missionary Herald* of Ka'ahumanu's experience surfriding on the Sabbath at Waikīkī.[16]

Honolulu, O'ahu
September/October, 1836

A change has taken place in certain customs, which must have influenced the physical development of the islanders. I allude to the variety of athletic exercises, such as swimming, with or without the surf-board, dancing, wrestling, throwing the jav[e]lin, &c., all of which games, being in opposition to the severe tenets of Calvinism, have been suppressed, without the substitution of other pursuits to fill up the time. Whether sinful or not, will depend upon the religious code by which they are measured. But let this be as it may, these exercises and games affect the health and longevity of the people, being deprived of these sports, they labour only to obtain food, which may be two days in the week, and having no mental relaxation, the remainder of the time is devoted to sleeping, or drinking, and other vicious practices. It must be borne in mind, that we are speaking of people whose blood has always moved beneath a tropic sun, from their most remotest ancestry to the present time. They cannot endure the same uninterrupted and incessant labour as Europeans or Americans, without a very much greater wear and tear; and though capable of very severe toil and great physical achievement, it is only for a short time together, and is generally followed by long periods of rest. Within the tropics, the inhabitants require longer periods of relaxation, both from mental and physical employment, than in temperate climates; and there are few who have not heard of the dangers which environ those of high latitudes, who reside in, or even visit the equatorial regions of the earth. Now, simply desisting from labour is not rest, particularly in young subjects; people, to enjoy life, require more; they want amusement, without which they flag, the spirits droop, disease follows, and they drag on a miserable, misanthropic existence, till death closes the scene. The practice in the middle and northern sections of the country, must not be taken as a rule, for there is perhaps no civilized people on earth, with the same opportunities, who spend so little time in sports and amusements. They all fix upon a time to come for enjoyment, which generally arrives when the vivacity and elasticity of mind and body have already disappeared, and the organism is no longer sensible to pleasure.

Would these games have been suppressed had the missionaries never arrived at the islands? It is fair to presume that they would have continued in use. Can the missionaries be fairly charged with suppressing these games? I believe they deny having done so. But they write and publicly express against the laws of God, and by a succession of reasoning, which may be readily traced, impress upon the minds of the chiefs and others, the idea that all who practise them, secure to themselves the displeasure of offended heaven. Then the chiefs, from a spontaneous benevolence, at once interrupt customs so hazardous to their vassals.

CHAPTER 26

Narrative of the United States Exploring Expedition (1845)[17]

Charles Wilkes
1798–1877

Another career U.S. naval officer, Charles Wilkes was commander of the U.S. ship *Vincennes* during an extended visit to the Hawaiian Islands on a surveying and exploring mission. He arrived in September 1840 and stayed until April of the following year. Along with a brief description of surfriding, which could have been taken from Ellis or numerous other sources, Wilkes targets the missionaries for their influence in putting a stop to activities like surfriding "to root out the licentiousness that pervaded the land." Given Wilkes's position in the navy, his opinions would have carried weight for a general audience.

1840–41

Playing in the surf was another of their amusements, and is still much practised. It is a beautiful sight to see them coming in on the top of a heavy roller, borne along with increasing rapidity until they suddenly disappear. What we should look upon as the most dangerous surf, is that they most delight in. The surf-board which they use is about six feet in length and eighteen inches wide, made of some light wood. After they have passed within the surf, they are seen buffeting the waves, to regain the outside, whence they again their course, with almost the speed of an aerial flight. They play for hours in this way, never seeming to tire; and the time to see a Hawaiian happy, is while he is gambolling and frolicking in the surf. I have stood for hours watching their sport with great interest, and, I must say, with no little envy. . . .

Since the introduction of Christianity, these amusements have been interdicted; for, although the missionaries were somewhat averse to destroying those of an innocent character, yet, such was the proneness of all to indulge in lascivious thoughts and actions, that it was deemed by them necessary to put a stop to the whole, in order to root out the licentiousness that pervaded the land. They therefore discourage any kind of nocturnal assemblies, as they are well satisfied that it would take but little to revive these immoral propensities with more force than ever. The watchfulness of the government, police, and missionaries, is constantly required to enforce the due observance of the laws.

CHAPTER 27

A Residence of Twenty-one Years in the Sandwich Islands (1847)

Hiram Bingham
1789–1869

> After leaving the Hawaiian Islands in 1840 because of his wife's ill health, Hiram Bingham set about writing his memoirs, an avenue, according to historian Gavan Daws, by which the missionary "fought the old battles over again and won them all."[18] After including a rewritten version of his description of surfriding, Bingham responds to the criticisms of writers like Ruschenberger and Wilkes by denying missionary influence in the decline of surfriding.

THE ADOPTION OF OUR COSTUME greatly diminishes their practice of swimming and sporting in the surf, for it is less convenient to wear it in the water than the native girdle, and less decorous and safe to lay it entirely off on every occasion they find for a plunge or swim or surf-board race. Less time, moreover, is found for amusement by those who earn or make cloth-garments for themselves like the more civilized nations.

The decline or discontinuance of the use of the surf-board, as civilization advances, may be accounted for by the increase of modesty, industry or religion, without supposing, as some have affected to believe, that missionaries caused oppressive enactments against it. These considerations are in part applicable to many other amusements. Indeed, the purchase of foreign vessels, at this time, required attention to the collecting and delivering of 450,000 lbs. of sandalwood, which those who were waiting for it might naturally suppose would, for a time, supersede their amusements.

TRAVELERS

CHAPTER 28

Mardi and a Voyage Thither (1849)

Herman Melville
1819–1891

Herman Melville landed at Lahaina, Maui, aboard a whaler in May 1843. He spent most of the summer in Honolulu working variously as a pin-setter in a bowling alley, a store clerk, and a bookkeeper. He left the Islands in August of the same year after enlisting in the U.S. Navy. Melville appears to be the first writer to incorporate surfriding into Western fiction. Although he borrows the surfboard description and mechanics of waveriding from the missionary William Ellis, his metaphorical language—waves as soldiers flinging themselves against the island and bombs exploding on the beach; surfboards as steeds mounted by riders—removes surfriding from a missionary context and begins a long tradition of popular writing that casts surfriding into plots of adventure and romance for Western audiences. In the following passage, the narrator and his companions (Braid-Beard and Media) stop at the island of Ohoono in the fanciful Mardi archipelago during their search for the narrator's lost lover, Yillah.

Rare Sport at Ohonoo

Approached from the Northward, Ohonoo, midway cloven down to the sea, one half a level plain; the other, three mountain terraces—Ohonoo looks like the first steps of a gigantic way to the sun. And such, if Braid-Beard spoke the truth, it had formerly been.

"Ere Mardi was made," said that true old chronicler, "Vivo, one of the genii, built a ladder of mountains whereby to go up and down. And of this ladder, the island of Ohonoo was the base. But wandering here and there, incognito in a vapor, so much wickedness did Vivo spy out, that in high dudgeon he hurried up his ladder, knocking the mountains from under him as he went. These here and there fell into the lagoon, forming many isles, now green and luxuriant; which, with those sprouting from seeds dropped by a bird from the moon, comprise all the groups in the reef."

Surely, oh surely, if I live till Mardi be forgotten by Mardi, I shall not forget the sight that greeted us, as we drew nigh the shores of this same island of Ohonoo; for was not all Ohonoo bathing in the surf of the sea?

But let the picture be painted.

Where eastward the ocean rolls surging against the outer reef of Mardi, there, facing a flood-gate in the barrier, stands cloven Ohonoo; her plains sloping outward to the sea, her mountains a bulwark behind. As at Juam, where the wild billows from seaward roll in upon its cliffs; much more at Ohonoo, in billowy battalions charge they hotly into the lagoon, and fall on the isle like an army from the deep. But charge they never so boldly, and charge they forever, old Ohonoo gallantly throws them back till all before her is one scud and rack. So charged the bright billows of cuirassiers at Waterloo; so hurled them off the long line of living walls, whose base was as the sea-beach, wreck-strown, in a gale.

Without the break in the reef, wide banks of coral shelve off, creating the bar, where the waves muster for the onset, thundering in water-bolts, that shake the whole reef, till its very spray trembles. And then it is, that the swimmers of Ohonoo most delight to gambol in the surf.

For this sport, a surf-board is indispensable: some five feet in length; the width of a man's body; convex on both sides; highly polished; and rounded at the ends. It is held in high estimation; invariably oiled after use; and hung up conspicuously in the dwelling of the owner.

Ranged on the beach, the bathers, by hundreds dash in; and diving under the swells, make straight for the outer sea, pausing not till the comparatively smooth expanse beyond has been gained. Here, throwing themselves upon their boards, tranquilly they wait for a billow that suits. Snatching them up, it hurries them landward, volume and speed both increasing, till it races along a watery wall, like the smooth, awful verge of Niagara. Hanging over this scroll, looking down from it as from a precipice, the bathers halloo; every limb in motion to preserve their place on the very crest of the wave. Should they fall behind, the squadrons that follow would whelm them; dismounted, and thrown forward, as certainly would they be run over by the steed they ride. 'Tis like charging at the head of cavalry: you must on.

An expert swimmer shifts his position on his plank; now half striding it; and anon, like a rider in the ring, poising himself upright in the scud, coming on like a man in the air.

At last all is lost in scud and vapor, as the overgrown billow bursts like a bomb. Adroitly emerging, the swimmers thread their way out; and like seals at the Orkneys, stand dripping upon the shore.

Landing in smooth water, some distance from the scene, we strolled forward; and meeting a group resting, inquired for Uhia, their king. He was pointed out in the foam. But presently drawing nigh, he embraced Media, bidding all welcome.

The bathing over, and evening at hand, Uhia and his subjects repaired to their canoes; and we to ours.

CHAPTER 29

Life in the Sandwich Islands (1851)

Henry T. Cheever
1814–1897

Henry T. Cheever published *Life in the Sandwich Islands* as "an humble attempt to furnish something better than the medley of Flash Literature usually found in the Cabin-Locker and the Sailor's Chest."[19] His work bridges the period between the declining influence of the missionaries and the growing number of travelers to the Islands: although his perspective is generally "moral" in nature and he supports the Protestant mission, his writing is mostly intended to offer historical and practical information to visitors. The large whaling fleets that descended upon the Islands every spring and fall may have been one of the inspirations for Cheever's writings (Cheever himself had arrived on a whaler). Whalers had been stopping in the Islands since the 1820s and their presence created much conflict with the missionaries, who saw the sailors as the prime reason for the fall of many natives into prostitution and drinking. In 1846, five years before the publication of Cheever's book, nearly six hundred whaling ships had arrived in island ports, the historical peak of whaling in the Pacific. Cheever offers an admirable description of surfriding in the following passage; in fact, he appears to be the first writer to use the term *surf-rider* in print. He both admonishes the missionaries for their overly severe view of the sport and reveals his own desires to "get balanced on a board just before a great rushing wave."

Lahaina, Maui
1843

It is highly amusing to a stranger to go out into the south part of this town, some day when the sea is rolling in heavily over the reef, and to observe there the evolutions and rapid career of a company of surf-players. The sport is so attractive and full of wild excitement to Hawaiians, and withal so healthful, that I cannot but hope it will be many years before civilization shall look it out of countenance, or make it disreputable to indulge in this manly, though it be dangerous, exercise.

Many a man from abroad who has witnessed this exhilarating play, has no doubt only wished that he were free and able to share in it himself. For my part, I should like nothing better, if I could do it, than to get balanced on a board just before a great rushing wave, and so be hurried in half or quarter of a mile landward with the speed of a race-horse, all the time enveloped in foam and spray, but without letting the roller break and tumble over my head.

In this consists the strength of muscle and sleight-of-hand, to keep the head and shoulders just ahead and clear of the great crested wall that is every moment impending over one, and threatening to bury the bold surf-rider in its watery ruin. The natives do this with admirable intrepidity and skill, riding in, as it were, upon the neck and mane of their furious charger; and when you look to see them, their swift race run, dashed upon the rocks or sand, behold, they have slipped under the belly of the wave they rode, and are away outside, waiting for a cruise upon another.

Both men and women, girls and boys, have their times for this diversion. Even the huge Premier (Auhea) has been known to commit her bulky person to a surf-board; and the chiefs generally, when they visit Lahaina, take a turn or two at this invigorating sport with billows and board. For a more accurate idea of it than can be conveyed by any description, the reader is referred to the engraving.

I have no doubt it would run away with dyspepsia from many a bather at Rockaway or Easthampton, if they would learn, and dare to use a surf-board on those great Atlantic rollers, as the Hawaiians do on the waves of the Pacific. But there is wanting on the Atlantic sea-board that delicious, bland temperature of the water, which within the tropics, while it makes sea-bathing equally a tonic, renders it always safe.

The missionaries at these Islands, and foreigners generally, are greatly at fault in that they do not avail themselves more of this easy and unequalled means of retaining health, or of restoring it when enfeebled.[20] Bathing in fresh water, in a close bath-house, is not to be compared to it as an invigorating and remedial agent; and it is unwise, not to say criminal, in such a climate, to neglect so natural a way of preserving health, as washing and swimming in the sea. In those who live close to the water, and on the leeward side of the Islands, it is the more inexcusable, for it could be enjoyed without exposure in the dewless evenings; or in some places, a small house might be built on stone abutments over the water, and facilities so contrived that both sexes could enjoy this great luxury of a life within the tropics.

CHAPTER 30

Around the Horn to the Sandwich Islands and California, 1845–1850 (1924)

Chester S. Lyman
1814–1890

Chester S. Lyman arrived in Honolulu on May 14, 1846, and remained in the Islands just over a year. During his stay, he taught at the Royal School for Young Chiefs and five of his students later became Hawaiian kings. During his career at Yale University, where he held chairships in physics and astronomy, Lyman maintained correspondence with such notable Hawaiian royalty as Queen Emma, Bernice Pauahi, and King Kalākaua. Lyman was one of the early *haoles* (Caucasians) to try surfriding. His journal description of the experience at Waikīkī indicates that surfriding traditions among royalty—twenty-six years after the arrival of the missionaries—were alive and well on Oʻahu. The description of the "thatched houses" at Waikīkī recalls the grass hut constructed for the original Outrigger Canoe Club, founded on the same beach in 1908 to preserve surfriding.

Waikīkī
June 3, 1846

By invitation of Mr Douglass took a ride with the young Chiefs, they very kindly offering me a horse. Rode to Waititi [Waikīkī] 3 miles where there is fine bathing in the surf. The premises there are in the hands of the Chiefs. Near the beach are fine groves of Coconut trees, & Kou trees, also several thatched houses one of which is occupied by the Y[oung] Chiefs as a dressing apartment while bathing. They have an attendant on the grounds. These youngsters are fond of riding & some of the way they put their horses on a run. Undressing at the house, I found a bath in the surf on the beach very refreshing. The Y[oung] Chiefs are all provided with surf boards, which are kept in the house above mentioned. They are from 12 to 20 feet long 1 ft wide & in the middle 5 or 6 thick, thinning off towards the sides & ends so as to form an edge. Some of these have been handed down in the royal family for years, as this is the royal bathing place. None of those belonging to Kamehameha Ist are now left, but one used by Kaahumanu & others belonging to other distinguished Chiefs & premiers are daily used by the boys, & on one of them (Kaahumanu's I believe) I had the pleasure of taking a surf ride towards the beach in the native style. Tho' the motion is swift it is very pleasant & by no means dangerous unless the surf be very strong.

CHAPTER 31

Travels in the Sandwich and Society Islands (1856)

Samuel S. Hill

Having read descriptions of the Islands by early explorers, Samuel S. Hill wrote: "Their very name to me was romance." As he traveled the paths of countless visitors before and after him—a visit to Kealakekua Bay, a trek through the volcanoes, a display of hula dancing—he encountered the realities of disease, depopulation, and the hardships faced by common Hawaiians as their wives and daughters were forced into prostitution to pay poll-taxes levied upon them. Hill included a report of a forlorn Kamehameha III (ruled 1824–1854) surfriding at Lahaina to escape the urban centers and "the scenes which continually reminded him of the decrease of nationality among his subjects, and the loss of independence, of his race." On his way to visit ancient tombs on Hawai'i, Hill passed through a nearly deserted village, Keauhua, and heard from several native women that most of the inhabitants were out surfriding. The description that follows provides a number of interesting observations: the natural amphitheater of the bay near Keauhua reminds us that surfriding—true for the first explorers as it is today—has always been a great spectator sport; we learn that natives strapped knives to their surfboards to combat sharks; and more than thirty years after the arrival of the missionaries, entire villages apparently still enjoyed surfriding together. Hill had commented that the ancient sport was "no longer played with the same spirit among the islanders where-ever the Europeans are mingled among them." His observation, along with his description of surfriding in this small village, reinforce an important historical point: while surfriding had declined in the areas populated by whites, outlying areas like Keauhua had kept the cultural traditions alive.

Keauhua, Hawai'i
1849

About mid-day we reached the village of Keauhua, where I had the satisfaction of witnessing, for the first time, the famous ancient sport of the country played in the water, upon what is termed by Europeans the surf-board. This is truly a famous and animating diversion, but, for what reason I know not, now discouraged by the missionaries, and no longer played with the same spirit among the islanders where-ever the Europeans are mingled among them. But as we are now so far removed from the seats of innovation upon former customs, the occasion may be as favourable to describe, as the opportunity we then had was of witnessing this sport. I shall, therefore, note all we observed from the best possible position for the purpose, with as much minuteness as the novelty of the diversion to an European, with the character of the sport and the place together, may seem to demand. . . .

After passing by one or two huts which had not an inhabitant within them, we met some women, who told us that all the men, women, and children of the place, save themselves, were sporting with their surf-boards in the water, and that the Government agent, for whom they supposed we were in search, had gone to the seat of government of the island. Upon hearing this, we determined to witness the national sport, and our new friends readily volunteered to conduct us to the most convenient spot for the purpose.

Upon issuing from the grove, we came opposite to a small bay formed by two promontories, and cliffs of no great elevation, and with a low beach at the bottom. Our guide led us on the left side of the bay, more than half the distance to the point of the promontory on that side, where we found five or six other women and some children seated upon the rocks, also contemplating the spectacle in the water, which thus affords at the same time a diversion for those who engage in it, and for those who witness the feats of agility and courage that are performed.

Had I not known that we were to see what I had heard much about since my arrival in the islands, or had we come accidentally upon this promontory without being prepared for what we were to see, I could scarcely have believed at the first sight of the natives, engaged as we now saw them, that we were looking upon creatures that were not absolute habitants of the sea, or at least amphibious. Three or four and twenty men, women, and children of all ages above seven or eight, were distributed over the bay and beyond the promontories, acting such a part amidst the turmoil of the breaking seas, as we might only suppose the beings of poets' imaginations to be capable of performing. Nature seemed to have formed this little bay for the express purpose of giving the natives the opportunity of carrying their feats in the water to the utmost verge of possibility, as well as for the spectators to witness the exhibition with the greatest advantage. The form of the bay, combined with the inequality in the depth of the water within and without, owing, doubtless, to the presence of the two coral reefs, caused the sea to break, first with terrible turmoil, half a quarter of a mile beyond the promontories, and again with less force within them, at something more than that distance from the bottom of the bay; and these two lines of broken water were each chosen for the basis of the performances of one of the two distinct parties into which these semi-amphibious beings were divided—that beyond the bay for the men, and that within for the women and children, the feats of both of which could be perfectly seen from the cliffs upon which we were now seated. . . .

While we sat watching them, the parties were distributed between the two lines of breakers, and within the inner line, in the act of rolling onward, or returning to the bars, or lying between the breaking seas, diving and reappearing, till the time seemed favourable for their long roll towards shore. The women, whom we could distinguish by their long hair, and also the girls and boys, appeared to us to perform their part amidst the turmoil of the minor line of breakers as dexterously as the men along the outer line. That they do not generally trust themselves farther from the shore, is rather on account of the sharks, which the men are prepared for, and seek to contend with, than from any distrust of their capabilities in the water. The sole weapon used by men in combating the shark is a dagger or knife, which on other occasions, when fishing, they stick in their maro [*malo*], to be used merely when, as it frequently happens, their canoe is upset, and they are attacked by the voracious fish before they can put their little craft again upon her bottom and resume their seats. But when they are engaged in this sport, the weapon is attached to the surf-board. If now attacked, the shark has no chance with them. At the approach of their enemy, they feign fear and swim away from him, at the same time exhibiting all sorts of awkwardness, until they give the equally cautious as voracious animal, sufficient confidence to approach them. Then they dive under him, for he is not an active fish in the water, and thrust their dagger into the under part of his body; upon which, even the stoutest of the species will turn and retreat, sometimes to escape, but often in such a condition as to be easily pursued and vanquished, and after the action triumphantly towed to shore.

It is the custom of the islanders, more especially when they have no other means of showing their hospitality, to make themselves as agreeable as possible to strangers, by placing by their side, one or two of the younger women, who, if a common language be wanting, will, at all events, laugh the most weary traveller out of the most sullen humour that ever accompanied fatigue. But on the present occasion we had in our good company, only several old men and women, and some children, and they seated by our side, the two elder among the girls, whose intelligence and quickness in answering questions put to them about the diversion we were witnessing, were as useful, to myself at least, as their merriment was refreshing to us both. We frequently expressed our admiration at what we saw, to the great delight of all the party; but upon asking the little girls near us, whose ages were probably between seven and nine, whether they intended, when a little older, to join in the sport, they declared it to be their daily amusement; and, without waiting to be asked to display their dexterity, they ran and picked up two small surf-boards that were lying near us, and set off in great haste to join one of the parties in the water.

Arrived at the beach, the girls slipped off their sole robe, and after leaping into the sea, soon reached and mingled with the rest in the exciting sport; and I confess, when I saw these little creatures sliding down the side of the swell which runs with such rapidity before the rolling surf, and diving to avoid its crash, when the curling wave was about to break over them, there seemed to me to be something absolutely superhuman in the feats they accomplished, so far were they above anything I had deemed possible for any creatures whatsoever to perform in an element not their own.

This bay, indeed, as before said, possesses peculiar advantages for the sport; and we, probably, saw the performances of the most expert swimmers in the islands. The healthful diversion is still the favourite of the few remaining national exercises of the natives throughout the group. I was informed by the missionaries and by others, in proof of its popularity, and of the constancy with which it must have been practiced for ages, that many of the natives spend whole days in enjoying themselves in this manner in the water. I was informed also, that Kamehameha III., then the reigning king, was known thus to divert himself even from sunrise to sunset, taking his meals of poi during the day without ever coming to shore. This was not, however, at the seat of innovation, and of the present government, but at or near Lahaina, in Mawhee [Maui], which his majesty made the place of his sojourn when disposed to quit the scenes which continually reminded him of the decrease of nationality among his subjects, and the loss of independence, of his race.

CHAPTER 32

The Victorian Visitors (1958)

Sophia Cracroft
1816–1892

Sophia Cracroft and Lady Jane Franklin (1792–1875), widow of Arctic explorer Sir John Franklin, arrived in the Islands in April 1861 and remained a little over two months. The English women had been traveling for enjoyment in San Francisco when rain and floods in California prompted them to sail for the milder climate of Hawai'i. During their stay, they grew acquainted with King Kamehameha IV (ruled 1854–1863) and Queen Emma. Queen Emma subsequently stayed with the women in London for four months on her western European tour in 1865–1866. Cracroft and Franklin also met "Colonel" David Kalākaua, the future king (ruled 1874–1891), who escorted them around the island of Hawai'i, where they visited Mauna Loa and Kealakekua Bay, and also witnessed a surfriding exhibition at Kailua.

Cracroft's journal entry allows us to make a couple of observations. First, it seems apparent that Kalākaua arranged the exhibition as a way of entertaining the ladies. Surfriding was thus no longer simply a way for natives to enjoy themselves when the swell rose, but had become by this time a staged show for the increasing number of island visitors. Cracroft also mentioned in this journal entry that the governess of Hawai'i, Princess Ruth Keelikolani, came riding up on horseback "with eight female attendants and probably at least as many men." "The whole population," she added, "seem to take to riding as much as to swimming." The event supports the recollections of Sereno Edwards Bishop (1827–1909), who commented that "as the horses became cheap and everyone had his horse, the people gave up surf riding."[21] One could well imagine the princess and her entourage, at an earlier date, stripping down and joining in the fun with their surfboards.

Kailua, Hawai‘i
May 9, 1861

At twelve, we started in our litters to a bay a little way below this, to see some surf riding. Seeing the R. Catholic Church open we looked in—the priest invited us in but we declined, stopping only long enough to observe that it was large, very well kept, and without any of the usual nonsense and frippery—only one picture was over the altar. There were several natives there praying—i.e., on their knees—and this made us regret that this act of outward homage does not prevail in the Presbyterian Church.[22] We were quite a cavalcade of horsemen and walkers—men, women, and children, some of whom accompanied us the whole way, some three miles—our bearers often running along merrily.

We alighted at a very nice native house belonging to a Chief of the lower grade, a very good-looking man whom Mr. Kalakaua had introduced to us yesterday. He is an excellent surf rider and joined in the succeeding sport, which was also witnessed by a great number of people belonging to the village, who clustered all round the house. I fear I can hardly give you a correct idea of surf riding but I must try.

A man or woman swims out to the line of breakers, having before him a thin board from 4 to 6 feet long and about 15 inches wide; this in swimming he carries before him with one arm, swimming with the other. The curling waves are nothing to these wonderful swimmers—they either dive under them or ride up the face of the liquid wall and appear on the top of or behind it. They choose their wave according to its height and the direction it will take in reaching the shore, and then instead of facing it they turn about, place the surfboard immediately in front, rise to the crest of the wave, and literally *ride* upon it with extended limbs until it has spent itself upon the beach. But if they perceive that it will cast itself against the rocks, then they turn round again and stop short. It is a really wonderful sight, and some are so expert that during their flying progress they can spring upright on the surfboard and come in erect! We saw one man do this.

All here living on the coast are as much at home in the water as on the land and seem to enjoy it thoroughly. The children begin from tender youth, three or four years old. You see them run in to the edge of the water and out again—a little older and they go farther and dance in the outer edge of the spent waves, throwing themselves down that the water may pass over them—older still and they have their tiny surfboards, being already good swimmers. Morning and noontime you see them here by the dozen in the water, shouting, playing, jumping in from the rocks head foremost or straight upright, diving, standing on their heads, and dashing their legs in the air—in fact, their antics are innumerable.

As we were watching the sport, who should come up with a goodly train all on horseback but the Governess, with eight female attendants and probably at least as many men. She wore a bright yellow petticoat after their fashion, of which I intend to learn the mysteries, but cannot describe at present, farther than to say that being astride, it falls in front on each side in sweeping folds and is kept down by going over the foot into the stirrup. All the ladies wore black cloth capes; the petticoats were either yellow or bright red, and the hats black or straw colour. Unfortunately, we did not see them dismount, nor would they mount until after we started to return. We would have given a good deal to see that enormous woman get into the saddle!

CHAPTER 33

"Ancient Sports of Hawaii: Such as Surfing, Jumping, Sledding, Betting and Boxing" (1865)

J. Waiamau

This article, first published in the Hawaiian-language newspaper *Kuokoa*, preceded a number of writings that described traditional Hawaiian culture, including surfriding, by Samuel Mānaiakalani Kamakau (in *Ke Au 'Oko 'a* from 1866 to 1871) and John Papa 'Ī'ī (in *Kuokoa* from 1868 to 1870). Interest in preserving Hawaiian language and cultural traditions led to contemporaneous works such as Lorrin Andrews's *A Dictionary of the Hawaiian Language* (1865) and Abraham Fornander's *An Account of the Polynesian Race: Its Origins and Migrations* (1879). Here the author presents new information on surfboard materials and surfriding competitions between chiefs. The commentary on coed surfriding—"Such riding in of the man and woman on the same surf is termed vanity, and results in sexual indulgence"—reveals a missionary influence and the dual legacy of their presence in the Islands, which included both the suppression of native traditions and the means to record those traditions for posterity through literacy and education.

VERY MANY WERE THE PRACTICES IN HAWAII here relative to this subject of pastimes, which has been termed the ancient sports of Hawaii here, such as those named above. Those are the sports it is desired to have described, therefore it is best perhaps for me to explain them singly, and their nature.

Of Surfing, that is a most popular sport of Hawaii here, from the chiefs to the common people. It is practiced in the following manner. The [surf] board is first prepared, it may be of koa (Acacia koa), kukui (Aleurites moluccana), ohe (Tetraplasandra Hawaiiensis), wiliwili (Erythrina monosperma), or some other wood suitable to furnish a board. In its first preparation, it is hewn while the wood is green, after which it is left to season, then it is worked down to a finish, with the smearing it with the black substance and well covered with kapa and put up in some suitable place till the time of surf sports arrive, when it is ready for surfriding. This however is the procedure: at the time of swimming out to reach the line of surf breaking, then watch for the surf suitable of landing [you], then enter it and be carried to the shore. There are three places in which to take the surf: to race with its spume, or surf at its end, and the third, surf in on top of the wave, and the [surf] board suitable for the top of the surf will not allow the wave to engulf the men.

If the surfing contest should be of chiefs, it is done in this manner: They go to the seashore, place the dog in the underground oven while the chiefs go surf-riding, on finishing that surfing contest they return, when the oven of dog baking is uncovered and all the chiefs have their meal, then go surf-riding again. Such is the surfing continued till their desire is satisfied.

If the surfing should be a contest of pride, it is done in this manner: The men are girded with red-dyed kapa malos, as they go leisurely and stand, looking fine, girded tight, like a company of soldiers of that day. Of women also, they are dressed with red-dyed kapa skirts, then they go and join together with the men in surf-riding. In their surfing, a man and a woman will ride in on the same surf. Such riding in of the man and woman on the same surf is termed vanity, and results in sexual indulgence.

Surf-riding is a means of deception with some people, and this is the way some charge their parents: "I am going with my sight-seeing companions, if you hear that I am dead on account of stealing, or other cause perhaps, then grieve both of you, but if you hear that I am dead through surf-riding desire, do not sit and mourn, nor indeed drop your tears." There are many things related to this pastime, but perhaps this unfolding thereof is sufficient in this place, so we will speak of leaping.

CHAPTER 34

Roughing It (1872)

Mark Twain
1835–1910

Mark Twain arrived in Honolulu in 1866 and spent four months writing a series of articles for the *Sacramento Union* newspaper describing his experiences in the Islands. Twain later added more material to the original letters—including the following account of his attempts at "surf-bathing"—when he collected the letters together and published them as *Roughing It*. The popular belief that only Hawaiian natives could "master the art of surf-bathing" would not be discredited until the early twentieth century and the founding of the Outrigger Canoe Club at Waikīkī.

Honaunau, Hawai'i
July, 1866[23]

In one place we came upon a large company of naked natives, of both sexes and all ages, amusing themselves with the national pastime of surf-bathing. Each heathen would paddle three or four hundred yards out to sea (taking a short board with him), then face the shore and wait for a particularly prodigious billow to come along; at the right moment he would fling his board upon its foamy crest and himself upon the board, and here he would come whizzing by like a bombshell! It did not seem that a lightning express train could shoot along at a more hair-lifting speed. I tried surf-bathing once, subsequently, but made a failure of it. I got the board placed right, and at the right moment, too; but missed the connection myself. The board struck the shore in three quarters of a second, without any cargo, and I struck the bottom about the same time, with a couple barrels of water in me. None but natives ever master the art of surf-bathing thoroughly.

CHAPTER **35**

Honolulu Directory and Historical Sketch of the Hawaiian or Sandwich Islands (1869)

Abraham Fornander

1812–1887

The following passage from the *Honolulu Directory* cites a letter from Abraham Fornander who, in describing the effects of a tidal wave that inundated the southern and eastern shores of Hawai'i on April 2, 1868, recounted an incident that has become legend in the Islands: a native named Holoua riding a tidal wave into shore.[24] Fornander indicated that eighty-one people were known to have perished in the disaster, "besides a number of the pulu pickers up in the mountains, back of Hilea; how many I am not yet advised, neither have I heard the number of those who perished at Kaalaala."[25] The *Directory* followed a number of publications throughout the nineteenth century that offered conflicting information on the state of surfriding: authors often insisted that surfriding was dying out while offering eyewitness accounts of natives surfriding. On one page the *Directory* mentioned surfriding as part of the "numerous games for amusement, which have long since fallen into disuse," and on another presented the story of Holoua, which clearly demonstrated that natives continued to harbor these skills within their communities—at least sufficiently enough to ride a tidal wave.[26]

Ninole, Hawai'i

April 6 & 7, 1868

I have just been told an incident that occurred at Ninole, during the inundation of that place. At the time of the shock on Thursday, a man named Holoua, and his wife, ran out of the house and started for the hills above, but remembering the money he had in the house, the man left his wife and returned to bring it away. Just as he had entered the house the sea broke on the shore, and, enveloping the building, first washed it several yards inland, and then, as the wave receded, swept if off to sea, with him in it. Being a powerful man, and one of the most expert swimmers in that region, he succeeded in wrenching off a board or a rafter, and with this as a *papa hee-nalu* (surf board,) he boldly struck out for the shore, and landed safely with the return wave. When we consider the prodigious height of the breaker on which he rode to the shore, (50, perhaps 60 feet,) the feat seems almost incredible, were it not that he is now alive to attest it, as well as the people on the hill-side who saw him.

CHAPTER 36

The Hawaiian Archipelago: Six Months among the Palm Groves, Coral Reefs and Volcanoes of the Sandwich Islands (1875)

Isabella Bird
1831–1904

An Englishwoman, Isabella Bird arrived in Hawai'i in January 1873 and remained until August of that year. She traveled extensively in her lifetime to combat chronic illness, visiting Australia, California, Colorado, Japan, China, and the Malay Peninsula. Bird wrote prolifically about her adventures, and her travel narratives were immensely popular during her lifetime and reprinted in numerous editions. The passage here throws into relief the problem of relying on personal narratives to gauge the state of surfriding in the latter half of the nineteenth century: her account appears entirely derived from previously published sources, notably those of missionary William Ellis and Charles Nordhoff.[27] She could well have seen an exhibition of surfriding during her time in the Islands, yet her narrative does not give the impression of an accurate firsthand account. In prose worthy of Jack London, Bird paints a scene of exotic danger, triumphant natives, and cheering crowds on the beaches of Hilo.[28] Ellis's influence renders much of her imagery of surfriding fifty years out of date, a portrait designed to capture a traveler's dream of the South Pacific rather than the realities of native life.

Hilo, Hawai'i
February, 1873

I had written thus far when Mr. Severance came in to say that a grand display of the national sport of surf-bathing was going on, and a large party of us went down to the beach for two hours to enjoy it.[29] It is really a most exciting pastime, and in a rough sea requires immense nerve. The surf-board is a tough plank shaped like a coffin lid, about two feet broad, and from six to nine feet long, well oiled and cared for. It is usually made of the erythrina, or the breadfruit tree. The surf was very heavy and favourable, and legions of natives were swimming and splashing in the sea, though not more than forty had their *Papa-he-nalu*, or "wave sliding boards," with them. The men, dressed only in *malos*, carrying their boards under their arms, waded out from some rocks on which the sea was breaking, and, pushing their boards before them, swam out to the first line of breakers, and then diving down were seen no more till they reappeared as a number of black heads bobbing about like corks in smooth water half a mile from shore.

What they seek is a very high roller, on the top of which they leap from behind, lying face downwards on their boards. As the wave speeds on, and the bottom strikes the ground, the top breaks into a huge comber. The swimmers appeared posing themselves on its highest edge by dexterous movements of their hands and feet, keeping just at the top of the curl, but always apparently coming down hill with a slanting motion. So they rode in majestically, always just ahead of the breaker, carried shorewards by its mighty impulse at the rate of forty miles an hour, yet seeming to have a volition of their own, as the more daring riders knelt and even stood on their surf-boards, waving their arms and uttering exultant cries. They were always apparently on the verge of engulfment by the fierce breaker whose towering white crest was ever above and just behind them, but when one expected to see them dashed to pieces, they either waded quietly ashore, or sliding off their boards, dived under the surf, taking advantage of the undertow, and were next seen far out to sea preparing for fresh exploits.

The great art seems to be to mount the roller precisely at the right time, and to keep exactly on its curl just before it breaks. Two or three athletes, who stood erect on their boards as they swept exultingly shorewards, were received with ringing cheers by the crowd. Many of the less expert failed to throw themselves on the crest, and slid back into smooth water, or were caught in the combers, which were fully ten feet high, and after being rolled over and over, ignominiously disappeared amidst roars of laughter, and shouts from the shore. At first I held my breath in terror, and then in a few seconds I saw the dark heads of the objects of my anxiety bobbing about behind the rollers waiting for another chance. The shore was thronged with spectators, and the presence of the *élite* of Hilo stimulated the swimmers to wonderful exploits.

These people are truly amphibious. Both sexes seem to swim by nature, and the children riot in the waves from their infancy. They dive apparently by a mere effort of the will. In the deep basin of the Wailuku River, a little below the Falls, the maidens swim, float, and dive with garlands of flowers round their heads and throats. The more furious and agitated the water is, the greater the excitement, and the love of these watery exploits is not confined to the young. I saw great fat men with their hair streaked with grey, balancing themselves on their narrow surf-boards, and riding the surges shorewards with as much enjoyment as if they were in their first youth. I enjoyed the afternoon thoroughly.

Is it "always afternoon" here, I wonder? The sea was so blue, the sunlight so soft, the air so sweet. There was no toil, clang, or hurry. People were all holiday-making (if that can be where there is no work), and enjoying themselves, the surf-bathers in the sea, and hundreds of gaily-dressed men and women galloping on the beach. It was serene and tropical. I sympathize with those who eat the lotus, and remain for ever on such enchanted shores.

CHAPTER 37

"Some Hawaiian Pastimes" (1891)

Henry Carrington Bolton
1843–1903

Henry Carrington Bolton, a noted chemist and bibliographer, traveled to the Hawaiian island of Niʻihau in 1890 to conduct research on the "musical sand" of Kaluakahua. Along the way he managed to fit in a surf session. Niʻihau offers a unique case study for surfriding. The Sinclairs, a family of New Zealand ranchers, purchased the island in 1864 and quickly took up surfriding. The Sinclairs and their descendants undoubtedly stand as the earliest non-natives to practice surfriding on a regular basis.[30] Although Ellis's influence is readily apparent in the second paragraph, Bolton essentially approached surfriding with a scientific turn of mind. He commented on the inaccuracies of past descriptions of the sport and, through photographs of natives and his own experience,[31] tried to demonstrate the mechanics of riding waves. Placing surfriding within a scientific framework was part of the steady Westernization of the sport that eventually led, in writers like Jack London, to an important shift in surfriding's image from an activity practiced by a community to one where the individual dominated and mastered nature.

Niʻihau
1890

Here I witnessed, by the courtesy of Mr. Gay, the sport of surf-riding, once so universally popular, and now but little seen. Six stalwart men, by previous appointment, assembled on the beach of a small cove, bearing with them their precious surf-boards, and accompanied by many women and a few children, all eager to see the strangers, and mildly interested in the sport. After standing for their photograph, the men removed all their garments, retaining only the malo, or loin-cloth, and walked into the sea, dragging, or pushing their surf-boards as they reached the deeper water.

These surf-boards, in Hawaiian "wave-sliding-boards" (Papa-he-nalu), are made from the wood of the viri-viri (Erythrina corallodendrum), or bread-fruit tree; they are eight or nine feet long, fifteen to twenty inches wide, rather thin, rounded at each end, and carefully smoothed. The boards are sometimes stained black, are frequently rubbed with cocoanut oil and are preserved with great solicitude, sometimes wrapped in cloths. Children use smaller boards.

Plunging through the nearer surf, the natives reached the outer line of breakers, and watching their opportunity they lay flat upon the board (the more expert kneeled), and, just as a high billow was about to brake over them, pushed landward in front of the combers. The waves rushing in were apparently always on the point of submerging the rider; but, unless some mishap occurred, they drove him forward with rapidity on to the beach, or into shallow water. At the time of the exhibition, the surf was very moderate, and the natives soon tired of the dull sport; but in a high surf it is, of course, exciting, and demands much skill born of experience.

As commonly described in the writings of travellers, an erroneous impression is conveyed, at least to my mind, as to the position which the rider occupies with respect to the combing wave. Some pictures, too, represent the surf-riders on the seaward slope of the wave, in positions which are incompatible with the results. I photographed the men of Niihau before they entered the water, while surf-riding, and after they came out. The second view shows plainly the position taken, although the figures are distant and consequently small.

A few days later, on another beach, I was initiated in the mysteries of surf-riding by my host, who is himself quite expert; and while I cannot boast of much success, I at least learned the principle, and believe that practice is only needed to gain a measure of skill. For persons accustomed to bathing in the surf, the process is far less difficult than usually represented.

CHAPTER 38

"Hawaiian Surf Riding" (1896)

Anonymous

This invaluable text was the first written source in English to describe surfriding's place in the traditional Hawaiian religion—what the editor, Thomas G. Thrum (1842–1932), termed "the ceremonies and superstitions of kahunaism"—and the particular practices, rituals, and tools of craftsmen who shaped the boards. Appearing in the *Hawaiian Almanac and Annual for 1896* (a reference book for travelers and the local business community), we learn from an anonymous "native of the Kona district of Hawaii" distinctions between surfboards and their riders, the names of different parts of waves and types of rides, how surfriders tried to raise swells during flat periods, and why *olo* boards were often ferried out on canoes. The appearance of such information, along with references to Hawaiian surf spots and the legends associated with them, shows the increasing interest by the *haole* community in native culture (Thrum himself would put out a number of books on Hawaiian legend in the following decades) and offers a unique look at a Hawaiian cultural tradition that, within a decade, would undergo an explosion of popularity not seen since the 1820s, when William Ellis described "fifty or a hundred persons riding on an immense billow."

AMONG THE FAVORITE PASTIMES of ancient Hawaiians that of surf riding was a most prominent and popular one with all classes. In favored localities throughout the group for the practice and exhibition of the sport, "high carnival" was frequently held at the spirited contests between rivals in this aquatic sport, to witness which the people would gather from near and far; especially if a famous surf-rider from another district, or island, was seeking to wrest honors from their own champion.

Native legends abound with the exploits of those who attained distinction among their fellows by their skill and daring in this sport; indulged in alike by both sexes, and frequently too—as in these days of intellectual development—the gentler sex carried off the highest honors.

These legendary accounts are usually interwoven with romantic incident, as in the abduction of Kalea, sister of Kawaokaohele, Moi of Maui, by emissaries of Lo-Lale chief of Lihue, in the Ewa district of Oahu; the exploit of Laie-ikawa, and Halaaniani at Keaau, Puna, Hawaii; or for chieftain supremacy, as instanced in the contest between Umi and Paiea in a surf swimming match at Laupahoehoe, which the former was challenged to, and won, upon a wager of four double canoes; also of Lonoikamakahiki at Hana, Maui, and others.[32]

How early in the history of the race surf riding became the science with them that it did is not known, though it is a well-acknowledged fact, that while other islanders may divide honors with Hawaiians for aquatic powers in other respects, none have attained the expertness of surf sport, which early visitors recognized as a national characteristic of the natives of this group. It would be interesting to know how the Hawaiians, over all others in the Pacific, developed this into the skillful or scientific sport which it became, to give them such eminence over their fellows, for we find similar traits of character, mode of life, mild temperature and like coast lines in many another "island world of the Pacific." That it became national in character can be understood when we learn that it was identified, to some extent at least, with the ceremonies and superstitions of kahunaism, especially in preparations therefor, while the indulgence of the exciting sport pandered to their gambling propensities.

The following descriptive account has been prepared for THE ANNUAL by a native of the Kona district of Hawaii, familiar with the subject. For assistance in its translation we are indebted to M.K. Nakuina, himself no stranger to the sport in earlier days.

Surf riding was one of the favorite Hawaiian sports, in which chiefs, men, women and youth, took a lively interest. Much valuable time was spent by them in this practice throughout the day. Necessary work for the maintenance of the family, such as farming, fishing, mat and kapa making and such other household duties required of them and needing attention, by either head of the family, was often neglected for the prosecution of the sport. Betting was made an accompaniment thereof, both by the chiefs and the common people, as was done in all other games, such as wrestling, foot racing, quoits, checkers, holua, and several others known only to the old Hawaiians. Canoes, nets, fishing lines, kapas, swine, poultry and all other property were staked, and in some instances life itself was put up as wagers, the property changing hands, and personal liberty, or even life itself, sacrificed according to the outcome of the match, the winners carrying off their riches and the losers and their families passing to a life of poverty or servitude.

Trees and Mode of Cutting

There were only three kinds of trees known to be used for making boards for surf riding, viz.: the wiliwili (*Erythrina monosperma*), ulu, or breadfruit (*Artocarpus incisa*), and koa (*Acacia koa*).

The uninitiated were naturally careless, or indifferent as to the method of cutting the chosen tree; but among those who desired success upon their labors the following rites were carefully observed.

Upon the selection of a suitable tree, a red fish called kumu was first procured, which was placed at its trunk. The tree was then cut down, after which a hole was dug at its root and the fish placed therein, with a prayer, as an offering in payment therefor. After this ceremony was performed, then the tree trunk was chipped away from each side until reduced to a board approximately of the dimensions desired, when it was pulled down to the beach and placed in the *halau* (canoe house) or other suitable place convenient for its finishing work.

Finishing Process

Coral of the corrugated variety termed *pohaku puna*, which could be gathered in abundance along the sea beach, and a rough kind of stone called *oahi* were the commonly used articles for reducing and smoothing the rough surfaces of the board until all marks of the stone adze were obliterated. As a finishing stain the root of the ti plant (*Cordyline terminalis*), called mole ki, or the pounded bark of the kukui (*Aleurites moluccana*), called *hili*, was the mordant used for a paint made with the root of burned kukui nuts. This furnished a durable, glossy black finish, far preferable to that made with the ashes of burned cane leaves, or amau fern, which had neither body nor gloss.

Before using the board there were other rites or ceremonies to be performed, for its dedication. As before, these were disregarded by the common people, but among those who followed the making of surf boards as a trade, they were religiously observed.

There are two kinds of boards for surf riding, one is called the *olo* and the other the *a-la-ia*, known also as *omo*. The *olo* was made of wiliwili—a very light buoyant wood—some three fathoms long, two to three feet wide, and from six to eight inches thick along the middle of the board, lengthwise, but rounding toward the edges on both upper and lower sides. It is well known that the *olo* was only for the use of chiefs; none of the common people used it. They used the *a-la-ia*, which was made of koa, or ulu. Its length and width was similar to the *olo*, except in thickness, it being but of one and a half to two inches thick alon[g] its center.

Breakers

The line of breakers is the place where the outer surf rises and breaks at deep sea. This is called the *kulana nalu*. Any place nearer or closer in where the surf rises and breaks again, as they sometimes do, is called the *ahua*, known also as *kipapa* or *puao*.

There are only two kinds of surf in which riding is indulged; these are called the *kakala*, known also as *lauloa*, or long surf, and the *ohu*, sometimes called *opuu*. The former is a surf that rises, covering the whole distance from one end of a beach to the other. These, at times, form in successive waves that roll in with high, threatening crest, finally falling over bodily. The first of a series of surf waves usually partake of this character, and is never taken by a rider, as will be mentioned later. The *ohu* is a very small comber that rises up without breaking, but of such strength that sends the board on speedily. This is considered the best, being low and smooth, and the riding thereon easy and pleasant, and is therefore preferred by ordinary surf riders. The lower portion of the breaker is called *honua*, or foundation, and the portion near a cresting wave is termed the *muku* side, while the distant, or clear side, as some express it, is known as the *lala*.

During calm weather when there was no surf there were two ways of making or coaxing it practiced by the ancient Hawaiians, the generally adopted method being for a swimming party to take several strands of the sea convolvulvus vine, and swinging it around the head lash it down unitedly upon the water until the desired result was obtained, at the same time chanting as follows:

> *Ho ae; ho ae iluna i ka pohuehue,*
> *Ka ipu nui lawe mai.*
> *Ka ipu iki waiho aku.*

Methods of Surf Riding

The swimmer, taking position at the line of breakers waits for the proper surf. As before mentioned the first one is allowed to pass by. It is never ridden, because its front is rough. If the second comber is seen to be a good one it is sometimes taken, but usually the third or fourth is best, both from the regularity of its breaking and the foam calmed surface of the sea through the travel of its predecessors.

In riding with the *olo* or thick board, on a big surf, the board is pointed landward and the rider, mounting it, paddles with his hands and impels with his feet to give the board a forward movement, and when it receives the momentum of the surf and begins to rush downward, the skilled rider will guide his course straight or obliquely, apparently at will, according to the spending character of the surf ridden, to land himself high and dry on the beach, or dismount on nearing it, as he may elect. This style of riding was called *kipapa*. In using the *olo* great care had to be exercised in its management, lest from the height of the wave—if coming in direct—the board would be forced into the base of the breaker, instead of floating lightly and riding on the surface of the water, in which case, the wave force being spent, reaction throws both rider and board into the air.

In the use of the *olo* the rider had to swim out around the line of surf to obtain position, or be conveyed thither by canoe. To swim out through the surf with such a buoyant bulk was not possible, though it was sometimes done with the thin boards, the *a-la-ia*. These latter are good for riding all kinds of surf, and are much easier to handle than the *olo*.

Expert Positions

Various positions used to be indulged in by old-time experts in this aquatic sport, such as standing, kneeling and sitting. These performances could only be indulged in after the board had taken on the surf momentum and in the following manner. Placing the hands on each side of the board, close to the edge, the weight of the body was thrown on the hands, and the feet brought up quickly to the kneeling position. The sitting position is attained in the same way, though the hands must not be removed from the board till the legs are thrown forward and the desired position is secured. From the kneeling to the standing position was obtained by placing both hands again on the board and with agility leaping up to the erect attitude, balancing the body on the swift-coursing board with the outstretched arms.

Surf Swimming Without a Board

Kaha nalu is the term used for surf swimming without the use of the board, and was done with the body only. The swimmer, as with a board, would go out for position and, watching his opportunity, would strike out with his hands and feet to obtain headway as the approaching comber with its breaking crest would catch him, and with his rapid swimming powers bear him onward with swift momentum, the body being submerged in the foam; the head and shoulders only being seen. Kaha experts could ride on the *lala* or top of the surf as if riding with a board.

Canoe Riding.—Pa-Ka Waa.

Canoe riding in the surf is another variety of this favorite sport, though not so general, nor perhaps so calculated to win the plaudits of an admiring throng, yet requiring dexterous skill and strength to avoid disastrous results.

Usually two or three persons would enter a canoe and paddle out to the line of breakers. They would pass the first, second, or third surf if they were *kakalas*, it being impossible to shoot such successfully with a canoe, but if an *ohu* is approaching, then they would take position and paddle quickly till the swell of the cresting surf would seize the craft and speed it onward without further aid of paddles, other than for the steersman to guide it straight to shore, but woe be to all if his paddle should get displaced.

Canoe riding has been practiced of late years in mild weather by a number of the Waikiki residents, several of whom are becoming expert in this exciting and exhilarating sport.

Names of Some Noted Surfs

1. *Huia* and *Ahua*, at Hilo, Hawaii, the former right abreast of Kaipalaoa, and the latter off Mokuola (Cocoanut Island). Punahoa, a chiefess, was the noted surf rider of Hilo during the time of Hiiakaikapoli.

2. *Kaloakaoma*, a deep sea surf at Keaau, Puna, Hawaii; famed through the feats of Laieikawai and Halaaiani, as also of Hiiakaikapoli and Hopoe.

3. *Huiha*, at Kailua, Kona, Hawaii, was the favorite surf whereon the chiefs were wont to disport themselves.

4. *Kaulu* and *Kalapu*, at Heie, Keauhou, Kona, Hawaii, were surfs enjoyed by Kauikeouli (Kamehameha III), and his sister the princess Nahienaena, whenever they visited this, their birthplace.

5. *Puhele* and *Keanini*, at Hana, and *Uo* at Lahaina, Maui were surfs made famous through the exploits of chiefs of early days.

6. *Kalehuawehe*, at Waikiki, Oahu, used to be the attraction for the congregating together of Oahu chiefs in the olden time.

7. *Makaiwa*, at Kapaa, Kauai, through Moikeha, a noted chief of that island is immortalized in the old meles as follows:

"I walea no Moikeha ia Kauai,
I ka la hiki ae a po iho.
O ke kee a ka nalu o Makaiwa—
O ke kahui mai a ke Kalukalu—
E noho ia Kauai a e make."

"Moikeha is contented with Kauai
Where the sun rises and sets.
The bend of the Makaiwa surf—
The waving of the Kalukalu—
Live and die at Kauai."

Part III

Surfriding Revival
(1907–1954)

Surfriding's revival in the early twentieth century began with the quiet athleticism of George Freeth, a celebrity endorsement by Jack London, and the enthusiasm and persistence of Alexander Hume Ford. The influence of each helped lay the groundwork for the founding of the Hawaiian Outrigger and Canoe Club in 1908, the first official organization devoted to "the purpose of preserving surfing on boards and in outrigger canoes."[1]

Waikīkī, historically the recreational area for Hawaiian chiefs, was the center of the surfriding world through the first half of the twentieth century: where George Freeth revived the practice of standing on a surfboard in 1902, where Jack London paddled his first surfboard in 1907, and where Tommy Zahn ended his record-setting paddleboard race from Moloka'i in 1953. Waikīkī was also the place where tourists like Minnie Crawford found adventure with the beachboys in the waves, where Tom Blake dedicated himself to a life based around the ocean, where every major surfboard innovation occurred up until World War II, and where every surfer or would-be surfer dreamed of making a pilgrimage to surf the long, gentle rollers off Diamond Head.

Although Jack London and Alexander Hume Ford may be credited with generating the spark of interest that ignited the popularity of surfriding, the day-to-day labor of maintaining that popularity rested, sometimes literally, on the shoulders of the Waikīkī beachboys. The beachboy life—or at least a romantic version of it—served as the model for a budding surf culture in temperate Southern California: spending all day at the beach surfriding, playing music, talking story, dancing, and drinking. From Jack London's masculine ideal of a "black Mercury" to Tom Blake's idealization of Duke Kahanamoku as a modern incarnation of Kamehameha I to the palm frond hats and grass shack at San Onofre, the Waikīkī beachboys were the source of the popular image and appeal of surfriding.

CHAPTER 39

"Riding the South Seas Surf" (1907)

Jack London
1876–1916

Jack London arrived in Hawai'i in May 1907 with his wife Charmian aboard the *Snark*, a ship on which the Londons planned to sail around the world. In Honolulu they met promoter Alexander Hume Ford—himself recently arrived in the Islands—who quickly introduced them to surfriding at Waikīkī. As part of a larger outdoors movement that saw Americans celebrating the "strenuous life" under President Theodore Roosevelt (1901–1909), London's experience in the surf—and his popularity as an adventure writer—helped attract attention to the sport in the United States and in Britain, where his account appeared in such magazines as *Woman's Home Companion* and *Pall Mall Magazine*. In Hawai'i, London's fame gave a boost to Ford as he helped found the first organization to preserve surfriding, the Outrigger Canoe Club (1908).

London drew upon his extensive skills as a fiction writer in the following account to transform a Hawaiian surfrider into the god Mercury, "a member of the kingly species that has mastered matter and the brutes and lorded it over creation." The detailed description preceding his own surfriding experience—what London called "the physics of surf riding"—demonstrates what he and many others of the time believed to be the central means by which humans achieved this domination of nature: a knowledge of science. London opened his account by quoting Mark Twain, a reference that served to dispel the popular belief that only native Hawaiians could master the sport. At a time when most Americans followed beliefs of white racial superiority, London urged his readers, "what that Kanaka can do you can do yourself. . . . Get in and wrestle with the sea; wing your heels with the skill and power that reside in you; bit the sea's breakers, master them, and ride upon their backs as a king should." Within a year or two of these words, surfriding became a fad among white island residents and tourists, thus launching the modern revival of the sport.

Waikīkī, Oʻahu
June 1–2, 1907

> *I tried surf riding once, but made a failure of it. I got the board placed right, and at the right moment, too, but missed the connection myself. The board struck the shore in three quarters of a second, without any cargo, and I struck the bottom about the same time, with a couple of barrels of water in me. None but the natives ever master the art of surf riding thoroughly.*
> —Mark Twain in *Roughing It*

THIS is what it is: a royal sport for the natural kings of earth. The grass grows right down to the water at Waikiki Beach and within fifty feet of the everlasting sea. The trees also grow down to the salty edge of things, and one sits in their shade and looks seaward at a majestic surf thundering in on the beach to one's very feet. Half a mile out, where is the reef, the white-headed combers thrust suddenly skyward out of the placid turquoise blue and come rolling in to shore. One after another they come, a mile long, with smoking crests, the white battalions of the infinite army of the sea. And one sits and listens to the perpetual roar, and watches the unending procession, and feels tiny and fragile before this tremendous force expressing itself in fury and foam and sound. Indeed, one feels microscopically small, and the thought that one may wrestle with this sea raises in one's imagination a thrill of apprehension, almost of fear. Why, they are a mile long, these bull-mouthed monsters, and they weigh a thousand tons, and they charge in to shore faster than a man may run. What chance? No chance at all, is the verdict of the shrinking ego; and one sits, and looks, and listens, and thinks the grass and the trees and the shade are a pretty good place in which to be.

A Master of the Bull-Mouthed Breaker

And suddenly out there where a big smoker lifts skyward, rising like a sea god from out of the welter of spume and churning white, on the giddy, toppling, overhanging and downfalling, precarious crest appears the dark head of a man. Swiftly he rises through the rushing white. His black shoulders, his chest, his loins, his limbs—all is abruptly projected on one's vision. Where but the moment before was only the ocean's wide desolation and invincible roar is now a man, erect, full-statured, not struggling frantically in that wild movement, not buried and crushed and buffeted by those mighty monsters, but standing above them all, calm and superb, poised on the giddy summit, his feet buried in the churning foam, the salt smoke rising to his knees, and all the rest of him in the free air and flashing sunlight, and he is flying through the air, flying forward, flying fast, as the surge on which he stands. He is a Mercury—a black Mercury. His heels are winged, and in them is the swiftness of the sea. In truth, from out of the sea he has leaped upon the back of the sea, and he is riding the sea that roars and bellows and cannot shake him from its back. But no frantic outreaching and balancing is his. He is impassive, motionless, as a statue carved suddenly by some miracle out of the sea's depth from which he rose. And straight on toward shore he flies on his winged heels and the white crest of the breaker. There is a wild burst of foam, a long, tumultuous, rushing sound, as the breaker falls futile and spent on the beach at your feet; and there at your feet steps calmly ashore a Kanaka, burnt black by the tropic sun. Several minutes ago he was a speck a quarter of a mile away. He has "bitted the bull-mouthed breaker" and ridden it in, and the pride in the feat shows in the carriage of his magnificent body as he glances for a moment carelessly at you who sit in the shade of the shore. He is a Kanaka—and more; he is a man, a natural king, a member of the kingly species that has mastered matter and the brutes and lorded it over creation.

How I Came to Tackle Surf Riding

And one sits and thinks of Tristram's last wrestle with the sea on that fatal morning; and one thinks further, to the fact that that Kanaka has done what Tristram never did, and that he knows a joy of the sea that Tristram never knew. And still further one thinks. It is all very well, sitting here in the cool shade of the beach; but you are a man, one of the kingly species, and what that Kanaka can do you can do yourself. Go to. Strip off your clothes, that are a nuisance in this mellow clime. Get in and wrestle with the sea; wing your heels with the skill and power that reside in you; bit the sea's breakers, master them, and ride upon their backs as a king should.

And that is how it came about that I tackled surf riding. And now that I have tackled it, more than ever do I hold it to be a royal sport. But first let me explain the physics of it. A wave is a communicated agitation. The water that composes the body of a wave does not move. If it did, when a stone is thrown into a pond, and the ripples spread away in an ever-widening circle, there would appear at the center an ever-increasing hole. No, the water that composes the body of a wave is stationary. Thus you may watch a particular portion of the ocean's surface and you will see the same water rise and fall a thousand times to the agitation communicated by a thousand successive waves. Now imagine this communicated agitation moving shoreward. As the bottom shoals, the lower portion of the wave strikes land first and is stopped. But water is fluid, and the upper portion has not struck anything, wherefore it keeps on communicating its agitation, keeps on going. And when the top of the wave keeps on going, while the bottom of it lags behind, something is bound to happen. The bottom of the wave drops out from under and the top of the wave falls over, forward and down, curling and cresting and roaring as it does so. It is the bottom of a wave striking against the top of the land that is the cause of all surfs.

But the transformation from a smooth undulation to a breaker is not abrupt except where the bottom shoals abruptly. Say the bottom shoals gradually for from a quarter of a mile to half a mile, then an equal distance will be occupied by the transformation. Such a bottom is that off the beach of Waikiki, and it produces a splendid surf-riding surf. One leaps upon the back of a breaker just as it begins to break, and stays on it as it continues to break all the way in to shore.

Just What Surf Riding Means

And now to the particular physics of surf riding. Get out on a flat board, six feet long, two feet wide and roughly oval in shape. Lie down upon it like a small boy on a coaster, and paddle with your hands out to deep water, where the waves begin to crest. Lie out there quietly on the board. Sea after sea breaks before, behind and under and over you, and rushes in to shore leaving you behind. When a wave crests it gets steeper. Imagine yourself, on your board, on the face of that steep slope. If it stood still you would slide down, just as a boy slides down a hill on his coaster. "But," you object, "the wave doesn't stand still." Very true; but the water composing the wave stands still, and there you have the secret. If ever you start sliding down the face of that wave you'll keep on sliding and you'll never reach the bottom. Please don't laugh. The face of that wave may be only six feet, yet you can slide down it a quarter of a mile, or half a mile, and not reach the bottom. For, see, since a wave is only a communicated agitation or impetus, and since the water that composes a wave is changing every instant, new water is rising into the wave as fast as the wave travels. You slide down this new water, and yet remain in your old position on the wave, sliding down the still newer water that is rising and forming the wave. You slide precisely as fast as the wave travels. If it travels fifteen miles an hour, you slide fifteen miles an hour. Between you and shore stretches a quarter of a mile of water. As the wave travels, this water obligingly heaps itself into the wave, gravity does the rest, and down you go, sliding the whole length of it. If you still cherish the notion, while sliding, that the water is moving with you, thrust your arms into it and attempt to paddle; you will find that you have to be remarkably quick to get a stroke, for that water is dropping astern just as fast as you are rushing ahead.

And now for another phase of the physics of surf riding. All rules have their exceptions. It is true that the water in a wave does not travel forward. But there is what may be called the send of the sea. The water in the overtoppling crest does move forward, as you will speedily realize if you are slapped in the face by it, for if you are caught under it and are pounded by one mighty blow down under the surface, panting and gasping, for half a minute. The water in the top of a wave rests upon the water in the bottom of the wave. But when the bottom of the wave strikes the land it stops, while the top goes on. It no longer has the bottom of the wave to hold it up. Where was solid water beneath it is now air, and for the first time it feels the grip of gravity, and down it falls, at the same time being torn asunder from the lagging bottom of the wave and being flung forward. And it is because of this that riding a surf board is something more than a mere placid sliding down a hill. In truth, one is caught up and hurled shoreward as by some Titan's hand.

My Ignominious Failure

I deserted the cool shade, put on a swimming suit, and got hold of a surf board. It was too small a board. But I didn't know, and nobody told me. I joined some little Kanaka boys in shallow water, where the breakers were well spent and small—a regular kindergarten school. I watched the little Kanaka boys. When a likely looking breaker came along they flopped upon their stomachs on their boards, kicked like mad with their feet, and rode the breaker in to the beach. I tried to emulate them. I watched them, tried to do everything that they did, and failed utterly. The breaker swept past, and I was not on it. I tried again and again. I kicked twice as madly as they did, and failed. Half a dozen would be around. We would all leap on our boards in front of a good breaker. Away our feet would churn like the stern wheels of river steamboats, and away the little rascals would scoot, while I remained in disgrace behind.

I tried for a solid hour, and not one wave could I persuade to boost me shoreward. And then arrived a friend, Alexander Hume Ford, a globe trotter by profession, bent ever on the pursuit of sensation. And he had found it at Waikiki. Heading for Australia, he had stopped off for a week to find out if there were any thrills in surf riding, and he became wedded to it. He had been at it every day for a month and could not yet see any symptoms of the fascination lessening up on him. He spoke with authority.

"Get off that board," he said. "Chuck it away at once. Look at the way you're trying to ride it. If ever the nose of that board hits bottom you'll be disemboweled. Here, take my board. It's a man's size."

I am always humble when confronted by knowledge. Ford knew. He showed me how properly to mount his board. Then he waited for a good breaker, gave me a shove at the right moment, and started me in. Ah, delicious moment when I felt that breaker grip and fling me! On I dashed, a hundred and fifty feet, and subsided with the breaker on the sand. From that moment I was lost. I waded back to Ford with his board. It was a large one, several inches thick, and weighed all of seventy-five pounds. He gave me advice, much of it. He had had no one to teach him, and all that he had laboriously learned in several weeks he communicated to me in half an hour. I really learned by proxy. And inside of half and hour I was able to start myself and ride in. I did it time after time, and Ford applauded and advised. For instance, he told me to get just so far forward on the board, and no farther. But I must have got some farther, for as I came charging in to land, that miserable board poked its nose down to bottom, stopped abruptly and turned a somersault, at the same time violently severing our relations. I was tossed through the air like a chip and buried ignominiously under the downfalling breaker. And I realized that if it hadn't been for Ford I'd have been disemboweled. That particular risk is part of the sport, Ford says. Maybe he'll have it happen to him before he leaves Waikiki, and then, I feel confident, his yearning for sensation will be satisfied for a time.

I Save a Life

When all is said and done, it is my steadfast belief that homicide is worse than suicide, especially if, in the former case, it is a woman. Ford saved me from being a homicide. "Imagine your legs are a rudder," he said. "Hold them close together, and steer with them." A few minutes later I came charging in on a comber. As I neared the beach, there, in the water, up to her waist, dead in front of me, appeared a woman. How was I to stop that comber on whose back I was? It looked like a dead woman. The board weighed seventy-five pounds. I weighed a hundred and sixty five. The added weight had a velocity of fifteen miles an hour. The board and I constituted a projectile. I leave it to the physicists to figure out the force of the impact upon that poor, tender woman. And then I remembered my guardian angel, Ford. "Steer with your legs!" rang through my reeling consciousness. I steered with my legs, I steered sharply, abruptly, with all my legs and with all my might. The board sheered around broadside on the crest. Many things happened simultaneously. The wave gave me a passing buffet, a light tap as the taps of waves go, but a tap sufficient to knock me off the board and smash me down through the rushing water to bottom, with which I came in violent collision and upon which I was rolled over and over. I got my head out for a breath of air, and then gained my feet. There stood the woman before me. I felt like a hero. I had saved her life. And she laughed at me. It was not hysteria. She had never dreamed of her danger. Anyway, I solaced myself, it was not I, but Ford, that saved her, and I didn't have to feel like a hero. And besides, that leg steering was great. In a few minutes of practise I was able to thread my way in and out past several bathers and to remain on top of my breaker instead of going under it.

"To-morrow," Ford said, "I am going to take you out into the blue water."

I looked seaward where he pointed, and saw the great smoking combers that made the breakers I had been riding look like ripples. I don't know what I might have said had I not recollected just then that I was one of a kingly species. So all that I did say was, "All right. I'll tackle them to-morrow."[2]

The Wonderful Hawaiian Water

The water that rolls in on Waikiki beach is just the same as the water that laves the shores of all the Hawaiian Islands; and in ways, especially from the swimmer's standpoint, it is wonderful water. It is cool enough to be comfortable, while it is warm enough to permit a swimmer to stay in all day without experiencing a chill. Under the sun or the stars, at high noon or at midnight, in mid-winter or in mid-summer, it does not matter when, it is always the same temperature—not too warm, not too cold, just right. It is wonderful water, salt as old ocean itself, pure, and crystal clear. When the nature of the water is considered, it is not so remarkable, after all, that the Kanakas are one of the most expert of swimming races.

So it was, next morning, when Ford came along, that I plunged into the wonderful water for a swim of indeterminate length. Astride of our surf boards, or, rather, flat down upon them on our stomachs, we paddled out through the kindergarten where the little Kanaka boys were at play. Soon we were out in deep water where the big smokers came roaring in. The mere struggle with them, facing them and paddling seaward over them and through them, was sport enough in itself. One had to have his wits about him, for it was a battle in which mighty blows were struck on one side, and in which cunning was used on the other side—a struggle between insensate force and intelligence. I soon learned a bit. When a breaker curled over my head, for a swift instant I could see the light of day through its emerald body; then down would go my head, and I would clutch the board with all my strength. Then would come the blow, and to the onlooker on shore I would be blotted out. In reality the board and I would have passed through the crest and emerged in the respite of the other side. I should not recommend those smashing blows to an invalid or delicate person. There is weight behind them, and the impact of the driven water is like a sand blast. Sometimes one passes through half a dozen combers in quick succession, and it is just about that time that he is liable to discover new merits in the stable land and new reasons for being on shore.

Out there in the midst of such a succession of big smoky ones a third man was added to our party, one Freeth. Shaking the water from my eyes as I emerged from one wave, and peering ahead to see what the next one looked like, I saw him tearing in on the back of it, standing upright on his board, carelessly poised, a young god bronzed with sunburn. We went through the wave on the back of which he rode. Ford called to him. He turned an airspring from his wave, rescued his board from its maw, paddled over to us and joined Ford in showing me things. One thing in particular I learned from Freeth—namely, how to encounter the occasional breaker of exceptional size that rolled in. Such breakers were really ferocious, and it was unsafe to meet them on top of the board. But Freeth showed me, so that whenever I saw one of that caliber rolling down on me I slid off the rear end of the board and dropped down beneath the surface, my arms over my head and holding my board. Thus, if the wave ripped the board out of my hands and tried to strike me with it (a common trick of such waves), there would be a cushion of water a foot or more in depth between my head and the blow. When the wave passed I climbed up on the board and paddled on. Many men have been terribly injured, I learn, by being struck by their boards.

The Trick is "Non-Resistance"

The whole method of surf riding and surf fighting, I learned, is one of non-resistance. Dodge the blow that is struck at you. Dive through the wave that is trying to slap you in the face. Sink down, feet first, deep under the surface, and let the big smoker that is trying to smash you go by far overhead. Never be rigid. Relax. Yield yourself to the waters that are ripping and tearing at you. When the undertow catches you and drags you seaward along the bottom, don't struggle against it. If you do you are liable to be drowned, for it is stronger than you. Yield yourself to that undertow. Swim with it, not against it, and you will find the pressure removed. And, swimming with it, fooling it so that it does not hold you, swim upward at the same time. It will be no trouble at all to reach the surface.

The man who wants to learn surf riding must be a strong swimmer, and he must be used to going under the water. After that, fair strength and common sense are all that is required. The force of the big combers is rather unexpected. There are mix-ups in which board and rider are torn apart and separated by several hundred feet. The surf rider must take care of himself. No matter how many riders swim out with him, he cannot depend upon any of them for aid. The fancied security I had in the presence of Ford and Freeth made me forget that it was my first swim out in deep water among the big ones. I recollected, however, and rather suddenly, for a big wave came in, and away went the two men on its back all the way to shore. I could have been drowned a dozen different ways before they got back to me.

One slides down the face of a breaker on his surf board, but he has to get started to sliding. Board and rider must be moving shoreward at a good rate before the wave overtakes them. When you see the wave coming that you want to ride in, you turn tail to it and paddle shoreward with all your strength, using what is called the windmill stroke. This is a sort of spurt performed immediately in front of the wave. If the board is going fast enough, the wave accelerates it and the board begins its quarter-of-a-mile ride.

A Gleam of Success—and the Price

I shall never forget the first big wave I caught out there in the deep water. I saw it coming, turned my back on it and paddled for dear life. Faster and faster my board went, until it seemed my arms would drop off. What was happening behind me I could not tell. One cannot look behind and paddle the windmill stroke. I heard the crest of the wave hissing and churning, and then my board was lifted and flung forward. I scarcely knew what happened the first half-minute. Though I kept my eyes open, I could not see anything, for I was buried in the rushing white of the crest. But I did not mind. I was chiefly conscious of ecstatic bliss at having caught the wave. At the end of the half-minute, however, I began to see things and to breathe. I saw that three feet of the nose of my board was clear out of water and riding on the air. I shifted my weight forward and made the nose come down. Then I lay, quite at rest in the midst of the wild movement, and watched the shore and the bathers on the beach grow distinct. I didn't cover quite a quarter of a mile on that wave, because, to prevent the board from diving, I shifted my weight back, but shifted it too far, and fell down the rear slope of the wave.

It was my second day at surf riding, and I was quite proud of myself. I stayed out there four hours, and when it was over I was resolved that on the morrow I'd come in standing up. But that resolution paved a distance place. On the morrow I was in bed. I was not sick, but I was very unhappy, and I was in bed. When describing the wonderful water of Hawaii, I forgot to describe the wonderful sun of Hawaii. It is a tropic sun, and, furthermore, in the first part of June it is an overhead sun. It is also an insidious, deceitful sun. For the first time in my life I was sunburned unawares. My arms, shoulders and back had been burned many times and were tough; but not so my legs. And for four hours I had exposed them at right angles to that perpendicular Hawaiian sun. It was not until after I got ashore that I discovered the sun had touched me. Sunburn at first is merely warm; after that it grows superlative and the blisters come out. Also, the joints, where the skin wrinkles, refuse to bend. That is why I spent the next day in bed. I couldn't walk. And that is why, to-day, I am writing this in bed. It is easier to than not to. But to-morrow, ah, to-morrow I shall be out in that wonderful water, and I shall come in standing up, even as Ford and Freeth. And if I fail to-morrow I shall do it the next day, or the next. Upon one thing I am resolved: the *Snark* shall not sail from Honolulu until I, too, wing my heels with the swiftness of the sea and become a sunburned, skin-peeling Mercury.

CHAPTER 40

"Aquatic Sports" (1908)

Alexander Hume Ford
1868–1945

Alexander Hume Ford arrived in Hawai'i in 1907 and made Honolulu his home base—in between periods of constant global travel—for the remainder of his life. Organizing support for the Hawaiian Outrigger Canoe Club at Waikīkī remains Ford's most enduring contribution to the history of surfriding. The Outrigger was the first official organization devoted "for the purpose of preserving surfing on boards and in outrigger canoes."[3] The club, almost exclusively Caucasian in membership, established institutional support for the sport by providing its members with access to surfboards and a place to ride waves. By generating interest in surfriding, the Outrigger also played an important role in the development of the beachboy tradition. The club opened the second, and eventually most important, beach service on Waikīkī, employing members of the rival Hui Nalu (a club almost exclusively for native Hawaiians or part-Hawaiians), many of whom were responsible for surfriding's growing popularity in the first half of the twentieth century.

After arriving in Honolulu, Ford quickly targeted the native sport as a way of drawing more tourists (and potential long-term residents) to the Islands; he learned how to surf himself and promoted the sport tirelessly through magazine articles and his editorship of the *Mid-Pacific Magazine* (founded in 1911) that spotlighted such local Hawaiians as Duke Kahanamoku, considered the father of modern surfriding. As Ford's publications promoted surfriding's revival at Waikīkī ("It is doubtful," he writes in the present article, "if the beginner would ever learn in any other surf in the world") and demonstrated his own aesthetic appreciation for riding a "billow that curls above the head within reach of a back-stretched hand," his account also reveals that the native surfriding traditions in both Tahiti and Hawai'i remained essentially unknown or ignored among the general Caucasian population who took a sudden interest in developing the sport.

HAWAII is the only place in the world, I believe, where man stands erect upon the crest of the billows, and, standing, rides toward the shore.

Riding the surf-board threatened to become a lost art, but today there are probably more people than ever before who can balance themselves on the incoming waves at Waikiki. I had always been taught, from childhood, that only Hawaiians born could ever expect to master the surf-board. Mark Twain came to Waikiki, made a single attempt, and gave up in despair. Six months ago, however, a new comer, seventy years of age, came to Waikiki, and with the third attempt, came in standing upon his surf-board. He declared that it was easier to ride standing on a board than to balance one's self on a log in a rushing stream, at which he was an adept. As a healthful sport and exercise, surf-riding has no equal in the world. Even swimming falls far behind surf-board riding as a developer of muscle. In the good old days it was the sport of the Hawaiian chiefs. Jack London came to Hawaii, learned the art, and dubbed it "The sport of kings." Anyone can learn to ride the surf-board at Waikiki. It is doubtful if the beginner would ever learn in any other surf in the world. The surf at Waikiki seems to be created by Divine Providence for the special purpose of permitting the beginner to learn the art of first starting his surf-board and then standing upon it.

A surf-board, or, in native parlance, papaheenalu, is a bit of board about six feet long, eighteen inches wide, and two inches thick, with a bow either round or sharp. This is taken out to where the waves generally fall, break, and rush inward, for one hundred yards or more. Given a start, it will rush before the waves at express speed, and if the operator be skillful, he will quickly learn to stand and balance himself upon this bit of wood as it shoots toward the beach.

There are three surfs at Waikiki. The little, or cornucopia, surf is in front of the Outrigger Club. Here, the young girls and beginners take their first lessons. The water at low tide is not more than two feet deep, and the waves, after breaking, run for perhaps a hundred yards. Standing upon the soft sandy bottom, the surfer holds his board so that he can give it an outward shove just as the wave is about to overwhelm him. If he judges his time, and the strength necessary, the board will be caught by the wave just as he throws himself full length upon it, and away he goes towards the beach, steering his board from side to side, or in a direct line, by the movement of his legs to the right or left. Although the speed is that of an express train, marvelous to relate, accidents are unknown, although at times there are hundreds in the surf with their boards. After the small boy has taken a few lessons in shallow water, he strikes out for the deep. It is a very long hoe, or pull, out to the nalu-nui, or big waves of the canoe surf. Lying full length on the board, the arms go round and round like a windmill. The inexperienced is soon fatigued, but this exercise kept up from day to day is a wonderful developer of muscle. The big waves are fully half a mile from shore, and sometimes give the surf-rider a run for a quarter of a mile before the wave dies out. If once the wave is pau, or finished, the board of the standing rider sinks beneath the water. Then there is a "Big surf" over in front of Queen's residence. There is no taking a standing start in that deep water. The arms must revolve with lightening speed. The great foaming billow rolls on, and if the speed of the board is sufficient, it is caught, lifted to the crest, and hurled forward with gigantic strength. Up leaps the rider, erect on his board, beating with his forefoot upon its bow to give it that tilt over the crest of the wave that will bring it down to the hollow in front of him. If it is a very high wave, he contracts his body until he has wriggled his board around so that it descends the wave on the bias. Once before the wave the board assumes a steady, straight, clear motion, and in all the world there is no more thrilling sport than this ride before a foaming, breaking, rushing, billow that curls above the head within reach of a back-stretched hand. Sometimes, owing to the lack of skill of the surfer, the board rises on that oncoming whirl of water, is caught on the crest of foam, and thrown high into the air, while the rider makes a more or less graceful dive to the coral.

It may seem a bold statement to make, nevertheless it is true, that it is easier to start and stand upon a surf-board than to correctly guide a fair sized canoe before the great billows that seem child's play to the surf-board rider. It takes nerve, grit, muscle, and a strong koa paddle to keep a canoe with six passengers, bow downward, at an angle of 45 degrees in the face of an on-rushing billow. A moment's loss of nerve, a little lack of strength upon the handle of the paddle, or any waning of skill, and the canoe swings around to the wave, which lifts its outrigger high in the air and capsizes the craft. The canoe, however, does not sink; it merely swamps; everyone climbs in again, there is a general bailing out and another try.

In all the world there are no such water sports as those at Waikiki, and today they are possibly being developed as never before. The Outrigger Canoe Club was organized in the summer of 1908. Already it has two hundred members, an acre and a half of property on Waikiki beach, several native grass houses, a score of Hawaiian canoes, half a hundred surf-boards belonging to members, bathhouses, a ladies' auxiliary with separate accommodations, a lagoon of clear water for the very little ones to use as practice grounds, and every facility for learning the water sports that were once exclusively Hawaiian. Since this Club was organized scores of boys and girls have learned to use the surf-board, and some of them to guide the surf-canoe. Surf-board games undreamed of by the Hawaiians are coming into vogue. Adepts at Waikiki now stand upon their boards and as they rush onward spear pigskins floating in the water. At night they go out into the waves with acetylene lamps attached to the bows of their boards so they appear like spirits riding on the water bathed in light. In every way the Outrigger Club is developing the great sport of surfing in Hawaii.

In Samoa, and in Fiji, as well as Tahiti, there are those who ride upon the surf-board but they do not stand. I once tried to show the natives of Fiji how it was done, and discovered, to my dismay, that neither the waves nor the coral were suitable to the sport of standing on the board. It is only in Hawaii, where the reefs are far out, and between them and the shore is a long stretch of sand, that the billows roll so evenly and so far, that this king of sports can be indulged in to perfection. I came to Hawaii for a day and lingered until the months rolled into years and I could stand upon my board and enjoy the sport that has no counterpart or equal in any part of the globe.

CHAPTER 41

Seven Weeks in Hawaii (1917)

M. Leola Crawford

M. Leola Crawford's short description of surfriding with Duke Kahanamoku provides a glimpse into the sport's popularity and growth
along with Hawai'i's tourist industry. In the post–Jack London era at
Waikīkī—a place that created the modern, carefree image of surfers and
served as surfriding's Mecca until World War II—visitors no longer simply watched surfriding but paddled out in the waves themselves. This was
made possible on a large scale through the instruction and surveillance of
the Waikīkī beachboys, who probably began working informally after the
first major resort, the Moana Hotel, opened in 1901. The first organized
beach service began around 1915 under the leadership of part-Hawaiian
Dude Miller. The same year Crawford published *Seven Weeks in Hawaii*,
Kahanamoku joined the Outrigger Canoe Club.[4]

   Kahanamoku's fame as an Olympic swimmer allowed him to break
down some racial barriers in the Islands and hold membership in both
the Outrigger and Hui Nalu. Tourists like Crawford flocked to have their
pictures taken with him and his surfboard, spreading the fame of Waikīkī
around the world. Although more of a goodwill ambassador for the Islands than a professional beachboy, Kahanamoku shows here how the
beachboys instructed, charmed, massaged, and rescued surfriding tourists in the waves, all for little or no pay. Although the beachboys were
responsible for spreading the enthusiasm for surfriding throughout the
first half of the twentieth century (and continue to do so today), most of
them endured lives of poverty as second-class citizens.

AT THREE O'CLOCK THEY DROPPED ME out at Waikiki, where I
had an appointment to go riding in an outrigger canoe. We had engaged
the services of the champion swimmer of the world to guide our boat. His
name is Duke Kahanamoku. He carried the honors at the Olympic Games
in Stockholm—one hundred yards in fifty-five and one-fifth seconds. He
is a splendid looking fellow, about six feet tall and dark as an Indian. I sat

directly in front of him in the boat, and he told me many interesting things about the fishes and the coral, and offered to teach me to ride the surf-board. I told him I would love to learn if I could keep from getting wet. He thought this a great joke, and when we finally returned, before I knew it, this Duke was carrying me to shore "to keep the lady from getting wet" as he said, and how he laughed and showed his pearly white teeth. I am quite fond of "the Duke"! . . .

TRULY, "The way of the transgressor is hard!"

My muscles are so sore that I can scarcely bend; my fingers so stiff that it is with difficulty I move my pen. Yea, verily, "Every rose has its thorn." It came about thusly:

A surf-board party was arranged for yesterday morning, to be superintended by Duke Kahanamoku (the champion swimmer). We met on the beach at eleven, and were each presented with a surf-board, upon which we lay flat, face down, our feet sticking over the square end, our chins resting on the board some twenty inches short of the pointed end. In this position the feet act as propeller, the hands as balancing power. Paddling far out we would wait for a wave and as it fell we were caught in its milky surf and washed with lightning speed to the beach. This is surely a reckless sport but, O, the wild joy of it! Even its dangers are fascinating, and after a few lessons from Duke I decided to venture alone. The frightful speed and driving spray caused me to close my eyes, so that I was unable to see an outrigger boat just ahead, and the collision introduced me to the coral reefs below. I rose! Duke reached the spot, clutched me by the back and spreading me out upon a surf-board gave me the famous Hawaiian *lomi-lomi*. This kind of rough massage, a sort of drubbing, which, though severe, is certainly effective, and in a few minutes I was able to join the party as good as new. Though our enthusiasm never for a moment waned, after two hours of this strenuous exercise our physical forces refused to act, so bidding Duke *aloha* we painfully wended our way homeward. And, as before stated, we are now but limping shadows of our former selves!

CHAPTER 42

Article from *The Evening Herald* (1917)[5]

George Freeth
1883–1919

The following article by George Freeth helps to situate surfriding's revival fairly precisely to the year 1902, when the nineteen-year-old part-Hawaiian began experimenting with standing on the surfboard in his home waters of Waikīkī. Although surfriding had occurred in Northern California as early as 1885 by visiting Hawaiians, Freeth is generally credited with sparking the interest in surfriding during his inaugural visit to Southern California in 1907.[6] Freeth also helped popularize swimming, diving, and water polo. According to historian Arthur C. Verge, "Freeth's greatest impact on California, however, remains his instrumental role in revolutionizing the profession of ocean lifesaving." Freeth's article in the *Evening Herald* was preceded by the following note, which outlined his contributions in this area:

> *Article written exclusively for* The Evening Herald *by George Freeth, life guard at Redondo Beach, who was commended by Congress and the United States Life Saving corps for the rescue of more than 250 lives during his career as a life-guard on the Southern California coast, and noted as the man who revived among the Hawaiians and introduced into the United States the lost art of surf board riding.*
>
> *Freeth has probably brought out and developed more swimmers of note than any other man in the country today, among them being the famous Sheffield sisters, Nita and Lyda, swimmers of the Golden Gate, Ludy Langer, long distance water dog, Doly Mings, the Newark sisters, Clifford Bowles, and others. The noted Hawaiian swimmer, Duke Kahanamoku who broke the world's record in the 100 meters race both at Stockholm and in Germany under the American colors, is one of Freeth's swimming companions who owes his success to the Redondo star.*

I CAN NOT REMEMBER THE DAY when I couldn't swim. The first days I can remember were those spent at Waikiki Beach, four miles distant from Honolulu, Hawaii, where, with hundreds of native boys, I swam and dove a greater part of the time. I was born at that beach, my father being a native of Cork, Ireland, and my mother, part English and part Hawaiian. Because of the location of my father's business, I remained there almost every day of my life up to the age of ten years.

Waikiki Beach is known the world over for its surf-board riders. Tourists go there from all over the world to watch the natives perform feats on the surf-board and I can name no sport that requires more daring, skill and dexterity than that of riding a surf-board at Waikiki Beach where the great breakers acquire a speed of sometimes thirty-five miles an hour.

I was born there November 8, 1883. When I began to swim and sport in the breakers with the native boys there was no standing surf-board riding. Every boy knew from the tales handed down from his father that the Hawaiians had at one time, ridden the waves but then not a one of them could stand. I listened to the tales told by the boys of how their ancestors could stand on a board speeding over the water at a terrific speed. I hardly believed it at first.

Not until I was nineteen and had made several trips to the United States, bathed at Atlantic City and learned a lot about water feats, did I attempt to ride a surf board. At that age, nineteen, I returned to Waikiki Beach, determined to learn the lost art of surf-board riding if it was within human possibility. I took a large board, shaped it to suit my weight and started.

I would get the board to riding well, then would stand up on my hands and knees, all the while guiding it with my feet. At last I was able to stand on my knees, going at full speed. My next move was to rest on one knee and one foot for short distances and was gradually able to work myself into longer distances. At last I was riding the entire length of the breaker range, a half mile, standing at full height on the board.

The native boys had laughed at me when I made my first efforts. Now they hailed me as the reviver of the lost art. They all took to riding while standing at full height and today the tourist at Waikiki can see hundreds of native boys riding these boards.

When I made my next trip to the United States I brought the surf-board art with me. Then not one person in this country could ride one. Today many of the life guards on our western coast are proficient riders and can do feats that make the spectator hold his breath. But ten years ago there was no surf board riding in America. It is an art that belongs to the natives of the Hawaiian islands.

CHAPTER 43

Hawaiian Surfboard (1935)

Tom Blake
1902–1994

Tom Blake visited Hawai'i for the first time in 1924 and proved to be a Renaissance man for surfriding. Intensely interested in the sport's history, including surfboard design, Blake began shaping replicas of the early Hawaiian *olo* and *alaia* boards housed in the Bishop Museum in Honolulu. Trying to reduce the great weight of these boards, some of which exceeded 150 pounds, Blake designed a hollow board in 1929 for both paddling and surfboard competitions, events in which he excelled. Blake is also credited with introducing the first surfboard fin in 1935, allowing riders to turn their boards more easily. *Hawaiian Surfboard* remains Blake's most enduring publication: it was the first book to offer a comprehensive treatment of surfriding, including chapters on Hawaiian legends and an early history of the sport.

It is hard to overestimate Blake's importance for the popular image of surfers today. Describing his idyllic life at Waikīkī in the 1920s and 1930s, Blake acted as a transitional figure between Hawaiian and *haole* surf cultures: he adopted an idealized version of the beachboy life and provided the most direct antecedent for the white, antiestablishment, "beach bum" surfer upon whom are based nearly all popular representations of surfers, beginning with Kahuna in the 1959 movie *Gidget*.

In the following excerpt, Blake provides information on the size, cost, and materials of surfboards in the 1930s. We see the perennial presence of Duke Kahanamoku and learn about such novelties as surfriding at night, an activity that inspired one of Blake's more poetic moments: "In the moonlight incoming swells creep up like great shadowy creatures. One cannot realize the silence of the ground swells until waiting for them at night." Blake helped the sport gain increased exposure on the mainland by publishing his surf photography in *National Geographic* and writing how-to articles in *Popular Science* and *Popular Mechanics* for surfboard construction and riding technique. In addition to these accomplishments, Blake had a profound impact on exporting Hawaiian surf culture to the burgeoning surf community in Southern California through such events as the Pacific Coast Surf Riding Championship, inaugurated in 1928.[7]

Within a mile of the crater's base (Diamond Head) is the old village of Waikiki. It stands in the center of a handsome cocoanut grove. There is a fine bay before the village, in whose water the vessels of Vancouver and other distinguished navigators have anchored.

There were no busy artizans wielding their implements of labor; no civilized vehicles bearing their loads of commerce, or any living occupant.

Beneath the cool shade of some evergreens, or in a thatched house reposed several canoes. Everything was so quiet as though it were the only village on earth; and the tennants, its only denizens.

A few natives were enjoying a promiscuous bath in a crystal clear stream that came directly from the mountains.

Some were steering their frail canoe seaward; others clad simply in Nature's robes, were wading out on the reefs in search of fish.

[G.W. Bates's *Sandwich Island Notes* (1854)]

This is a very pretty picture of Waikiki beach. I would give my best surfboard to find it like that again some bright morning when I come down from Kaimuki. Instead, I come to the modern looking suburb of Honolulu with its fine hotels, Piggly Wiggly stores, shops, and private residences. Only the palm groves remain unchanged, the bay of Waikiki and the eternal breakers.

I really get more pleasure from Waikiki beach than the "not so idle rich" get on their short vacations here. Someone expresses my sentiment very well in these simple lines:

Along the shore I wander, free,
A beach comber at Waikiki,
Where time worn souls who seek in vain,
Hearts ease, in vagrant, wondering train.

A beach comber from choice, am I,
Content to let the world drift by,
Its strife and envy, pomp and pride,
I've tasted, and am satisfied.

Waikiki beach has been kind to me. The native Hawaiians have been kind. I have had the honor of riding the big surfs with these Hawaiians—I have sat at their luaus—watched their most beautiful women dance the hulas—I have been invited into their exclusive Hui Nalu surfriding club—a club for natives only. I have held the honor position (bow seat) riding waves in the outrigger canoe—the honor position (holding down the outrigger) on the sailing canoe. I have been initiated into the secrets of spear fishing far out on the coral reefs.

I have learned much from these people.

Acquaintances in the States have asked me why I bury myself in the Hawaiian Islands. The reason is because I like it. It fits my nature, it is life's compensation for such a nature as mine. I like it because I can live simple and quietly here. I can live well, without the social life. I can dress as I please, for comfort, usually it's a pair of canvas sneakers, light trousers and a sleeveless polo shirt with swimming trunks all day. I like the Islands because I can keep one hundred percent sun-tan here the year around, rest and sleep for hours in the wonderful sunshine each day.

Although I live 3 miles away from the beach, up near the mountains, I enjoy the exercise of the three-mile walk each day from and to my cottage. In my yard grow bananas, avocados, mangoes, papaia and luxurious ferns and flowers including a stately Royal palm which is majesty in itself in the moonlight.

I like it because of the natural beauty of everything here, the very blue sky, very white clouds, very green mountains, clothed in foliage in their ridges. My greatest pleasure in life is through my eyes so why should I stay around Main Street or Broadway? The coco palms waving in the clean trade winds, the colors of the water on the coral reef, greet my eyes each day as I near the beach, and when the giant waves of the Kalahuewe-he surf are breaking white, far from shore, it means royal sport is waiting and I actually break into a run to get to the Outrigger Club, don trunks and get out my favorite surfboard of teak wood. I like the opportunity of studying and seeing the great mixture of races gathered here, each one retaining many of their old customs of eating, dress and living. I pick a custom or two from each race to use at my convenience. Perhaps it is the Buddhist religion of the Chinese—the poi eating and surfriding of the Hawaiians—the raw peanut eating of the Filipinoes—the happiness, enthusiasm and appreciation with which the Japanese meet their daily duties. I like it here because I can live conservatively and find the habit interesting and a pleasure. It's a great place for a bachelor.

Aside from the charm of Bates' description of old Waikiki it establishes the fact that under those conditions, surfriding was, indeed a lost art. I feel, however, that there was always surfriding at Waikiki beach, on some kind of board. Waikiki's condition in 1854 indicates that the great popularity of the national pastime, surfriding, was but a memory. . . .

Now to get to surfriding today. The Outrigger Canoe Club, built in 1907, is the center of surfriding at Waikiki.[8] At the club is to be found a row of some two hundred upright surfboard lockers, filled with boards of all sizes, shades and colors; the average being ten feet long, twenty-three inches wide, three inches thick; quite flat on top and bottom, with edges rounded and weighing up to seventy-five pounds.

They are made of California redwood, white cedar, white sugar pine and a few of balsa wood. Ninety percent being of redwood because of its lightness, strength and cheapness. Ten dollars will buy the rough plank to make a redwood board. Some of the boards are hollowed out and decked over to lighten them.

In the latter part of 1929, after three years experimenting, I introduced at Waikiki a new type of surfboard; new so the papers said, and so the beach boys said, but in reality the design was taken from the ancient Hawaiian type of board, also from the English racing shell. It was called a "cigar board," because a newspaper reporter thought it was shaped like a giant cigar. This board was really graceful and beautiful to look at, and in performance was so good that officials of the Annual Surfboard Paddling Championship immediately had a set of nine of them built for use during the 1930 Hawaiian Paddling Championship races. The half mile record of seven minutes and two seconds, was cut that year to four minutes and forty-nine seconds and the hundred yard dash was reduced from thirty-six and two-fifths seconds to thirty-one and three-fifths seconds. This made me the 1930 champion in the senior events and, incidentally, the new record holder. But as is true in yacht and other similar racing, I won because I had a superior board. This was the first cured or hollowed out board to appear at Waikiki. As the racing rules allowed unrestricted size and design, I staked my chances on this hollow racer whose points were proven for now all racing boards are hollow.

This type of board was purely for racing and I soon followed it with a riding board sixteen feet long. The new riding board model was a great success and Duke Kahanamoku built his great 16-foot hollow redwood board along about the same time. He is an excellent craftsman and shapes the lines and balance of his boards with the eye; he detects its irregularities by touch of the hand.

I feel, however, that Duke had some appreciation of the old museum boards and from his wide experience in surfriding and his constructive turn of mind would have eventually duplicated them, regardless of precedent. . . .

During ou[r] last big surf, which comes only three or four times a year, the Duke did some of the most beautiful riding I have ever seen on his new long board. In one instance, at zero break, he caught a twenty-five foot wave and rode across the face of it, through first break, clear into Queen's surf at a speed of about thirty miles an hour. On this four hundred yard ride Duke was able to catch the wave out farther than the boys with the short ten-foot boards and the weight of his one hundred and thirty pound board gave him additional speed which enabled him to beat the break to Queen's.

Take Sunday; good surf running, not big surf, and plenty of action is to be found out in the breakers. I'll go out as an observer.

The surfers gather around a certain dark patch of water. This is because the coral is higher there and the wave breaks steeper and is easier to catch. In the lull of the surf they have drifted with the tide and wind some ten or fifteen yards from the proper position and when a set of ground swells are sighted a few hundred yards outside general commotion prevails as they all maneuver for what they consider the best position to catch the wave.

As the swells approach they get steeper and most of the riders paddle for the first one but only seven manage to get it. They stand up on their boards and speed shoreward at an angle. About one hundred feet back is the second wave. Everyone left paddles for this. It proves very steep and easy to catch. Nearly all catch it, including two of the tandem parties.

Starting at the extreme right to describe the different riders here is what one sees. The first boy is no doubt inexperienced for he was too far over in the break which caused him and his board to "pearl dive," or go straight down towards the bottom, giving him a severe ducking and some valuable experience. This dive was caused partly because he did not slide or turn his board at an angle soon enough and partly because the wave was too steep and about to break at that point. The second rider just squeezed out of the steep part by a sharp tack to the left. He straightens out a bit to avoid colliding with the third board—a tandem. The boy on this board has a passenger. He stands up first, then assists his partner to her feet.

The fourth board also contains a tandem party. On this one the girl rises first, then the boy stands up with her on his shoulders—very thrilling, indeed, for the girl. The next board has two girls for riders. They "jam up," after a short fifteen yard ride, with an inexperienced surfer and all three lose their boards and get ducked, barely missing getting hit by the loose boards. Rather brave these girls to be out there. The rest of the riders have pulled away some twenty yards. They are on the same wave and all manage to hold their boards, as this is one of the first rules of surfing. To loose [*sic*] a board means to swim maybe a hundred yards for it and also a loose board is dangerous to the other surfers. Of the dozen or so on this wave only two on the extreme left ride through the various breaks and do not get caught in the foam. Their ride has been a good one, perhaps two hundred yards long at a speed of about twenty-five miles an hour—eighteen miles an hour for the wave and seven for the slide.

There is another lull and all gather outside again to repeat the performance. It is good sport and the time flies. The water is so warm one is not conscious of it. The view of the palm trees on shore, the hotels, the mountains and clouds is marvelous and to me it is part of the pleasure of surfing. The hour before sunset is best of all for then the mountains take on all the shades of white and gray. Gayly colored rainbows are often seen in far off valleys.

Moonlight surfing is enjoyed for a few nights each month in the summer time when the big yellow tropical moon is at its fullest. It is truly a rare sport. In the moonlight incoming swells creep up like great shadowy creatures. One cannot realize the silence of the ground swells until waiting for them at night.

From the shore surfriders in the moonlight look strange and unreal when riding in on a breaker. One is never sure what it is until a rider lets out a yell. At night it is easy to yell because a person's nerves are on edge in spite of the fun and beauty of the scene.

CHAPTER 44

"Lessons in Surfing for Everyman" (1936)

C. P. L. Nicholls

C. P. L. Nicholls provides one of the earlier records of the California surf scene as it gathered momentum in the 1930s. In truth, there is little written record of surfriding's adolescent years in California between George Freeth's first visit in 1907 and the publication of Doc Ball's *California Surfriders* in 1946. Much more research in local newspapers and magazines, including interviews with those who lived through the era, is needed to establish a more complete record of this important time in surf history. Southern California certainly remained in the shadow of Waikīkī until well after World War II. The entire surf culture in California derived from the Islands, from the paddle board club mentioned here by Nicholls to the Waikīkī-like San Onofre surf scene complete with a grass hut on the beach, palm frond hats, and weekend luaus.

Nicholls gives a sense of the scope of the early California surf scene (which probably comprised no more than a couple hundred surfers in the entire state) as he noted the first surfriding clubs and the most popular spots in Santa Monica, Palos Verdes, and Long Beach. Nicholls's article paints a very different picture of surfriding, and of surfriders, than the one of disaffected youth that arises after World War II: here surfriders act as responsible sportsmen who prefer to build their own boards and whose clubs "have rigid tests for prospective members." Doc Ball provides another example of the upstanding surfers of this era in the Palos Verdes Surfing Club creed, which was recited in unison at the beginning of each club meeting by all members:

> I as a member of the Palos Verdes Surfing Club do solemnly swear to be ever steadfast in my allegiance to the club and its members. To respect and adhere to the aims and ideals set forth in its constitution. To cheerfully meet and accept my responsibilities hereby incurred and to at all times strive to conduct myself in a manner becoming a club member and a gentleman so help me God.[9]

TO THE AVERAGE CITIZEN WATCHING a surf rider, the impression is that these stalwart, sun-tanned youths are gifted with superhuman daring and are some species of duck or fish, or that they are reckless youngsters who have not sufficient experience in life to know the meaning of danger. He perhaps has seen surf riders depicted in Sunday rotogravure sections or has read of the thrill of riding in an outrigger canoe. Our beach visitor, watching a dozen or so surfers ride in on a white-tipped wave of six to eight feet high, which eventually crashes on the beach, can only marvel at the agility and skill they exhibit.

It is difficult to describe the thrill of surfing. It must be experienced to be appreciated fully. Skill and agility to a marked degree are necessary, coupled with expert swimming ability. However, any strong swimmer can enjoy the sport if he learns it one step at a time. The cost is mainly a large quantity of personal effort together with the ability to take a few spills along the way.

Motorists driving along the Southern California seashore past the mouth of Santa Monica Canyon at any time of the year, will probably see from fifteen to twenty husky young surfers sitting astride their boards waiting for a good wave to carry them shoreward on its peak. Passing on down the coast towards Palos Verdes the week-end driver will see another group of similarly browned, well-built young surfers riding steeper and longer waves into the pebbly beach of Palos Verdes Cove. If the day happens to be one on which heavy ground swells are running and the motorist carries on with his beach excursion to the Long Beach Flood Control channel, it is likely that he will spot still another group of these ardent surfing enthusiasts practicing their act on the large waves to be found at this location.

The reason that these locations above mentioned are suited for surfing is that the ocean bottom remains level for a considerable distance so that the incoming swells hold their form for a length of a quarter of a mile or more before breaking on the beach. This enables the surfer to get his desired long ride.

For many years past the Balboa-Newport Harbor entrance channel has been an ideal location for surfers, but due to the fine development of the recent harbor improvement the channel has been deepened and the shoals have been dredged out so that the waves formed are not suitable for surfing.

The Cove at Palos Verdes is perhaps the best location at the present time for the practice of surfing. There are two organized surfing clubs in Southern California. One may be found at Santa Monica and is organized under the name of Santa Monica Paddle Board Club. The other club is located with its center of activity at the Palos Verdes Cove and is organized under the name of the Palos Verdes Surfing Club. Both clubs have rigid tests for prospective members. These tests are entirely necessary in order to provide for the mutual safety of its members. First of all, the prospective surfer must be not only a good swimmer, but an excellent swimmer who can swim long distances if perchance he is caught in an ongoing tide or rip. He must know the intricacies of wave action and must have sufficient hardihood to withstand many spills before he accomplishes any degree of proficiency in this sport.

There are two types of so-called surf boards used on the beaches in Southern California. They are the paddle board, which is a surface speed paddling board, and the true surf board which is essentially a wave riding board. The racing board first mentioned is constructed to make speed over the top of the water. It is constructed of varying lengths, thirteen feet and over, according to personal preference and design. Its width varies up to a maximum of twenty inches and it is usually constructed with a round, oval, "V", or flat bottom. It may have a round or square stern and be either hollow in construction or made of balsa wood. A board of this type will make, with a good paddler riding it, an average of around four or more miles per hour.

The surfboard constructed particularly for riding waves is of a different design from that used for paddling on the surface of the water. The bow or nose of the board has a slight rise in order that the board may be paddled through the waves and prevent digging in as a surfer rides his wave towards the beach. It also has an average width of twenty inches. The stern or tail comes to a point so that it may act as a rudder. As a surfer stands up on the board for his ride a slight leaning of the body to the right or left directs this rudder-like action of the tail to either one side or the other. This enables the surf board rider to ride in on his wave at an angle thereby enabling him to have a long ride, but this is only accomplished by experienced surfers after much tedious practice and many spills.

The prospective surfer should first provide himself with a well-constructed board which he can make himself, in any home workshop at a cost of between eight and ten dollars. Commercial boards may be purchased, but usually a surfer desires to make his own board suited to his individual weight and preference. . . .

Surfing is truly a year around sport for the hardy and it is so because it is only occasionally that the rider is wholly submerged in the water. Southern California water rarely drops below the temperature of 55 degrees Fahrenheit, and since the surfers are on top of their boards most of the time and continually active, they enjoy an exhilarating tingle rather than clammy cold, and the sport becomes an all-year-round activity.

CHAPTER 45

"Surf boarding from Molokai to Waikiki" (1954)

Thomas C. Zahn
1924–1991

Tommy Zahn was a career lifeguard in Los Angeles and helped introduce, along with Joe Quigg and Dale Velzy, the lighter, more maneuverable balsa boards to Southern California in the early 1950s. Zahn also formed part of a contingent of lifeguards who introduced the balsa boards to Australia in 1957, sparking a renewed interest in surfriding that has since become a national sport in that country. Zahn's article shows the strong connection between paddleboard racing and surfriding in the formative era of California surf culture. Tom Blake's inaugural Pacific Coast Surf Riding Championship in Corona del Mar (1928) was in fact a combination of the two events. The Waikīkī beachboys had popularized the tradition of the Hawaiian waterman: a person whose skill in surfriding formed part of a larger expertise in all ocean activities, including outrigger canoe paddling, swimming, diving, spear fishing, and what Zahn terms here "surfboarding." Zahn was at the tail-end of a waterman tradition—transplanted from Hawai'i by George Freeth, Duke Kahanamoku, and Tom Blake—that would all but disappear from mainstream California surf culture by the end of the 1950s. Zahn was also at a critical point in surfriding history in terms of surfboard equipment: the same World War II technology that provided fiberglass for his balsa paddleboard also produced polyurethane foam, a product that would replace balsa as the primary surfboard material also by the end of the 1950s. Although Southern California, and Malibu in particular, soon replaced Waikīkī as the epicenter of surf culture, Zahn captures here the general enthusiasm that surfriders still had in the 1940s and 1950s for Waikīkī and "the famed surfs of Oahu."

ON OCTOBER 24, 1953, during the annual Aloha Week Molokai-to-Oahu Outrigger Canoe Race, I paddled my surfboard from Point Ilio,

Molokai, to Waikiki beach, Oahu. This was accomplished in nine hours and twenty minutes; the course was thirty-six miles with an actual total of some forty miles, after allowing for wind and drift. The Kaiwi channel, popularly known as the Molokai channel, is considered by many to be one of the roughest bodies of water in the world. This is caused by a combination of very deep and shoal waters; abrupt island shorelines causing heavy backwash and crosswells; a prevailing northeast tradewind in the middle of the channel, but continually shifting as one approaches shoreward due to the mountains, valleys, and passes. The result: an ugly, choppy, restless body of water.

The reasons for attempting this type of project deserve some explanation. I was born in Santa Monica, California, a locality where many types of aquatic activities flourish, much as they do in Hawaii. When I was eight years old, I fell in love with the sport of surfriding. The thrill I got from my first ride on a little redwood "belly" board I have never forgotten and is little exceeded by riding much larger deepwater swells today.

After surfing the California coastline for years, and under the influence of such champions as Tom Blake and Preston Peterson, I developed an ambition to try the famed surfs of Oahu. My first experience was in 1945 enroute to the invasion of Okinawa. Our ship had a one-day stopover at Pearl Harbor, allowing me about four frantic hours at Waikiki. My first impression was all that I'd hoped for; a friendly reception, beautiful water and weather conditions, and a promising surf. Following this "brief encounter," watching Diamond Head fade into the distance as we sailed southward, I resolved I would come back someday, which I did as a civilian in October, 1947.

I moved in with Gene (Tarzan) Smith, then Hawaiian Surfboard Champion and began one of the happiest portions of my aquatic career. Gene had paddled his board between virtually all of the islands. His personal accounts of these expeditions and his training methods intrigued me. The crossing that brought him recognition and interested me the most was that from Molokai to Makapuu Point, Oahu, in the time of eight hours and thirty-seven minutes.[10]

I began to prepare for the event. As the project became more of a reality—my plan was to better the existing time, go the entire distance to Waikiki beach and evaluate the surfboard as a means of deep water rescue and survival equipment.

In April, 1953, I resigned from the Santa Monica Lifeguard Service where I had been a lieutenant and worked eleven years to return for the fourth time to Hawaii. When I heard of the approaching 2nd

Annual Molokai to Oahu Outrigger Canoe Race, I knew the time and circumstances were right for the crossing. I wrote Joseph M. Quigg, the Malibu sailboat designer to design and build what he considered the ideal board for the crossing. This he agreed to do in his spare time.

Then I began a routine of surfing four hours a day and swimming every night to develop the endurance and speed for the coming test. I enjoyed myself immensely that summer surfing Waikiki, and Makaha beach at Waianae in the early fall. A month before the race I began polishing up the process of preparation under the expert advice of my friend and coach, Tom Blake. Everyday he would take me up the channel coast of Oahu and I would paddle back to Waikiki. We went further until we were at Hanauma bay twelve miles from Waikiki. It was in these workouts I developed the long relaxed stroke I was to use, and accustom myself to the short, nasty chop that would be so characteristic of the rip.

I learned at this time that in accomplishing anything of this nature, preparation is nine-tenths of the battle. My conditioning and diet required thought. Getting a suitable escort craft was a problem. The greatest problem, however, was weather conditions; on this unpredictable phenomenon the success of the project was dependent. I studied the reports daily; I stared at the ocean surface and clouds whenever possible. If the wind were to shift from trades to Kona (southwest), my plans would be seriously affected. I desired a moderate trade which would provide a favorable current and a quartering wind-chop that would assist my progress.

Quigg air-freighted my new board to me the day before the race. He had many delays in its completions due to other commitments, plus details and experiments he made while in construction. I uncrated the board that morning, October 23, and gave it a short test try. I was thrilled and delighted with the finished product. It is sixteen feet long, nineteen inches wide, made of hollow balsa-wood construction, with a one-eighth inch plywood deck. The board is covered with a thin layer of fiberglass, and is equipped with a foot operated rudder. It cost one-hundred and forty dollars. As an afterthought, Tom Blake attached a chin-rest that was to save me later by relieving my neck and shoulders of the weight of my head. The board has stability and maneuverability, and I would now say it is the ideal board for offshore work.

We re-crafted the board and loaded it on the charter boat Hula-Girl, at the Ala Moana Yacht Basin, that afternoon. We were to rendezvous that night at Molokai with the boat that was to be my escort. At this time it was still indefinite who my escort would be, as this was a courtesy of the Aloha Week Committee.

This contributed to my growing anxiety, together with such thoughts as what conditions I would encounter, such as fish. I had read every account of shark activity in the Hawaiian Islands, trying to separate fact from fiction and superstition. I read all the books I could obtain on the matter. I was comforted by the knowledge that the deadly killer-whale does not frequent these waters due to a lack of suitable prey. My fear of sharks diminished as it became apparent that virtually all humans attacked were engaged in one form or another of fishing. So, barring a freak accident, I felt reassured.

The yacht, Hula-Girl, a converted PT craft, owned by Jim Lee and skippered by Spike Simpson, had been chartered by the Hawaii Visitors Bureau to cover the entire canoe race, and to accommodate a party of casual observers. At 4:30 p.m. we left the shelter of Diamond Head to plow into the channel swells enroute to Molokai. I concentrated on the wind and water conditions until it was too dark to see. Then I went below and slept soundly for several hours. When I awoke, a beautiful moon was over Oahu illuminating the silver of the breaking whitecaps. The flash of the Makapuu lighthouse was directly astern. Ahead was the low silhouette of Point Ilio, Molokai. The keen anticipation of the task that lay ahead the next day dulled my appetite and I ate lightly of beef-stew, tomatoes, and fruit. It was a lovely night on deck as I tried to sleep, but the pressure of my plans, the advance publicity I'd received, the "well-meaning" but dubious warnings and advice I'd heard, made sleep come slowly. I wanted to be off as soon as possible. The actual performance would be a release.

Dawn broke clear with ideal conditions. I ate a light breakfast of cornflakes, honey, condensed milk and applesauce. This was to be the last food or drink I was to receive until I finished, although I had a supply of food and orange juice in the event I was in the water longer than anticipated.

We waited for the "escort craft." It did not appear. We heard, then saw the canoes get underway. I became fearful that I had been forgotten, which was apparently the case. After a hasty conference on the Hula-Girl, the group informed me with no hesitation that I was to get underway immediately, which I did at 6:20 a.m.

I actually started in the water, in the lee of Point Ilio, about one-hundred yards offshore. I paddled toward the open sea, increasing my speed as I warmed up. Just as I hit the first open water I struck a "Portu-guese-man-of war" (a form of jellyfish) which inflicted a minor sting on my left arm. I didn't break stroke, however, but wondered if there would be a repetition of this. As it turned out, there was one other minor sting somewhere in mid-channel.

I believe there may have been many among the skeptical of the outcome of my trip, perhaps a few on board the Hula-Girl. At this point I determined to relieve them of any doubts they might have. I maintained my practiced pace with success, following the boat about fifty to a hundred yards astern and a little to windward to avoid the exhaust from twin diesels. I would look astern every twenty minutes or so to see if the dark outline of Molokai had diminished any. My pace was calculated to a point that I could determine my position reasonably close whenever I could hear the time from Tom Blake, who was watching my progress carefully from the Hula-Girl's taffrail. He had an auxiliary board ready in case anything happened to mine. He also had a rescue tube ready in case of an accident. He scanned the surface continually with binoculars for dangerous fish, and also photographed my progress with a Rolleiflex camera.

As the sun rose higher and I approached the Oahu shoreline, I headed for Makapuu Point, so that we might work as far as possible to windward. Also I wanted my time at the point, to break the existing record, if possible.

Toward eleven a.m., the distance stretched interminably. I neither ate nor drank, as I didn't want to lose the time involved in doing so. The Hula-Girl would follow me, then lead for a while, then change sides. This was relaxing for me, as each change afforded me some relief of the rhythmic monotony I was undergoing. I no longer needed her to set my course, as the Oahu landmarks were clearly visible.

Past the mid-channel mark I ran across several schools of flying fish. They sailed across my bow about twenty feet away, giving me ample room. I later saw what I believed to be a mahimahi break water in a foaming whitecap several yards away. These were the only signs of marine life I saw during the trip. Now and then a curious sea-bird would hover slowly overhead, inspecting this strange form of travel.

I became anxious concerning my time as we reached Makapuu Point, as I wanted to be well under the record, and yet paced enough to finish at Waikiki. My fastest speed was the last hour out of Makapuu Point, and I was delighted to learn that I had made my mark, and was inspired to finish at Waikiki. I changed my course to Koko Head; and it was in the approach to this headland I found the roughest water of the entire trip, caused by the sheer cliffs between Sandy beach and Koko Head. There was an hour of this messy cross-chop and changing winds, but at no point did I doubt that I would make my goal. Upon rounding Koko Head by Portlock, I could see the wonderful outline of Diamond Head, as I entered the relatively smooth waters of Maunalua bay.

The trip then became a series of obstacles to hurdle. First, Kuliouou, then Aina Haina, its comfortable homes clearly visible. Wailupe, and finally Black Point which I passed so close I could see people walking about. I set my course just outside the breakerline fringing Diamond Head, where I left the loyal Hula-Girl, who had to skirt the reef to seaward. Here I was escorted by a fishing canoe until I brushed the surf at Elks club. With little more than a mile to go, I pulled myself together for the final stretch.

This last portion also had its obstacles. First, the Elk's club, the Natatorium, Cunha surf, and finally Canoe surf where I picked up a short ride shoreward. Already the beachboys in canoes were welcoming me—I could see a large crowd in front of the Moana hotel and could hear the announcer speaking over the sound system. I evidently slipped up on them unnoticed, as they were all staring out to sea, until the last few yards.

My board touched the beach at 3:40 p.m., a total of nine hours and twenty minutes since I left Molokai. I rolled off my board into the warm, blue water, and was assisted to the platform there on the beach to receive the greatest welcome and applause I have ever known. Hawaiians I'd never met were giving me leis of flowers and maili, kissing me and shaking my hands. Edwin Adolphson of the Oahu Lifesaving Service presented me with a silver cup, and my board was brought up on the platform and exhibited to the friendly crowd.

I was then walked, or rather, half carried down the beach to my apartment by friends and well-wishers. Other than a slight numb sensation through my body, I felt quite normal but sleepy. I took a long warm shower interrupted by many friendly callers. I was given hot soup and milk to eat, but found eating difficult due to the pressure from the weight of my body on the board, that had caused a general muscular tension.

My first act was to telephone Joe Quigg in Santa Monica and thank him for the wonderful job of construction and design, and for making the air-freight deadline.

I slept a few hours, dressed, and ate a huge steak dinner. After a three-day rest I was more or less restored to normal activity.

The newspapers were warm in their comment with front page stories and pictures that Mainland papers picked up. The Quarterdeck club selected me for their Williams "Player of the Week" award at a very hospitable luncheon the following week. Rex Wills, KHON sportscaster, invited me to appear on a thirty minute interview, at which time I was joined by Tom Blake. Later, at a dinner-dance held by the Waikiki Surf club, I received a beautiful trophy made of Hawaiian woods and silver to commemorate the occasion.

I learned many new things about the sea, the human body, and the surfboard. I was satisfied for the time being with what I had set out to do; but perhaps the most memorable sensation was the wholehearted Aloha I felt at my reception at Waikiki.

Part IV

Youth Culture
(1957–1979)

UNDER THE INFLUENCE OF JACK LONDON'S literary imagination, the communal act of surfriding among Polynesians of all ages became an individualized sport narrowed to the exploits of heroic males. This image narrowed further in the late 1950s and early 1960s to a very specific stratum of society: teenagers. The adventures of fifteen-year-old Franzie ("Gidget") and the teenage pop tunes of the Beach Boys and Jan and Dean carried this popular image for the better part of three decades. Surfing as an activity for the young—or at least the young at heart—is the dominant image of the sport today.

Tom Wolfe's articles on The Pump House Gang chronicled a more jaded version of youth culture in the mid-1960s as certain segments of that population transitioned into the counterculture. Although surfing retained much of the summer sun and fun image, surfers became associated with the more radicalized stance of West Coast counterculture: antiestablishment drop-outs whose protests took the form of long hair, Eastern religions, and psychedelic drugs. Mickey Dora's report on the Malibu contest in 1968 offers one of the era's strongest protests against the packaging and commodification of America's newest recreational fad.

Two voices from Down Under added another facet to surfing's image: the competitive, professional surfer. Australian journalist John Witzig criticized the judging system of surf contests in California in the mid-1960s, though for very different reasons than Mickey Dora. Rather than questioning the entire enterprise, Witzig lampooned a decadent competitive scene that revolved around expertise in a single maneuver: nose riding. The new school of power he championed resurfaced a decade later in the person of Ian Cairns, one of a small group of primarily Australian, South African, and Hawaiian surfers who looked to polish the rough edges of surfing's countercultural image as they launched an international professional tour. At the local level, Hawaiian surfer Kimo

Hollinger offered an impassioned counterpoint to the emerging trend of global competition.

The Australians' enormous influence on competitive surfing during this time resulted directly from a cross-pollination of ideas on surfboard design that arose when surfers began to take to the road. Inspired by such films as Bruce Brown's *The Endless Summer*, surfers fanned out around the globe in increasing numbers in the late 1960s and early 1970s. The travelogues published by Kevin Naughton, Craig Peterson, and Erik Aeder epitomized the "follow the waves" philosophy that has become an important part of both the reality and the image of riding waves.

CHAPTER 46

Gidget (1957)
Frederick Kohner
1905–1986

Frederick Kohner, a Czechoslovakian Jew, studied in Paris and Vienna before emigrating to the United States following the rise of Nazi Germany. A longtime screenwriter in Hollywood, Kohner enjoyed his most success with the novel *Gidget*, based on his teenage daughter's experiences at Malibu in the late 1950s. The popularity of the novel inspired a series of movies, additional novels (*Gidget Goes Hawaiian*, 1961; *Gidget Goes to Rome*, 1962), television shows, and a play. *Gidget* was the initial spark for the enormous popularity of surfing in mainstream culture that began in the early 1960s and continues today; because Kohner was not a surfer himself, *Gidget* has also become synonymous with the exploitation of the sport by non-surfers. Part of the novel's appeal is its precocious heroine, fifteen-year-old Gidget, who recalls Princess Kelea of Maui in her dedication to surfing. As Kelea, in one version of the story, insists that "the surf-board was her husband, and she would never embrace any other," so Gidget concludes about her summer at Malibu: "All things considered—maybe I was just a woman in love with a surfboard."[1]

[Editor's note: In the opening chapters, Gidget is swimming at Malibu Beach and must be rescued by Moondoggie on his surfboard; so begins her romantic interest with both Moondoggie and surfing. The story develops Gidget's acceptance by the Malibu surfers (including their leader, Kahoona) and her on-again off-again relationship with Moondoggie. The action culminates in a wild beach party and an out-of-control brush fire. The next morning, Moondoggie discovers that Gidget has spent the night in Kahoona's beach hut.]

Fourteen

I must have been sleeping way into the morning because when I opened my eyes the sun was filtering into the hut and I heard a roar from the outside as if all hell was loose.

The great Kahoona was nowhere in sight.

My blouse and skirt looked a mess, all wrinkled up, and I decided to go out and have a morning swim before breakfast.

I slipped out of my clothes and threw them on the cot and just as I was about to head out, the door to the hut opened.

The sudden impact of the sun blinded me for a moment.

"Morning, Cass," I called out.

Anybody could have made that crazy mistake. The guy who stood in the door frame was almost as tall as Cass and he wore jeans and a T-shirt like him.

It wasn't the great operator, however. It was one of his sponsors. It was no other than Moondoggie.

But it wasn't only me who hadn't recognized him at first. There seemed to be something wrong with Jeff's eyesight too. He gazed about as if he couldn't focus very well, then he saw my skirt and blouse and I guess it was then that he recognized me.

"Gidget," he said flatly. "What in hell . . . ."

My mind was jumping around so quickly—I hardly could keep track of it. Has he been looking for me? Did he think I had been sleeping with the great Kahoona? And if so—what would I tell him? I didn't know what to say so I just gave a fine imitation of a deaf mute and tried to brush past him and get outside.

"Hey, wait a moment . . ." He had grabbed me by the wrist.

Well, here it comes, I thought.

"I want you to answer me . . ."

"Why should I?" I said. "You didn't even talk to me last night."

"But now, *now* I want you to tell me . . ."

For a moment I felt an impulse to call for help, when I spotted the great Kahoona. He had just come out of the surf which was something tremendous. Waves about twenty feet high. That's the way it must look at Makaha at Zero break, I thought. I wished I could have seen him coming riding in. I had never seen them that bitchen, on my word of honor.

Jeff still had me by the wrist when the Kahoona came towards us, his board shouldered.

"Hi, man," he said, quite calmly. "What a surf!"

Only then he noticed the way Jeff was almost crushing my wrist. He didn't say anything. He put the board down and leaned it against the hut. Then of all things he started to whistle.

I guess it was the whistling that brought out the beast in Geoffrey Griffin. He released the grip on my wrist. I noticed that all the tan had faded from his face. It was real white now. He made a couple of steps towards Cass. His right fist traveled in a short arc and he hit the great Kahoona solidly on the chin.

"Jeff!" I yelled.

"Shut up," he yelled back.

Cass had stumbled, but it seemed as if the jab had merely shook him up a little. It also had cleared his head.

There was a moment of silence as those two giants faced each other. Then the Kahoona's face spread out like an accordion; he really laughed, and at the same time he hit back at Jeff with a haymaker that sent him backwards, ricocheting into the wall of the hut. The Kahoona's surfboard started to sway and it would have crashed right down on Moondoggie if I hadn't had the presence of mind to hold out my hands and catch it at the last second.

Jeff stared up at the Kahoona. He was panting. And the Kahoona looked down at him and he kept smiling. And I stood there, gripping the surfboard in my hands, just staring.

Suddenly it hit me. I guess "like lightning" is too corny to write down but, Jeez, it fits to a T. It hit me that this wasn't a crummy movie I was watching. Two grown-up men had almost killed each other on account of little me—the gnomie—the shortie—the gidget!

I noticed some blood trickling from Jeff's nose as he lay stymied and bleary-eyed against the wall of the hut but instead of feeling compassion nothing but a pang of joy went through me. This was the pinnacle, this was the most. Surely nothing more wonderful would ever happen to me, ever.

Had I shouted they would certainly have thought I had gone crazy. So I did the next best thing to give vent to my soaring spirits. I lifted the board in my hands over my head and ran down to the water.

The board felt like feathers, all twenty-five pounds of it. The waves smashed against the dunes like one long, noisy, mad steam roller. I slid on the board and dug my hands into the water and shot over the foam like a speedboat. The cold water tingled about me—sharp and like cold fire. A wave and another wave, high as houses, but I didn't care. Once I glanced back over my shoulder and saw Cass and Jeff. They had obviously run after me and they yelled something I couldn't hear and they waved their arms crazily, urging me to come back.

No, I wouldn't go back. Not for the life of me. The scenery had been all set up for me like an opening performance. This was the final testing ground I had picked for myself.

A few more strokes and I was beyond the surfline. I couldn't see the coast any more, so high rose the wall of waves before me. I whirled around and brought the board in position. There was no waiting. I shot towards the first set of forming waves and rose.

I stood it. I have to come in standing, I told myself. I gritted my teeth.

"Shoot it," I yelled.

I was lifted up, sky high . . . and went down. But I stood it. One wave, another one.

"Olé!" I yelled. "Olé!"

Up I was—and down I went.

And still standing.

I was so jazzed up I didn't care whether I would break my neck or ever see Jeff again—or the great Kahoona.

I stood, high like on a mountain peak and dove down, but I stood it.

The only sound in the vast moving green was the hissing of the board over the water. A couple of times it almost dropped away under my feet, but I found it again and stood my ground.

"Shoot it, Gidget. Shoot the curl!!"

My own voice had broken away from me and I could only hear the echo coming from a great distance.

"Shoot it . . . shoot it . . . shoot it, Gidget!"

There was the shore, right there. I could almost reach out and touch it.

Fifteen

Well, this is it.

This was the summer I wanted to write about, the memory of which I wouldn't part with for anything.

Now I'm middle-aged, going on seventeen. I've learned so much in between. I've learned that virtue has its points. That you can grow up even if you don't grow. That men are wonderful.

I'm beholden to the big operator—ever since that night in August when he gave me a second helping of his profound philosophy. It's a quaint word, beholden, but that's what I am and I think Mister Glicksberg would appreciate my using it . . . more than many other words I have put down. That's why I'm not going to read these pages back. I might get red in the face and tear them up—the way I tore up the letter I once wrote to Jeff.

Oh, yes—we're writing steady now. He's shooting the curl at some boot-camp in Texas, being sponsored by the supreme commander himself.

I got his fraternity pin before he left and—brother—do I make the most of it with those squares who think they're just *it*, because they have a few more inches upwards and sideways.

As for the great Kahoona: he had to fold up his stand after the fire and now he's probably pushing some green water down in Peru, operating with a new set of sponsors.

My big love is still out Malibuways with some bitchen surf going.

When it struck me this summer with Jeff it could have been just the dream. With Cass curiosity. But with the board and the sun and the waves it was for real.

All things considered—maybe I was just a woman in love with a surfboard.

It's as simple as that.

CHAPTER 47

"The Pump House Gang Meets the Black Panthers—or Silver Threads among the Gold in Surf City" (1966)

Tom Wolfe
1931–

Tom Wolfe became known in the mid-1960s for his writings on car culture, collected in *The Kandy-Kolored Tangerine-Flake Streamline Baby* (1965), for his portrayal of the 1960s counterculture in *The Electric Kool-Aid Acid Test* (1968), and for his association with writers who formed part of the New Journalism school of writing (*The New Journalism*, 1973). Later successful works include *The Right Stuff* (1979), *The Bonfire of the Vanities* (1987), and *A Man in Full* (1998). In this essay (the first of a two-part article), Wolfe made the important link between economic prosperity in Southern California and the growth of surf culture, which, like the car culture he described in *The Kandy-Kolored Tangerine-Flake Streamline Baby,* showed the great impact of teenage culture on American society. In his introduction to the collection of stories *The Pump House Gang* (1968), Wolfe captured other important shifts in surf culture of the time. He tracked the first movements of surfers into the counterculture and argued that their lifestyle had in fact established the foundation for the later generation of hippies. Wolfe also correctly foresaw that the generation of surfers from the boom years in the early 1960s would manage to hold on to that lifestyle past their teens and early twenties:

> The day I met the Pump House Gang, a group of them had just been thrown out of "Tom Coman's garage," as it was known. The next summer they moved up from the garage life to a group of apartments near the beach, a complex they named "La Colonia Tijuana." By this time some were shifting from the surfing life to the advance guard of something else—the psychedelic *head* world of California. That is another story. But even the *hippies*, as

the heads came to be known, did not develop *sui generis*. Their so-called "dropping out" was nothing more than a still further elaboration of the kind of worlds that the surfers and the car kids I met—"The Hair Boys"—had been creating the decade before.

The Pump House Gang lived as though age segregation were a permanent state, as if it were inconceivable that any of them would ever grow old, i.e. 25. I foresaw the day when the California coastline would be littered with the bodies of aged and abandoned *Surferkinder*, like so many beached whales.

In fact, however, many of these kids seem to be able to bring the mental atmosphere of the surfer life forward with them into adulthood—even the adult world where you have to make a living.

As evidence of this last comment, Wolfe focused (in the second install-ment of the essay) on what he called the "surfing millionaires"—John Severson (founder of *Surfer* magazine), Hobie Alter (early surf shop owner and inventor of the Hobie Cat), and Bruce Brown (director of *The Endless Summer*)—surfers over twenty-five who had managed to mold tremendously successful livings from the surfer lifestyle. The trend has continued today with a multibillion-dollar surf industry that furnishes myriad surfers both young and old with the means to continue living what Wolfe calls "*The Life.*"

OUR BOYS NEVER HAIR OUT. The black panther has black feet. Black feet on the crumbling black panther. Pan-thuh. Mee-dah. Pam Sta-cy, 16 years old, a cute girl here in La Jolla, California, with a pair of or-ange bell-bottom hip-huggers on, sits on a step about four steps down the stairway to the beach and she can see a pair of revolting black feet without lifting her head. So she says it out loud, "The black panther."

Somebody farther down the stairs, one of the boys with the *major* hair and khaki shorts, says, "The black feet of the black panther."

"Mee-dah," says another kid. This happens to be the cry of a, well, *underground* society known as the Mac Meda Destruction Company.

"The pan-thuh."

"The poon-thuh."

All these kids, seventeen of them, members of the Pump House crowd, are lollygagging around the stairs down to Windansea Beach, La Jolla, California, about 11 a.m., and they all look at the black feet, which are a woman's pair of black street shoes, out of which stick a pair of old veiny white ankles, which lead up like a senile cone to a fudge of tallowy, edematous flesh, her thighs, squeezing out of her bathing suit, with old faded yellow bruises on them, which she probably got from running eight feet to catch a bus or something. She is standing with her old work-a-hubby, who has on *san*dals: you know, a pair of navy-blue anklet socks and these sandals with big, wide, new-smelling tan straps going this way and that, *for keeps*. Man, they look like orthopedic sandals, if one can imagine that. Obviously, these people come from Tucson or Albuquerque or one of those hincty adobe towns. All these hincty, crumbling black feet come to La Jolla-by-the-sea from the adobe towns for the weekend. They even drive in cars all full of thermos bottles and mayonnaisey sandwiches and some kind of latticework wooden-back support for the old crock who drives and Venetian blinds on the back window.

"The black panther."

"Pan-thuh."

"Poon-thuh."

"Mee-dah."

Nobody says it to the two old crocks directly. God, they must be practically 50 years old. Naturally, they're carrying every piece of garbage imaginable: the folding aluminum chairs, the newspapers, the lending-library book with the clear plastic wrapper on it, the sunglasses, the sun ointment, about a vat of goo—

It is a Mexican standoff. In a Mexican standoff, both parties narrow their eyes and glare but nobody throws a punch. Of course, nobody in the Pump House crowd would ever even jostle these people or say anything right to them; they are too cool for that.

Everybody in the Pump House crowd looks over, even Tom Co-man, who is a cool person. Tom Coman, 16 years old, got thrown out of his garage last night. He is sitting up on top of the railing, near the stairs, up over the beach, with his legs apart. Some nice long willowy girl in yellow slacks is standing on the sidewalk but leaning into him with her arms around his body, just resting. Neale Jones, 16, a boy with great lank perfect surfer's hair, is standing nearby with a Band-Aid on his upper lip, where the sun has burnt it raw. Little Vicki Ballard is up on the sidewalk. Her older sister, Liz, is down the stairs by the Pump House itself, a concrete block, 15 feet high, full of machinery for the La Jolla water system. Liz is wearing her great "Liz" styles, a hulking rabbit-fur vest and black-leather boots over her Levis, even though it is about 85 out here and the sun is plugged in up there like God's own dentist lamp and the Pacific is heaving in with some fair-to-middling surf. Kit Tilden is lollygagging around, and

Tom Jones, Connie Carter, Roger Johnson, Sharon Sandquist, Mary Beth White, Rupert Fellows, Glenn Jackson, Dan Watson from San Diego, they are all out here, and everybody takes a look at the panthers.

The old guy, one means, you know, he must be practically 50 years old, he says to his wife, "Come on, let's go farther up," and he takes her by her fat upper arm as if to wheel her around and aim her away from here.

But she says, "No! We have just as much right to be here as they do."

"That's *not the point*—"

"Are you going to—"

"*Mrs. Roberts,*" the work-a-hubby says, calling his own wife by her official married name, as if to say she took a vow once and his word is law, even if he is not testing it with the blond kids here—"farther up, *Mrs. Roberts.*"

They start to walk up the sidewalk, but one kid won't move his feet, and, oh, god, her work-a-hubby breaks into a terrible shaking Jello smile as she steps over them, as if to say, Excuse me, sir, I don't mean to make trouble, please, and don't you and your colleagues rise up and jump on me, screaming *Gotcha*—

Mee-dah!

<hr />

But exactly! This beach *is* verboten for people practically 50 years old. This is a segregated beach. They can look down on Windansea Beach and see nothing but lean tan kids. It is posted "no swimming" (for safety reasons), meaning surfing only. In effect, it is segregated by age. From Los Angeles on down the California coast, this is an era of age segregation. People have always tended to segregate themselves by age, teenagers hanging around with teenagers, old people with old people, like the old men who sit on the benches up near the Bronx Zoo and smoke black cigars. But before, age segregation has gone on within a larger community. Sooner or later during the day everybody has melted back into the old community network that embraces practically everyone, all ages.

But in California today surfers, not to mention rock 'n' roll kids and the hot-rodders or Hair Boys, named for their fanciful pompadours—all sorts of sets of kids—they don't merely hang around together. They establish whole little societies for themselves. In some cases they live with one another for months at a time. The "Sunset Strip" on Sunset Boulevard used to be a kind of Times Square for Hollywood hot dogs of all ages, anyone who wanted to promenade in his version of the high life. Today, "The Strip" is almost completely the preserve of kids from about

16 to 25. It is lined with go-go clubs. One of them, a place called It's Boss, is set up for people 16 to 25 and won't let in anybody over 25, and there are some terrible I'm-dying-a-thousand-deaths scenes when a girl comes up with her boyfriend and the guy at the door at It's Boss doesn't think she looks under 25 and tells her she will have to produce some identification proving she is young enough to come in here and live The Strip kind of life and—she's *had* it, because she can't get up the I.D. and nothing in the world is going to make a woman look stupider than to stand around trying to argue *I'm younger than I look, I'm younger than I look.* So she practically shrivels up like a Peruvian shrunken head in front of her boyfriend and he trundles her off, looking for some place you can get an old doll like this into. One of the few remaining clubs for "older people," curiously, is the Playboy Club. There are apartment houses for people 20 to 30 only, such as the Sheri Plaza in Hollywood and the E'Questre Inn in Burbank. There are whole suburban housing developments, mostly private developments, where only people over 45 or 50 can buy a house. Whole towns, meantime, have become identified as "young": Venice, Newport Beach, Balboa—or "old": Pasadena, Riverside, Coronado Island.

<hr/>

Behind much of it—especially something like a whole nightclub district of a major city, "The Strip," going teenage—is, simply, money. World War II and the prosperity that followed pumped incredible amounts of money into the population, the white population at least, at every class level. All of a sudden here is an area with thousands of people from 16 to 25 who can get their hands on enough money to support a whole nightclub belt and to have the cars to get there and to set up autonomous worlds of their own in a fairly posh resort community like La Jolla—

—Tom Coman's garage. Some old bastard took Tom Coman's garage away from him, and that means eight or nine surfers are out of a place to stay.

"I went by there this morning, you ought to see the guy," Tom Coman says. Yellow Stretch Pants doesn't move. She has him around the waist. "He was out there painting and he had this brush and about a thousand gallons of ammonia. He was really going to scrub me out of there."

"What did he do with the furniture?"

"I don't know. He threw it out."

"What are you going to do?"

"I don't know."

"Where are you going to stay?"

"I don't know. I'll stay on the beach. It wouldn't be the first time. I haven't had a place to stay for three years, so I'm not going to start worrying now."

Everybody thinks that over awhile. Yellow Stretch just hangs on and smiles. Tom Coman, 16 years old, piping fate again. One of the girls says, "You can stay at my place, Tom."

"Um. Who's got a cigarette?"

Pam Stacy says, "You can have these."

Tom Coman lights a cigarette and says, "Let's have a destructo." A destructo is what can happen in a garage after eight or 10 surfers are kicked out of it.

"Mee-dah!"

"Wouldn't that be bitchen?" says Tom Coman. Bitchen is a surfer's term that means "great," usually.

"Bitchen!"

"Mee-dah!"

It's incredible—that old guy out there trying to scour the whole surfing life out of that garage. He's a pathetic figure. His shoulders are hunched over and he's dousing and scrubbing away and the sun doesn't give him a tan, it gives him these . . . *mottles* on the back of his neck. But never mind! The hell with destructo. One only has a destructo spontaneously, a Dionysian . . . *bursting out*, like those holes through the wall during the Mac Meda Destruction Company Convention in Manhattan Beach—Mee-dah!

Something will pan out. It's a magic economy—yes!—all up and down the coast from Los Angeles to Baja California kids can go to one of these beach towns and live the complete surfing life. They take off from home and get to the beach, and if they need a place to stay, well, somebody rents a garage for twenty bucks a month and everybody moves in, girls and boys. Furniture—it's like, one means, you know, one *appropriates* furniture from here and there. It's like the Volkswagen buses a lot of kids now use as beach wagons instead of woodies. Woodies are old station wagons, usually Fords, with wooden bodies, from back before 1953. One of the great things about a Volkswagen bus is that one can . . . *exchange* motors in about three minutes. A good VW motor exchanger can go up to a parked Volkswagen, and a few ratchets of the old wrench here and it's up and out and he has a new motor. There must be a few nice old black panthers around wondering why their nice hubby-mommy VWs don't run so good anymore—but—then—they—are—probably—puzzled—about—a—lot—of—things. Yes.

Cash—it's practically in the air. Around the beach in La Jolla a guy can walk right out in the street and stand there, stop cars and make the candid move. Mister, I've got a quarter, how about 50 cents so I can get a *large* draft. Or, I need some after-ski boots. And the panthers give one a Jello smile and hand it over. Or a guy who knows how to do it can get $40 from a single night digging clams, and it's nice out there. Or he can go around and take up a collection for a keg party, a keg of beer. Man, anybody who won't kick in a quarter for a keg is a jerk. A couple of good keg collections—that's a trip to Hawaii, which is the surfer's version of a trip to Europe: there is a great surf and great everything there. Neale spent three weeks in Hawaii last year. He got $30 from a girl friend, he scrounged a little here and there and got $70 more and he headed off for Hawaii with $100.02, that being the exact plane fare, and borrowed 25 cents when he got there to . . . blast the place up. He spent the 25 cents in a photo booth, showed the photos to the people on the set of *Hawaii* and got a job in the movie. What's the big orgy about money? It's warm, nobody even wears shoes, nobody is starving.

All right, Mother gets worried about all this, but it is limited worry, as John Shine says. Mainly, Mother says, *Sayonara*, you all, and you head off for the beach.

The thing is, everybody, practically everybody, comes from a good family. Everyone has been . . . *reared well*, as they say. Everybody is very upper-middle, if you want to bring it down to that. It's just that this is a new order. Why hang around in the hubby-mommy household with everybody getting neurotic hang-ups with each other and slamming doors and saying, Why can't they have some privacy? Or, it doesn't mean anything that I have to work for a living, does it? It doesn't mean a thing to you. All of you just lie around here sitting in the big orange easy chair smoking cigarettes. I'd hate for you to have to smoke standing up, you'd probably get phlebitis from it—Listen to me, Sarah—

—why go through all that? It's a good life out here. Nobody is mugging everybody for money and affection. There are a lot of bright people out here, and there are a lot of interesting things. One night there was a toga party in a garage, and everybody dressed in sheets, like togas, boys and girls and they put on the appropriated television set to an old Deanna Durbin movie and turned off the sound and put on Rolling Stones records, and you should have seen Deanna Durbin opening her puckered kumquat mouth with Mick Jagger's voice bawling out, *I ain't got no satisfaction*. Of course, finally everybody started pulling the togas off each other, but that is another thing. And one time they had a keg party down on the beach in Mission Bay and the lights from the amusement park were reflected all over the water and that, the whole design of the thing, those nutty lights, that was part of the party. Liz put out the fire throwing a "sand potion" or something on it. One can laugh at Liz and her potions, her necromancy and everything, but there is a lot of thought going into it, a lot of, well, mysticism.

You can even laugh at mysticism if you want to, but there is a kid like Larry Alderson, who spent two years with a monk, and he learned a lot of stuff, and Artie Nelander is going to spend next summer with some Outer Mongolian tribe; he really means to do that. Maybe the "mysterioso" stuff is a lot of garbage, but still, it is interesting. The surfers around the Pump House use that word, mysterioso, quite a lot. It refers to the mystery of the Oh Mighty Hulking Pacific Ocean and everything. Sometimes a guy will stare at the surf and say, "Mysterioso." They keep telling the story of Bob Simmons' wipeout, and somebody will say "mysterioso."

Simmons was a fantastic surfer. He was fantastic even though he had a bad leg. He rode the really big waves. One day he got wiped out at Windansea. When a big wave overtakes a surfer, it drives him right to the bottom. The board came in but he never came up and they never found his body. Very mysterioso. The black panthers all talked about what happened to "the Simmons boy." But the mysterioso thing was how he could have died at all. If he had been one of the old pan-thuhs, hell, sure he could have got killed. But Simmons was, well, one's own age, he was the kind of guy who could have been in the Pump House gang, he was . . . *immune*, he was plugged into the whole pattern, he could feel the whole Oh Mighty Hulking Sea, he didn't have to think it out step by step. But he got wiped out and killed. Very mysteriso.[2]

<hr style="width:15%"/>

Immune! If one is in the Pump House gang and really keyed in to this whole thing, it's—well, one is . . . *immune*, one is not full of black pan-thuh panic. Two kids, a 14-year-old girl and a 16-year-old boy, go out to Windansea at dawn, in the middle of winter, cold as hell, and take on 12-foot waves all by themselves. The girl, Jackie Haddad, daughter of a certified public accountant, wrote a composition about it, just for herself, called "My Ultimate Journey":

"It was six o'clock in the morning, damp, foggy and cold. We could feel the bitter air biting at our cheeks. The night before, my friend Tommy and I had seen one of the greatest surf films, *Surf Classics*. The film had excited us so much we made up our minds to go surfing the following morning. That is what brought us down on the cold, wet, soggy sand of Windansea early on a December morning.

"We were the first surfers on the beach. The sets were rolling in at eight to 10, filled with occasional 12-footers. We waxed up and waited for a break in the waves. The break came, neither of us said a word, but instantly grabbed our boards and ran into the water. The paddle out was difficult, not being used to the freezing water.

"We barely made it over the first wave of the set, a large set. Suddenly Tommy put on a burst of speed and shot past me. He cleared the biggest wave of the set. It didn't hit me hard as I rolled under it. It dragged me almost 20 yards before exhausting its strength. I climbed on my board gasping for air. I paddled out to where Tommy was resting. He laughed at me for being wet already. I almost hit him but I began laughing, too. We rested a few minutes and then lined up our position with a well known spot on the shore.

"I took off first. I bottom-turned hard and started climbing up the wave. A radical cut-back caught me off balance and I fell, barely hanging onto my board. I recovered in time to see Tommy go straight over the falls on a 10-footer. His board shot nearly 30 feet in the air. Luckily, I could get it before the next set came in, so Tommy didn't have to make the long swim in. I pushed it to him and then laughed. All of a sudden Tommy yelled, 'Outside!'

"Both of us paddled furiously. We barely made it up to the last wave, it was a monster. In precision timing we wheeled around and I took off. I cut left in reverse stance, then cut back, driving hard toward the famous Windansea bowl. As I crouched, a huge wall of energy came down over me, covering me up. I moved toward the nose to gain more speed and shot out of the fast-flowing suction just in time to kick out as the wave closed out.[3]

"As I turned around I saw Tommy make a beautiful drop-in, then the wave peaked and fell all at once. Miraculously he beat the suction. He cut back and did a spinner, which followed with a reverse kick-up.

"Our last wave was the biggest. When we got to shore, we rested, neither of us saying a word, but each lost in his own private world of thoughts. After we had rested, we began to walk home. We were about half way and the rain came pouring down. That night we both had bad colds, but we agreed it was worth having them after the thrill and satisfaction of an extra good day surfing."

〰〰〰〰〰〰〰

John Shine and Artie Nelander are out there right now. They are just "outside," about one fifth of a mile out from the shore, beyond where the waves start breaking. They are straddling their surfboards with their backs to the shore, looking out toward the horizon, waiting for a good set. Their backs look like some kind of salmon-colored porcelain shells, a couple of tiny shells bobbing up and down as the swells roll under them, staring out to sea like Phrygian sacristans looking for a sign.

John and Artie! They are—they are what one means when one talks about the surfing life. It's like, you know, one means, they have this life all of their own; it's like a glass-bottom boat, and it floats over the "real" world, or the square world or whatever one wants to call it. They are not exactly off in a world of their own, they are and they aren't. What it is, they float right through the real world, but it can't touch them. They do these things, like the time they went to Malibu, and there was this party in some guy's apartment, and there wasn't enough *legal* parking space for everybody, and so somebody went out and painted the red curbs white and everybody parked. Then the cops came. Everybody ran out. Artie and John took an airport bus to the Los Angeles Airport, just like they were going to take a plane, in khaki shorts and T-shirts with Mac Meda Destruction Company stenciled on them. Then they took a helicopter to Disneyland. At Disneyland crazy Ditch had his big raincoat on and a lot of flasks strapped onto his body underneath, Scotch, bourbon, all kinds of stuff. He had plastic tubes from the flasks sticking out of the flyfront of his raincoat and everybody was sipping whiskey through the tubes—

—Ooooo-eee—Mee-dah! They chant this chant, Mee-dah, in a real fakey deep voice, and it *really bugs people*. They don't know what the hell it is. It is the cry of the Mac Meda Destruction Company. The Mac Meda Destruction Company is . . . an *underground* society that started in La Jolla about three years ago. Nobody can remember exactly how; they have arguments about it. Anyhow, it is mainly something to *bug* people with and organize huge beer orgies with. They have their own complete, bogus phone number in La Jolla. They have Mac Meda Destruction Company decals. They stick them on phone booths, on cars, any place. Some mommy-hubby will come out of the shopping plaza and walk up to his Mustang, which is supposed to make him a hell of a tiger now, and he'll see a sticker on the side of it saying, "Mac Meda Destruction Company," and for about two days or something he'll think the sky is going to fall in.

But the big thing is the parties, the "conventions." Anybody can join, any kid, anybody can come, as long as they've heard about it, and they can only hear about it by word of mouth. One was in the Sorrento

Valley, in the gulches and arroyos, and the fuzz came, and so the older guys put the young ones and the basket cases, the ones just too stoned out of their gourds, into the tule grass, and the cops shined their searchlights and all they saw was tule grass, while the basket cases moaned scarlet and oozed on their bellies like reptiles and everybody else ran down the arroyos, yelling Mee-dah.

The last one was at Manhattan Beach, inside somebody's poor hulking house. The party got *very Dionysian* that night and somebody put a hole through one wall, and everybody else decided to see if they could make it bigger. Everybody was stoned out of their hulking gourds, and it got to be about 3:30 a.m. and everybody decided to go see the riots. These were the riots in Watts. The Los Angeles *Times* and the San Diego *Union* were saying, WATTS NO-MAN'S LAND and STAY WAY FROM WATTS YOU GET YO' SE'F KILLED, but naturally nobody believed that. Watts was a blast, and the Pump House gang was immune to the trembling gourd panic rattles of the L.A. *Times* black pan-thuhs. Immune!

CHAPTER 48

"We're Tops Now" (1967)

John Witzig
1944–

John Witzig, an Australian surf journalist, heralded with this article a new era of surfing dominated by Australians and characterized by power and aggression rather than style and poise. His initial diatribe against California surfers, and David Nuuhiwa in particular, transformed into a pointed critique of the then-current judging system that he felt had restricted surfers and narrowly defined the best surfing as nose riding. The Australian "school of involvement" offered a much-needed antidote, Witzig believed, to the nose-riding obsession prevalent among top California surfers. Within a year of Witzig's article, Australian shaper Bob McTavish, inspired by California kneeboarder George Greenough, would be the primary architect of the shortboard revolution. Surfboards not only dropped drastically in size and weight, but, melding with the influence of the counterculture, surfers began to reassess why they rode waves in the first place. The new shorter designs of surfboards privileged tube riding over nose riding, an experience that surfers felt gave them a fuller, more intimate experience with the ocean. Witzig's claim that Australians would stay on top panned out in the decades following the establishment of a world professional circuit: from 1976 (the inaugural year) to 1991, eleven of sixteen titles in the men's division were won by Australians. It is also worth mentioning that McTavish's description of this new surfing—"to place yourself in a critical position, under, in, over, around the curl, quite often in contact with it"—essentially serves as the core of pro surfing judging criteria today.

"THE HIGH PERFORMERS?" RUBBISH! That's all that can be said about that story in the last issue—rubbish! Rubbish! Rubbish![4]

After our Nat Young completely dominated competition at the World Surfing Championships at San Diego, we might have expected a more accurate assessment of California surfing than "The High Performers." Yet not, since this history is indicative to an absolute degree of the California scene as a whole. Has everyone forgotten that David was beaten? Thrashed?

Up pours the smoke. To laud, to deify, to obscure. To obscure the fact that everything the pedestal of California surfing is being built upon means—nothing!

"The whole sport is following Nuuhiwa now" . . . "and another thing was my rollercoaster" . . . My rollercoaster, David? MY? Ha! McTavish has been doing rollercoasters for years.

Off with the rose-colored spectacles and look beyond the David. If everyone is not too conditioned by the propaganda: STOP. Reassess. Establish the real value in California surfing.

"Tell us, David . . . how does it feel to be told that the whole sport of surfing is following you?"

Are you kidding?

Tom Morey said that his nose riding contest at Ventura was just a game, but it seems a pity that he didn't tell all the surfers in California. For when this "game" has come to be accepted as "surfing" then the time has come for re-evaluation. It appears to me that a largely false set of values has been created in California surfing. The East Coast, following blindly along the path that has been set, has not only emulated the mistakes that have been made, but have taken it upon their own shoulders to take this "Californian" type of surfing to a further ridiculous extreme.

"Nat will thrash Nuuhiwa and make Bigler look like a pansy." These were the words of Bob Cooper when he saw Nat at Rincon in the week prior to the World Championships at San Diego. It was far more than a superficial comment when Cooper noted "I haven't seen power surfing since I was in Australia." Cooper knew that Nat and [Peter] Drouyn were not two isolated instances, but were indicative of the new school of thought in Australia.

Those of us who were conversant with the present trend of surfing in Australia were astonished at the corresponding lack of development in this direction in the United States. Probably nothing has had such a profound influence in leading California surfing out on a limb than has the nose riding fixation.

I need no justification to claim that this obsession with nose riding has been initiated and vigorously promoted by the commercial interests in the sport. The number of "nose riders" that have been sold gives more than credence to this argument. The real aim of surfing has been lost in a morass of concaves and the idolatry of David Nuuhiwa.

There can be no greater indictment of Californian surfing than the fact that Nuuhiwa took only his nose rider to San Diego for the World Championships. Surfers had been telling themselves for so long that they were right and that they were good that they had come to absolutely believe in it. How much a shock has it been to see the idols, the graven images, fall so unceremoniously to the ranks of the also rans.

What was it that made Nuuhiwa take only his specialist board to San Diego? If this can be honestly answered, then this curious ailment that has stricken Californian surfing will have been partly remedied. Not only did Nuuhiwa think that all he had to do to win the World Championships was to perch on the front of his board: not only did he know that everyone in California would agree with him: but he thought that the rest of the world could not see through his self-induced delusion. This delusion has been expressed, and I suppose partly caused, by a second great anomaly in the California surfing system. While the nose riding preoccupation has produced surfing specialists on a scale never before envisaged, the restricted wave system used in contests has produced a group of the most ordinary and average surfers that I imagine have ever "led" Californian surfing.

What has happened to surfing? On one hand, there are specialists who have made "surfing" "nose riding"; on the other, an uninspired personification of normalcy, neutrality, and mediocrity. In the middle somewhere are the group who are not really good at either.

I cannot state that there are no good surfers in California. I cannot state that David Nuuhiwa cannot surf well according to the standards which I seek to establish. I do state that the "system" has created a standard of surfing, a pattern of riding, that does not allow surfers to perform to the full extent of their ability. Nuuhiwa is simply a product of the system.

A contest system should work to draw from the competing surfers their best. When the surfers have to work for, to surf for the system, then the system has defeated its purpose. The Huntington contest is a prime example of a restricted wave contest. Through Australian eyes, this was the most tedious and uninteresting contest that I have ever seen. Even the stupidity of the mass public enthusiasm for nose work did little to arouse interest. The surfers, restricted and confined to the system, did not attempt anything which would constitute a chance. Indeed, they could not.

A contest system must simulate as closely as possible those conditions that are experienced in the ocean. If the freedom that we find so inherent in riding waves is not expressed in our competitions, then these are not true contests of surfing. If we are to derive any value from contests, then they should encourage the surfer to draw on greater things and make a mistake in the process. To my knowledge, achievement has never been laid at the door of the ordinary person. Consistency becomes mediocrity unless measured in terms of challenge and achievement.

This, then, is Californian surfing. But what of Australia? What is this surfing that I find so exciting and dynamic? The theme is involvement. How bitterly ironic it is that the person who has been most influential in the progress of Australian surfing should be a Californian. A Californian that most surfers in the United States would never have seen nor heard of. George Greenough of Santa Barbara is probably one of the unsung geniuses of surfing. Technically, there is possibly nobody who can surpass him. He has a working knowledge of hydrodynamics and has expressed it in his design of surfing equipment. It was Greenough that gave impetus to the smoldering dissatisfaction with the "Farrelly era" in Australia.

The surfer with whom Greenough first came into contact was Bob McTavish. A theoretician in his own right, it was only reasonable that he and Greenough talked and surfed and began applying their principles to surfboard design. While everyone else in Australia was turning to longer boards, McTavish built short and more maneuverable boards which he could use to place himself in the best part of the wave. McTavish's words best describe his principal motive: "The direction is involvement. Getting into tight spots and getting back out of them. This is, of course, a supplement direction to the all-powerful 'make the wave' motive. The way to get involved, obviously, is to place yourself in a critical position, under, in, over, around the curl, quite often in contact with it." The trend is to push things to the limit: "The tighter you push them, the longer you hold them, the more involved you are, the more situations you can overcome, the hotter you are." This, then, is the McTavish philosophy. The desire to attempt the impossible, to transgress into the realm of the unattainable, to power.

McTavish, the master tactician of the perfect wave, saw his personal limitations in the transference of his thoughts into general surfing. He chose then to infuse with his enthusiasm and his aggression a number of other surfers in Australia. The results of this union was the surfer that the world saw as the best in San Diego.

Nat has an enormous reservoir of surfing talent. He has a feeling for the surf that he can express in his riding. He possesses that superb control under all circumstances that mark him as a fine surfer. He is part of this "power" school of surfing: he has crushed the "pansy" surfers of California and the East Coast: the mediocre "competition surfers" have paled into insignificance in the face of his aggression.

Nat is the best surfer in Australia. Australia is represented by its best. How is it that the United States is not? Of the ten Californian surfers, only John Peck showed some sort of aggression, and David Nuuhiwa showed that he was capable of it. While Australia presented its finest, the U.S. had only its run of the mill ordinary and its specialists. Surfboards expressed as clearly as any other item the extent of the deviation in direction that has occurred in Californian surfing. There was the ever present list of models proposing to make the rider a genius in some surfing maneuver. Against an imposing lineup we put the small, light, thin and sensitive Australian board. It is the concern of this Australian surfer that his board should express, as he himself sees it, the whole rather than a series of unrelated or specialists maneuvers. The Australian board is designed with this purpose in mind. The direction is positive. It is towards dynamic and controlled aggression in surfing.

What is the future? We're on top and will continue to dominate world surfing. Californian surfing is so tied and stifled by restrictions that are its own creation, and the other countries simply do not have the necessary ability.

What chance is there that California will free itself of its encumbrances? This is something that I cannot answer. General social conditions will continue to exercise an influence over the surfing scene. The drug situation is something which cannot be ignored. While surfing progress, the creative era, is being credited to those who participate, and indirectly, because they participate, I cannot foresee much change. Strangely enough, the effect of these stimulants seems to have a depressant effect on challenge and aggression. I felt like yelling "let yourself go, take a chance." But as is the pattern, this was not to be. Everyone was so confined, so under control, so absolutely without the apparent freedom to express.

An end must come to this monotony. Vigor will replace lassitude: aggression will replace meek submission. The dynamic will force an end to the commonplace. Power will be the word, and surfing will be surfing.

CHAPTER 49

"Mickey on Malibu" (1968)

Mickey Dora
1934–2002

Mickey Dora is a controversial figure in surf culture. Alternately my-thologized and despised, he ranted against the commercialism of the sport while profiting from stunt work in such Hollywood films as *Gidget* (1959) and *Beach Party* (1963) and also promoting his own line of sig-nature surfboards. Dora is known as the quintessential Malibu maestro, a nimble and stylish longboard rider whose quickness earned him the nick-name "Da Cat." Dora considered Malibu his territory and was not above pushing people off waves or kicking his board at them if they dropped in front of him. Like John Witzig's "We're Tops Now," Dora began his article with personal attacks yet moved on to criticize a judging system that he felt only rewarded those whose surfing fit into a predetermined package that could then be conveniently exploited and sold to main-stream America through the media. For both writers, the effect of this oppressive system was to restrict the act of surfing itself, a sport whose ul-timate value was self-expression. Although Dora himself is typically hard to locate through the cynical, sarcastic "Dora character" he habitually played, a genuine voice surfaces toward the end of the article to mark the cultural changes that were happening around him—"New philosophies are taking hold"—and to hope that these changes would alter the course of the Vietnam War and of the commercialization of surfing.

MALIBU AND MICKEY . . . the famous surfing break and the famous surfing non-conformist have been going steady quite a while . . . Mickey is considered by many as "Mr. Malibu" . . . and so, SURFER asked Mr. Malibu to give out with his thoughts on this year's Malibu Invitational Club Contest . . . and here they are . . .

When I say the Malibu Contest, I mean it in the simplest form of mass boredom and unimpeachable incompetence due to the power struc-ture of the people who control these events. Someday I may have the opportunity to expose the mentality of these contest organizers. It may prove to be quite interesting.

It's quite an occasion when the untouchable SURFER Magazine, the so-called bible of the surfing world, calls me for an interview. Once again this gives me faith in the free enterprise system. So I'm thinking to myself already, "Vat you wanting from me dis time?" Maybe you came to hear the truth—or maybe not. Maybe it's basic masochism.

But I'm grateful SURFER came to the source this time. Usually they obtain information about the Dora character from their paid stooges on the Play Surf editorial staff. Cheap gossip usually is the rule—especially with that star reporter Bill Cleary—one of the great frauds of our time. This guy deserves the SURFER Pulitzer Prize for double-talk, hot air articles he contrives about me. Sometimes I wonder how many minds believe the lies he writes about me—for example, the so-called reporting job he did on the Malibu contest a year ago.

You know, Cleary old boy, someday you're going to find out I'm not public property and my private life is my own business. I'm not a commodity of yours to use in your cheap quick-buck articles. Last year's contest is a perfect example of using my name to save a no-wave, miserable day's judging on your part. Remember, Cleary, I'm not obligated to you or anybody else. I ride waves for my own kicks, not yours.

I know SURFER must be jammed up for a deadline. The annual Huntington Beach best seller was a smashing flop. What is the magazine going to do without those straight-off photos in the white water? All those thousands of inland slave mentality imbeciles who go goose stepping into that helmeted restrictive lifeguard state take over that they call a contest.

All right, why not express myself? The price is just about right for what it's worth.

Malibu, personally, is my perfect wave. Naturally, when it's breaking correctly. And when it's right, it's right in the palm of my hand. These waves will never change, only the people on them. And that's what I remember, the waves I ride, not the crud that floats around them. Somebody out there must understand what I'm saying, and others won't. Like any good thing, the idealism can't last forever, and that's what's happening to Malibu (understatement of the decade).

When I talk to guys I think are in the know, who are still riding waves for the sheer freedom they offer all of us, these same guys look at me as if I were out of my mind to run that gauntlet every time I want to express myself in the water. Their concept of Malibu today is a complete Valley takeover, a fantasy of insanity filled with kooks of all colors, super ego mania running rampant, fags, finks, and pork chop-ism and a thousand other social deviations. The tragic thing is they're true; these guys are right, up to a point.

It's very hard to stand up to all the put-downs and heat I go through to work a few waves over. But, I do have my moments, and that neutralizes this whole illusion.

Understand, there are a few unknown kids who ride the place very well and probably understand what I'm talking about. Kids who might be able to save Malibu. For myself, I gave up years ago.

For what I really think of the contest, there isn't a magazine in existence that would print what I'm thinking. So let's take it really easy without going into the mechanics of how things are run or stepping on any toes or insulting anyone.

I can only speak for myself, naturally, and I do go into contests once or twice a year for the sheer pleasure of shaking up the status quo. The way I see things, wave riding talent and abilities on the scale of a thousand, is batting a thousand—on judging, one goose egg. Judging was the greatest insult to the exceptional talent that turned out to enter this conveyor belt gamble factor. With this three-quarter system setup, it's obvious what limitations prevail. I'd rather play Russian roulette with the C.I.A. My odds of survival would be greater.

This year was my second immersion in this pay toilet thing they call California's finest. Two years ago I almost had the savages on the beach rioting, practically destroying themselves while I was getting my satisfaction shaking up these little pigmeo Faines, ego heroes in their famous Stan Richards backbends.

It figures this year, due to restrictive, oppressive rules, they wanted more conformity. These judges are the judge and jury of all of us. For one day only, thank God. They are boring people with a boring job. The more restrictive they can make a contest, the less they have to think or know about what you're accomplishing in the water, thus making an easy job easier, at our expense. What do these people care about your subtle, split-second maneuvers, years of perfecting your talents?

First of all, they're fat and out of shape, and I'm positive they've never been in the right position while riding in their lives. Maybe by accident, and they never got over it. They wouldn't know what's going on even if Channel 9 would have their video playback stop action screen; they still wouldn't know what's happening due to their beer drinking stupor mentality of the late '50s. These judges care less if the south winds blows your heat all to hell or there aren't enough waves in your time slot or some rich Okie tourist in his weekend power boat screws things up. Postponement or delay a few minutes, until conditions improve, is completely out of the question. They want their little winner as quick as possible—at the expense of all of us. So it should be obvious to everyone the types which emerge victorious in these miscarriages of talent.

I've been fighting these people *alone* for the past ten years with no help from any one of you out there. If I had my way, I would take all of them, including Channel 9 and Stan Richards in his Roaring Wheels costume, take those hula hoops, deadbeats and herd them in their psychedelic Groovy truck and ship them to the Mojave desert where they can start subdividing their sick little culture again.

Someday the youth of this country is going to wake up to what's really happening around them and do something on their own for once. The same thing must occur in surfing before things are going to improve. Eventually, the time will come when the guys who are riding and expressing themselves for the free truth will take over from the TV-land backwardness and will put together something way out enough to bring us out of these dark ages we're in now. It's up to the youth to rise up and take over and do everything on their own, NOW.

There I was killing time in my semifinal heat as some idiot water skier churned up the wave. Time was running out and with it my utter frustration with the high tide junk. I was observing the crowd on the beach, as I do on many occasions—what a fantastically picturesque place with the beautiful hills in the background. I was remembering how things were before the subdividers, concessionaires, lifeguards—before exploiters polluted the beaches like they do everything else.

I found the crowd very interesting. There was something I had never seen before in surfing. Aside from the ugly tourist and TV, there were the usual surf dopes, magazine and photo exploiters, the lap dog surf star club rah-rah boys, the same old story year after year.

But, toward the point, strange, strange things were happening, faces and people I knew casually over the years with new costumes and appurtenances, maybe new philosophies. Something in their euphoric chemistry has been transformed into a new dimension. I can't put my finger on it exactly, but I begin to comprehend and come around. This subject is difficult to discuss openly, for I'm not an authority on human nature. If anything, I'm a freak of nature and don't fit in with anybody.

However, I can't help feeling there's something happening and things are not going to stay the same. New philosophies are taking hold. There is a great deal of change accruing in certain segments of the sport, and I hope you want the same things I want, freedom to live and ride nature's waves, without the oppressive hang-up of the mad insane complex that runs the world and this sick, sick war.

Things are going to change drastically in the next year or so, for all of us whether we like it or not. Maybe a few will go forward and make it a better world.

These are incredible times.

Thank God for a few free waves.

CHAPTER 50

"Centroamerica" (1973)

Kevin Naughton
1953–

Craig Peterson
1955–

Greg Carpenter

Kevin Naughton and Craig Peterson's travel dispatches, published in *Surfer* magazine on a regular basis between 1973 and 1978, came to typify, even glorify, the era's notion of a surf safari: escaping crowded, hostile lineups in search of the perfect wave. This ideal had first captured the popular imagination with the nationwide release of Bruce Brown's *The Endless Summer* in 1966. The authors offered a grittier version of surf travel than *The Endless Summer*, detailing the realities of life on the road in Central America, Africa, and Europe. Along the way they established a basic formula for surf travel articles that included a wry narrative filled with mishaps, various physical hardships and dangers, the occasional local ruffian (or uncompassionate authority figure, or alluring woman)—all of which must be negotiated as the surfers realize their dream of living simply with friendly natives and discovering perfect, uncrowded waves. Naughton and Peterson also touched upon a critical paradox that remains a touchy issue for surfers and surf magazines today: exploiting untapped wave resources in glossy magazines that virtually guarantees creating what the authors had been escaping in the first place—an influx of crowds. In this their inaugural article, the first of a four-part installment for *Surfer*, Naughton and Peterson are joined by Greg Carpenter as they visit the relatively unknown surf destination of El Salvador.

Winter was announcing itself in California with a barrage of bad vibes from irate locals guarding "their" secret spots. Surfing was turning into a battle of wits with Darwin's and Dora's survival-of-the-fittest theory dominating the atmosphere. The water was so cold the seals were wearing wetsuits, and the smog was as stifling as the crowds. With this in mind, we three adventurous

*young surfers packed our belongings, bid farewells, and started a long jour-
ney to a land of Eden and intrigue.*

ALIVE, WE LAY IN OUR HAMMOCKS, swaying as leaves in a gentle
breath of wind. We set our minds back three weeks into the recent past
to remember (as everyone does who has survived the long trek here) the
hellish nightmare it took for us to follow our dreams to surf. It's easy to
bring back to life all the bad things—worry, heat, frustrations, boredom,
expenses, troubles, sweat, hunger, lack of sleep, mosquitoes, filth, confu-
sions and transfusions; and hard to recall from their grave the good experiences—sharing, down-to-earth people, and arrivals. Yet here we are,
timelessly swinging, back and forth, to and fro, hither and yonder, with
thoughts on that first night . . .

Third time's a charm, they say? For us it took an extra charm to
get us going, the first charm being used up by engine trouble, the second
charm shot four nights later when the rear wheel fell off en route from
Greg's house to Craig's, rolled down the street beyond view—scratch one
brake drum. On the mythical "third charm," we actually did leave—for
about five hours and thirty miles—'til the engine blew up. So we returned,
watched the surf while munching on our supply of tootsie pops, and con-
templated our dilemma. Final verdict: rebuild the engine.

And so, for the next week, we turned ourselves into grease monkeys, rebuilt our engine *twice*, the first time being a half-assed job of it.
For our fourth charm, the motor finally ran, we bid our farewells and left
for good.

With the Mexican border in front of us and home behind us, we
journeyed on. After the usual confusion with the Federales at the border,
we passed through. After a quick snack at Colonel Sanchez' Kentucky
Fried Chicken De Mexico, we worried about Mexico's bad reputation of
mean country, intense heat, many rip-offs, crooked Federales, and wondered what we were getting into. But it was the gateway to escape. We
had to pass on Mexico's surf because of the rush we were in to make it
south before the rainy season began (April-October). For now, just us and
a long, lonesome highway, on the threshold of a dream.

The Sonora Desert is huge. A baked expanse of rocks, dirt, and
shrubs, with a pitiful road through its interior. In the summer, a boiling
pot of heat so fiery everything seems to melt together on the horizon.
In winter, we met with an unending gray mass of droning rain, constant,
a brain-warping dull mist enveloped us. For three days and two nights,
it was like a Chinese water torture incessantly tapping on the roof, al-

ways the same, piercing the mind and nerves into slow breakdown. These days went by almost uneventfully, with the exception of one particular instance. While on a detour around a village, we had to punch the car to get through this pond which lay in our path. When we hit, it turned out to be deeper than anticipated. Muddy water covered the car on impact, windows became brown, we could see nothing—then we were floating! Greg hit the wipers, we searched in back for something to paddle with, while Greg carefully piloted our ship to high land, and we drove off rolling with laughter.

Another day of straight roads full of potholes, a boring drive. That night, we gulped down our meal of the day (we were on a tight budget). We dined on a "Mexican hamburger" (a can of something like Skippy dog food cooked medium rare, between two slices of bread) and a glass of warm milk. It was the only thing we'd eaten all day, so there were few moans and groans at the taste. After dinner, we decided to catch a few z's in the car that night, conserving money.

Sleeping arrangements were exceptionally tight for three people in a packed VW bug, but after we discovered a spot underneath a tree in the middle of a bushy field (which, much to our dismay, turned out to be a city dump, when we woke in the morning with a putrid smell all about), we soon became dazed into sleep. Our bodies were mixed all around, fingers in eyes, elbows in ribs, etc. So there we were, three red-eyed surfers asleep in a VW, under a tree with a full moon out, in the middle of a Mexican dump.

Our next few days were marred by car trouble in the tropical port of Mazatlan. A result of bad Mexican gas. The surf was nonexistent and windblown, so we decided to drop our engine in the hotel parking lot and take it to a machine shop to be repaired. After a few other problems with our axle, the engine was repaired (for an outrageous cost) and putting along. With a few minor adjustments made, we cleaned our grease off and struggled back to the land of the living. A short confrontation with the hotel manager about cramming three people in a singles room (economy) for three nights. He felt he'd been taken, so a few dollars later we saw our last of Mazatlan and the hotel's now greasy parking lot, and sped away under the secrecy of the nocturnal hours.

Nothing but full-on, conscious-corroding driving along the asphalt snake through cloud-breaking mountains 'til Mexico City, with a small hassle in between. A few maids, one morning, screeched at us to return all the motel towels to them. We had none, and soon cleared that up with minimal confusion.

As we descended down into a vast expanse of buildings, houses and people, commonly referred to as Mexico City, we knew it was going to be bad—a huge city we had zero knowledge of in the middle of their 5 o'clock rush-hour traffic. Driving was like a demolition derby, with more misses than hits, cars coming inches apart, everybody wailing around the traffic circles in utter confusion, zipping in and out on radical lane changes that would make Mario Andretti turn in his racing gloves and sell lasagna, everybody running lights, stop signs (special note: after halting at many stop signs like you're supposed to do and nearly being rear-ended by the bug-eyed maniac drivers behind us, we came to realize that stop signs in Mexico are something to look at, not something to do). It's like millions of ants coming and going from one sugar pile to another, mass mania of crash-crazed, go-cart drivers, totally insane!

Eventually we got onto this freeway and fifteen minutes later we were pulled off on the side, paying off a crooked motorcycle Federale, screaming in his foreign gibberish that he was taking us to the station, claiming we gringo surfers in a beat-up, bogged down old VW Bug were flying down his freeway at a preposterous 65 mph in a 55 mph zone (the Bug can only do 50 mph)! But, as he put it, being a nice, honest cop, he would gladly let us pay the $20 ticket to him now so we wouldn't have to go downtown. Of course, we didn't want to go downtown, and he knew this by the terrified look on our grubby faces! We were an easy $20 to him. It was easy to see dollar signs in his eyes and gold in his pointed teeth, while forking over the money into his sweating palms. Crime doesn't pay, but it sure would be profitable being the law in Mexico.

On the freeway again after an exchange of a false showing of teeth as a friendly farewell gesture to our greedy, green-eyed amigo, facing a problem of getting off one freeway to another, we blew it righteously. We exited the freeway all right, went onto the other freeway going north when we wanted to go south, so we turned around, now going south, but when it came to a fork, we took the right fork which went onto the wrong freeway, turned around, got back onto the other freeway, going north again, U-turned to a southbound lane, proceeded south and made the left fork to the right freeway (if this confused you just reading it, just think how it was doing it!), and went our way dazed and dizzy.

Late that afternoon, our windshield wipers went out with a dull whirr and fizzle. We took it all in stride, realizing that bad karma clung to us. At dusk, we turned on the lights to discover they too refused to function. Forced into getting down the mountain to find a safe place to park, we ingeniously shined a flashlight out the front window as a headlight so oncoming cars knew we were there, and followed the taillights of trucks ahead down the winding snake to the bottom. After fixing the lights, we pushed on to a toll house where once again we crammed ourselves in the car and dozed the darkness away in their parking lot.

This stretch of snake was long, 350 miles long through endless mountain ranges, night and day driving thru nondescript scenery. One afternoon we raced ahead of a fast-moving storm front, fearing rain which would make driving an impossible feat without wipers. Beating it out and following the asphalt serpent until reaching flat land. Along with flat land was the dreaded La Vientosa winds, a hurricane-force breeze that blows several times a year. We felt it hitting our car broadside at 70 mph, tilting us at a 30-degree angle to the road, with us leaning in the opposite direction as a counter balance until finding shelter.

Half-heartedly we entered the tropics, into the heat and heavy air. We survived all the rip-'em-up, throw-it-out microscopic border inspections encountered at every border crossing, which is a challenge to one's nerves. These border guards have nothing to do all day, and when a gringo Americano's mobile pulls up, it's like giving candy to a baby—they love every hour of tearing apart your car, asking what everything is and does.

At one border, a guard, duly dubbed Rocky Rococo, looking his meanest and raunchiest, gave us the evil eye while flexing his blubbery biceps, sharpening bullets with a knife, during which time his cohorts in crime went bananas over our surf bomb. Soon enough we escaped Rocky's evil clutches and ended up here, reminiscing in our drifting hammocks in one form of paradise.

We lived in an old wiped-out Volkswagen Bug, crammed together like molecules for (statistics now) 12 days, 1 hour, 23 minutes and timeless seconds, driving a sweaty, enduring 3,385.4 miles along a treacherously crooked and badly pitted snake of a road in ill-tempered weather. The excursion exhausted $239.05 hard-earned coinage, used 131.7 gallons of gas, consumed $38.34 worth of food, $39.28 for hotels and trailer parks, $29.77 for auto goods, $29.86 for auto insurance, $20 to a Federale's liquor fund, $8.40 spent at borders, $3.50 worth of "contributions to the Mexican government," miscellaneous bucks for miscellaneous stuff, and 10¢ for parking. Along with this we shunned our long locks for the straight look, excreted 3 1/2 quarts of sweat, 2 pints of blood, exchanged 1,847 dirty words and wasted away numerous cells in our craniums! All this for the sweet taste of paradise!

Paradise to us meant several things that every surfer dreams about, but few get to experience. It's a combination of warm, transparent ocean, mixed with repetitioning infinite tubes, unpopulated in a tropical setting. We found all this here, with the exception of crowds. It has multiplied enough here to bring the bad vibes and hustling for waves out from the closets back home, with the hassling being its worst between locals and newcoming surfers. But we came to get away from bad vibes and crowded tubes, two ingredients which create a bitter taste in the sweet nectar of paradise.

Native people of the land here are overly friendly and trust gringos the same as their own family. How long this will last with a continuing high tide of wayfaring surfers pulling in is questionable, as some natives have already been abused by a few asinine surfers. The women down here are beautiful—long, straight silky hair, dark tanned and always smiling. But, for their nightly entertainment, most gringos just settle for second best, The Panama House, a local establishment.

The tropics, in all its splendor, lives up to its legendary fierceness: intense heat, flooding rains, king-size killer mosquitoes one can't even pick off with a flick of a finger, complete with their hypodermic blood-rendering tools, mass swarms of deadly bugs, wild animals, and cannibals, all in full force. The heat is inescapable, sweat flows from your body, draining all energy from you, creating an exhausted feeling 24 hours a day.

Taking all in stride, the good is here to be enjoyed too. Palm and coconut trees merge with white sandy beaches, untouched by man, which melds into the warm 85-degree green-blue ocean with ease. Listening to a daily chorus of various birds of the jungle, relishing the Hawaii-type weather, peace is all about.

Food is another benefit down here, with succulent fruits of different types in abundance. Meat is tough and hard to come by, but shellfish and fish are our daily ecstasies. All of these earthly delights are either free for the taking or can be bought for a pittance.

We live in a small house with two really fine surfers, Bob Levy and Juan Sverko, two good friends to have anywhere. They are the original locals in this area, and have been returning here for the past several years, ripping apart all the spots. But this is their last visit, compliments of crowded waters. The house is a short stroll through a jungly path, ending up at a good reef break, a rarity you can't find in many places around the world. A small pool in front, a few poker tables that are in constant use, outdoor shower and bathroom, coconut, papaya, banana trees scattered about, gardener and his quarters, good clean water, three parrots: all for $50 a month!

As for the surf, well, if the photos don't show it, it's as good (if not better) than anyplace. A random surf check on a medium swell in a four-mile stretch produces: Rocky Point; L.A.; a Rinconish right, a heavy throw-out lip that forms into a constant tube, breaking boards and bodies on rocks covered with urchins a few feet below the impact zone—a low tide and they become a few inches under.

Further up this point lies Lucifers, a take-off-go-for-it wave with tricky sections and nasty hollows. Around the point and down the sandy beach lies Michelle's in all its graceful beauty . . . A beach break. Many peaks around, all a hollow start-to-finish tube, just beautiful. A little way from that, Juan's and Bob's secret spot, good waves to be found quite often and hard to get to but well worth it. Powerful swells create a hard-turning surface with vicious wipeouts. Another point, Margaritas, a right tubey section wave, good, mellow atmosphere on a tree-lined point. On down a ways, a reef titled Randy B.'s, good peak, takes an exact swell. But it works with two round bowls—a challenge to anybody. Secreto Mancho, a rivermouth break with high qualities but a hard grind to get to.

The waters are infested with sharks; you never get accustomed to the fins that prowl around waiting beyond the surf line. Enough people have not returned from a go-out on account of them to warrant leaving the water as soon as that certain type of fin appears. Their sizes range from 3 to 15 feet, with one 30-foot tiger shark locally nicknamed "La Gata," that devours everything around when it appears. Other monsters lurking beneath are barracuda, rays, manta rays, a deadly form of sea snake, and other fish of a size that'll make anybody shriek while doing a two-second paddle in. It all adds a little spice to the surfing life if you're willing to risk it.

To wake up to the crowing of roosters at sunrise, snatching your board from the rack and walking down to crystal waters with see-through tubes, sometimes perfection, sometimes less than perfection, seven days a week, is an easy task. But for us, we've about used up this paradise and are moving on towards a better land, searching for a perfect wave yet to be discovered, yet to be ridden. This is in the future, and what happens there nobody knows. That will be another adventure, another joy, another tale.

CHAPTER 51

"An Alternate Viewpoint" (1975)

Kimo Hollinger
1939–

> In this article for *Surfer* magazine, Kimo Hollinger offered a dissent-
> ing opinion to the growing professionalization of the sport in the mid-
> 1970s. Hollinger's nostalgic description of earning his place among a
> small cadre of big-wave surfers in 1958 contrasts strongly with his ac-
> count of another day in 1975 when he was asked to leave the water
> because of a surf contest. As Hollinger protests the increasing commer-
> cialization of the sport and ensuing loss of individual freedom, he draws
> out a very personal connection to the ocean and the spirituality among
> those who dedicated their lives to big-wave surfing.

PARADISE, 1958: I WAS A FRESHMAN at the University of Hawaii.
I was finished for the day, and was on my way home. My car radio was
on, the usual mixture of music and news, when the announcer mentioned
that giant surf was at that moment hitting the north and west shores of
the island. The mood I was in immediately transformed from lethargy to
agitation. I made it home as fast as I could, loaded my board on the car,
convinced my parents that this was something they couldn't miss, and
headed for Makaha.

Once we made it through the cane fields and could see the ocean, I
knew that this was surf like I had never seen before in my life. The ehukai
(sea mist) was so heavy in the air that my mother was positive it was coral
dust from some road construction. We were coming through Waianae
town when I noticed Buzzy Trent's car at the local market. We pulled in
and I found Buzzy, still with his wet sprint shorts on, buying some grocer-
ies. I said, "God, Buzzy, don't tell me you guys rode that shit." He tried
to appear as nonchalant as possible, and said, "Yeah, we got a few waves."
I almost collapsed. We arrived at Makaha and it was awesome. Nobody
was out, it was getting late, my mother was screaming at me, "You're not
going out, you're not going out." I didn't.

That night, I called Paul (Gebauer) and made plans for the next day. We got there early in the morning. It didn't look as big; yet, as we were taking our boards off the car, Ethel and Joe (Kukea) tried to warn us that perhaps it was too dangerous for us. (Paul was still in high school at the time.) Paul kind of looked at them, and we hit it. We weren't halfway out when a giant set came through. It closed off the whole Makaha Bay. It was like we were at some spot we had never surfed before. All the breaks and lineups that we were accustomed to didn't exist. The white water had dissipated most of its power by the time it reached us, and we were able to roll it; but still, I wanted out. I'm sure that had I been alone, I would have gone in but I didn't want to lose face with Paul. Perhaps it was the same with him. When we finally made it to the lineup, I couldn't believe how far out we were. Makaha Point was someplace way inside, where normally it was outside or even with you. Buzzy, who was already out, screamed at me to stay away from him (I was on a 9'2" semi-pig Velzy). The rest of the crew, George (Downing), Wally (Froiseth), Pat (Curren), Charley (Reimers), and John (Serverson), simply ignored us. I positioned myself on the shoulder, took a deep breath, and waited. The waves came. We scratched for the horizon, and something I've always had took over. It's like the bell had rung, the butterflies were gone; it was survival. How was I to outwit these awesome waves and these six or seven guys who wanted to ride them as much as I did. I took off in front of George and Wally. Unlike North Shore waves, it's possible to ride high at Makaha. I made a turn, and for the first time in my years of surfing experience, my knees dragged in the wave. Then it was down, down, down like it would never end. My heart was in my throat. I can't remember if Wally was talking to me, steadying me. We made the wave, and as we glided over the shoulder, Wally smiled. I guess George was thinking "Damn kid, one more guy I got to put up with." The ice had been broken. Paul and I rode our share of waves that day, and also took some terrible wipeouts. The wipeouts were so bad that you actually gave up struggling and began looking forward to death as a release from the punishment; and then somehow you floated to the surface. And it wasn't like you could breathe there. You had to first clear a hole in the foam that must have been a foot thick before you could take a breath. I actually think that this "giving up" tendency saved our lives, because we then conserved what little oxygen we had until we surfaced. Our boards ended up in the most ungodly places, like in front of some guy's garage a mile down the beach towards Lahilahi Point. Another thing I've always had is the ability to immediately erase a wipeout from my mind, grab my board, and head out again. Towards the end of the day, the wind turned onshore, and I was left alone out there. It was neat because I knew I was going in. I didn't have to catch any more of those monsters. I could sit and just watch them roll by, huge, beautiful, unridden waves.

Nature is so beautiful, it knocks me out. As I reflect on that day, it seems that we all wonderingly gazed at the bigger sets, not wanting to disturb or contaminate their majesty with our petty human flailings. George was in his prime at this time, and got the day's best waves. Buzzy was talking about getting a boat and going out to Maile, and I thought he was crazy. John served notice (he broke a rib on one of those days, and went on to become a successful publisher). The others rode well. Paul and I took up space, but we were dedicated to and loved what we were doing. Paul and I were so proud to belong. It was great to be young and to feel unique. [*La*] *joie de vivre*.

Progress

Thanksgiving Day, 1975: (The day of the Smirnoff at Waimea.) I woke up to the sound of the surf. I grabbed a light and pointed it out on the water. All I could see was white. I set my alarm to awaken at daybreak and tried to go back to sleep. It wasn't easy. At the jingling of my alarm, I bolted out of bed. The ocean was in turmoil. As I loaded my board in the truck, this eerie feeling overwhelmed me. It said, "You are suicide prone, you are suicide prone." I recently had suffered a severe setback in my life, and it was like I was methodically preparing myself to do myself in. As I drove down Kam Highway, this feeling persisted. Then, at Velzyland, I looked up towards the verdant hills and down towards the green pastures with cattle and sheep grazing, and then towards the ocean, which was putting on this most fantastic show like it only does on the North Shore, and I realized who I was and what I was doing. I was a surfer, and I was about to communicate with Nature, my God, in the most ultimate way I know how, riding the big surf. I began crying to myself.

At the Bay, the crowds had begun to gather. I parked in the parking lot and took out my board. I asked Sam Hawk how it was, and he said, "good." As I carried my board towards the beach, I pretended not to see the stands, the signs, the trucks, the workers, the roped-off areas. I tried to tell myself to be civil to these people, to mask my true feelings, even though we were, in that situation, of opposite ilks. Also, I did not want to cause a scene, for many of those people were, in other ways, my friends. As I waxed my board, Fred (Hemmings) came over and talked to me. I joked with him. I like Fred. I said hello to Rabbit (Kekai), and hit it. I paddled out in total confusion. This was Waimea Bay, a very spiritual place for me and those like me. What were they doing to it? Just then a huge closeout set came through, and it was suddenly 1958 all over again. I was still far enough in so that I was able to roll this set, which must have closed out the Bay about six times. I made it out and recognized Sam (Lee), Jeff (Hackman), and Jimmy (Jones). For chrissake, where were Jose (Angel) and Peter (Cole)? I soon realized why they weren't out. Sets now began to pour in, and they were huge. These were closeout sets that were breaking top to bottom. Jimmy and I pushed over one that must have been 40-feet high. I was laughing so hard I could hardly paddle. What a ridiculous situation. What was I doing out there? There just isn't enough room at the Bay to ride surf that big. Plus, there was a horrendous chop. I wanted in. But how? I vowed that I'd never surf anywhere again without checking it out first. Here I was, a guy who was supposed to be so concerned with water safety, about to start waving for help. I decided to wait for a lull and try and sneak in. I couldn't stop laughing.

Gradually, the surf diminished, the offshore wind started, and the Bay became rideable. The few waves that I did catch were big, steep, and exciting. The line between a good wave and a terrible wipeout at Waimea at this size is very thin. That's what makes it the place it is. As the conditions improved, the regulars made their way out. Everyone agreed that it was the best it had been for five or maybe ten years.

As stoked as everyone was, we also feared the worst, that they would soon start the contest. The consensus was that we would all stay out and screw 'em. (We didn't.) The crowds were getting bigger, the traffic more backed up, the contest people must have been doing their thing. Soon, powerboats and helicopters appeared, and Fred started warming up on the loudspeaker. A blaring horn and a waving of flags, and the contest began. The kids started paddling out with numbers on their bodies. Numbers! It was incongruous to the point of being blasphemous. I wondered about myself. I had been a contestant and a judge in a few of those contests when it all seemed innocent and fun. But it never is. The system is like an octopus with long legs and suckers that envelope you and suck you down. The free and easy surfer, with his ability to communicate so personally and intensely with his God, is conned into playing the plastic numbers game with the squares, losing his freedom, his identity, and his vitality, becoming a virtual prostitute. And what is worse, the surfers fall for it. I felt sick. The guy I felt the sorriest for was Mike (Miller). We, the old timers, were reminiscing while sitting out there. (On one wave, Jose and I took off behind Peter Townend. The official boat came over to tell us to get out of the water. Jose was like coiled steel spring. I think the boatman realized that they would be getting into something more than they could handle if they tangled with Jose. They wisely backed off.) But

Mike was right on top of it. It was his time. He, probably better than anyone else out there, could have communicated like George and Buzzy had done in the '50s, like Pat, Eddie (Aikau), Jose and Peter had done in the '60s, but they wouldn't let him. Our friend, Ricky (Grigg), told him not to take off in front of Jeff (Hackman). Granted, Jeff is a hell of a surfer, but he isn't the waterman Mike is, and that's what it takes to ride really big surf. I couldn't believe it. Telling us who could ride and who couldn't ride; the squares had invaded one of our last sanctuaries, big surf at the Bay. And, it wasn't the end.

I asked you, the editors, if I could write an article for you. I needed a vehicle to express this pent-up feeling that I harbored inside of me. I would like to end it thusly; A storm brews in the North Pacific; its high winds cause waves to start towards Hawaii. These waves hurdle towards the North Shore of Oahu, which because of its unique configuration, causes them to break bigger and better than anywhere in the world. A surfer has trained himself all his life to ride these waves. It is all he asks of life. Who the hell is Smirnoff or Hang Ten or the Duke or anyone else to tell him he can't. God created those waves. *Auwe* (Alas).

CHAPTER **52**

"We're Number One—
Interview: Ian Cairns" (1976)

Jack McCoy
1948–

The following interview with professional Australian surfer Ian Cairns
introduced a new era in surfing, much as John Witzig's "We're Tops
Now" article did nearly a decade earlier. Cairns formed part of a group
of young surfers from Australia, South Africa, and Hawai'i who dreamed
of making a living out of a lifestyle. In 1976, they decided to link various international contests to form the first world professional tour. As
Cairns predicted, Australians dominated professional surfing through
the late 1970s and 1980s. Much like their compatriot Nat Young at the
1966 World Championships, the Australians showed an aggressiveness,
especially in the big-wave arena of O'ahu, which earned them the respect—and subsequently the enmity—of local Hawaiian surfers. Fellow
Australian Wayne "Rabbit" Bartholomew's article in *Surfer* later that
same year, "Bustin' Down the Door," prompted violent confrontations
between the Australians and the Hawaiians during the winter of 1977,
but the new aggressive style of surfing, and the budding image of surfers
as professional athletes, gained momentum. A well-respected big-wave
surfer, Cairns also touches upon a recurring phenomenon among members of that small but elite group: the inevitable moment that comes after
a near-death wipeout. Cairns was interviewed by Jack McCoy, who went
on to become the sport's premier cinemaphotographer. Cairns himself,
after a number of years on the professional tour, became a successful
coach and contest promoter.

IT WAS A SURPRISE SEEING IAN WHEN I did on the North Shore
in October. I hadn't seen him for over nine months, and in that time he
had put on a few pounds during his winter stay in his home state of Western Australia. I started kidding him about the L-B's, and asking him if he

213

thought he could get his ten pounds overweight around enough in the water to win a bloody contest. "You bet! This is nothing. I'll lose that in nothing flat . . . and when I do, look out!" The last few words were directed at his good friend, surfing pal, and ice cream eating partner Rabbit Bartholomew. Buggs laughed, but lying slightly under the surface of Ian's joking attitude, I sensed a seriousness that sounded like he almost had it all planned.

"I am serious. I've watched it for the past year, and this year I'm sure the Aussies are going to make a strong statement about today's surfing. I can feel it."

And that's just what has happened. This year it came together. With his ten pounds shed in a matter of weeks, Kanga was tuning into the North Shore rapidly and getting ready for the contest program. During the Duke, he took over.

After Ian's win at Waimea, the Australian Broadcasting Commission asked us to do an interview with the two local lads who had made good in the Islands—Ian and Mark Richards. It wasn't till the year's contests were over and Ian was on his way home that I finally stuck my mike in front of the dreaded Kangaroo—a nickname that has stuck with him for years because of the size of the Roos that breed in Western Australia. They often pass the six-foot level—Ian is 6'1".

I sat down with him specifically to do an interview for all the Aussie fans who would be watching "Sports Night," with their can of Fosters in one hand and a meat pie (the Australian equivalent of the American hamburger) in the other.

Jack: Why do you think the Aussies have been so successful this year?

Ian: The Australians are a really competitive bunch. Out in the water we're all sort of competing against each other continually. Once you get a group of guys who are consistently pushing themselves further and further, the standards are undoubtedly going to rise. That's what happened over the last few years. There's been a resurgence of interest in Hawaiian surfing contests, because we seem to be able to push ourselves harder than the Hawaiians do. Our surfing, as a group, has improved outrageously; whereas theirs, as a group, has stagnated a fraction. We've all been working hard to get into contests over here, and now that we've got a stack of Australians in them, we're super keen to do well.

Jack: Most of the contests this year were held in big surf. Do you enjoy riding big waves?

Ian: It's tremendously exciting. It's one of the few challenges I've ever been faced with. Here's this phenomenally huge body of water coming at you, which, if it breaks on you, you know has the potential to crush and maim and do whatever it wants to you. And you're sitting there facing it, and you know you're going to take off on it and ride it and control it.

Jack: What about control?

Ian: You have to control your adrenaline, your heart pumping, your terror . . . you have to swing around and paddle into the thing forcefully and with confidence, and ride the bloody thing. You can't let it beat you.

Jack: This year you astounded spectators by hotdogging at Waimea. Is this part of your approach to big-wave riding?

Ian: The classic old-style Hawaiian approach is entirely divorced from the way performance surfing has evolved. I thought to myself, "Why are all these people going straight?" Here we've been practicing all these turns, and here's the ultimate medium for doing them—a giant face with more room to correct your errors. So I went out and endeavored to ride 20'-25' waves in the same manner as if I was riding a four-foot wave.

Jack: How did you feel winning the Duke? I know you have a lot of respect for Duke Kahanamoku.

Ian: It's a tremendous honor for an Australian to win a contest in the Duke's memory. It was one of my ambitions to be able to compete in it, and then to actually win was a dream come true.

Jack: Were you surprised that you won?

Ian: In the finals of the Duke, I went out feeling really good after winning the semi, started to get a few waves . . . I felt really confident I could win it. I gradually began to build up my aggression and my confidence, getting further and further inside, taking off later and later, getting steeper and steeper on the borderline of impossible, insane maneuvers, and I was making it. I thought, "I'm invincible. Here we go." So I took off on this wave, and it was the biggest wave I'd seen; and I was taking off, and all of a sudden I wasn't taking off. I wasn't going down; I was being pulled backwards up the face of the wave. It was impossible! I was invincible! "My God, I've made a bit of a bad judgement here." So I jumped off about twenty feet straight down the face, went over the falls, which took an incredible amount of time, 'cause you go from the bottom of the wave up inside the wave back down, about a forty-foot circular trip, and when I hit the bottom, I thought, "Now, this is a big wave. I've made a terrible error. I'm going to have an incredible wipeout." And when the wave hit me . . . I just didn't think any wave could be *that* heavy.

That's one thing in surfing that continually astounds me—that you can have such an incredible force and pressure put on you, and yet your body is so strong and flexible. The power of that wave must have been like getting run over by a semi-trailer or a train. I thought, "My God, that's just terrible. I shouldn't have done that." And I eventually came up, and that was sufficient to drain my confidence. I rode a couple of dribblers after that, and fortunately the waves before that wipeout had been good enough to let me win.

Jack: How do you feel about professional surfing?

Ian: We put our lives on the line; we go out there and take insane risks; we go over the falls and get annihilated, impress the crowd, yet we make such a measly amount of money. It's astounding that a sport as impressive as surfing can't engender enough excitement in the sponsorship circle to organize more prize money.

Jack: Are you satisfied with your performance this season?

Ian: I haven't surfed anywhere near the goal I set for myself at the beginning of the season. I don't surf religiously every day. I'm more into surfing for my own pleasure and enjoyment. That's when I surf well and really feel enthused and excited.

Jack: Could you comment on some of the top riders on the North Shore?

Ian: Mark Richards is one of the most explosive, radical, and incredible surfers I've seen. And he's going to improve outrageously. He's got an untapped amount of talent. He's emotionally sound—he won't be a one-day fizzle. He'll be around for a long time. He's a tremendous surfer. And he'll be the guy to beat consistently in the future anywhere in the world. He's good in small waves. He's good in big waves. He's just a well-rounded, incredibly hot surfer. I don't go for his style; it's not relaxed or eye pleasing, but the maneuvers and positions he gets into on the wave are phenomenal. I reckon he's a progressively exceptional surfer.

Jack: What about Shaun [Tomson]?

Ian: Of all the surfers I've ever seen, I'd say Shaun is the best tube rider because of his control and his ability to turn around sections in the tube. He's an incredibly strong, powerful surfer. He's got his fluid turn, cutback maneuvers down unbelievably. He's fantastic. He's the one person who is a real strong threat to the Australians.

Jack: Does that mean you think the Australians are the best?

Ian: We've had a really strong competitive record over the years. It slumped a fraction in the early '70s, but since then a new crop that has come up to take over from Nat Young and Midget Farrelly has consistently improved and improved each year until now—we're number one.

After I had gathered all of my recording equipment and started walking down the road to my plane, I couldn't help but look back to the first time I saw Ian back in early October, and think that he had made his prediction come true. As professional surfing develops and grows, the realization that there are confident, progressive surfers like Ian representing the sport is sure to attract respect and interest for the contest circuit. That means money . . . and money means food. Ian will like that.

CHAPTER 53

Articles from *Skateboarder* Magazine (1976–1977)

C. R. Stecyk III
1950–

C. R. Stecyk's writing and interviews for *Skateboarder* magazine in the mid-1970s helped establish the historical connection between surfing and skateboarding, an influence that reversed in the 1990s as skate-inspired aerial maneuvers became standard fare for a younger generation of progressive surfers. Stecyk's articles in particular located the influence of post–shortboard revolution surfers like Larry Bertlemann on young skateboarders in west Los Angeles. His chronicle of the radical innovations of the Z-Boys in DogTown linked their unique skating and surfing styles to the specific environment of Southern California. As Stecyk wrote in "Aspects of the Downhill Slide" (Fall 1975 issue of *Skateboarder*): "Two hundred years of American technology has unwittingly created a massive cement playground of unlimited potential. But it was the minds of 11 year olds that could see that potential." The confluence of environmental and architectural factors provided the surfers/skaters of DogTown with the raw ingredients for creating a new image—urbanized and grittier—for both sports.

The Westside Style or Under the SkateTown Influence (August 1976)

Traditionally, on the Westside, the varied beach and adjacent communities have been a hotbed of skate action. In the 60's, the Santa Monica Bay area spawned both the original Makaha and Hobie Vita Pak teams. Personalities like Fries, Johnson, Bearer, Woodward, Saens, Blank, Archer, the Hiltons, Trafton, et al., established the freestyle standard for the world. They wowed the masses in innumerable demos at department stores throughout the land, showing city slicks and farm boys alike a glimpse of the Westside style. Even today their exploits are regarded with awe. After all, people still mention "Skater Dater."

There are explanations offered for the area's early emergence as a skate power. The most common is the "origin of the species" proposal. Simply stated, it goes that since skateboarding itself originated in the mid-50's as an invention of the Malibu surf crew, the people who lived in the vicinity were naturally more proficient. Other reasons may be found in the region's diverse topographic contours. Canyon runs, storm dams, banked slopes, swimming pools, dams, concrete pipes, and parking lots abound. Consequently, all sorts of skating situations were readily accessible.

Well, the spots are still there, and over the last decade new faces, drawing heavily upon this local heritage, have pioneered some radical new approaches. This style made its public debut at the Del Mar Nationals eighteen months ago in the incarnation of the now notorious Z-Boys. The boys made quite an impression with their hard-driving, low-slung, pivotal, bank-oriented moves. In the words of the Mellow Cat himself, "There was so much aggression, they were more like a street gang than a skate team," or as the reporter from the *Evening Sentinel* put it, "While everyone else was standing up, these kids were turning all over the ground."

Since the stepping forth of the SkateTown-based Z-Boys and their innovative trips they have been widely imitated, but no one yet seems to have mastered the finer points. "I see guys who have copied one or two moves, but they don't have it . . . they just skate, get down, slide, stand up, and move on to their next trick—the problem is that their approaches are not integrated."—N. Pratt.

On any given day, practitioners of the new Westside style such as Adams, Alva, Biniak, Cullen, Constantineau, Muir, Oldham, Cahill, Oki, Kubo, Peralta, Pratt, Ruml, Hoffman, etc., can be seen on the streets where you live (at least if you dwell in SkateTown), carving out new legends for an even newer era.

"The whole thing has been going on up here for a long time; now the trip is out of the bag, and the influence is spreading . . ."—Tony Alva

Excerpt from Skateboarder Interview Highlights: Stacy Peralta (October 1976)

Q: The people in your area have a different style from those of other areas; in fact, it even differs from the older skaters in your own region. How did the low, pivotal, ground-contact style originate?

It came from riding banks more than anything. How better to ride a wave of cement than to surf-skate it? Besides, the style we have is related to short-board surfing, while I think the older guys have more of a long-board skate style. It's just different attitudes. In the old days you moved on the board, while now you move with the board and the board moves with you. It's much more integrated. Bertleman[n]'s surfing was a real influence on it. People came on it individually at first. Nathan Pratt and I were skating Ocean View one night a couple of years ago, and we just started doing S-turn cutbacks, using our arms as pivots. Down at the beach, Tony and Jay Adams were doing the same things. Different approaches, same conclusions. People all over the area were skating more or less similarly. It really jelled, as far as everyone else was concerned, with the Zephyr team.

Q: How so?

The Zephyr team showed a lot of people what sort of skating we were into up here. At the Del Mar Contest, we blew a lot of minds. The way we skated was really advanced. It was a total surf-skate with no tricks. People, in general, didn't understand it because they had never seen anything like it before. The surfers in the audience got off on it while everyone else was into handstands. We were so far ahead of what was going on in that zone it was amazing. I never realized we were different before that contest; the way we skated was the only way we knew how.

Excerpt from Skateboarder Interview Highlights: Tony Alva (February 1977)

Q: Your style differs markedly from these older skaters. When did you develop your current approach?

I was hanging out with Jay Adams, who is like my younger brother. He's always been a radical little rat. When he was 8, he was already into surfing at places like Malibu and Pitas Point. We both had these superhyperactive personalities, and so we always had to be doing something, and that "something" was usually causing trouble, being rowdy, surfing and skating. Jay was always a good skater, and I passed on what I had learned from the Hobie Team to him. Gradually we both evolved into a kind of a mutual style. At that time, we were to such an extreme in our skating that we didn't do any flat freestyle tricks at all. We'd ride the banks, get low and turn over like we were surfing . . . totally into the Bertleman[n] style. All of the people we hung with were into the same surf-skate approach, and we all surfed Jeff Ho's sticks out of the Zephyr shop. Jeff, Skip Engblom, and Jay's dad, Kent Sherwood, designed a low-center-of-gravity flex board to go along with the new style of skating. The Z-Boys happened through all of that. There wasn't a tryout for the skate team or anything like that; you were only on the team if you belonged. We were all friends, into the same kind of skating, and that was the basis of the whole trip. It just sort of set itself up, and Jeff and Skip backed us. It was a total skate trip . . . no bullshit tricks. People are just now starting to flash on how heavy it all was.

CHAPTER 54

"Indonesia: Just Another Paradise" (1979)

Erik Aeder
1955–

Erik Aeder, a photographer at *Surfer* since the late 1970s, introduced the 1980s version of Cape St. Francis (from *The Endless Summer*) to most of the surfing world, "a fabled perfect right point break" called Nias in the wave-rich region of Indonesia. An entire industry has since developed around surfing in the area—surf shops, pro contests, yacht tours, media promotions, travel packages, private surf camps—inundating this latest Mecca with surfers trying to fulfill the dream of finding the perfect, uncrowded wave. Beyond the discomforts and dangers expected in such narratives since the days of Naughton and Peterson, amenities to Aeder's dream include the same ideals that drew travelers to the Hawaiian Islands in the nineteenth century: the sensual experience of life pared down to the basics, the friendly welcome of curious natives, and the exotic allure of island women. Rather than ending, like Naughton and Peterson, with the continuing search for another perfect wave, Aeder returns from his surreal experience in a tropical daze, completely sated on paradise.

Dream Wave Discoveries in the World's Largest Tropical Archipelago

As soon as the Thai Airlines 707 left the ground, my friend Mark Oswin and I each stretched out on some empty seats to catch up on some very needed sleep. As I drifted off, I dreamed of a beautiful stewardess laying a blanket over me, which I pulled around my neck and fell deeper to sleep.

We were landing sooner than I expected and switching planes to a small twelve-seater, which would take us a bit nearer our destination. After an hour's flight, we landed at the village from which we would catch a boat the following day to the other side of the island.

The morning broke clear, and we were soon chugging along, the diesel engine hammering into my head even after I stuffed my ears with cotton. After eight hours, the boat docked in a small village, and we quickly found the local accommodations, and I attempted to sleep except for the ringing in my ears.

The next morning the coconut truck drove us up to another village for the final leg of our trip to a fabled perfect right point break. A hired fisherman was soon paddling us down a river that slid noiselessly through the tangle of bush at its edges. We approached a large hill that the river seemed to flow directly through and then the cave appeared. Dripping, jagged teeth cluttered its yawn which the boat was drawn to. We passed slowly through the cavity, ducking and pushing the hanging pinnacles until we emerged into flat water at the mouth of the river. There all my imaginings solidified as a set swept across the reef outside. I nearly fell out of the boat in excitement, and couldn't get dropped on the beach quick enough to stash my belongings in the village and head for the point with my board.

Life in the village became a routine of surfing in the morning, then eating, reading, writing, napping and surfing again in the evening. An incredibly simple existence revolving around how much energy we had to surf. Since there was little else to do and we were heading inland after we left there, surf was about all we did. The weather didn't assist my photography, being nearly always overcast or rainy, and I was convinced the area wasn't meant to be photographed for fear of exposure, with easy justification.

The family with whom we stayed had a young boy, Johnny, who would greet us with "Gidday mate." The Aussies had taught him well. He was like a monkey, and would raid our food supply or get into anything his curiosity might compel him to. They also had a beautiful 13-year-old daughter who I fell foolishly in love with, and who could persuade me out of anything with one of her flirting smiles and long, deep looks. The father asks with sign language if I've brought any gunja with me, and I tell him unfortunately not. He shakes his head, too bad, and offers me a beetle nut instead.

The sisters prepared all our meals, which consisted almost entirely of rice. Luckily, we had brought some essentials like peanut butter, honey, raisins, dried apricots and a tin of Milo chocolate mix. The peanut butter and honey went well on the coconut bread they baked, and when we scored a stalk of bananas, our sandwiches were complete. Occasionally they turned us onto a lobster dinner with veggies cooked in coconut milk, and with a Heineken beer cooled off in the well to top it off. We ate like kings.

Each morning I would crawl out from my mosquito net and bang my head as I walked through the low doorway, which would wake me up smartly. A fifty-yard dash through the jungle to avoid the mozzies put us on the long beach looking at the early waves out on the point. During the one-mile walk to the beach, I was tempted to start running when a wave would spit across the reef. But a look around at the empty beach and knowing that there probably wasn't another surfer within a hundred miles let me have a casual walk, picking up an occasional transparent pink shell on the way. If the tide was out, a touchy walk across the inside reef was necessary. The end of the reef dropped away in a series of caves and ledges into blue, bottomless water into which we jumped. Even at low tide, the waves broke in deep water on the level reef outside, changing slightly in characteristic to a longer down-the-line tube. Since the reef is part way inside the long bay, the swell is drawn out before it breaks, making a clean line up. These were the best waves I'd surfed since leaving Hawaii, and better since there were no crowds.

As the tide came in, the bowl at the end would wrap in more, causing an unexpected climax to the rush. Coming in over the reef at a higher tide, I turn my board fin up and pull myself along by the scant weed in the shallower water. With my feet scratched enough, I walk on the reef as little as possible.

With the wet season starting, the rain persisted, sometimes refreshing and sometimes annoying us. We would catch as much rainwater as we could, since drinking the cool well water meant risking cholera. One night when I was asleep, dreaming vividly of a girl in Bangkok, the rain began pounding so heavily on the tin roofing that I awoke suddenly and bolted from my bed to end up on the floor tangled in my mosquito net. The rain puts a fever into the young kids, who run laughing and screaming through the shallow pools like we used to run through the sprinklers on the front lawn during a hot summer's day. One day while out surfing, it began raining so heavily that a one-foot-deep fog was thrown up from the splashing water. The sets moved in like rolling clouds, and the only place to hide from the rain was in the tube. With the rains, temperature about 70° and the ocean about 85°, we got off our boards and swam to stay warm.

One morning after a surf, we made a two kilometer walk to a nearby village to replenish our supply of bananas. We were the center of attraction as we walked down the laid cut-stone street, flanked by our troop of kids each clinging to a corner of our clothing or one hand on each finger. Several beautiful, dark pairs of eyes were caught peering through slats of wood, and would quickly duck away when seen. The very young kids would take one look and start screaming, while running for cover behind mama's long dress. At the center of town in an obvious place were a couple of sacrificial stone tables carved by the ancestors of these people several centuries ago. Before the missionaries came and had their red churches constructed on the top of the hills and tamed this violent society, human sacrifices and head hunting were practiced.

After securing a stock of bananas for 35¢ from a gentleman with a long knife, we leave when I noticed a boy with a huge flying beetle tied onto a piece of string and the bug flying around his head like a rubberband airplane. He offered it to me for a nickel, and I gave him two bananas instead.

Since nothing lasts forever, the waves had to drop to two feet for several days. With the heat, boredom set in, as it was too hot to walk anywhere, too hot to sleep, and I'd been in the ocean for three swims by noon. As our visas were running out soon, but the full moon was approaching, a decision had to be made about leaving. The wounds on my body were pleading me to stay out of the water for a few days so they could heal up. My stomach longed for good food, and my tongue cried for some ice cream, but I knew that once I was leaving here, I'd be regretting it. I wanted one more chance at the waves, and with the full moon near, we had to stay.

As the moon enlarged, the weather grew dark and the rain came down in torrents segmented by cracks of thunder. The palms were whipped and bent over near the point of breaking, and occasionally a set of coconuts would crash down on the tin roofing. The ocean was stained brown by the flooding river, and the waves were hopelessly unridable. That evening the wind quieted to a purr and the sky broke clear to reveal the full moon rising behind a curtain of palm trees. After an easy sleep that night, the morning presented us with a good seven-foot swell under overcast skies and a slight drizzle. The rain gave the water surface that texture so you could feel your board through the turns. I stayed out till my arms were jellied, then let a wave wash me over the reef for the last time. As we walked back up the beach, I looked over my shoulder through the mist of the shorebreak at another wave on the point that seemed blurringly surrealistic. I rubbed my eyes, then turned and started the short jog through the boonies.

A gentle nudge opened my eyes to a pretty smile and the stewardess saying we were landing soon. I gazed glassy-eyed out the window at the palm-fringed beach passing under us; just another paradise. She asked if I had my customs form ready, and I reached in my pocket to pull out a transparent pink shell which I handed her. She looked at me, but I was looking out the window again, wondering where I had been.

Part V

Surfing Today

THE SIGNIFICANT IMPACT OF TECHNOLOGY on surfing over the past fifteen years—represented here by Bruce Jenkins's profile of Laird Hamilton and tow-in surfing—has fundamentally changed the practice and perception of surfing. Continued innovations in surfboard building materials, wave forecasting, portable wave machines, and the building of artificial reefs promise not only to redefine the sport but to make surfing accessible to more people than ever before. The twentieth-century revival of surfing opened with Jack London championing an individual-ist, man-versus-nature ethos. The century closed with an equally hyper-masculinized Laird Hamilton, a lightning-rod figure who, along with a small group of dedicated big-wave riders, helped expand surfing into a team sport complete with personal watercraft, foot straps, and tow-in ropes.

The passing of Mickey Dora in 2002 closed a chapter on perhaps the most captivating figure in surf culture of the latter half of the twentieth century. Beyond conveying the importance Dora holds for surfers who came of age in the 1950s and 1960s, Steve Pezman's "The Cat's Ninth Life" demonstrates the sustained role surfing plays in the lives of surf-ers now in their sixties. When not actually riding waves, Pezman and his surf companions—Mickey Muñoz and Yvon Chouinard (both of whom make an appearance in Bob Shacochis's "Return of the Prodigal Surfer" in Part VI)—are picking up surfboards, scouting the surf, or involved in any number of ancillary projects that revolve around riding waves, from building boards and selling apparel to publishing magazines and books. A whole generation—now expanding to several generations—may not spend as much time in the waves as formerly, yet surfing remains a compelling force in their lives.

Susan Orlean's profile of teenage surfer girls on Maui captures one of the most important shifts in contemporary surfing: the enormous movement of women into the sport that began in the 1990s. Aided by user-friendly modern longboards and fueled by apparel-giant Quiksilver's financial resources (the women's fashion line Roxy was launched in 1990), the women's movement produced its own bona fide star in Lisa Anderson (world champion from 1994 to 1997) and its own surf magazine (*Wahine*, founded in 1994). More women surf now than ever before (comprising an estimated 15 to 20 percent of the surf population worldwide), creating a critical shift in both the practice and image of surfing as daughters, mothers, and grandmothers rejoin men in the line-up.

Surf journalist Steve Barilotti offers a powerful counterpoint to the exuberant narratives penned by Kevin Naughton and Craig Peterson during the early years of surf travel in the 1970s. A popular conception during that era was the non-depletive nature of riding waves: "The surfer leaves at the end of the day, and there's no trace."[1] Barilotti's visit to Bali shows the traces that three decades of surfers have in fact left behind in their pursuit of riding the perfect wave. Marketed worldwide for its health aspects and sex appeal, surfing does not slip unscathed through the unsavory sex-trade industry that afflicts many ports of call on the exotic-wave circuit. Barilotti also implicitly ruminates over his own responsibility as a traveling reporter for *Surfer* magazine, one whose job it is to spotlight surf outposts around the globe only to watch the local cultures steadily degrade under the onslaught of eager, barrel-eyed surfers, the twenty-first-century messengers of globalism.

This part of the book concludes with a poignant article by Matt Warshaw on aging big-wave surfer Fred Van Dyke. Set in the context of how surfing priorities have shifted in the author's own life, Warshaw chronicles Van Dyke as an extreme example of a phenomenon that nevertheless touches upon all aging surfers: the moment when their hard-core dedication—so crucial to the image surfers have of themselves—begins to wane.

CHAPTER 55

"Laird Hamilton: 20th Century Man" (1997)

Bruce Jenkins
1948–

Bruce Jenkins, a sportswriter for the *San Francisco Chronicle* since 1973, has published numerous articles on surfing. His *North Shore Chronicles* (1990) offers the most comprehensive collection of essays on a locale that has been, for the past three decades, the epicenter of big-wave surf competition: O'ahu's North Shore. Jenkins's lengthy profile of pro surfer Laird Hamilton, from which the following excerpt is taken, provides an engrossing account of the tow-in surfing movement that began in the early 1990s and continues to be the most acclaimed innovation to hit the sport since the shortboard revolution of the late 1960s. Tow-in surfing has, as with any far-reaching innovation, generated its share of boundless praise and sharp criticism, divergent perspectives that Jenkins represents well. Above all, Jenkins takes measure of perhaps the world's most recognizable waverider—Laird Hamilton—a larger-than-life figure whose intensity, innovativeness, and consummate waterman skills cast him as both the rearguard of bygone surf traditions and the point man in the most extreme of today's extreme sports.

THERE IS NO GREATER PRIVILEGE than standing on the bluffs at Peahi, watching Laird and his crew dictate the future of surfing. It's not a place you find by accident; even an earnest set of directions won't work too well. You must be led there, through a maze of bumpy roads and a "Hey brah, you're trespassing" vibe that stays with you from start to finish.

The place was empty when I got there around 10 a.m. Not a soul in the water as a set of thick, heaving 15-footers rolled in. I realized then that Laird had found his sanctuary, a forum for his creativity and an escape from frauds. He's seldom seen at conventional surf breaks, preferring to ride longboards (shaped by his father) at more isolated settings. He rarely even considers nearby Honolua Bay, "because it brings out the aggressive side of me, and I really like putting that part to sleep," he says. "Enthusiasm is everything. That's your fuel."

The morning had been spent on preparation. Skeptics see tow-in surfing as a sell-your-soul cakewalk on a water-ski line, but in fact it's an endless amount of work. In surf of this caliber, there's an exact science to boards, footstraps, rope, sleds, inserts and a battery of safety equipment from neck braces to hospital-grade oxygen. The right-sized truck makes for ideal loading and unloading at the docks. The jet ski is your life, and must be regularly tuned, tested and flushed. On certain days, the preparation and wind-down take longer than the actual session.

The arena is at once breathtaking and frightful. Billy Hamilton calls Peahi "probably the most wicked reef setup I've ever seen for big waves. It turns the white water into these big strands of rope." In the wake of a broken wave, says Lopez, "The aftermath boiling in the impact zone is actually nauseating to look at. Taking a hit out there could mean dismemberment." There is no beach, just a steep cliffside bordered by rocks the size of Volkswagens. According to Laird, in the days before Peahi was ridden, "I sat up there watching 80-foot faces spitting every single time, like a cannon. We haven't seen that yet. But it exists. That's what we're waiting for."

Nobody's going to hand you a map, a jet ski and a reference guide if you show up at Peahi. The first thing you'll get is a massive dose of skepticism, from the Strapped crew to the boys at the dock to the hand-picked group of photographers. Bodyboarder Mike Stewart is one of the most full-on chargers in the history of surfing (Brock Little chose him as a tow-in partner), but when Stewart went to Peahi, "The vibe was pretty thick," he says. "Not one guy in particular. Laird was cool. But I'm new, I'm on a sponge . . . I did not feel welcome there."

So here's what Ken Bradshaw wants to know, and he speaks for a lot of people in the surfing community: "These guys have their spot, and they control it. I can understand that. But they've chosen to expose it. They've put out these incredible videos and everyone's seen 'em. So they're trying to protect it *and* expose it. You can't have it both ways."

Laird's response: "Yeah, we came out with a video—and not once did we say where it was. Did it even say Maui? Did it even say Peahi? Did it even say (sarcastically) 'Jaws'? It didn't say anything. It didn't even show jet skis. It just shows surfing, with music. We're not trying to be so sly that we're trying to hide anything, but we're not promoting the spot. We're promoting the evolution of surfing.

"It's a hard question, I'll admit. We do feel some loyalty to the spot, and now other people are showing up, and we're not ecstatic about that. If somebody like Brian Keaulana wants to come over, with the kind of big-wave credentials he's got, wonderful. I'll personally take him up there and tow him into a wave. But if some unknown kid decides he's a big-wave rider and comes over, I got another opinion for him. I'll say, go to Oahu and surf Pipeline for the next 10 years, and maybe we'll talk about it.

"See, nobody's gonna admit he's not a big-wave rider. Especially if he's been saying how easy this tow-in thing looks. So he wants to come right in here. Wrong. Excuse me. You might have the capabilities, but we don't know that yet, and we're not gonna wait to find out on that big day. That's something people forget. We have a sense of obligation to be around, to see who's out there, because one mistake and you're dead. Period. Put aside the legitimate big-wave riders, and this place is gonna spit out anything else that gets in the way. Do we want to be responsible for that? We've got enough to worry about. Better I punch you in the face than you die, or I die trying to go get you."

To set the record straight, the proposed tow-in contest at Peahi was not postponed because of the Strapped boycott. Contest organizer Rodney Kilborn lost the battle of permit rights to Sony Pictures, which is backing production of the full-length surfing film, *In God's Hands*. As Kilborn said, "I'm a local boy. I can't fight a billionaire company." But the contest was already losing momentum. Potential entrants Ken Bradshaw, Buzzy Kerbox, Brock Little, Cheyne Horan, Charlie Walker and Clyde Aikau had serious reservations when they learned that the Hamilton-Kalama-Doerner element would not be involved. Worse yet, Kilborn had promised the support of Brian Keaulana and Terry Ahue for contest water safety, and those two backed off, as well.

"We'll come back stronger next year," says Kilborn.

And if the Strapped element isn't involved? "OK, then they take themselves off the list," he says. "If Laird and those guys change their mind, they can compete for empty slots in the trials, not the main event."

Laird in the "trials?" Nutty concept.

"Well, that's a joke, but I don't see myself involved at all," said Hamilton. "I know this contest is gonna happen eventually, but it promotes the idea of going against your better judgment. Period. If you ever saw a big day around here, you know it's way too early to start having contests. It reminds me of an extreme snowboarding contest they used to have in Alaska. All the best snowboarders would go throw their bodies down the mountain. Guys broke legs, one guy died. They finally decided they were pushing people into areas they shouldn't go."

The people from *In God's Hands* have scored big-time, locking up priceless footage from some of the best days at Peahi. You'll see Doerner, Randle and Cabrinha in that film, but you won't see Laird. "To me, the only thing more back stabbing than the contest is that movie," he says. "First of all, this whole thing about (director) Zalman King is bullshit. He's a beautiful, sweet man, but he's like a 'C' director. I read the script. It's terrible. And if the quality of the film is substandard, then I pay directly.

"Kalama's not involved, either. We have nothing to do with it. If Darrick wants to be involved and make some money, great. I don't hold that against him. But to me, it feels a little bit like rape. They might film me, but I've got people that'll look out for me and go after 'em if they try to use it."

More than anything, Hamilton is weary of the obsession with Peahi, saying surfers should broaden their tow-in vision. "You've got outside Pipeline, Pupukea, Sunset, Ke Waena, all lined up," he says. "So do all the other islands. I want to see those 15-foot waves in Indonesia, breaking way outside, that people always talk about. I want to see Tahiti, Fiji, Western Oz, Mexico, Northern California. There's always some mysto spot, 'Oh, that one's too big, too fast.' Not any more. There's no such thing as too big or fast."

Nobody questions the surrealistic beauty of Laird Hamilton carving up a 50-foot face on a feathery, 7-4 Brewer. But what did it take to get him there? Is that surfing? Dave Parmenter has struggled with the issue, detesting it in his traditionalist's soul but finding himself captivated by the videos. "As a designer, I think it's fantastic," Parmenter said on the beach at Makaha last winter. "After watching Laird Hamilton surf those waves, I changed everything I'd previously thought about guns. I love the speed and where they're going with it.

"But no, it's not surfing. Did you ever see the movie *Hatari*? They're hunting rhinos in Kenya and they have this special truck with a seat on the hood, and as they go alongside the rhino at 50 mph, the guy in front drags him in with a noose. To me, surfing is having the rhino charge *you,* and you're there by yourself in a pair of trunks. It's Greg Noll, a solitary guy facing his ultimate fear, and here comes a big black one around the point. You have to choke back that fear, turn around, match the speed of the wave and choke over that ledge. These tow-in guys have the truck, and they're chasing right along with the rhino, at its speed. That's the big thing. They're going faster than the wave right off the bat. Plus its motors and noise, the smell of octane—that doesn't appeal to me at all. And this extreme surfing, you've got to have a partnership, your gear, your walkie-talkies. I've never thought of surfing as teamwork."

In the view of Peter Cole, in his early 60s and still surfing Sunset, "The whole thing is the takeoff. That's the challenge. Saying you're gonna do it, then charging straight down that thing. It's relaxing once you get to the bottom. These guys are missing the best part."

Martin Potter has called it "cheating." Tommy Carroll says there's nothing to true surfing but "blood and flesh. Add all that other stuff, and you're giving up a hell of a lot." Purist-minded North Shore surfers like Keoni Watson and Chris Malloy have been repulsed by the presence of tow-in crews at their favorite outer reefs, dismissing most of them as phonies.

"It's not even real," says Watson. "It's not even necessary. But Jaws is a whole different thing. Laird is a whole different thing. I'm totally in awe of what he's doing. If you're talking about an athlete with sheer balls, he's off the scale. What really scares me is that so many people will want to be like Laird."

"That's a real danger," Parmenter agreed. "Laird's an amazing waterman. Very close to the modern-day version of Pete Peterson, one of the real forgotten heroes. These are guys who can do everything: stunt man, diver, handy in boats, ride any kind of board. But Laird's much more of a daredevil. I see a wild-eyed look and a bit of self-promotion there, using big waves as a vehicle. And Laird is a very, very tough act to follow. It's like when Spielberg and George Lucas made *Jaws* and *Star Wars*, they set the standard for the greatest action movies ever. But they also spawned a million terrible imitations, and that ruined the industry. Somebody, down the line, is gonna try to be like Laird. And he's gonna die."

Laird could make his own movie on tow-in surfing. If necessary, he could spend the first hour in passionate defense of his position. Here is a condensed version:

"I won't say that you absolutely can't paddle into these waves. I run from that kind of thinking. But the high performance and efficiency just end the argument, in my opinion. I don't care if it's perfect 8-foot Pipeline or Western Australia, you're still gonna ride the wave from deeper back, pull in, have footstraps on so you can do a bunch of sick stuff you could never imagine, won't need the rail-grab, and you can ride the wave twice as far *and* be back to catch another wave. Not only that, towing is totally superior as far as physical exertion. Most of the time paddle surfing, you're just sitting around. Try to go water skiing and tow behind the boat for an hour. I mean, we are worked—because it's non-stop. We've all gone to a whole new level of being in shape.

"Look at someone like Dave Kalama. He's probably ridden more 20-foot waves in the last three years than I rode in my whole life before I started towing. Dave's really ripping now. He's the most improved surfer I've ever seen. He said, 'It's your fault.' I said, 'It's not my fault how fast you learn.' This is a phenomenal athlete riding dozens and dozens of big waves. The kids will realize it after a while. After they've had footstraps, they'll realize it's like trying to ski without bindings. My friend Rush Randle's doing stuff that Kelly Slater dreams of. Nobody's even heard of Rush, and he's doing some of the most innovative shortboard surfing in history.

"The first Maverick's video I saw blew my mind. Best wipeout video of all time. Period. Those guys are nuts, they're catching giant waves, total respect across the board, but they're sheep being led to the slaughter. Then, hey! Guy makes the drop! Then he gets nailed at the bottom! I'm here to surf, OK? I've done enough wiping out. I want to make the wave now. Most guys think tow-in surfing is weak, or it's not manly or something, which is great. Killer. They'll just be that much farther behind when they see the light."

There's a real purity to Peahi, sort of like walking through the baseball Hall of Fame. Nearly every face is significant, every deed a historical contribution. A sentimentalist could be moved to tears watching Randle, Waltze and Angulo windsurf the place with such consummate skill. Cabrinha has consistently performed the steadiest backside survival surfing in memory. Darrick Doerner was the first man to get in the tube, and later that day in February of '96, Laird came out of one. Brock Little jumped immediately into the fray, disappearing inside a giant room and getting savagely hammered. Stewart set a bodyboarding standard that may never be equaled. On the biggest day ever ridden, the 60-foot faces of Thanksgiving '95, Kalama had a solid, 10-wave session. Last February, on a day Laird was off-island, Kalama towed Brian Keaulana into an 18 footer, and after spending what observers described as a gut-wrenching five seconds inside the tube, Keaulana came flying out.

This is how Laird wants it: Great watermen only, no pretenders. He wants to see Clyde Aikau and Titus Kinimaka at Peahi. He wants Johnny Boy Gomes and Tommy Carroll—"the guys with the concrete stances," he says. "Pour all kinds of shit on those guys, and they never move. Yeah, Carroll with the good Tiki stance (laughter). I love that kind of power surfing. I'd love to have seen Jose and Butch out here, riding the kind of equipment we have now. They never had the chance to ride these little tiny boards.

"I'll tell you why Brian Keaulana is the best kind of guy to come over here," Laird went on. "This guy's a king, man. A beautiful person. But he came in here like a rookie, with an open mind, basically saying, 'I don't know what I'm doing.' Of all people! Think about that. He knows the most about big water, and he just wants to observe and learn. What does that make you if you're doing all this talking and you've never even done it?"

Kelly Slater, a prince of humility, would seem to be a natural for Peahi. Lord knows, the world would love to see it. "I think Kelly's reluctant to do it, and I'm not sure why," says Hamilton. "Maybe because he knows he's not gonna be the bull. Over here he'd be at the back of the pack, and I don't think he'd be willing to put the time in. Maybe his sponsors wouldn't want that. Anything that would make him look less than he is."

Slater was disappointed by that comment, responding, "I don't understand. That's kind of strange. You mean, are my sponsors protecting me? That's not the case at all. I'd love to try it. That would be wild. I know Laird, he's cool. He's invited me to come over."

"I tell you, it would blow his mind," said Laird. "He's one of the most phenomenal surfers we've ever seen, but one or two days with us would change his life. He'd know that what he's doing isn't the ultimate thing in the world."

One mainstay has been conspicuously missing from Laird's world lately, and that's Buzzy Kerbox. They were partners for years, in surfing and the world of high-fashion modeling, and it was Buzzy's inspiration that triggered the tow-in movement—at both Peahi and outside Backyards, where Kerbox, Hamilton and Doerner made history in the early '90s.

Kerbox has a new tow-in partner now in Victor Lopez (Gerry's brother), and they coexist smoothly with the Strapped crew. But Kerbox admits to a "falling-out" with Laird over a property settlement on Maui, a dispute that has affected their relationship.

"We had some disagreements in our dealings with the property," he says. "It's unfortunate. Laird and I paddled the English Channel together, did a lot of things together. We were like brothers. To lose a friendship over something silly is frustrating, but Laird's tough to compromise with. You're either with him or you're not. We had to go our own way." Kerbox feels he's been short-changed in recognition, saying, "When the tow-in thing started, I had the boat, and basically the idea, and Laird was one of the guys I picked to pull it all together. Now, Laird's basically stolen the whole deal. Laird invented it and pioneered it. And that's a little bit frustrating. It's sort of like having Michael Jordan on your basketball team. Every bit of credit goes to him. I'm the Scottie Pippen."

Kerbox said he teamed up with Lopez because, "I wasn't interested in being one of the Strapped gang. I'm in this to get away from everyone. Laird surrounded himself with a big group that travels together, launches from the docks together, eats lunch together, and I didn't want to be a part of that. Laird will never go surfing without tipping off five photographers, and I'm not worried about getting the pictures."

Not that Kerbox wouldn't mind the occasional recognition. "I've seen stacks of photos from these great sessions we've had, and when it gets to the magazine, it's all Laird and I get nothing," he says. "Laird gets the cover, the double-spread, and my shots don't get printed. Once again, it's that Jordan thing. Everything else seems mild in comparison. Laird's in a position where he can do no wrong—and hey, Laird *is* the Michael Jordan of big-wave riding. In my mind or anybody else's. He puts it all together like no person on earth."

Laird was mostly amused by Buzzy's comments, hinting that their friendship is far from over. "I see Buzzy out in the water and we're all edgy with each other, and I tell him, 'You know what, you and I are like a couple of sisters. The only reason we give each other such a hard time is because we care about each other.' If Buzzy got in a fight, I'd be the first guy over there pounding on the other guy. At the same time, we'll sit there and be shitty to each other. It's like, I can be shitty to you but no one else can (laughter)."

As for the photo angle—*Laird only surfs for the cameras*—he's heard that one before. "I have to laugh," he says. "I'm the furthest thing from that. If anything, I try to avoid it. But you're talking about specific jobs and things that are required by sponsors so you can make a living. It's not my fault that (photographers) are seeing and finding. It's not because I'm making them aware of it."

In the early days, Laird felt comfortable with Kerbox and Doerner because he knew they'd be there in a crisis. Today, that is his sole criterion for determining partners. "You never really know until you get out there," he says. "I can't tell you how many guys I thought were my friend, but when a really heavy situation came down and they didn't come get me, I never looked at 'em the same. They didn't cross the fine line, where it goes from courageous to the next level.

"I can tell you who'll come and get me. I won't tell you who won't (laughter). I can tell you that Dave Kalama is there every time. And Darrick Doerner is there every time. A guy like Mark Angulo will come and get you, and Brian Keaulana and a lot of lifeguards. Those are my guys, and I hope they feel the same way. If they don't, something's wrong. The unit's broken."

When the worst kind of crisis arrives, Laird attacks with an unbridled ferocity—pure animal. There was a terrifying scene one winter when Victor Lopez was caught inside, being dragged into oblivion by his leash. Mike Waltze motored quickly into the white water to make a pass. Lopez got onto the sled but the leash was still connected, anchoring them all in the worst possible place. They were crushed by the remnants of a set wave, left to float without equipment. As Kalama rushed in to rescue Lopez and Waltze, Laird jumped off the ski and let the white water push him onto the rocks, where Waltze's craft was being mangled. It was a lost cause, but Laird was up there battling, yanking, ducking huge surges of white water, ignoring the blood streaming down his legs, risking his life for his friend's equipment.

Hamilton had another harrowing situation with Doerner, the same day Darrick had broken ground with Peahi's first tube ride. "He got in a situation where he hadn't come up for a long time," said Laird. "And when he did, he came up right in front of the next wave. I was trying to muster some speed in this pile of foam, and when he got on the sled, we were barely moving. The wave broke right behind us when I gassed it. We did sort of a wheelie—the guys on the cliff said they saw the whole bottom of the ski and sled. I wasn't sure if Darrick was still on, but when we got into the channel, he had a big grin on his face, like, 'You think I was gonna let go?'"

So that's how it is. Make a pass in a crisis, or fall out of the loop. "You can say this guy's the best waterman or whatever, but if he turns the other way in that kind of situation . . . I've lost a couple of friends that way," Hamilton says. "Won't ever look at 'em the same. And they know that. Not a thing they can do about it. It's like a brand (makes a sizzling noise). And there won't be another chance."

So what else is there to know about Laird? Well, he doesn't sit down to a plate of sprouts and avocado after a rip-roaring session. I saw him sit down with Waltze and Gabrielle Reece and devour the two biggest cheeseburgers I've ever seen, complete with fries and a coke.

Is he like the rest of us out there, gliding across waves with music running through his head? Absolutely: "A lot of Hendrix. He's the only guy who ever made surf music. I hear chick singers, going off hard; that's always pretty hot. Sometimes I'll be singin' to myself when I'm riding. It might even affect the way I ride. Like today, my song was 'Free-Fallin' by Tom Petty. Yeah, that was pretty appropriate."

As Laird's truck rumbled along the Hana Highway, a Van Morrison tune came on the radio. "This is a good one to be stuck with, right here," he said.

And the wind catches your feet, sets you flyin'.

This struck me as a defining moment with Hamilton, infinitely more relevant than his critics' comments about ego and attitude. This was Laird in his element, the hair still wet, a smile on his face, a soul-stirring session in his wake.

As I spoke with some of the most respected figures in surfing, I found they had stripped away the excess, as well.

Lopez: "When you put it all together, the power, grace and finesse, nobody does it better. To see him up close at Jaws is the ultimate. He finally found a place where he can match power with the wave. It's an environment that matches everything he is. I think he's been bred to ride the biggest wave ever ridden, and I think he's gonna do it. Who cares about the rest?"

Little: "On the Easter Island trip we had a lot of down time, and I remember Laird lifting me up from the neck—just for fun, to do curls with me (laughs). That's how he is in the water. He's not the best surfer I've ever seen, but he doesn't try to flow with the power like the rest of us. He tries to screw with it. Just growling, right in front of the beast coming at him. Laird can actually challenge the wave. Whereas I'm forced to ride it."

Watson: "One year we're right in the middle of the opening ceremony for the Aikau contest, introducing all the surfers, when we hear this car pull up in the parking lot. Right as Steve Pezman announces Johnny Boy Gomes—the name before 'Hamilton'—we hear the door shut. And Laird walks right into his place, right as Pezman speaks his name. Turns out he'd been running people off the highway trying to get there on time, but that was Laird: big, crazy, perfect timing, gnarly presence. Everything he does is like that."

Bradshaw: "I remember apologizing to Laird one time about a comment I'd made. I said if it wasn't for Laird and Darrick, the outer reefs wouldn't be exposed, and the world wouldn't know about them. I didn't know how the conversation was gonna go. I've gotten in fights over stuff like that. But he said, 'You know what, Ken? I don't know why I'm the one. I don't know why it's my time to be here. But I'll tell you for sure, I'm here, I'm now, and I'm gonna take full advantage of my situation for as long as it lasts.' That was a rational, mature side of Laird I hadn't seen before. I walked out of there thinking, there's no doubt in my mind. This is the guy who will ride a 40-foot wave."

Angulo: "If it wasn't for Laird, I don't think any of us (in the Strapped crew) would have gotten this far, this quickly. There are certain days when you're a little scared to go out, but if he feels you're good enough, he'll say, 'Come on. Ride a couple.' And you'll go. And afterward you'll brag to your chick how bad you were (laughter). But Laird truly loves it. When that giant wave comes, and Laird gets right into the top of that big ol' thing . . . nobody does it like that."

Ricky Grigg: "Every so often somebody comes along with the talent and that other thing: the charisma, the magic. That extra dimension that sets him apart, like Carl Lewis or Muhammad Ali. I can't even put into words my admiration for this guy, how he came out of nowhere. He's the phantom, coming out of the mist, the abyss. It's very spiritual."

Terry Ahue: "When we worked on the set of *Water World*, Laird was blowing the stunt guys away. They couldn't believe what he was doing. They're all jumpin' for a kickback—'cause every time you do a stunt, you get paid for it—and Laird's like, 'Shit, I can do that for free.' He's one of a kind, this guy. Everybody thinks he's egotistic, but if he says he's gonna do something, he's gonna *kill* it. And in all the years I've known him, I've never had a bad experience with him."

Through all the tributes, it was a comment from Ahue's partner, Brian Keaulana, that really hit the target. Brian wasn't expecting the question. He hadn't rehearsed an answer. But when I asked him to sum up Laird, this is what he said, without hesitation:

"Laird is like every single element known to man. Raw power that the ocean has. Strong foundation of mother earth. He can be as calm as the sea, as strong and swift as the wind."

The big swell will come one day, holding within it the biggest wave. There will be plenty of notice, but funny things will happen. Dentist appointments. Gotta go pick up the kids. Absences unexplained.

Laird Hamilton will be up before dawn, preparing for the day he's awaited all his life. He will bring together all the elements, from Butch and Jose to his mother's memory to the legacy of the Hamilton name. And then he will surf. As strong and swift as the wind.

CHAPTER 56

"The Cat's Ninth Life... On Visiting Miki Dora Near the End" (2002)

Steve Pezman
1941–

> Steve Pezman edited *Surfer* magazine from 1971 to 1991, then began the *Surfer's Journal* in 1992 with his wife, Debbee. The *Surfer's Journal* has served for more than fifteen years as the spiritual leader of what might be called surfing's heritage movement: an attempt to delineate an authentic cultural history for surfing amid a globalized marketing industry that uses surf images to sell products far removed from the beach lifestyle. Pezman's dramatic account of visiting Mickey Dora before Dora's imminent death captures well the reverence with which surf heroes from a bygone era are now treated. As the baby boom generation takes stock of its formative years—and surfing's contribution to that formation—figures like Dora, who so strongly captured surfers' imaginations of the period with his personal style and iconoclasm, will continue to grow in importance.

I HAD AN APPOINTMENT WITH Yvon Chouinard to meet early morning on December 18th, a Tuesday, at his beachfront home north of Ventura. Yvon had suggested timing the drive up from San Clemente to coincide with a good swell, but it was late in the year and I wanted to present him with a thank you gift for his consistent support over The Journal's first ten years while it was still our tenth year. (The item being a self-portrait taken by Doc Ball in 1935 on which Doc had written, "Enjoy your years while you still have them." Doc Ball, 2001.)

Mickey Muñoz was riding along because he needed to pick up a large gasoline generator he'd bought from Yvon, so he could haul it down to his second home in Mexico, and a new Rocket Fish that was awaiting him at Clyde Beatty's board works in Santa Barbara. I drive a cargo-friendly, heavy-duty pickup, so the joint mission made sense. Mickey and I have been friends since he employed me as his assistant at Ole Surfboards (after Hobie bought it) on Bay Blvd. in Seal Beach back in 1963. These days, we enjoy any excuse to spend rare time together, especially a coastal cruise. While discussing the trip, I suggested to Mickey that he might want to call Miki Dora's father in Montecito and see if we could stop by and visit the failing Cat while he was still able to take visitors.

By now, word had spread that Dora was in the final stages of terminal cancer. Just two to three weeks previously, he had been flown first-class from Biarritz, France, to Loma Linda Clinic in Redlands, California, by Quiksilver Europe's Harry Hodge, who had been putting Miki up in France. Dora had been quickly screened and judged untreatable, riddled with an illness too long ignored. Miki had refused the option of surgeries, radiation, chemotherapy, and had been moved to his father's to fight the last fight. He had been given two months.

Word of Miki's affliction had been the underground buzz for much of the last year, the news spreading like tendrils throughout a surfing world scattered with old friends and acquaintances. It was said that Miki had been reaching out via phone to certain individuals known to him as being either ill themselves, or with some basis for knowledge of treatments, in his hour of need. The shocking reality of a terminal Dora struck hard into the psyche of the surfing community; a subculture that has seen itself age from its early 1960s popularity explosion when it comprised 99% teenagers, to today's current demographic, weighed heavily with aging boomers and pre-boomers dropping dead, quite naturally all around us. Only six months ago, a still rakishly tan, handsome, and fit Miki had reportedly received the doctor's reports and chose to turn away from conventional debilitating treatments, preferring more homeopathic dietary strategies, juice fasts, golf, tennis, and surfing. Who could blame him?

To digress, over recent years, Dora had played cat and mouse with various film industry figures who had expressed interest in making a picture based on his life story, while others wanted him to do the autobiographical tell-all book. At one point, it was reported that Dora had turned down 50 grand cash up front to do "the book." But it was the elusive movie deals that Miki chased in his own seemingly passive/aggressive way. For the most part, they were fostered by producer/directors who were themselves part of the Malibu scene, well versed in the Dora mystique, and now were bankable industry figures powerful enough to choose their own projects. With some understanding of the difficulty of two such supreme egos trying to mate, Dora coming to a contractual agreement with a filmmaker was a process doomed to failure. It went like this: The light bulb would go on for the Hollywood guys and they would put word out that they were interested. Even we would occasionally field "searching for Miki" calls at The Journal. We'd generally send them to Greg Noll, who would have a chuckle, then pass them on to Miki. Contact would eventually occur; meetings would be set up. Negotiations would progress between Miki, his lawyer, and the surfer/producer type until Dora's suspicious nature and/or sense of propriety would revolt when faced with the Hollywood guy's ideas for how it should be. Once the Hollywood guys experienced the reality of Miki's persona in full bloom, the light bulb would burn out and the deal would die. Finally, there were none left calling.

Miki was aging; it seemed as if the moment of opportunity might be passing him by. Why Miki wanted a film of his life to be made, it's hard to be sure. Originally, it had to be the money, plain and simple. Eventually, as interest waned, he came to see "the book" as a vehicle to rekindle interest in "the film." By this point, Tom Adler, a Santa Barbara surfer, graphic designer, and marketing consultant who had created the acclaimed, small-format book, *San Onofre to Point Dume, 1926–1942,* of seminal Don James' images that Dora much admired, had proposed a similar book to Miki, with long-time Dora confidant Craig Stecyk as writer. To this, Miki finally agreed. In fact, he even pursued Adler's book. When his illness advanced and his time became short, Miki's motivation for doing the book was no longer about the money and selling a movie deal, but about leaving a high quality statement as a legacy.

To this end, Adler and Stecyk both became personally dedicated as well. For weeks, in November and December 2001, Stecyk had been frequenting Dora's father's house in Montecito, taping interviews when Miki's energy level allowed. All the while, Adler, who had been visiting Dora in France to discuss the book and who lived nearby Miki's father in Montecito, had become close to Miki and a constant support presence.

This was the scene that awaited Muñoz and I on our run up the coast.

We arrived at Chouinard's house around 8:30 a.m. The surf was small and glassy, with occasional sets revealing signs of a freshening swell. The tide was too high out front, so Mickey and I followed Yvon down to C-Street in Ventura where they enjoyed an hour in light-offshore, waist-to-shoulder conditions up on the far point. Both surfed with easy competence: Muñoz, in his traditional way, picking off inside waves, doing stand-up fade turns stiff-legged off the bottom then flowing through section after section on down the beach, and Chouinard, who with a direct, unadorned body language, pulled deep takeoffs and easily made the zippy little outside curls. After the surf, we proceeded to Point Blank, Chouinard's surfboard factory, where we horsed the heavy gasoline generator into the back of my truck and headed north onto 101.

The Dora family home is, by Montecito standards, a relatively modest but very comfortable cottage located on a small lane just inland of the highway. We followed Mr. Dora's directions off the freeway and parked my big white Ford diesel against a hedge along the front of the house, behind a clean showroom-stock El Camino that looked like Craig Stecyk's. On the drive up, Mickey and I had speculated on what we'd encounter. Visiting a terminal patient can be excruciatingly uncomfortable. Make that person the intimidating Miki Dora and the normal tension is magnified. While I had been of some assistance to Miki from a distance during his illness, as this day had approached, my not being an intimate friend of Miki's made me feel awkward about violating his private space at such an intensely personal time. I had troubled over this and decided that if it felt inappropriate for me to go in, I'd wait in the car. However, Mickey had clearly mentioned to Mr. Dora that we were riding up together and he had been enthusiastic, telling Muñoz when queried about what he could bring, to "bring your sense of humor," so we ended up figuring it would be OK. As a gift, Mickey had selected a silly surfing Santa that danced hula on a surfboard. Muñoz ventured that it represented perfectly everything that Miki hated about surfing, hopefully providing the perfect bit of levity. I had brought three never-before-printed-let-alone-published, mid-'60s, Ron Stoner b&ws of The Cat at Rincon, in his prime.

We both got out and walked to the front porch. While approaching the house through the yard, suddenly we could see Miki about 60 feet away reclined in a sunny patch of patio off to the left side of the house with a lady (who turned out to be his stepmother, Christina) in attendance. Miklos Dora Sr. came to greet us at the door. We introduced ourselves, and he invited us in while apologizing that Miki was at the moment indisposed, taking sun out back. He bid us into the front room and we sat down, joining Craig Stecyk who nodded to us from the couch. The room was dominated by a large modern/impressionist landscape hanging over the fireplace. Glancing around at the inner sanctum of Miki's parents, a space that under normal circumstances I never, ever would have intruded on, I observed the roots of Miki's sophisticated tastes expressed by the assembly of family objets d'art, all of them time appropriate to the senior Doras. This was obviously the well-appointed home of a financially-secure elderly couple. I had heard that Mr. Dora was a retired wine merchant, and there indeed were framed, autographed Grand Cru labels from significant French vintages adorning the wall in the hall. But the most striking aspect of meeting Miki's father was that he looked exactly like his famous surfer son: the shape of the head, the tight curls of the hair, the impish eyes, the nose and mouth, the facial structure and expressions. His precise English was spoken with a Hungarian accent, and the use of hands and shoulders to emphasize meanings. All of it immediately added up.

Mr. Dora went out to announce to Miki that he had visitors. I squirmed. We heard Miki exclaim, "Not now," then more soft words. Mr. Dora returned to say that Muñoz was invited to join Miki in the garden. By way of preparing us for Miki's gaunt appearance, he forewarned us that Miki was eating almost nothing—just taking sips of papaya juice at most. Mickey rose, glanced over at me, and followed Mr. Dora out the door, carrying the absurd Santa. Craig and I glanced at each other. Mr. Dora returned to keep us company while the two Mickeys visited. He sat down and we made small talk. What did I do? Oh, The Journal; he believed he had seen a copy. Silence. I questioned a trophy sitting on a sideboard, and with sudden enthusiasm, Mr. Dora launched into a description of his own tennis past. He had played at a top-ranked amateur level in the '40s and '50s, able to hold his own playing social matches at the L.A. Tennis Club with such period stars as Jack Kramer and Pancho Gonzales. The foundation for Miki's considerable tennis ability suddenly came clear. Mr. Dora politely excused himself and left the room.

By now, Muñoz had returned back inside. Miki had tired. Mickey looked at me and Craig and shook his head. It had been tough. He whispered to us that he had felt foolish giving Miki the funny Santa, that Miki had not reacted to it, but that when he reached down to take it with him as he left, Miki had put his hand on Mickey's indicating that he should leave it. Mr. Dora returned and invited us into the den where the walls were covered with family photos. Pointing to an image on the wall, he explained the young boy and young man in surf trunks standing on the sand in front of a bluff, "Here I am with Miki on our first day at San Onofre in 1940. Miki is six in the photo." Surprised, Muñoz asks, "Did you surf?" Miklos answers, "Oh, yes. I wasn't ever that good, but I frequented the Cove and San Onofre back in the '30s and '40s. I took Miki to the Cove for his first surf at age four." We had both always assumed that it was Miki's stepdad, Gard Chapin, who had launched his surfing, that his real father was more the city sophisticate, removed from the beach scene. But no, not at all. More pieces fell into place. I noticed another small image of a grade-school-aged Dora looking angelic: parted hair, soft smile. And yet another: a defused, Johnny Mathis-style portrait of an adult Miki dressed in all white, sweater, slacks, white slip-ons, holding his beloved dog Scooter (named for the famous 1940s Waikiki surfing dog, Scooter-Boy) on his lap. (Miki would reputedly scam the pooch a seat next to him on plane flights by wearing dark glasses and claiming he was a seeing-eye dog.) The photo was made all the more poignant by the knowledge that Scooter had died in a house fire at Jeffrey's Bay just a few years ago. When we returned to the front room, Mr. Dora scurried out to check on his son. I could hear Mr. Dora asking Miki if he could see a Mr. Pezman, who was here with Mickey. "Pezman? Is he here? Oh, god." Then some more muffled words. Suddenly, Mr. Dora appeared in the doorway and invited me out to see Miki. Not wanting to make an uncomfortable scene worse by protesting, I rose and followed him out to the patio. There lay The Cat, on a padded chaise lounge, tanned to a dark hue, but with extremely emaciated shoulders and arms. He was nude, draped with a small white towel over his groin, a plastic catheter tube ran out from under the towel into a container on the ground at his side. Miki seemed unselfconscious of his state. His countenance looked like the Dora I had known but was gaunt, his eyes dark hollows, his hair gray specked and shaggy around his darkly-tanned features. Miki was resting head down, in apparent slumber. I sat and waited. He slowly looked up, registered on me, and said, "Pezman, sorry to have you see me in this wretched state." With an abbreviated wave of his hand he said, "I can't hold anything down." I uttered a few inane words in reply, I can't remember what, then said, "I had these prints made—Ron Stoner shots, of you—Rincon, back in the . . ." I trailed off as he reached out and took the three 8 x 10s and shuffled through them, inspecting each carefully. After a moment, he looked up into my eyes, handed them back to me, and asked, "How much?" Caught off guard, I again fumbled for words. Was he joking or being serious? "I had them made for you." He gestured for me to put them down. I set them on the ground. He said, "No, put them inside." (Indicating a copy of The Journal I had brought along.) Then, tired from the exchange, his eyes closed and his head dropped. Christina came close and suggested we return to the front room, to let Miki move inside. It had grown chilly on the patio.

I returned to join the others and we waited while Miki walked slowly to his bedroom, put on a robe, and then moved to the front room to continue our audience from the couch. Miki rested from the effort, then looked up and gazed at each of us as if assessing our presence. He looked at me, then his hand moved to his forehead in that familiar Dora-esque gesture, and he spoke, "I spent my life traveling the world, looking for a good wave to ride by myself . . . I found a few . . . ten years before anyone else." I nodded. Another pause, "I want to apologize for my past behaviors . . . the whole thing just got too big for me . . . the commercialism." I was stunned. After a longer pause, "I'm fighting this thing, but it looks like it may beat me." Yet a longer pause, "Don't make a big deal out of my obituary . . . if you must write something, a few simple words. Just leave it at that." Miki slowly got up to return to his room. It was time. Muñoz, myself, Stecyk, we all rose as did Miki, and we moved toward the door. Miki stopped and turned to face us and he and Stecyk hugged. Then he and Muñoz hugged. Then Miki stopped in front of me and slowly extended his hand. His grasp was strong and firm, he looked into my eyes for a brief instant, searching for something, then moved away down the hall.

〰〰〰〰〰〰

Three weeks later, at 9:30 a.m., on January 3, 2002, I was sitting at my computer at home writing these words when Greg Noll called to tell me that Miki Dora had passed at 6:00 a.m. He had died peacefully in his sleep. His doctor had reportedly marveled that for being so sick, he had passed away easily and relatively pain-free.

CHAPTER 57

"The Maui Surfer Girls" (2002)

Susan Orlean

Susan Orlean, an author and staff writer for the *New Yorker*, provides an updated version of "*The Life*" that Tom Wolfe first described in his articles on The Pump House Gang (1966). Bunking with teenage surfer girls on Maui, Orlean draws out "the moment," a state of pure surfing adolescence, as she writes, that is as utopian as it is ephemeral: a life revolving around the beach and dreams of surf-stardom that, like the life of Wolfe's La Jolla teenagers, ends all too quickly in the realities of adulthood. Part of today's realities for female surfers that Orlean touches upon include inequalities in everything from sponsorship to competitive respect. Another sign of the times for surfing that Orlean records is the appearance of surf moms and surf dads. Increased mainstreaming of the sport has drawn surfing into the realm of suburban soccer carpools, with parents moving groups of kids from one contest to the next in pursuit of trophies and future stardom.

THE MAUI SURFER GIRLS LOVE ONE another's hair. It is awesome hair, long and bleached by the sun, and it falls over their shoulders straight, like water, or in squiggles, like seaweed, or in waves. They are forever playing with it—yanking it up into ponytails, or twisting handfuls and securing them with chopsticks or pencils, or dividing it as carefully as you would divide a pile of coins and then weaving it into tight, yellow plaits. Not long ago I was on the beach in Maui watching the surfer girls surf, and when they came out of the water they sat in a row facing the ocean, and each girl took the hair of the girl in front of her and combed it with her fingers and crisscrossed it into braids. The Maui surfer girls even love the kind of hair that I dreaded when I was their age, fourteen or so—they love wild, knotty, bright hair, as big and stiff as carpet, the most un-straight, un-sleek, un-ordinary hair you could imagine, and they can love it, I suppose, because when you are young and on top of the world you can love anything you want, and just the fact that you love it makes it cool and fabulous. A Maui surfer girl named Gloria Madden has that kind of hair—thick red corkscrews striped orange and silver from the sun, hair that if you weren't beautiful and fearless you'd consider an affliction that you would try to iron flat or stuff under a hat. One afternoon I was driving two of the girls to Blockbuster Video in Kahului. It was the day before a surfing competition, and the girls were going to spend the night at their coach's house up the coast so they'd be ready for the contest at dawn. On contest nights, they fill their time by eating a lot of food and watching hours of surf videos, but on this particular occasion they decided they needed to rent a movie, too, in case they found themselves with ten or twenty seconds of unoccupied time. On our way to the video store, the girls told me they admired my rental car and said that they thought rental cars totally ripped and that they each wanted to get one. My car, which until then I had sort of hated, suddenly took on a glow. I asked what else they would have if they could have anything in the world. They thought for a moment, and then the girl in the backseat said, "A moped and thousands of new clothes. You know, stuff like thousands of bathing suits and thousands of new board shorts."

"I'd want a Baby-G watch and new flip-flops, and one of those cool sports bras like the one Iris just got," the other said. She was in the front passenger seat, barefoot, sand caked, twirling her hair into a French knot. It was a half-cloudy day with weird light that made the green Hawaiian hills look black and the ocean look like zinc. It was also, in fact, a school day, but these were the luckiest of all the surfer girls because they are home-schooled so that they can surf any time at all. The girl making the French knot stopped knotting. "Oh, and also," she said, "I'd really *definitely* want crazy hair like Gloria's."

The girl in the backseat leaned forward and said, "Yeah, and hair like Gloria's, for sure."

A LOT OF the Maui surfer girls live in Hana, the little town at the end of the Hana Highway, a fraying thread of a road that winds from Kahului, Maui's primary city, over a dozen deep gulches and dead-drop waterfalls and around the backside of the Haleakala Crater to the village. Hana is far away and feels even farther. It is only fifty-five miles from Kahului, but the biggest maniac in the world couldn't make the drive in less than two hours. There is nothing much to do in Hana except wander through the screw pines and the candlenut trees or go surfing. There is no mall in Hana, no Starbucks, no shoe store, no Hello Kitty store, no movie theater—just trees, bushes, flowers, and gnarly surf that breaks rough at the bottom of the rocky beach. Before women were encouraged to surf, the girls in Hana must have been unbelievably bored. Lucky for these Hana girls, surfing has changed. In the sixties, Joyce Hoffman became one of the first female surf aces, and she was followed by Rell Sunn and Jericho Poppler in the seventies and Frieda Zamba in the eighties and Lisa Andersen in this decade, and thousands of girls and women followed by example. In fact, the surfer girls of this generation have never known a time in their lives when some woman champion wasn't ripping surf.

The Hana girls dominate Maui surfing these days. Theory has it that they grow up riding such mangy waves that they're ready for anything. Also, they are exposed to few distractions and can practically live in the water. Crazy-haired Gloria is not one of the Hana girls. She grew up near the city, in Haiku, where there were high school race riots—Samoans beating on Filipinos, Hawaiians beating on Anglos—and the mighty pull of the mall at Kaahumanu Center. By contrast, a Hana girl can have herself an almost pure surf adolescence.

One afternoon I went to Hana to meet Theresa McGregor, one of the best surfers in town. I missed our rendezvous and was despairing because Theresa lived with her mother, two brothers, and sister in a one-room shack with no phone and I couldn't think of how I'd find her. There is one store in Hana, amazingly enough called the General Store, where you can buy milk and barbecue sauce and snack bags of dried cuttlefish; once I realized I'd missed Theresa I went into the store because there was no other place to go. The cashier looked kindly, so I asked whether by any wild chance she knew a surfer girl named Theresa McGregor. I had not yet come to appreciate what a small town Hana really was. "She was just in here a minute ago," the cashier said. "Usually around this time of the day she's on her way to the beach to go surfing." She dialed the McGregors' neighbor—she knew the number by heart—to find out which beach Theresa had gone to. A customer overheard the cashier talking to me, and she came over and added that she'd just seen Theresa down at Ko'ki beach and that Theresa's mom, Angie, was there too, and that some of the other Hana surfer girls would probably be down any minute but they had a History Day project due at the end of the week so they might not be done yet at school.

I went down to Ko'ki. Angie McGregor was indeed there, and she pointed out Theresa bobbing in the swells. There were about a dozen other people in the water, kids mostly. A few other surfer parents were up on the grass with Angie—fathers with hairy chests and ponytails and saddle leather sandals, and mothers wearing board shorts and bikini tops, passing around snacks of unpeeled carrots and whole-wheat cook-ies and sour cream Pringles—and even as they spoke to one another, they had their eyes fixed on the ocean, watching their kids, who seemed like they were a thousand miles away, taking quick rides on the tattered waves.

After a few minutes, Theresa appeared up on dry land. She was a big, broad-shouldered girl, sixteen years old, fierce faced, somewhat feline, and quite beautiful. Water was streaming off of her, out of her shorts, out of her long hair, which was plastered to her shoulders. The water made it look inky, but you could still tell that an inch from her scalp her hair had been stripped of all color by the sun. In Haiku, where the McGregors lived until four years ago, Theresa had been a superstar soccer player, but Hana was too small to support a soccer league, so after they moved there Theresa first devoted herself to becoming something of a juvenile delinquent and then gave that up for surfing. Her first triumph came right away, in 1996, when she won the open women's division at the Maui Hana Mango competition. She was one of the few fortunate amateur surfer girls who had sponsors. She got free boards from Matt Kinoshita, her coach, who owns and designs Kazuma Surfboards; clothes from Honolua Surf Company; board leashes and bags from Da Kine Hawaii; skateboards from Flexdex. Boys who surfed got a lot more for free. Even a little bit of sponsorship made the difference between surfing and not surfing. As rich a life as it seemed, among the bougainvillea and the green hills and the passionflowers of Hana, there was hardly any money. In the past few years the Hawaiian economy had sagged terribly, and Hana had never had much of an economy to begin with. Last year, the surfer moms in town held a fundraiser bake sale to send Theresa and two Hana boys to the national surfing competition in California.

Theresa said she was done surfing for the day. "The waves totally suck now," she said to Angie. "They're just real trash." They talked for a moment and agreed that Theresa should leave in the morning and spend the next day or two with her coach, Matt, at his house in Haiku, to prepare for the Hawaiian Amateur Surf Association contest that weekend at Ho'okipa Beach near Kahului. Logistics became the topic. One of the biggest riddles facing a surfer girl, especially a surfer girl in far-removed Hana, is how to get from point A to point B, particularly when carrying a large surfboard. The legal driving age in Hawaii is fifteen, but the probable car ownership age, unless you're wealthy, is much beyond that; also, it seemed that nearly every surfer kid I met in Maui lived in a single-parent, single- or no-car household in which spare drivers and vehicles were rare. I was planning to go back around the volcano anyway to see the contest, so I said I'd take Theresa and another surfer, Lilia

Boerner, with me, and someone else would make it from Hana to Haiku with their boards. That night I met Theresa, Angie, and Lilia and a few of their surfer friends at a take-out shop in town, and then I went to the room I'd rented at Joe's Rooming House. I stayed up late reading about how Christian missionaries had banned surfing when they got to Hawaii in the late 1800s, but how by 1908 general longing for the sport overrode spiritual censure and surfing resumed.[2] I dozed off with the history book in my lap and the hotel television tuned to a Sprint ad showing a Hawaiian man and his granddaughter running hand in hand into the waves.

〰〰〰〰〰

THE NEXT MORNING I met Lilia and Theresa at Koʻki Beach at eight, after they'd had a short session on the waves. When I arrived they were standing under a monkeypod tree beside a stack of backpacks. Both of them were soaking wet, and I realized then that a surfer is always in one of two conditions: wet or about to be wet. Also, they are almost always dressed in something that can go directly into the water: halter tops, board shorts, bikini tops, jeans. Lilia was twelve and a squirt, with a sweet, powdery face and round hazel eyes and golden fuzz on her arms and legs. She was younger and much smaller than Theresa, less plainly athletic but very game. Unlike Theresa, she was home-schooled, so she could surf all the time. So far Lilia was sponsored by a surf shop and by Matt Kinoshita's Kazuma Surfboards. She has a twin brother who was also a crafty surfer, but a year ago the two of them came upon their grandfather after he suffered a fatal tractor accident, and the boy hadn't competed since. Their family owned a large and prosperous organic fruit farm in Hana. I once asked Lilia if it was fun to live on a farm. "No," she said abruptly. "Too much fruit."

We took a back road from Hana to Haiku, as if the main road wasn't bad enough. The road edged around the back of the volcano, through sere yellow hills. The girls talked about surfing and about one surfer girl's mom, whom they described as a full bitch, and a surfer's dad, who according to Theresa "was a freak and a half because he took too much acid and he tweaked." I wondered if they had any other hobbies besides surfing. Lilia said she used to study hula.

"Is it fun?"

"Not if you have a witch for a teacher, like I did," she said. "Just *screaming* and *yelling* at us all the time. I'll never do hula again. Surfing's cooler, anyway."

"You're the man, Lilia," Theresa said tartly. "Hey, how close are we to Grandma's Coffee Shop? I'm starving." Surfers are always starving. They had eaten breakfast before they surfed; it was now only an hour or two later, and they were hungry again. They favor breakfast cereal, teri-yaki chicken, French fries, rice, ice cream, candy, and a Hawaiian specialty called Spam Masubi, which is a rice ball topped with a hunk of Spam and seaweed. If they suffered from the typical teenage girl obsession with their weight, they didn't talk about it and they didn't act like it. They were so active that whatever they ate probably melted away.

"We love staying at Matt's," Lilia said, "because he always takes us to Taco Bell." We came around the side of a long hill and stopped at Grandma's. Lilia ordered a garden burger and Theresa had an "I'm Hungry" sandwich with turkey, ham, and avocado. It was 10:30 a.m. As she was eating, Lilia said, "You know, the Olympics are going to have surfing, either in the year 2000 or 2004, for sure."

"I'm so on that, dude," Theresa said. "If I can do well in the nationals this year, then . . ." She swallowed the last of her sandwich. She told me that eventually she wanted to become an ambulance driver, and I could picture her doing it, riding on dry land the same waves of adrenaline that she rides now. I spent a lot of time trying to picture where these girls might be in ten years. Hardly any are likely to make it as pro surfers—even though women have made a place for themselves in pro surfing, the number who really make it is still small, and even though the Hana girls rule Maui surfing, the island's soft-shell waves and easygoing competitions have produced very few world-class surfers in recent years. It doesn't seem to matter to them. At various cultural moments, surfing has appeared as the embodiment of everything cool and wild and free; this is one of those moments. To be a girl surfer is even cooler, wilder, and more modern than being a guy surfer: Surfing has always been such a male sport that for a man to do it doesn't defy any perceived ideas; to be a girl surfer is to be all that surfing represents, *plus* the extra charge of being a girl in a tough guy's domain. To be a surfer girl in a cool place like Hawaii is perhaps the apogee of all that is cool and wild and modern and sexy and defiant. The Hana girls, therefore, exist at that highest point—the point where being brave, tan, capable, and independent, and having a real reason to wear all those surf-inspired clothes that other girls wear for fashion, is what matters completely. It is, though, just a moment. It must be hard to imagine an ordinary future and something other than a lunar calendar to consider if you've grown up in a small town in Hawaii, surfing all day and night, spending half your time on sand, thinking in terms of point breaks and barrels and roundhouse cutbacks. Or maybe they don't think about it at all. Maybe these girls are still young enough and in love enough with their lives that they have no special foreboding about their futures, no uneasy presentiment that the kind of life they are leading now might eventually have to end.

〰〰〰〰〰〰〰

MATT KINOSHITA LIVES in a fresh, sunny ranch at the top of a hill in Haiku. The house has a big living room with a fold-out couch and plenty of floor space. Often, one or two or ten surfer girls camp in his living room because they are in a competition that starts at seven the next morning, or because they are practicing intensively and it is too far to go back and forth from Hana, or because they want to plow through Matt's stacks of surfing magazines and Matt's library of surfing videos and Matt's piles of water sports clothing catalogs. Many of the surfer girls I met didn't live with their fathers, or in some cases didn't even have relationships with their fathers, so sometimes, maybe, they stayed at Matt's just because they were in the mood to be around a concerned older male. Matt was in his late twenties. As a surfer he was talented enough to compete on the world tour but had decided to skip it in favor of an actual life with his wife, Annie, and their baby son, Chaz. Now he was one of the best surfboard shapers on Maui, a coach, and head of a construction company with his dad. He sponsored a few grown-up surfers and still competed himself, but his preoccupation was with kids. *Surfing* magazine once asked him what he liked most about being a surfboard shaper, and he answered, "Always being around stoked groms!" He coached a stoked-grom boys' team as well as a stoked-grom girls' team. The girls' team was an innovation. There had been no girls' surfing team on Maui before Matt established his three years ago. There was no money in it for him—it actually cost him many thousands of dollars each year—but he loved to do it. He thought the girls were the greatest. The girls thought he was the greatest, too. In build, Matt looked a lot like the men in those old Hawaiian surfing prints—small, chesty, gravity-bound. He had perfect features and hair as shiny as an otter's. When he listened to the girls he kept his head tilted, eyebrows slightly raised, jaw set in a grin. Not like a brother, exactly—more like the cutest, nicest teacher at school, who could say stern, urgent things without their stinging. When I pulled into the driveway with the girls, Matt was in the yard loading surfboards into a pickup. "Hey, dudes," he called to Lilia and Theresa. "Where are your boards?"

"Someone's going to bring them tonight from Hana," Theresa said. She jiggled her foot. "Matt, come on, let's go surfing already."

"Hey, Lilia," Matt said. He squeezed her shoulders. "How're you doing, champ? Is your dad going to surf in the contest this weekend?"

Lilia shrugged and looked up at him solemnly. "Come on, Matt," she said. "Let's go surfing already. . . ."

〰〰〰〰〰〰

THE FIRST HEATS of the contest had right-handed waves, three or four feet high, silky but soft on the ends so that they collapsed into whitewash as they broke. You couldn't make much of an impression riding something like that, and one after another the Hana girls came out of the water scowling. "I couldn't get any kind of footing," Theresa said to Matt. "I was, like, so on it, but I looked like some kind of kook sliding around."

"My last wave was a full-out[3] closeout," Lilia said. She looked exasperated. "Hey, someone bust me a towel." She blotted her face. "I really blew it," she groaned. "I'm lucky if I even got five waves."

The girls were on the beach below the judges' stand, under Matt's cabana, along with Matt's boys' team and a number of kids he didn't sponsor but who liked hanging out with him more than with their own sponsors. The kids spun like atoms. They ran up and down the beach and stuffed sand in one another's shorts and fought over pieces of last night's chicken that Annie had packed for them in a cooler. During a break between heats, Gloria with the crazy hair strolled over and suddenly the incessant motion paused. This was like an imperial visitation. After all, Gloria was a seasoned-seeming nineteen-year-old who had just spent the year surfing the monstrous waves on Oahu's North Shore, plus she did occasional work for Rodney Kilborn, the contest promoter, plus she had a sea turtle tattooed on her ankle, and most important, according to the Hana girls, she was an absolutely dauntless bodyboarder who would paddle out into midsize waves, even farther out than a lot of guys would go.

"Hey, haoles!" Gloria called out. She hopped into the shade of the cabana. That day, her famous hair was woven into a long red braid that hung over her left shoulder. Even with her hair tamed, Gloria was an amazing looking person. She had a hardy build, melon-colored skin, and a wide, round face speckled with light brown freckles. Her voice was light and tinkly, and had that arched, rising-up, quizzical inflection that made everything she said sound like a jokey, good-natured question. "Hey, Theresa?" she said. "Hey, girl, you got it going *on*? You've got great wave strategy? Just keep it up, yeah? Oh, Elise? You should paddle out harder? Okay? You're doing great, yeah? And Christie?" She looked around for a surfer girl named Christie Wiekey, who got a ride in at four that morning from Hana. "Hey, Christie?" Gloria said when she spotted her. "You should go out further, yeah? That way you'll be in better position for your wave, okay? You guys are the greatest, *seriously?* You rule, yeah? You totally rule, yeah?"

At last the junior women's division preliminary results were posted. Theresa, Elise, and two other girls on Matt's team made the cut, as well as a girl whom Matt knew but didn't coach. Lilia had not made it. As soon as she heard, she tucked her blond head in the crook of her elbow and cried. Matt sat with her and talked quietly for a while, and then one by one the other girls drifted up to her and murmured consoling things, but she was inconsolable. She hardly spoke for the rest of the afternoon until the open men's division, which Matt had entered. When his heat was announced, she lifted her head and brushed her hand across her swollen eyes. "Hey, Matt!" she called as he headed for the water. "Rip it for the girls!"

<hr/>

THAT NIGHT, a whole pack of them slept at Matt's—Theresa, Lilia, Christie, Elise, Monica Cardoza from Lahaina, and sisters from Hana named Iris Moon and Lily Morningstar, who had arrived too late to surf in the junior women's preliminaries. There hadn't been enough entrants in the open women's division to require preliminaries, so the competition was going to be held entirely on Sunday, and Iris would be able to enter. Lily wasn't planning to surf at all, but as long as she was able to get a ride out of Hana she took it. This added up to too many girls at Matt's for Cheyne's liking, so he had fled to another boy's house for the night. Lilia was still blue. She was quiet through dinner, and then as soon as she finished she slid into her sleeping bag and pulled it over her head. The other girls stayed up for hours, watching videos and slamming one another with pillows and talking about the contest. At some point someone asked where Lilia was. Theresa shot a glance at her sleeping bag and said quietly, "Did you guys see how upset she got today? I'm like, 'Take it easy, Lilia!' and she's all 'Leave me *alone*, bitch.' So I'm like, 'Whatever.'"

They whispered for a while about how sensitive Lilia was, about how hard she took it if she didn't win, about how she thought one of them had wrecked a bathing suit she'd loaned her, about how funny it was that she even *cared* since she had so many bathing suits and for that matter always had money for snacks, which most of them did not. When I said a Hana girl could have a pure surfing adolescence, I knew it was part daydream, because no matter how sweet the position of a beautiful, groovy Hawaiian teenager might be in the world of perceptions, the mean measures of the human world don't ever go away. There would always be something else to want and be denied. More snack money, even. Lilia hadn't been sleeping. Suddenly she bolted out of her sleeping bag and screamed, "Fuck you, I *hate* you stupid bitches!" and stormed toward the bathroom, slugging Theresa on the way.

〰〰〰〰〰〰

THE WAVES ON SUNDAY came from the left, and they were stiff and smallish, with crisp, curling lips. The men's and boys' heats were narrated over the PA system, but during the girls' and women's heats the announcer was silent, and the biggest racket was the cheering of Matt's team. Lilia had toughened up since last night. Now she seemed grudgeless but remote. Her composure made her look more grown up than twelve. When I first got down to the beach she was staring out at the waves, chewing a hunk of dried papaya and sucking on a candy pacifier. A few of the girls were far off to the right of the break where the beach disappeared and lustrous black rocks stretched into the water. Christie told me later that they hated being bored more than anything in the world and between heats they were afraid they might be getting a little weary, so they decided to perk themselves up by playing on the rocks. It had worked. They charged back from the rocks shrieking and panting. "We got all *dangerous*," she said. "We jumped off this huge rock into the water. We almost got killed, which was great." Sometimes watching them I couldn't believe that they could head out so offhandedly into the ocean—*this* ocean, which had rolls of white water coming in as fast as you could count them, and had a razorblade reef hidden just below the surface, and was full of sharks. The girls, on the other hand, couldn't believe I'd never surfed—never ridden a wave standing up or lying down, never cut back across the whitewash and sent up a lacy veil of spray, never felt a longboard slip out from under me and then felt myself pitched forward and under for that immaculate, quiet, black instant when all the weight in the world presses you down toward the ocean bottom until the moment passes and you get spat up on the beach. I explained I'd grown up in Ohio, where there is no surf, but that didn't satisfy them; what I didn't say was that I'm not sure that at fifteen I had the abandon or the indomitable sense of myself that you seem to need in order to look at this wild water and think, I will glide on top of those waves. Theresa made me promise I'd try to surf at least once someday. I promised, but this Sunday was not going to be that day. I wanted to sit on the sand and watch the end of the contest, to see the Hana girls take their divisions, including Lilia, who placed third in the open women's division, and Theresa, who won the open women's and the junior women's division that day. Even if it was just a moment, it was a perfect one, and who wouldn't choose it over never having the moment at all? When I left Maui that afternoon, my plane circled over Ho'okipa, and I wanted to believe I could still see them down there and always would see them down there, snapping back and forth across the waves.

CHAPTER 58

"Lost Horizons: Surfer Colonialism in the 21st Century" (2002)

Steve Barilotti
1955–

A photojournalist and editor at *Surfer* magazine for nearly twenty years, Steve Barilotti has logged a good portion of his life in exotic surf locales like Bali that he describes in the following article. After an absence of six years, Barilotti returned to the fabled waves at Bali only to experience the fallout from the global tourism industry, a significant portion of which (at least in Bali) includes surfers on their continual search for the perfect, uncrowded wave. More than anything else, Barilotti charts here in thoughtful, dynamic prose nothing less than the transformation of surfing—and surfers themselves—from adolescence to maturity, from a pastime that begins in youthful hedonism to a global recreation whose members must acknowledge how profoundly and often detrimentally their practices and ideals impact other cultures. As Barilotti updates readers on the numbers of surfers worldwide and such newfound institutions as Surf Aid, he ponders the future of the growing surf tourism industry and the opportunities (and responsibilities) its affluent members have to act as beacons for positive social change.

> *"All is clouded by desire, Arjuna—as fire by smoke, as a mirror by dust . . . through these it blinds the soul."*
> —Lord Krishna, Bhagavad-Gita

MADE, THE KUTA HACK, broke down the price list for me as we crept along Jalan Legian in the crush of early-evening traffic.

"I know nice place, very clean, in Sanur," opined Made ("Mahday"), craning his broad grinning face around to assess me. A small florid Balinese man in his early 30s, his flat, filed teeth sported a single gold incisor that winked at me like a lighthouse beacon. "Girls very clean, very young, very clean all the time. I take you—you get very good one-hour price. Get massage, karaoke, jiggy jig, shower. I bring you back to hotel after. Or I bring girl to hotel. But maybe problem for you. Better you come with me."

For diversion, I did the math. The cost for the evening's erotic entertainment came to 100,000 rupiah—roughly $10 not including the beers served in the brothel's in-room minibar. I asked why the girls would want to sing to me. Made giggled at my sexual illiteracy. By way of explanation he mimed his fist into a microphone and made a universal head-bobbing sign. His earnest googly-eyed leer broke me up.

Bali's burgeoning sex industry had taken off markedly since I'd last visited Kuta six years ago. Every cab driver I encountered, it seemed, had become a skilled tout for one of the countless brothels that had sprung up around Sanur and Denpasar. Balinese sex tours are advertised via "Asian gentlemen's clubs" on the net to Tokyo salary men and any solo surfer weaving home late from the Double Six or Sari Club is fair game to one of the ubiquitous moped whores working the tourist losmans along Poppies Lane. The Indonesian AIDS rate has understandably tripled since 1999.

A dense equatorial darkness flowed up the bustling boulevard as the neon signs powered up and sputtering scooters darted in and out of traffic like feeder fish. Jalan Legian, Kuta's main business conduit, is a hustling Dickensian warren of curio shops, bars, restaurants, massage parlors, tattoo studios, Internet cafes and cut-rate backpacker hostels that seems to run on dollars and pure low-rent desire.

Kuta Beach started out as a drowsy little fishing village in the 1930s catering to a small number of vacationing European colonialists. Its surf potential was discovered by Australian surfers in the mid 1960s. Since then it has morphed into a fully developed surf ghetto on a par with Huntington Beach or the North Shore. Every major surf house—Quiksilver, Rusty, Billabong, Volcom—has a marquee shop flying giant banners to lure in the overseas tourist dollar. Surf imagery and fetishes abound—from countless racks of surf-logo tank tops to a life-size fiberglass Kodak wave sited outside the infamous Tubes bar.

Made's cab edged towards the traffic light. We passed throngs of Japanese tourists milling outside the three-tiered McDonald's. Ronald McDonald had been transmogrified into a squat little concrete demon sporting a lurid smirk and an apropos set of devil fangs. A nearby video arcade bathed everything in flashing red epileptic lights. Balinese teenagers wearing sunglasses scowled from their mopeds while bobbing their heads to Metallica. A street hawker wearing a Billabong t-shirt sidled up to the window. Grinning conspiratorially, he proffered a pungent brown lump of hashish in one palm, a tab of Ecstasy in the other.

Kuta is a socio-anthropologist's dream research thesis. Premise: four thousand years of ancient animistic squat culture smacks straight into Western tech-heavy materialism in the late 20th century. The paradoxes fairly slap you upside the head.

But rather than the West automatically implanting the flesh-eating maggot of consumerism in Bali's paralyzed carcass, the Balinese have somehow managed to transfigure their belief system to mix high-tech wizardry into part of their daily religious rituals. Sanskrit cyber prayers are carried up to the gods via incense and sat links.

I was back in Bali for a few days to regain my cultural land legs after a fortnight spent boat exploring an overlooked portion of northern Indonesia. Photographer Ted Grambeau, myself and three professional surfers had sailed a 60-foot catamaran a thousand nautical miles over the top of Indonesia through shallow reef-spiked waters that hadn't been adequately charted since WWII.

To score a decent uncrowded wave, we'd endured seasickness, malarial mosquitoes, pirate threat, suffocating humidity, and the occasional warning shot over our bow from some understandably nervous survivors of a recent jihad massacre. Afterwards I learned that the US State Department had issued a blanket warning against any travel by US citizens to the region. The entire trip—underwritten by *Surfer* magazine, the charter company and two major surfwear sponsors—had cost roughly $10,000.

In the space of ten days, however, we had managed to sift out a handful of above-average surf breaks and survey a dozen more with promise. We'd passed dozens of uninhabited atolls and met naked nappy-headed Melanesian villagers who were as intrigued with our pale sun-burned skin as they were with our bizarre mission to ride the waves breaking near their fishing reef.

As proof I had a pile of log notes and damp coffee-stained charts back in my sea bag back at the hotel.

But the maps—and to varying degrees large parts of my account—were to be used for my back reference only. I'd promised Ted, who maintains a strict no-tell policy on the places he explores, that I would not get any more specific than the region known in Dutch colonial days as the "Celebes." Much of my job as a travelling surf journalist these days involves cleverly encoding the exact geographic co-ordinates of the places we discover while at the same time attempting to give a reasonably truthful rendering of the coastlines and cultures we encounter.

Of course, the word gets out. It always does. And ironically not by us, the crass media exploiters, but usually by the same local guide who made us swear a blood oath of secrecy. Like an old prospector who's finally hit the motherlode, surfers who score pristine remote locations are compelled after a few rounds back at the saloon to brag about their good luck to the wrong hombre. Maps get drawn on the back of a bar napkin and soon another gold rush is on.

"So for you, my friend, I give you one-time good friend price . . ."

On Made's dash, next to a sun-faded photo of his family, was the ubiquitous palm-tray offering of sweets and incense for the ordinary gods of commerce. Through Hinduism's wondrously cosmic balancing act Made was able to rationalize being both a spiritual man, a father and a pimp. Sex to the Balinese is as natural as any other body function so they find it amusing that tourist men should be so obsessed with it. And besides, reasoned Made, all the girls were Javanese anyway—bred from birth to be whores of one kind or another. The Balinese can smile in a hundred different ways and in the end give you exactly what they feel is appropriate.

As Made chattered on trying to close the sale I settled into the old Toyota's weary seats and savored the intense radiant heat rising from my sore sunburned back.

Earlier that day I'd surfed Uluwatu for the first time. It was a random touchstone moment of long-postponed exotica—akin to pulling over to take a leak on the motorway down to Cornwall and suddenly encountering Stonehenge. I'd wanted to surf Uluwatu since first seeing shots in 1975 of Gerry Lopez and Rory Russell streaking along Uluwatu's green roping walls in the shadow of an ancient Hindu temple. Uluwatu, or at least the idea of Uluwatu, represented the ultimate outpost of the surfing universe, a serene dream world so far removed from my pre-packaged Southern California existence as to be on another planet altogether.

But after a decade of sporadically covering the ASP tour and visiting a chain of rutted-out surf paradises I'd subsequently abandoned the dream. I'd heard of the tawdry development, severe overcrowding and the rancorous, sometimes violent localism that had metastasized around Uluwatu.

But an unseasonable winter south swell had caught most of the locals napping, and in a pique of surf lust and rationalization I hired a bemo for the day and headed up the narrow windy road leading to the craggy Bukit peninsula. As we pulled into the dirt lot of the newly constructed Uluwatu Resort I was greeted with the sight of endless four-to-six foot lines bending into the Suluban Bay bight. A cursory wax up and suddenly I was down the trail and paddling out of the same ghostly limestone cave that Rusty Miller and Steven Cooney—Uluwatu's first surfers—had ventured out of 30 years ago.

No more than a dozen surfers had chanced the trip from Kuta that morning so the lineup was eerily deserted. The sun, even at 10 a.m., was searing through my white rashguard like a laser and the glare off the green steamy water made little fluorescent worms of light dance in my periphery. Surrealistic glowing waves looped over and spun down the reef at an elegant pace. It was a scene of such intense phosphorescent beauty as to approach a hallucination. After a short paddle up the line I found a likely takeoff zone near a small pod of Brazilian surfers. I waited for an auspicious wave with a foreseeable end to stand up, and stroked into my dream. . . .

"So, you not like girl? That's okay, I have boy. Very good massage, very strong, good all-night price. Bagus!"

We pulled up to my hotel, a three-story thatched affair brimming with chubby Australian girls seared from a day by the pool and sporting freshly beaded hair and henna tattoos. I paid three dollars for a two-dollar fare and Made's tooth danced in the lobby lights. He handed me a card with a cel number on it and told me to call later if I changed my mind.

"Hey maybe you hungry. I know good fish restaurant in Jimbaran. Best night-market price. I take you now, okay?"

> *In the bye and bye, we float. Float over the politics, the guns,*
> *the disease, the corruption and the relentless need. We throw*
> *off the anchors of humanity, of caring, and drift on a sea of*
> *bland numb indifference searching for a transient high in*
> *surfing. By not caring, we float. Heather T., Santa Cruz*
> —Bathroom grafitti at Tubes Bar, Kuta, Bali.

Long before every Silicon Valley startup began using surf imagery to hawk their decidedly prosaic products, novelist and erstwhile surfer Jack London divined surfing's appeal as an effective marketing tool. "Take surfboarding for instance . . . " wrote London in 1916, ". . . a California real estate agent, with that one asset could make the barren desert of the Sahara into an oasis for kings."

His claim was no doubt based on direct experience. His friend George Freeth, the famed Irish-Hawaiian waterman and surfer, was employed by railroad-baron Henry Huntington in 1907 to give surfing exhibitions at the newly built Hotel Redondo in Redondo Beach. The upscale Angelenos, who had ridden out from the Los Angeles basin on Huntington's Red Line trolley, were suitably impressed by Freeth's daring mastery of the "Polynesian Arts." After the show people were exhorted to buy one of the small holiday lots staked out on the coastal dunes. They sold out quickly. Huntington's other land scheme down the coast, Huntington Beach, would later bear the honorific, "Surf City."

Surfing Macroeconomic Theory: Waves attract surfers. Surfing attracts energy. Energy attracts people. People attract capital. Investment attracts development. And so it goes. A quick survey from outer space would likely show an inordinate number of major coastal cities expanding outwards in concentric waves from a quality surf break.

Self-affirming mysticism aside, there is something instinctually compelling about watching a fellow human hitching a ride on such a wild avatar of primeval energy. Or, as Tom Morey puts it: "the heart loves the shape of a wave."

With surfers, however, the disembodied platonic love of nature quickly turns to an eerily lopsided obsession. In their insatiable quest to find uncrowded quality surf surfers have trekked to the most remote spots of the planet via every conveyance possible. They've braved civil war, disease, bandits, shipwreck, grizzly attack and rackety flying deathtraps flown by inebriated pilots.

But in the wake of the explorers inevitably follow the settlers. Outposts are set up, then villages, eventually full-blown surfburbs. While the baseline activity of surfing is essentially non-exploitative, once surfers set up a collective around a marquee surf break such as Jeffreys Bay or Uluwatu, the impacts of human colonialisation—trash, roads, erosion, water pollution, development, environmental degradation, resource depletion—inevitably follows. In our blind zeal to set up insular surf enclaves, we parachute advanced technologies into third-world economies and set up brittle unsustainable infrastructures. The list of soiled third-world surf paradises—Cloud Nine, Tamarindo, Nias, Puerto Escondido, Baja Malibu, Cactus—is long and growing.

"Ironically these refugees from modernity carry their disease [of escapism] with them," writes anthropologist John McCarthy about the adventure-oriented tourist explosion in Indonesia. "Anticipating change, tourists race to remote places to out-pace the tourism frontier. Yet as they travel to isolated places, they carry the frontier of development outwards: Lombok, Sulawesi, Flores, Maluku and Irian Jaya. Backpackers and independent travelers, the advance scouts of tourist development, usually discover the locations which later become popular resorts."

On Nias, the effect of surf tourism on the Niah, a proud warlike tribe once notorious for their headhunting and elaborate costumed rituals, has sped the erosion and disappearance of traditional ways. Twenty-five

years of cashed-up westerners tramping through Lagundi village has se-
duced the local youth with lurid Baywatch fantasies of the North American high life. A surf ghetto of ramshackle losmans now line the point. Raw
sewage from the losmans seeps into the bay and the beach is littered with
plastic debris. The severe crowding in the lineup makes for a testy scene.
Localism among the local surf kids has reared its myopic little head. Bla-
tant drop-ins have become rampant and often backed up with insidious
death threats.

Peter Reeves, one of the first regulars to live at Nias for extended
stints in the early 1980s, reflected on surfing's mixed blessing to the Niah
villagers, a subsistence culture suddenly yanked into 20th century consumerism by well-meaning but clueless young surf tourists.

"Surfing has certainly boosted the Lagundi Bay economy but I
feel it's come at a huge price," said Reeves. "The alcoholism, gambling,
crime, and on my last trip there, the small kid I taught to surf in 1981 is
now a pimp for working girls on the point. I wonder if the simple life of
harvesting coconuts and rice would have been a better destiny for these
people?"

Surfers pride themselves on being a global culture. The beach is
not a place, it is said, but a state of mind; a transitional, highly porous
border between the primeval terrestrial and aquatic. Surfers cross through
this evolutionary no-man's land with ease.

But surfers seem ill-equipped to handle the big questions of geo-
politics and globalization. The surfing gestalt is based on cool indiffer-
ence to concerns of politics, religion or class. Surfing is one of the most
viciously democratic endeavors around, wherein the neurotic confines of
arrested adolescence one's social-desirability index can yaw wildly based
solely on the strength of one's cutback.

Yet by our very gregarious roaming nature we find ourselves in
the frontlines of some of the most fundamental problems facing the human race today—wealth inequity, resource distribution, racism, genocide,
religious conflict. We are not divorced from this world or its problems. In
fact, as surfers we often find ourselves enmeshed in the heart of conflict.

In 1965, most U.S. surfers would have been hard pressed to correctly pronounce apartheid, much less explain a particularly clumsy and
brutal form of institutionalized racism rammed down the collective throats
of a nation that was four-fifths non-white.

Yet, by the closing reel of the *Endless Summer*, many U.S. surfers
were scrambling to their atlases to book a flight to a far-away continent
they knew little about other than it had a perfect empty Malibu-type right
peeling off at some spot called Cape St. Francis. A few years later, Jeffreys

Bay was discovered, and the international surfing gold rush was on. Apartheid simply came with the scenery—along with game parks and Zambezi sharks.

Not surprisingly, it's been observed by outsiders that many surfers tend to carry a remarkably narrow view of the world around with them—judging a people or its culture solely by what they don't have rather than what they may have to offer. Most surfers travel not to experience another culture but to find waves similar to their home breaks but without the crowds. In many cases the indigenous people are an obstacle or a friendly nuisance to sidestep on the way to the water.

Every surfer carries a naïve secret hope of finding the Forgotten Island of Santosha—a utopian warm-water idyll where the waves are perfectly shaped and most of all blessedly uncrowded. Accommodation is Spartan but elegant and includes all the latest consumer entertainment electronics. Add in pretty girls to make burritos and banana-rum smoothies and the fantasy is complete. A simple escapist dream of the vaguely dissatisfied Western bourgeoisie. . . .

So how does one create sustainable surf tourism that benefits the surfer, the local, and does as little damage to the environment as possible?

In the case of Bali and Nias, unfettered access has led to hodge-podge development, lineup crowding, and a general degradation of the environment and surfing experience. At G-land, the two camps are capable of accommodating up to 180 people. Surfers are paying an average of $100 a day for the privilege of sharing the Moneytrees lineup with 60 other surfers. In the Mentawais there are currently up to 30 boats plying the waters, each capable of holding six to 12 surfers. Boat-in surfers pay up to $250 a day to surf perfect empty waves at a Kodak-friendly spot like HT's, but within minutes of another boat or two pulling up can have a crowd factor that exceeds the one they left back in California or Kanagawa.

Tavarua Island resort, now approaching its 20th anniversary, provides a case study on the long-term impact and benefits of resort-style surf tourism. The founding team, Americans Scott Funk and Dave Clark, discovered the surf potential of Tavarua and nearby Cloudbreak in the late 1970s. Seeing the possibility of a surf camp they secured exclusive use of the island and the surrounding reefs from the local villages (Cuvu, Nabila, Momi). They set up a long-term lease arrangement where the villages received an income and the guarantee of a certain number of jobs as resort help.

While there have been sporadic dustups over wave rights and repeated charges of yuppie "ego-tourism," Cuvu tribal chief Ratu Sakiusa Nadruku ("Druku") asserts that the lease arrangement has benefited the villages overall. They now have electricity, improved sanitation and better health and dental care due to the efforts of the Surf Docs who have worked closely with the camp since its inception.

The Mentawais have proven a fascinating test case on the cumulative impact of the information age. Advances in satellite navigation, internet advertising and digital-media have compressed the exploitation curve from decades down to a few years. Currently, three main companies run charters to the Mentawais—Rick Cameron's Great Breaks International, Martin Daly's Indies Trader Marine Adventures, and Paul King's venerable Surf Tour Company. A smattering of other small operators have also joined the industry including some local fisherman-turned-tour-guides.

How lucrative is the Mentawai trade? Thirty boats, each capable of carrying eight passengers or more at an average $150-250 a day can potentially generate over $48,000 a day. Conservative total revenues at half-capacity for a six-month season topped $4.5 million. Last year, an estimated $325,000 was spent on last year's Op/*Surfer* magazine Boat Challenge contest, with $90,000 in prize money. Countless photos generated from various Mentawai boat trips are used in ad and editorial to promote the surfers sponsored by multimillion-dollar surfwear companies.

While the boat charters are relatively benign compared to the multinational loggers decimating the Siberut rainforests or the Indonesian government's transmigration schemes, they've proven at best to be symbiotic parasites. Some of the wealthiest cultures in the world are using the surrounding reefs as aquatic playgrounds while at the same time returning little or nothing to the host cultures that exist a few hundred yards onshore. Sam George, *Surfer* magazine's editor, observed during the last OP Boat Challenge contest held in the Mentawais—a delux catered media event where pros were pampered with back massages and air-conditioned cabins—that "we are mining this place."

The Mentawai people, only a couple generations out of the Stone Age, are some of the most impoverished in the world. The head of a family of four makes less than $15 a month harvesting copra. Health conditions are appalling. Half the villagers are infected with malaria and the chances of any Mentawai child surviving measles, tetanus, hepatitis, tuberculosis or polio to his or her fifth birthday is the literal flip of a coin.

Surf Aid International, a surfer-run NGO, has been struggling to provide basic health care and disease prevention to the Mentawai villagers for the last two years. Surf Aid was started by New Zealand M.D./surfer Dave Jenkins who had a crisis of conscience while surfing in the Mentawais a few years ago. Together with Andrew Griffiths and a small staff of local nurses Jenkins has run a shoestring clinic from Taileleu, a large village on the main Mentawai island of Siberut. His most pressing task is basic mosquito and malaria control, training local nurses and shamans to diagnose malaria and giving out mosquito nets as funds trickle in to buy them.

Jenkins, who has been working without a salary since he started Surf Aid, says although at times he feels like despairing at the monumental task ahead of him, he is constantly astounded by the gracious, happy spirit of the Mentawai people that seems to transcend their precarious existence.

"We believe that everyone who partakes in the surfing culture, be it from reading, writing or advertising in a magazine, watching or producing a video or wearing a label, has a role to play in helping these people," says Jenkins. "We know that most surfers care—but in the past have lacked a relevant vehicle for helping."

To date, however, Surf Aid has garnered less than $8,000 from the surf industry worldwide. Rick Cameron's permit scheme to tax surfers five dollars per day per surfer to benefit the Mentawai people was met with vehement opposition from his competitors.

Of the main Mentawai tour operators, only Cameron has attempted—at least on paper—to talk the politically-correct talk of the sustainable surf tourism. Although he has been traduced by his competitors in the surfing media, Cameron has gone to great lengths to outline the plight of the Mentawai people and has helped Surf Aid with in-kind donations and free advertising. He's also developed the Mentawai Sanctuary program to set up a code of socially responsible ecotourism to ensure that real benefits go to the Mentawaians while protecting the area from over-development. Both Cameron and Paul King have secured permits to build land-based surf resorts, which would give them exclusive right, à la Tavarua, to the waves within a designated radius of the camps.

Is it too big a leap to ask surfers—a culture that honors the antihero maverick and treasures the bare-assing rebel—to adopt a socially responsible attitude? Perhaps. Then again, things change as one becomes one's parents. And who's to say one can't bare-ass the world by doing the right thing? Perhaps the first step is to find one's personal bili bili board and pass on some stoke.

Pierce Flynn, Surfrider Foundation's former executive director, pondered whether surfers are up to the task of managing their own future at a *Surfer* magazine round table discussion on wave rights.

"The question is, are surfers maturing as a tribe, as coastal stewards?" asked Flynn. "Do we have the ability to look long term and ask

'What is it we want for our kids to have? How do we stop the trend among surfers to leave devastation behind? How do we balance the freedom of surfing with long-term preservation of the real values that we're all after, that include other people too?'"

We live in the most amazing time to be a surfer. The whole of technological advances in design, materials, travel, swell prediction and athletic performance are all just a keystroke away. Surfers, once considered fringe characters akin to outlaw bikers, are now integrated role models in mainstream society and have infiltrated every occupational niche from teachers to firemen to space-shuttle astronauts and Nobel Prize-winning gene scientists. We have our own culture, our own dress, our own music and art, even our own language. And to its credit or peril, everybody, it seems, wants to be us.

In 1984 pop sociologist Alvin Toffler wrote in *The Third Wave*: "Surfers are the signposts of the future," meaning that surfers defined a new paradigm of existence—aligning themselves not behind a flag or a race, but a rare, shared passion.

Surfing, with its race of stoked entrepreneurial mavericks, has proven a dynamic and adaptable culture. With over four million surfers on the planet one could only speculate what might be attainable if we actually worked together. The world might be ruled by surfers. What a profoundly disturbing thought.

But at the same time. Tom Morey—inventor, jazz musician and surfing's own barefoot futurist—offered this perspective:

"The art of living, surfing life as it comes, without trying to capture and hold the waves, just riding them. Living a balanced life whereby one doesn't have excess fat, possessions, wealth and takes it day by day. All of us just surfing along, enjoying each other's company and not at all paying any attention to religions, nations, states, cities or any of the rest of the man-made gizmos."

"That's where we are supposed to be."

CHAPTER 59

"Winterland: Fred Van Dyke, and the Blissful, Stressful, Unpredictable Life of the Older Surfer" (2005)

Matt Warshaw

1960–

A former professional surfer and editor at *Surfer* magazine, Matt Warshaw has authored half a dozen books on the sport, including *Maverick's: The Story of Big-Wave Surfing* (2000), *Surf Movie Tonite!* (2005), and the momentous *The Encyclopedia of Surfing* (2003). In "Winterland," Warshaw tackles in his honest, thoughtful way the troughs and peaks of what it means for one of the sport's most recognized names to confront—and at times condemn—the image he created of himself as a big-wave surfer. Warshaw's article, along with the *Surfing for Life* documentary he mentions below, are a reflection of how a generation that established surfing as a youth-oriented activity in the 1950s and 1960s is now helping to redefine surfing's image to encompass the realities of an increasingly aging demographic.

OLDER SURFERS ARE NOW MORE INTERESTING *to me than younger surfers. I don't know exactly when this happened—ten or 15 years ago, somewhere back in the early '90s—but whenever it was, whenever the scales tipped, at that moment I suppose I became an older surfer myself. I'm still a TransWorld Surf subscriber. I check periodically to see how Andy's world title run is going. Yesterday I downloaded a QuickTime clip of Jamie O'Brien at Pipeline and ran it three times in a row, quietly rocking back and forth in my office chair like an autistic child. But for the most part my connection to the younger generation has become small and narrow, almost vestigial, like my connection to bars and clubs, or new British import bands. As it should be. Andy and Jamie and the rest of surfing's hot young guns are all conviction, certainty, and rude good health, while I'm 45 with sore knees, a growing liver spot on my left cheek, eyebrow hairs that are beginning to corkscrew out over the tops of my glasses, and a creeping doubt about what it's meant to devote that big of a chunk of my life to surfing. I'm still inspired by younger surfers. I'm still at times, and usually to a pretty shameful end, trying to surf like I'm 25. But I'm paying more and more attention to older surfers—for inspiration of a different sort, and for reassurance that our version of the life aquatic hasn't been a waste of time.*

I visited Fred Van Dyke in Hawaii last January for a lot of reasons. He tells great stories about surfing Santa Cruz in the pre-wetsuit era. He rode Waimea the first day it was surfed, and more or less created the Duke contest. Van Dyke told a Sports Illustrated reporter in 1965 that most big-wave riders were "latent homosexuals," which is still surfing's funniest quote—made even better by the fact that Van Dyke has spent 40 years trying to explain that he didn't mean it that way. I'd fly to Hawaii just to get Fred to wrestle with that one again.

But mostly I went to Hawaii because I watched two slightly different versions of the 2001 documentary Surfing for Life. *I saw the PBS-aired version where Van Dyke and another half-dozen senior surfers with twinkly eyes and big smiles talk about riding waves into their 60s, 70s, even 80s. And I saw a working print where Van Dyke suddenly begins to cry, calls himself a "macho tough surfer" in a disparaging voice, then says he's "scared shitless" about growing older and dying. That scene didn't make the final cut. I wanted to see what Van Dyke thought about that, and what he thought about becoming an older surfer. Everything, surfing included, is more complicated for me at 45 than 25. How about 30 years from now? Fred, what's it like?*

Seventy-two, Van Dyke tells me with a sigh, was easy. Seventy-five is hard. It *looks* hard. He was in poor health for much of 2003 and 2004, and the effects linger in his eyes, his build, his skin, his posture. Four years ago he posed for a *Prevention* magazine article, bare-chested and biceps flaring, surfboard cocked against a fat-free hip, and the slightly agog caption read, "In his 70s—yes, his 70s!" Van Dyke at 71 looked like a super-fit man of 50. At 75 he looks 75.

We're sitting in the living room of Van Dyke's airy one-story house in Lanikai, a palmy cul-de-sac neighborhood in Kailua, adjacent to a near-waveless bay on the east side of Oahu. It's a comfortable room, with white throw rugs, a few semi-abstract art pieces, bright tropical flowers in a glass vase. I ask Van Dyke who got the house looking so good, him or his wife Joan, already knowing the answer, and he doesn't even glance around. "It's all Joan," he answers. "Or 99% Joan."

Van Dyke's soft voice has also changed over the past few years, becoming slower and thicker, although his conversational stamina is fine. He begins with an overview. Surfing, he says, was his real career—more so than the 32 years he spent as a primary and secondary school teacher. He pulls a dismissive face when talking about the various "living legend" surf events that he occasionally attends, but "living legend" nonetheless rolls comfortably from his mouth, and he plainly enjoys being included with Greg Noll, Ricky Grigg, Buzzy Trent, Peter Cole, George Downing, and the rest of the Eisenhower-age surfers from California and Hawaii who more or less invented big-wave riding. (The preface to Van Dyke's 1989 book, *30 Years of Riding the World's Biggest Waves*" takes the "legend" motif a lot further, as Santa Cruz writer James Hall first compares Van Dyke to Babe Ruth, Charles Lindbergh and Jack Dempsey, then says he has the intellectual traits of an "ancient philosopher.") Scenes from big-wave surfing's Genesis story are right there on Van Dyke's living room wall, which is covered with oversized wood-framed photographs from the glory days, including a 1959 color shot of him at the bottom of a heaving Waimea wall, arms extended, fists clenched, determination stamped on his features, and looking like a cross between Charles Atlas and Montgomery Clift.

But if surfing made Fred Van Dyke, it nearly unmade him as well, turning him into a bad husband, a so-so father, and an unreliable worker. The sport owned him for a long time, he says. Now it doesn't, but even so he keeps some distance. He's healthy enough these days to surf, and has two boards hanging from the rafters of his garage, but he rarely gets in the water, and hasn't been hardcore about it for years. I ask when he last went surfing, and he first says "a long time ago," then pauses and says it's been a few months, then changes his mind again and says he went week before last. He shakes his head, frustrated, as he often is these days at his balky memory. "Surfing was my life for so many years," he says, dismissing the question of when he last got in the water and moving to the bigger point, "now I've just found other things." . . .

Fred Van Dyke landed in Honolulu during the summer of 1955. At 26, he was old enough to have missed the rock-and-roll-fueled youth culture launch—old enough, in fact, by the day's standards, to be thought of as early middle-aged. A few weeks earlier he'd been interviewed in Palo Alto by the visiting president of Oahu's private and moderately exclusive Punahou School, who gave the athletic, sun-darkened teacher a narrow look and asked if he was a surfer. Van Dyke shook his head and lied, saying "I've tried it, but it's not a serious part of my life," and got a job teaching seventh-grade math and science. New forces were in play. Van Dyke had married three years earlier, and his wife had given birth to a severely retarded daughter, who was soon given up to foster care. The experience badly damaged the marriage, and Van Dyke hoped that the move to Hawaii would help. It didn't, and the couple soon divorced.

By this time, Van Dyke had been surfing for five years. He was fit and tremendously determined, but not possessed of any great natural talent. Gene Van Dyke was the best surfer in the family, closely followed by Peter, seven years Fred's junior, who was a powerful all-arounder with a flamboyant drop-knee cutback. "Fred was sort of tense out there," Ricky Grigg told me over the phone when I asked about Van Dyke's surfing ability, "like he was ready to get wiped out pretty much all the time." Peter Cole said the same thing, that Fred "was kind of stiff." Cole was a nationally ranked middle-distance swimmer at Stanford when he met Van Dyke at Steamer Lane in '53. Five years later he also left for Hawaii on a big-wave mission and moved into Van Dyke's Waikiki house, as did Grigg—a fellow Stanford alum and future Duke Invitational winner. Cole and Van Dyke lived together for three years; Grigg roomed with them for a year, as did Buzzy Trent, another expat California big-wave rider.

"Fred has short muscles, and couldn't paddle or swim as fast as a lot of us," Cole continued. "There were times when we'd wipe out on the same wave, more or less at the same time, and I'd make it to the surface five or ten seconds before Fred." (Van Dyke himself never seemed to think much of his surfing ability. "I was becoming adept at riding Steamer Lane, it being my favorite spot," he wrote in his 2001 memoir *Once Upon Abundance*. "I took off on the shoulder of a twelve-foot wave, made it to the bottom, turned and wiped out." Ricky Grigg, the most cocksure big-wave surfer of the era—no mean accomplishment in a field that includes Buzzy Trent and Greg Noll—couldn't write that sentence about himself if you put a gun to his head.)

Van Dyke rode big Makaha early during his first winter in Hawaii, and the experience was so powerful that the guiding principle of his life for the next 20 years was to be there, every time, without fail, when the surf came up. He obsessed over how it felt to transition into the flats after a huge drop, his board knifing through the water, the pressure radiating up through the deck of his board into his feet and legs. He daydreamed about the view from the lineup, watching an incoming set wave inflate as it rolled over the outer reefs, the trades putting a stipple of white along the apex, the cataract of water spilling over into the trough, the cloudsplitting roar of whitewater. A mildly sadistic Catholic school education had turned Van Dyke into a lifelong agnostic, but he had moments in the water, in huge surf, when he felt spiritually connected to the ocean, the planet, the universe. One such moment came in late 1957, when Greg Noll broke a long-standing North Shore taboo and led a group of surfers, Van Dyke included, into the lineup at Waimea Bay. Van Dyke's final wave that morning was a giant, and he recalls that as he hit the trough and looked up, "time just froze . . . and I could see everything, the water droplets, the sunlight bouncing off the wave face, the little ripples and chops—all of it. It lasted just a second, but it was total perfection." Van Dyke has a beatific look on his face as he tells the story, which not surprisingly ends with another round of big-wave abuse: "Then I ate it and just got completely destroyed."

He was featured in *Surf Crazy* and *Surf Safari* and a lot of other first-generation surf movies. The 1960 debut issue of *Surfer* has two classic Van Dyke black-and-white photos: a doomed late takeoff at Waimea, and the follow-up shot of him standing bare-chested off Kam Highway, a look of macho disgust on his face, each arm holding a splintered half of his just-broken surfboard.

The rest of his life during that period, Van Dyke says, was more or less spent marking time between big-wave events. He moved to the North Shore in 1959, and the following year he got married for the second time, to a Punahou art teacher. He'd switched departments—from math and science to English—and had become one of Punahou's most popular teachers, partly because he was an easy grader, but also because he was patient and easygoing, and an excellent listener. His student roster of famous surfers includes Jeff Hakman, Gerry Lopez, Fred Hemmings, James Jones and Brock Little. He moonlighted by writing articles for *Surfer*, *Surf Guide* and *International Surfing*. . . .

Funny things turn up when you do research on older surfers. There's a Doonesbury cartoon where surfer-turned-nanny Zonker Harris gets a call from Ol' Surfer Dude, his former mentor, who tells Zonker that there's "some mad spray off Malibu," and asks if he wants to fly out for a surf. "Good thought, Master," Zonker replies. "Except I'm in Connecticut and you're 87." Then there's a short essay from last year by surf journalist Chris Cote: "I felt my age creeping up on me during the middle of my session," he writes in the opening paragraph. "I felt all its problems slink into my knees and back. I started surfing slower, my turns started getting weak." Cote is the editor for the grom-targeted *TransWorld Surf*. He's 27, the poor fermenting old thing.

Surfing, in a lot of ways, is a good sport to grow old in. Water is the most forgiving of all playing fields, and basic surfing maneuvers (aerials excepted) are low-impact, almost to the point of *no*-impact. Surfing doesn't have an equivalent to tennis elbow. Furthermore, the complexities of wind, tide, and swell, along with all the tics and quirks of any given break, mean that an older surfer's knowledge can to some degree substitute for dwindling strength, slower reactions, stiffening muscles, and a longer post-surf recovery time. Finally, surfing itself—the actual wave-riding part—is measured out in such tiny little time-packets, usually just a few seconds per ride, that it's an almost impossible thing to fill up on. Tom Curren, Kelly Slater, and other older pros go through periods of burnout. Not so for the rest of us, older surfers included (older surfers in *particular*, in a lot of cases), who surf through the decades feeling as if we never get enough. Not even *close*. Hunger feeds longevity. I couldn't even guess how many tens of thousands of waves Dorian Paskowitz has ridden over the course of his 72-year (*72-year!*) surfing career, but when we talked last summer he was still trying to figure out how to bump up his wave-riding time. "Get a bigger board, I think. Because two waves, three waves, that's pretty much all I'm good for now, plus I can barely get to my feet. I catch it, get to my knees, then the thing knocks me over just about every time—and I don't give a fuck, I just love it so much."

But a case can just as easily be made that surfing isn't at all kind to its seniors. The wave-hunger that feeds longevity also feeds selfishness: Darwinian law begins to take over once there are more than a dozen surfers in the water and in a crowded lineup it's the rare gentleman who cuts any slack to someone older, slower, weaker. Even legend status only goes so far. Gerry Lopez has his choice of waves on the rare occasion when he paddles out at Pipeline, but I'm told that Lance Carson can't get one to himself at Malibu, and Ricky Grigg grew so tired of riding scraps on the North Shore, his home for more than 30 years, that he finally gave up and moved to Oahu's East Side, where he gets to ride as many crappy, windblown three-footers as he can catch. And while the surf media has broadened its target demographic (data here is sketchy, but I'd guess the surfer's average age has jumped from 18 or 19 in 1970 to somewhere in the late 20s today), more often than not the older surfer is presented as a greyer, balder, thicker-waisted version of the 22-year-old surfer. *Surfer* recently interviewed 83-year-old Rabbit Kekai, cocked his baseball hat off to the side for his portrait photograph, called him "the world's oldest grom," and said that he's "proof positive that while surfers may grow older, they never grow up."

The hardest thing about becoming an older surfer often has less to do with physical deterioration, crowded lineups, and a faintly ridiculous surf media, and more do with all the balancing, weighting, apportioning and bargaining that goes into adult life. Part of it is a straightforward, time-allotment problem, where surfing has to vie for hours with career and family. Part of it, for some of us, is coming to terms with the idea that the sport just doesn't mean as much as it once did, that the fires are burning lower—a pretty small worry, as far as these things go, but tricky nonetheless if you've gone around for 20 years or more proudly and primarily identifying yourself as a surfer. Marc Theodore, my best friend since high school and one of South Bay's finest goofyfooters, told me in a slightly defeated voice at age 31 that he was pretty sure he'd "never love anything the way I used to love surfing." Which didn't mean he'd fallen *out* of love with surfing, but that it was now a lesser thing, and had to be acknowledged as such. And then what? You either work out a new relationship with the sport (as Marc did), or become an ex-surfer.

Or the third option: remain a full-timer and take your chances. I first saw the Mickey Dora segment in *Surfers: The Movie*, in 1990, and the part I remember best was his grinning rap about "my whole life is escape," and how "all the shit goes over my back . . . the screaming parents, the teachers, police, priests, politicians." Dora, 55 at the time, was staking his claim as an uncompromised and fully committed late-middle-aged surfer, and it was thrilling for those of us in our late 20s or 30s, still doing it hardcore. But watching *Surfers* today, I'm more struck at how non-socialized Dora looks: eating by himself in a Baja cantina, or walking alone with his dog on the beach at Shipwrecks, looking not so much like the fabled antihero, but more like the sad graying surfer as described all those years ago by Doctor Powelson in *Sports Illustrated*. "I don't expect anybody to live my life," Dora says in a *Surfers* voice-over, honest enough to acknowledge the down side. "Why should they? It's pretty lonely."

<hr />

Fred Van Dyke lived for 28 years in a beachfront house in front of Pupukea on the North Shore, and at some point in the early '70s he put a sign on his front porch that read "Old Surf Star's Home." He remembers sitting on the porch and talking with neighbor Jose Angel, another big-wave riding schoolteacher, about how much time they had left at places like Sunset and Waimea. "We figured we could do it until 70," Fred Van Dyke tells me in his quiet voice. "All of us did." We then go down the list and talk about how many of his big-wave friends from the '50s and '60s actually stuck with it: Peter Cole did, and became big-wave surfing's model senior, riding Waimea until he was 65, and still riding Sunset today at 74. Ricky Grigg hung in there for a long time as well, but not with anything like Cole's devotion. Everyone else gave it up. Buzzy Trent, Greg Noll and Kimo Hollinger quit 30 or more years ago—Trent and Noll of their own accord, Hollinger after a near-death experience in the Waimea shorebreak. Jose Angel died in a free-diving accident in 1976 that his daughter said was probably a suicide, in response to his aging. (Why did Cole hang in when the others all dropped off? "Skill-wise," he told me, "you're just going in reverse after a certain point." So it all comes down to if you can or can't accept that each year you become more of a kook. I don't really have a problem with that.")

Van Dyke himself found a kind of tortured middle ground between Cole and guys like Trent and Noll, keeping his place in the lineup, but not very happy about it. In his 1968 *Life Australia* article, right about the time his second marriage began to falter and his big-wave drive began to implode, he asks himself, "Where does it end? How many times do I have to prove myself out there?" It wasn't so much an answerable question as the beginning of a long midlife crisis. On a visit to the Bay Area that same year he learned that the woman to whom he'd lost his virginity back in 1944, "the love of my life for decades," had killed herself, and he drove brokenhearted to the hills above Santa Cruz and dropped a giant hit of acid. The following year, at age 40, he ran his first and only marathon, which he hated. In 1972 he took a sabbatical from his job at Punahou, resigned his post as Duke contest director, kissed his wife and three adopted children goodbye, and spent three months walking 1,300 miles from Wyoming's Grand Tetons to the California/Oregon border. The following year he was divorced. Not long afterwards he turned and paddled for a Waimea set wave, with everyone in the water screaming at him to go, then put the brakes on just before getting to his feet, "totally overcome with fear," and paddled to the beach knowing his days in 20-foot surf were finished.

He remained a gentle sort of oddity. Fitness continued to be an obsession: he ran and swam daily, did endless push-ups and leg-lifts, and rounded out his low-fat diet with brimming tablespoons of wheat germ, bone meal, brewer's yeast, or whatever health-food-store supplementary fad was in vogue. Peter Cole remembers driving south on the H2 freeway, during morning rush hour, and looking over to see Van Dyke one lane over, wearing a gas mask as protection against car exhaust. At Punahou he allowed his students to decorate the classroom walls with paintings of daisies and peace signs. (He continued to be one of the school's most popular teachers, and former students will still pick him out in a crowd, run up and introduce themselves, sometimes hug him, and briefly fill him in on their lives to date while Van Dyke smiles and listens closely, like he always did in class. That said, he was never invested heart and soul in his work like most other teachers, and in 1985 he took an early retirement.)

It's strange to talk with Van Dyke about this period of his life. He's wrestled with himself for long enough, and with enough success, that he can revisit difficult times almost without flinching. He's learned how to look back and savor the high points. That said, his early-middle adult years all seem to return through a filter of self-recrimination. "The bottom line is I never really wanted to get married, and I never wanted to have children. I enjoyed teaching, but I could have lived without it. Owning a surfboard was the only responsibility I did want. Just . . . be a big-wave hero. And I thought I was such a big shit at the time." He gives a contemptuous little laugh, shaking his head. "But I never was." . . .

Van Dyke's father lived to be 89, and his mother lived to be 86. Van Dyke himself is confident that he'll make it to 90, but says he thinks about death all the time. It's an issue between he and Joan who, in addition to her varied and sundry New Age beliefs, is also bedrock Catholic and has no doubt that we're all just passing through, on our way to and from other lives. "She says that being afraid of dying is really just a way of being afraid of living," Van Dyke tells me, adding with a touch of skepticism, "maybe there's some truth to that." Ten years ago he called himself an atheist. Now he wavers slightly, wanting to believe in the afterlife, but for the most part holding on to the wholly terrifying idea that this is it: one life, and a terminating death.

Because of that, Van Dyke tells me he tries to live entirely in the present. But in fact he spends a lot of time doing what nearly all sentient old people do: reviewing and sifting the years of a lifetime, framing and editing, looking for order, rhythm, meaning, definition. He's right to call himself an honest, truth-telling person, but honesty and truth will sometimes run hard against this reviewing/defining process. He tells me, for example, that he's a "loner, and always has been," but I think he just likes the way that sounds, that it appeals to his sense of cool, and that what he *really* means is that he's okay spending a few hours by himself. Lifelong friend Peter Cole laughs when I bring up Van Dyke's "loner" remark. "He loves to think that about himself. Fred's not a loner. He's loves to talk, and loves to be around people."

These are slow days for Van Dyke. It's been 20 years since he left Punahou, and up until 2002 he spent much of his time writing, which he calls "the second love of my life, after Joan." He's published four books, including the comically mistitled *Surfing Huge Waves With Ease*, in which Van Dyke reviews his big-wave career with characteristic *un*ease, and writes things like "checking Waimea in the early morning always smelled like death." His typing and handwriting skills have deteriorated since his illness, which he says blocks the flow of ideas; he finished a book-length manuscript recently, but claims it's no good, and doesn't know what he'll write about next.

Surfing these days is no more than a low background hum in Van Dyke's life. Occasionally he'll pick up a surf magazine or video, but the surf industry as a whole turns him off. His interest in surf contests ranges from nonexistent to something close to hostile. (His meet director job for the Duke contest went sour pretty quickly after the event's 1965 debut, and during one of our phone conversations he called the whole idea of surfing competition "totally ridiculous.") But surfing in general sits well with him—maybe even better than he knows. I wouldn't gainsay Van Dyke when he talks about surfing-related costs in his life: the marriage woes, the compromised career, the big-wave night-sweats, the therapy sessions that often focused on what Van Dyke has called his "sick addiction" to surfing. I would never say that hardcore surfing is anything *but* an indulgent and frequently selfish pursuit. But at the same time, I wonder if Van Dyke hasn't consciously or unconsciously promoted surfing a bit too aggressively as the cause for problems that might well have existed no matter what direction his life had taken.

Or look at it another way: Van Dyke comes off as an essentially content person (he clocks eight deep and drug-free hours of sleep a night, a high-score mark among all seniors I know), and surfing played a huge part in shaping his life. So how corrosive could it have been, really? So many of Van Dyke's admirable morals and values were at the very least enhanced, if not created outright, by surfing: his high regard for nature, the way he holds experience and freedom over money, property, and rank. Could you go so far as to suggest that surfing itself contained the seedpod of enlightenment that eventually allowed Van Dyke to put love before recreation? That's a stretch. Probably not. But the transition was made; Van Dyke at least advanced to full adulthood, and I don't think it's wrong to say that his surfing life was symptomatic of a problem, not the problem itself.

<hr/>

Fred Van Dyke now has two favorite ocean-related activities. The first begins with a flight to San Francisco, where he rents a car and drives north along the coast on Highway One, sometimes all the way to the Oregon border, stopping often to get out to watch the waves sweep across the reefs and points. His wave judgment is as good as ever, he says, and he'll focus on a place in the lineup, wait for a set wave, mind-surf it for as long as it holds shape, then shift his eyes back to the lineup and pick out another one. Hawaii has been home for 50 years now, but he's always preferred northern California, and still hopes to someday move back.

The other thing Van Dyke likes to do is put on his trunks, take a pair of fins from the garage, and swim along the beach near his house. "Swimming in the ocean," he told me near the end of my visit, "was always my real joy anyway."

Two weeks later, rereading *Once Upon Abundance*, I came to the part where Cliff Kamaka, the Hawaiian-born Mormon lifeguard and bodysurfer, teaches young Fred Van Dyke how to ride waves. I'd already taken note of Van Dyke's first ride: how he'd hit the shorebreak, gotten walloped, and came up screaming with pleasure—the birth of a surfer. Reading the passage again, I stopped where Van Dyke and Kamaka push through the surf and reach the flat water beyond the waves. Kamaka turns and rides one in, leaving Van Dyke out alone, at which point the 18-year-old future big-wave legend, instead of looking around for a set wave, just stares out across the glassy water. "It was peaceful and quiet," he recalled, "and I could see the sky reflected on the surface of the ocean." As a child he'd dreamed of what it was like out beyond the surf. Now, out there at last, "it was even better than I fantasized."

Van Dyke turned, rode that first wave, and for 30 years came back to the water almost daily loading then overloading the experience with meaning, dragging along fear and ambition and self-worth as he paddled out, then returning to shore with the adventures of a lifetime, as well as a kind of hairshirt identity— the muscle-flexing waterman who secretly couldn't wait to get his feet back in the sand. But no regrets, he says, and I believe him. I'll bet he replays all the great rides and terrible wipeouts while swimming through the calm blue-green shallows off Lanikai. And I'll bet that at the end of a swim he lets the memories go, turns over to face the sky, and asks what his younger self never could have asked, that the water do nothing more than support his weight.

Part VI

What Is Surfing?

IN *CAUGHT INSIDE: A SURFER'S YEAR on the California Coast* (1996), Daniel Duane reflects poetically on "the peeling wave as an ideal of perfection." "The surfer's object of passion," Duane writes, "becomes the very essence of ephemerality—not a thing to be owned or a goal to be attained but rather a fleeting state to inhabit." He concludes: "while one might, I suppose, wish for a bloom to remain in blossom, for a ripening grape to hang always on the vine . . . the wave's plenitude is rather in the peeling of the petal, the very motion of the falling fruit" (98–99). Since riding waves is above all concerned with motion—and multiple, simultaneous motions at that—reflections on gliding through time and space come into play in nearly all the works represented in this part. The act of surfing ultimately serves these writers as a catalyst for personal insights, epiphanies, perceptual breakthroughs, the "highly conscious life" as LSD-Guru Timothy Leary once stated in a *Surfer* magazine interview with Steve Pezman. In this same interview, Pezman writes: "Surfing gives you very elemental illustrations of broader truths by serving as a microcosm that we can grasp."[1]

Surfing, then, provides the opportunity to get a handhold on the world around us, even the world above us, and to assess our precarious place within these worlds. So strongly a function of place itself—how waves break against rock and reef and sand—surfing ties us irrevocably to specific landscapes; to the histories, dreams, and myths embodied by those landscapes; and to unsettling notions of escape—from land, from responsibility, from our commitments—all for a nonproductive, personal pleasure. "Is surfing enough," frets Thomas Farber, "to define—to defend—a life?"

Ineffable as the surfing experience will ever be, storytellers and writers have been stubbornly compelled over the centuries to try and capture its alluring essence. The most successful among them know their most sincere and dedicated exertions will fail marvelously. They resort to analogy, to metaphor, to repetition in hopes of conveying a sense of the physical and sensual through the abstract medium of language. Inventive, beautiful, and insufficient. Words alone can never contain such a simple act and the complex universe of feelings and emotions that surfing has engendered in wave riders for perhaps thousands of years.

And yet the ongoing trials are sufficient evidence of surfing's unique place in human culture.

This final part of the book stands as the literary equivalent of an Expression Session wherein the sport's elite gather on the same field of play to perform all their best maneuvers and tricks, to watch and derive inspiration from one another, and to break down the limits of what is known and acceptable. There are no winners in such an event, only a tribute to surfing and a reckless expansion of our collective imagination.

CHAPTER 60

"Playing Doc's Games—I" (1992)

William Finnegan
1952–

THE RAIN PUDDLES are like small powder-blue windows scattered on the muddy farm road as I hurry down to the beach at Four Mile. It's a soft, clear morning, with not a breath of wind, and a north swell. It looks to have sneaked in overnight. Remarkably, there's no one around. Four Mile is a reef break in a pristine cove between San Francisco and Santa Cruz. The break isn't visible from the highway, but it's a short walk from the road to a vantage point, and the spot is popular with surfers from Santa Cruz. I have caught Four Mile good before, but have never surfed it alone. While I pick my way across a creek behind the beach, I find myself listening anxiously for howls from the hillside behind me—other surfers arriving and seeing the swell. But the only sound is a tractor chugging down long rows of Brussels sprouts that stretch away to the south.

A deep, reliable channel runs out through the middle of the cove at Four Mile; the wave is on the north side. It's a quirky right, with sections that change with the tide or with any shift in the size and direction of the swell. It can get quite big, and very spooky, but the surf this morning looks benign. I paddle out through the channel, hands stinging, and my heart starts to pound when a good-sized wave hits the outside reef, stands up—bottle-green against the pale-blue sky—pitches out, explodes, and begins to wind down the reef in fine, peeling sections. This may be the best wave I've ever seen break at Four Mile. Two more nearly as good follow, and I take deep breaths to try to control the flurry of adrenaline. Carried on the back of a swift seaward current, I reach the lineup with my hair still dry. I move along a line of broad boils, paddling slowly, watching the horizon for a set, looking for a likely takeoff spot near the head of a chunk of reef, checking my position against a cypress tree on the bluff. Still nobody in sight on shore. Just one wave, I find myself praying, just one wave.

A wave comes. It swings silently through the kelp bed, a long, tapering wall, darkening upcoast. I paddle across the grain of the water streaming toward the wave across the reef, angling to meet the hollow of a small peak ghosting across the face. For a moment, in the gully just in front of the wave, my board loses forward momentum as the water rushing off the reef sucks it back up the face. Then the wave lifts me up—I've met the steepest part of the peak, and swerved into its shoreward track—and with two hard strokes I'm aboard. It's a clean takeoff: a sudden sense of height fusing with a deep surge of speed. I hop to my feet and drive to the bottom, drawing out the turn and sensing, more than seeing, what the wave plans to do ahead—the low sun is blinding off the water looking south. Halfway through the first turn, I can feel the wave starting to stand up ahead. I change rails, bank off the lower part of the face, and start driving down the line. The first section flies past, and the wave—it's slightly overhead, and changing angle as it breaks, so that it now blocks the sun—stands revealed: a long, steep, satiny arc curving all the way to the channel. I work my board from rail to rail for speed, trimming carefully through two more short sections. Gaining confidence that I will in fact make this wave, I start turning harder, slicing higher up the face and, when a last bowl section looms beside the channel, stalling briefly before driving through in a half crouch, my face pressed close to the glassy, rumbling, pea-green wall. The silver edge of the lip's axe flashes harmlessly past on my left. A second later, I'm coasting onto flat water, leaning into a pullout, and mindlessly shouting "My God!"

The unridden waves behind mine send me windmilling greedily back outside, but the set is over before I can reach the lineup. I resume my search for a takeoff spot, lining up the cypress tree on the crown of a forested hill farther inland. When the next set comes, a few minutes later, the wave I catch is smaller and slower than that first one, but I ride with more confidence, my board loose and quick under my feet, and the last section is again a fine, swift flourish. From that point, the session settles into a rhythm of paddling, positioning, waiting, and riding—and my recollection of this morning at Four Mile begins to blur, its colors running into other sessions, other mornings, other waves. A similar but more dramatic wave in Indonesia, for instance, bleeds into the picture. There the reef was coral and perfectly straight, making an immaculate wave, and the water was warm—the island where the wave broke straddled the equator, a hundred miles west of Sumatra—but the last section before the channel there also wrapped around luxuriously, inviting a sharp last maneuver, although on a larger scale. The same rare sense of surfeit, of leisure, also suffuses the memory of that quiet, palm-lined bay in Indonesia: if I didn't often surf it alone, neither did I worry much about getting my share of waves. There were more than enough waves to go around among the few surfers who had managed to find the place. (Later, after the surf magazines discovered it, that changed.)

The places I've surfed sometimes seem like so many beads on a memory string, a rosary of hundreds of small stereopticons, wherein the multicolored waves break in amber. More often, they seem like stations on some looping, ragged pilgrimage, my wave hound's *Wanderjahre*—a long search through a fallen world for shards of a lost bliss. I tend to locate this primal bliss, both for myself and for surfing as a whole, somewhere off Waikiki. At the turn of the century, when there were half a dozen surfers in the world, they were all to be found at Waikiki. Its wide, gentle swells were the womb of modern surfing—the warm, turquoise bowl of beginning. In my own case, my family lived in Honolulu when I was a young teen-ager, and I lived in the water off Waikiki. Things on land were complicated, and Waikiki itself was by then a dense nest of skyscrapers, hucksterism, and crime, but the waves, while crowded, hadn't changed since the days when Duke Kahanamoku and Dad Center rode the "bluebirds" out at Castle Surf on great hardwood boards. And the tradewinds were the same, sweet and soft off Diamond Head. And it all made a profound impression on me, and my lasting attachment to surfing was largely forged then.

Ocean Beach is the polar opposite of Waikiki—cold, gritty, scary, not for beginners. I find beauty in it, but an utterly different, more challenging, modernist beauty. Captain Cook, when he first saw surfing, compared its effects to those of listening to music. When I think of Waikiki, I hear early classical compositions: fugues and Bach concertos, sacred music. Being out at Ocean Beach is like surfing to Mahler. This glistening morning at Four Mile has a score by Handel. That wave in Indonesia might have been composed by Mozart. Sunset Beach is pure Beethoven. Strangely, when I think of the best wave I've ever surfed—the one breaking off an uninhabited island in Fiji—I hear no music at all.

But this metaphor is about mood and memory, not about the waves themselves, which dance to an infinitely more complex tune. To someone sitting in the lineup trying to decipher the structure of a swell, the problem can, in fact, present itself musically. Are these waves in 13/16 time, perhaps, with seven sets an hour, and the third wave of every second set swinging wide in a sort of minor chord crescendo? Or is this swell one of God's jazz solos, whose structure is beyond our understanding? When the surf is very big, or in some other way humbling, such questions tend to fall away. The heightened sense of a vast, unknowable design silences the effort to understand. You feel honored simply to be out there. I've been reduced on certain magnificent days to just drifting on the shoulder, gawking at the transformation of ordinary seawater into muscled swell, into feathering urgency, into pure energy—impossibly sculpted, ecstatically edged—and, finally, into violent foam. This solitary session at Four Mile does not contain that level of grandeur. It does, however, have a sweet, jewelled quality that leaves me peering from the channel into the last, cracking section, trying to hear what oceanographers call the entrainment of air burst free as the wave breaks—millions of air bubbles collapsing into smaller and smaller bubbles, from which the entrained air finally escapes with a barely audible hiss.

The most memorable aspect of this session, however, is just that, for the longest time, no one else shows up. The waves change as the tide drops, getting smaller and breaking slightly farther out, but the wind stays down, and, for all my glancing at the bluff, no one appears. After a time, I stop glancing, and my surfing goes into a trance. My concentration is unusually good: I find I'm correctly anticipating the behavior of even the trickiest sections. More than that, I'm riding at the outer edge of my ability, recovering consistently from maneuvers that under normal circumstances would be long shots. After two hours of high-amp wailing—the only real soundtrack for aggressive surfing is, in truth, rock and roll—I realize I haven't fallen off once.

A howl from the hillside finally ends this idyll. Ten minutes later, two guys are furiously paddling out through the channel, with two more hurrying across the beach, shaking their boards and hooting like monkeys. I decide that my next wave will be my last. I catch a shoulder-high peak, driving across the inside shelf. As I near the channel, I can see the two paddlers there pause to watch me ride. Rather than coast through the last section, I bank hard off the bottom and try a showy maneuver known as a reentry. I've been making more difficult moves all morning, but my concentration is flawed now. I fall off, and get washed through the shallows to shore.

CHAPTER 61

On Water (1994)

Thomas Farber
1944–

JACK THE SURFER. Surfing for him something about hunting the waves, or, occasionally, being hunted by them. Turning forty, still living right across from the beach in Carlsbad, in the water on dawn patrol nearly every morning. Not a beach bum, however: he has a job selling fine mountain gear, a good job as jobs go—flexible workdays, ample vacation time. Work chosen to allow him to continue to surf. Work long since pleasant, boring, unfulfilling.

When his wife accuses him yet again of being a Peter Pan, he finally goes to see his wife's psychologist, a woman. A compulsive triathlete, the therapist concludes that Jack's responsible enough, says his wife is lucky to have someone so physically fit with a passion for nature. Pleased, relieved, Jack nonetheless wonders. At a meeting of the sales force at his company, one of the managers notices that Jack's monthly calendar is also a tide chart, and teases him. Jack can read the component of envy, of course, but still . . . is surfing enough to define—to defend—a life?

Jack at forty, remembering surfing as a way to leave behind an overworked mother and an absent father. Being out on the water, thinking only of the waves. Remembering Tavarua, in Fiji, bunking with surf nazis from the States and Australia, riding almost perfect sets day after day. Being the only one there reading a book. Reading anything. And, now, turning forty, wondering why it should be more strange to know the time of the next high tide than to know, say, that the network news will be on at seven.

CHAPTER 62

Caught Inside: A Surfer's Year on the California Coast (1996)

Daniel Duane
1967–

"IF SOMEONE ASKS," Vince said suddenly, standing up, "what I've done with my life, what'll I say? Surfed the Point and taught math?" He shook his head with a laugh. "Raw mediocrity." It didn't, of course, strike me that way, and I wanted to tell him but couldn't think of how. I also wanted to ask if I could meet him surfing some time, maybe share the drive; but I knew it was too soon. The fog now well offshore, and fingers of wind printing deep-blue splotches on the light-blue sea, we started back and I got to wondering about a culture that marked his life that way, a man who'd mastered a skill he deeply loved, learned to truly know an element. On campus, he explained as we walked, boards under our arms, he had to lie about irregularities of schedule, fabricate false travel itineraries for sabbaticals; the frivolous aura of surfing having invalidated the great achievement of his life. No social cachet at all—just a guy who couldn't grow up. And then the oddest thing happened: a cougar stood in the road, a hundred yards off, its long, supple tail swinging slowly from side to side. As we walked closer, it stepped into the dead hemlock on the side of the road, looked back out with its brown head, and then disappeared. As we approached the point where the cat had entered the brush, Vince suggested that the petting-zoo concept might not be appropriate, thought we ought to give the beast a little room. We stepped off the far side of the road, and as we came even with the bush, Vince said, "Is that it? There it is, right?"

Ten feet away, waiting under a willow: a cat the size of a very large dog, a wild thing on a scale quite different from the raptors and their rodents. We both froze. And suddenly it vanished like a ghost—unafraid, unhurried. One second it lay watching, the next it was gone. None of the coyote's slinking or the deer's bolting. A visitation in a backwater place, all part of the wet skin and salty eyelashes, draining sinuses and muscles loose in the way only water can make them. We were both stunned, and Vince said that in thirty years he'd never seen a cougar before. Big predators change your whole sense of an ecology: sharks in the water, lions on the land, a hawk overhead.

"By the way," Vince said, as we walked back up the path, "get a new surfboard." A few hippie farming interns stood smiling in the field, having fun—not, after all, getting paid.

"Because of the lion?"

"No, because you need one." Surfboard shape changes constantly in a blend of technical advancement and fashion; Vince made a point of eschewing whatever the current trend. At the moment, the young pros had made wafer-thin little blades the craze; Vince told me to steer clear of that baloney, get something with a little heft. "Nobody in their right mind rides one of those ridiculous potato chips," he said, "but as long as they do, guys like you and me will paddle circles around them, which is fine." As we got our last glimpse of ocean, Vince said an evening surf was out of the question.

Why? How could he tell? The winds seemed right, plenty of swell . . .

"Color—wind'll be onshore." The gradations in the ocean's blue had tipped him off; not genius, but an intimate knowledge of place, an eye adapted to particular minutiae. Still, nothing learned, gained, or earned in a public way, just his secret discipline, his private pleasure.

CHAPTER 63

"Ground Swell" (1997)

Mark Jarman
1952–

IS NOTHING REAL but when I was fifteen,
Going on sixteen, like a corny song?
I see myself so clearly then, and painfully—
Knees bleeding through my usher's uniform
Behind the candy counter in the theater
After a morning's surfing; paddling frantically
To top the brisk outsiders coming to wreck me,
Trundle me clumsily along the beach floor's
Gravel and sand; my knees aching with salt.
Is that all that I have to write about?
You write about the life that's vividest.
And if that is your own, that is your subject.
And if the years before and after sixteen
Are colorless as salt and taste like sand—
Return to those remembered chilly mornings,
The light spreading like a great skin on the water,
And the blue water scalloped with wind-ridges,
And—what was it exactly?—that slow waiting
When, to invigorate yourself, you peed
Inside your bathing suit and felt the warmth
Crawl all around your hips and thighs,
And the first set rolled in and the water level
Rose in expectancy, and the sun struck
The water surface like a brassy palm,
Flat and gonglike, and the wave face formed.
Yes. But that was a summer so removed
In time, so specially peculiar to my life,
Why would I want to write about it again?

There was a day or two when, paddling out,
An older boy who had just graduated
And grown a great blonde moustache, like a walrus,
Skimmed past me like a smooth machine on the water,
And said my name. I was so much younger,
To be identified by one like him—
The easy deference of a kind of god
Who also went to church where I did—made me
Reconsider my worth. I had been noticed.
He soon was a small figure crossing waves,
The shawling crest surrounding him with spray,
Whiter than gull feathers. He had said my name
Without scorn, just with a bit of surprise
To notice me among those trying the big waves
Of the morning break. His name is carved now
On the black wall in Washington, the frozen wave
That grievers cross to find a name or names.
I knew him as I say I knew him, then,
Which wasn't very well. My father preached
His funeral. He came home in a bag
That may have mixed in pieces of his squad.
Yes, I can write about a lot of things
Besides the summer that I turned sixteen.
But that's my ground swell, I must start
Where things began to happen and I knew it.

CHAPTER **64**

"The Surfer" (1998)

Richard Katrovas
1953–

> Father, you needn't punish me anymore.
> I shall punish myself now.
>
> —Sigmund Freud

COLD APRIL OCEAN thrilled the surfer's skin
And shocked his brain alert; graphing the flow,
The first full minute after he'd sliced in,
Undulating upon the drift below
The shifting drifts of salty morning air,
He (serpentine) stared out at the charmed swells,
Forgot mere physics of how they could tear
White dripping roots that blurred to green then fell
To curling spread of aqua-smooth release.
That storied movement was destination.
Like one issued grim orders to police
A turbulent range defining nations,
Between the gray, brake-boulders at his lee
And a thin, sweeping sandbar, he shuttled
Parallel, as grieving to memory.
Sensation palpable as passion pulled
A part of him passion was not meant to reach,
The quiet, dry center where balance gripped
His spine, grapneled his will onto the beach.
A buoy frigged upon the line where currents ripped
A quarter mile beyond the breakers rise.
He'd seen a tourist paddle out that far
To dumb-show for a lover, then heard the cries,
High rasps of terror diminished in air
Weighted with the ocean's contrabass.

Sex and dancing define repetition
In lyric terms of mirroring and pace.
This is what he does, what must be done,
When doing must be felt so he may feel.
Others waken to their dread and live it;
Dreading life, he wakens squatting in the peel
Of water pushing water to a limit
His mother voiced in pain when he was born.
His longest ride he always dreams his last.
Young men look back upon themselves and mourn
Futures in repetitions that are past.

CHAPTER **65**

"Surfing Accident at Trestles Beach" (2000)

Richard Robbins
1953–

WHEN JAMES ARNESS fractured his skull, my mom
took all the names and numbers, she

got the son's autograph, an X-ray tech
laying that cracked head down.

Sand in his hair turned up as tangled stars
awaiting diagnosis. All

around his brain on the light table,
a universe held, the victim

conscious now in the next room, cracking jokes,
asking for Doc and Kitty. He reached

for my mom, faked hallucination.
He offered to sign his wrecked board,

snapped in half and fluttering over tide pools.
By the time the on-call came,

he'd recited Yeats and Robert Service,
lost his balance once, invited

everyone to his house, took those loose words
back, ordered ten Shakey's pizzas

for the crew. Near as ever after that,
Dodge city boiled up once a week,

and I watched for the lawman's cracks to show.
Would he kill Chester

or take a bribe? Would he turn to gardening?
Instead I saw him cut and slice

through kelp beds of violence, free-falling
wave-tip to base in pursuit

of the cruel. He guarded home and gold,
bright beach of our dream. And so

it came to pass that tropical storms
arrived regularly

in Kansas. Pier timber rattled straighter
than train or slug toward bent palms

inside the Longbranch Saloon. I was too
young to understand, but these were

the early days of metaphor. It was
the end of the West as I knew it.

CHAPTER 66

In Search of Captain Zero (2001)
Allan C. Weisbecker
1948–

OFTEN THESE DAYS I'LL FIND MYSELF sitting on the cliffs under the lighthouse or taking a beach walk with Honey and thinking about things. One of my recurring thoughts is of a particular wave I rode around this time last summer, at Pavones. The break there is amazing. It's not thick, nasty and barreling like Salsa Brava, but fast and very, very long; thought, in fact, to be the longest point break in the Northern Hemisphere. On a well-overhead day with a pure, long-period south swell the ride can be up to 1,000 yards or better, well over half a mile. Rather than assaulting the land head-on, like Salsa, and expelling its energy all in one sudden and final heave, the Pavones wave breaks along the shore at an acute angle, which accounts for its astounding length. It seems to be conserving itself, putting off its inevitable expiration for as long as possible. The wave at Pavones is much more suited to me than the one at Salsa Brava, which is more of a young man's wave.

In spite of the increasing tension of the local squatter problem, I found myself quite taken with the area, which is much more primitive than Puerto Viejo and very definitely has a frontier feel. (Electricity had come only a year or so before my arrival.) There are only two structures on shore visible to someone sitting in the lineup: a cantina at about the midpoint of the wave and, a few hundred yards further along, a fish camp at the far northern end.

I paddled out early the day I rode this particular wave, just after sunrise. There was only a handful of other guys in the water, well to the south of me, surfing off the mouth of El Rio Claro. The swell was shoulder to head high; not big enough to form those thousand-yard miracles, but, still, a longer wave than you'll find almost anywhere on the planet.

My takeoff was just to the south of the cantina. At first the wave didn't feel like anything special—it wasn't even a set wave—but as I stepped to the nose and looked down the line ahead of me, I could see that the wave face was organizing itself perfectly for a sustained tipride.

The noseride, The Glide, is an unstable situation, not easy to maintain. This is principally due to the ephemerality of the moving niche where unbroken, green water steepens past the vertical and where the energy of the wave is released in the form of falling white water: this is the position on the wave the surfer must sustain in order to prolong the noseride. What eventually happens is that either the wave overruns the surfer or the surfer outruns the wave. In both situations a backpedal to the rear of the longboard is called for, so a change of direction and/or alteration of board speed can be accomplished; the noseride is over.

Most noserides are very brief, often no more than the time it takes to plant the front foot, or both feet, on the tip, then immediately back off. The average noseride lasts somewhere around three, maybe four seconds at most. In general, a noseride of over ten or so yards will get the attention of those lazing on shore; over 20 will have them sitting up and taking serious note; anything much over that will likely have them on their feet hooting in amazement. A noseride of 50 yards lasts about 10 seconds and is considered about the practical limit, even at extra-long breaks like Malibu and Rincon, California's two best-known points. At the World Contest in 1966, legendary tiprider David Nuuhiwa sustained a hang-five for about that length of time and distance. His ride was scored a perfect 10 and is still remembered today.

The wave in question afforded me a continuous nose position from my takeoff point to the shore break in front of the fish camp around the corner in the next bay, a distance of about 500 yards. The ride lasted upwards of one minute.

Five hundred yards, one minute, of continuous Glide time.

Imagine hitting a baseball 450 feet over the center field wall and into the seats. Imagine the sensation of the bat striking the ball. Imagine that sensation lasting *one minute*.

Imagine seeing something so beautiful that for an instant your breath is literally taken away. Imagine that emotion lasting *one minute*.

Imagine the peak of orgasm lasting *one minute*.

You don't generally paddle right back out after riding a wave at Pavones; it's too far. You hoof it along the beach or, at high tide, through the bush, then across the cantina grounds and on to your original paddle-out spot further down the shore.

Emerging from the shore break after that ride, I felt too weak in the knees to make the walk right away, so I sat down on a rock by the fish camp. There didn't seem to be anyone around, but then I noticed a guy in surf trunks on the rocky beach by the cantina. He just stood there staring at me. Shiner was trotting toward me on the beach. She'd learned to recognize me surfing and would watch me in the water from a particular spot by the cantina. When I caught a wave, she'd run along the shore and then accompany me on the walk back.

I was feeling strange, a little disoriented, as if I'd just awakened from a deep sleep and was unsure of whether I was still dreaming.

Shiner arrived and sat down on my foot. Then the other surfer walked up and said, "You didn't backpedal until the shore break, did you?"

I had to think about it. "That's right," I said. He'd watched the first couple hundred yards of my noseride from the seawall by the cantina, he said, then ran down the beach when I rounded the corner into the next bay to see how far I'd go without backpedaling.

"The wave was perfect," I said, still feeling dreamy. "It lined up perfectly."

I focused hard on the ride, trying to remember. I knew I had to remember now or I'd lose all traces of what had just happened. Something remarkable had occurred, I mean apart from the ride itself, even apart from the perfection of the wave.

I remember the take-off and having the thought that the first section of the wave was lining up well.

I remembered making an adjustment—shifting my back foot to the inside rail to bring the board more parallel to the wave face—and barely getting through the fast section adjacent to the cantina.

I remembered having a fleeting thought that I'd been on the nose for a long time. A *really* long time. And ahead of me, the wave face continued to build and taper endlessly into the distance. It was as if each new section of the wave was self-replicating from the one before it, doing so continuously, with flawless elegance and symmetry.

I remembered that I'd made another adjustment, a slight stall—a weight shift to the outside rail—at a flattening section some distance past the threshold to the next bay; then, sensing my board accelerating as the wave steepened again in front of me, I shifted my weight back again to the inside rail for speed. What I experienced—and adjusted for—was a tiny wrinkle in the otherwise absolute perfection of the wave.

But I could remember nothing of the final couple hundred yards of the ride, except an odd sensation, which I can only describe as one of suspension. I was flying and I was walking on water, yet it was also as if

I were standing still—as if I were *stillness itself*—and *everything else* was moving past *me*.

This sort of illusion is of course a common perceptual quirk. You look out the window of a train that you thought was stationary but in reality is moving slowly, and you hallucinate that it's the scenery that's moving.

This was the difference, though: everything *but the wave itself* was moving. The water beneath my board, the sea around me, the sky above, the distant shore, maybe the earth itself, were moving past me, but not the wave.

It is not the water, not the sea itself, that is ridden when one surfs. The water is only the medium that carries the energy that *is* the wave, much as one's body is the medium, the carrier, of one's consciousness. I had perceived, in a deeply intuitive way, the seamless integration of matter and energy—without the artificial duality, the either/or-ness the human mind is prone to.

Having spent so much uninterrupted time in the place and state of mind I refer to as The Glide, I had achieved a perceptual breakthrough of some sort and was experiencing the wave on a new level of the here-and-now.

I tried to extend my understanding of this visceral insight but found I could not; I could probe no further. Then it hit me. The barrier to added insight was of a practical nature:

I did not know how surfing worked.

Walking back toward the cantina with Shiner and the other surfer, I voiced this thought aloud.

The other surfer, thinking I was speaking to him, asked me what I meant.

"I know how that wave brought me in to shore," I said to him. "But how did I ride *across* it from all the way out there?"

I looked out at the distant lineup. Someone else had paddled out and was sitting at about the same spot where I'd caught the wave. Although we'd walked nearly a hundred yards back in his direction along the shore, he still seemed very far away.

By what means *had* I traveled down the coast?

"The wave pushed you," the other surfer said, tentatively.

No, the wave didn't push me *across* it. It only pushed me toward shore.

"Gravity," the guy said. "You surfed *down* the wave."

I'd started at sea level and wound up at sea level. The concept of "down" did not apply.

The more I thought about it, the less I understood the mechanism of what I'd just done. It wasn't that I couldn't grasp the complexity of it; quite the reverse. My limitation was that some essential simplicity eluded me.

All I really knew was that I had found the perfect place on a perfect wave, and I had remained there endlessly. *Forever.*

CHAPTER 67

"Return of the Prodigal Surfer" (2001)

Bob Shacochis
1951–

KIRITIMATI, CHRISTMAS ISLAND, erstwhile thermonuclear play-ground in the mid-Pacific. Neither the beginning nor the end of a journey toward the lightness of being but, for me, more of the same, surfwise, self-wise, further evidence of the cosmic truth inherent in the mocking axiom, *You should have been here yesterday.* Yesterday, in fact, is the stale cake of many an aging surfer. Yesterday is what I walked away from, determined to someday again lick the frosting from the sea-blue bowl.

Out there on the Kiritimati atoll, we were a small, neoprene-booted family of silverbacks—Mickey Muñoz, Yvon Chouinard, Chip Post—and brazen cubs—Yvon's son and daughter, her boyfriend, Chip's son. Mick-ey, 61, was the first maniac to surf Waimea Bay, back in 1957. Yvon, 60, founder of Patagonia Inc. and legendary climber, had surfed just about every break on earth, starting with Malibu in 1954. Chip, 60, a lawyer in L.A., had seniority in almost every lineup from Baja to San Francisco. Our Generation Xers, in their late twenties, were already dismantling breaks all over the planet. In years (middle), condition (non splendid), experience (moderate), and ability (rusted), I was the odd watermonkey in the clan, neither out nor in, and the only one dragging an existential crisis to the beach. The only one who had opted out of The Life, the juice. Maybe I wanted back in, but maybe not. I felt like an amputee contemplating the return of his legs, but long accustomed to the stumps.

In the coral rubble of the point we stood brooding, muttering, trying to conjure what was not there. The glorious, mythical break had been crosswired by La Niña, and the deformed shoulder-high waves now advanced across the reef erratically, convulsed with spasms, closing pre-maturely, like grand ideas that never quite take shape or cohere to mean-ing. In years past at this same spot, Yvon had been graced with an endless supply of standard Christmas Island beauties—precise double-overhead rights, shining high-pocketed barrel tubes that spit you out into the postcoital calm of the harbor. We'd come all this way for Oceania's interpretation of euclidean geometry and we got this: bad poetry, illiterate verse.

Yeah, well . . . this was a hungry crew, and you never know what's inedible until you put it in your mouth.

The Xers flung themselves into the channel; the rip ferried them out to the reef. Chip goes. Then Yvon, but less enthusiastically. "I'm not going," said Mickey, squatting on his heels. I sat too, thunderstruck with relief. Forget that it had been more than seven or eight years since I surfed, almost 15 since I surfed steady, daily, with the seriousness and joy of a suntanned dervish. With or without its perfect waves one thing about this break horrified me: As each swell approached the reef, the trough began to boil in two sections, and when the wall steepened to its full height, thinning to emerald translucence, the two boils morphed into thick fence posts of coral.

We watched Yvon muscle onto an unreliable peak, gnarled and hurried by the onshore wind. The drop was clean, exhilarating, but without potential. He trimmed and surged past the first spike of coral, the fins of his board visible only a few scant inches above the crown before the wave sectioned and crumbled over the second spike. He exited and paddled in.

"Those coral heads really spook me," I confessed.

The stay-alive technique, Yvon assured me, was glide shallow when you left your board, protect your head, avoid disembowelment or the tearing off of your balls.

"Yeah, I guess," I said.

For a half-hour we watched the rodeo out on the reef, Chip and the Xers rocketing out of the chute, tossed and bucked into the slop. Mickey kept looking up the coast, across the scoop of bay to a reef I had named, ingloriously, Caca's, because the locals in the nearby village mined the beach with their morning turds. The tide had begun to ebb.

"Caca's going off!" Mickey cheered. Yvon and I squinted at the froth zippering in the distance.

"Yeah?" we said, unconvinced. But off we trudged to check it out.

<hr>

So. There is a pathology to my romance with surfing that contains a malarial rhythm; its recurrence can catch me unaware, bring fevers. For a day or two I'll wonder what's wrong with me, and then, of course, I'll know.

I would like to tell you that I remain a surfer but that would mostly be a lie, even though I grew up surfing, changed my life for surfing, lived and breathed and exhaled surfing for many years. Now I can barely address the subject without feeling that I've swallowed bitter medicine. I avoid surf shops with the same furtiveness with which I steer clear of underage girls, and I wouldn't dare flip through a surf magazine's exquisite pornography of waves, unless I had it in mind to make myself miserable with desire.

My life only started when I became infected with surfing, moonsick with surfing, a 14-year-old East Coast gremmie with his first board, a Greg Noll slab of lumber, begging my older brothers for a ride to Ocean City. Before that, I was just some kid-form of animated protoplasm, my amphibian brain stem unconnected to any encompassing reality, skateboarding around suburbia like an orphan.

I remember the spraying rapture of the first time I got wrapped—seriously, profoundly, amniotically wrapped—by an overhead tube, an extended moment when all the pistons of the universe seemed to fire for the sole purpose of my pleasure. It was at Frisco Beach, south of the cape on Hatteras. I remember the hard vertical slash of the drop, the gravitational punch of the bottom turn and that divine sense of inevitability that comes from trimming up to find yourself in the pocket hammered into a long beautiful cliffside of feathering water. It only got better. There, pinned on the wall in front of me, entirely unexpected and smack in my face, was a magnificent wahine-ass-valentine, tucked into a paper yellow bikini. For a moment I thought I was experiencing a puberty-triggered hallucination, but there she was in the flesh, whoever she was, wet as my dreams, locked on a line about two feet above me. Surgasm—can that be a word? The wave vaulted above us and came down as neat and transparent as glass and we were bottled in brilliant motion, in the racing sea. And friends, that ride never ended, unto this day. Boy, girl, wave—whew. On earth, I could ask no greater reward from heaven, nor define any other cosmology as complete as this.

The first time I declared my irreversible independence and defied my father, it was to go surfing. I joined the Peace Corps to go surfing in the Windward Islands. Later I moved my household from the ocean-lonely prairies of Iowa, where I was teaching, to the Outer Banks to go surfing. I chased spectacular waves off Long Island, New Jersey, Virginia Beach, North Carolina, Florida, Hawaii, Puerto Rico, waves that when I kicked out, through the sizzle of the whitewater I could hear hoots of astonishment on the beach, which felt like your ecstasy was shouting back at you, and beyond you, to a future where one day you might recollect that once, for a time, you had been a great lover in your affair with the world. You weren't just sniffing around.

※※※※※※※※

NOW, YEARS LATER, on Christmas Island, I didn't know if I wanted to surf again, to become reinfected, because I knew there was a chance I would stop living one life and start living another, that I would uproot everything, and I didn't particularly think that was possible. Still, Mickey designed me a new board, which Fletcher, Yvon's son, shaped and glassed for me. Still, I flew 6,000 miles to Christmas Island, artificially mellowed by some kind of depresso's drug to make me stop smoking. Still, I gulped back the dread that the point break had induced and walked down to Caca's with Mickey and Yvon.

What we found was surfing's equivalent of a petting zoo—little giddyup waves, pony waves, knee-high and forgiving. The silverbacks made every wave they wanted; I made maybe one out of five. I felt clownish, hesitant, my judgment blurred by bad eyesight. But finally none of that mattered, finally I started hopping into the saddle, having fun. That I considered to be a mercy.

I had collided head-on with my youth and with what needed resurrection, though not in the boomer sense of never letting go. I had already let go. But the dialectic of my transformation had reached a standstill: Surf = No Surf = ??? I wanted more waves. I wanted more waves the way a priest wants miracles, the desert wants rain. Throughout my celibacy, living a counterpoint life, I had prayed hard to be welcomed home again to waves, and these tame ponies would, I hoped, serve as that invitation. I have since surfed San Onofre with limited success. Florida too, but only once. I have yet to find the equation that will spring open my life, rearrange my freedoms. My resources are modest, my obligations many; my dreams are still the right dreams but veined with a fatty ambivalence. Maybe the season has passed, but I don't think so.

The thing about surfing, Chip told me, is that "you leave no trail." Yessir, Mickey agreed: "It's like music—you play it and it's done."

The strategy you're looking for is the one that teaches you to hold the note.

Permissions

Grateful acknowledgment is due to the following individuals and publishers for the right to reprint copyrighted material.

Erik Aeder for "Indonesia: Just Another Paradise" from *Surfer* 20, no. 3 (March 1979).

Steve Barilotti for excerpt from "Lost Horizons: Surfer Colonialism in the 21st Century" from *The Surfer's Journal* 11, no. 3 (Summer 2002).

Nona Beamer for "'Auhea 'O Ka Lani (Where Is the Royal Chief?)" from *Nā Mele Hula: A Collection of Hawaiian Hula Chants*. Vol. 1. Honolulu: Institute for Polynesian Studies/Brigham Young University, 1987.

The Bishop Museum Archives for items found in the Hawaiian Ethnological Notes (HEN) collection, including "Ancient Sports of Hawaii Such As Surfing, Jumping, Sledding, Betting and Boxing" by J. Waiamau from *Kuokoa*, December 23, 1865 (Thrum # 49); "He Inoa no Naihe" [Name chant for Naihe], trans. Mary K. Pukui (Part III); the George Freeth article from *The Evening Herald* from the Charles Kenn collection (Box 18, folder 7).

The Bishop Museum Press for "Kelea-nui-noho-'ana-'api'api" by Samuel M. Kamakau from *Tales and Traditions of the People of Old: Na Mo'olelo a ka Po'e Kahiko*. Trans. Mary K. Pukui; ed. Dorothy B. Barrère. Honolulu: Bishop Museum Press, 1991; for proverbs from *Ōlelo No'eau: Hawaiian Proverbs & Poetical Sayings*. Trans. Mary K. Pukui. Honolulu: Bishop Museum, Special Publication 71, 1983; for "Activities in Court Circles" from *Fragments of Hawaiian History* by John Papa 'Ī'ī. Trans. Mary K. Pukui; ed. Dorothy B. Barrère. Honolulu: Bishop Museum Press, 1959.

Daniel Duane for excerpt from *Caught Inside: A Surfer's Year on the California Coast*. New York: North Point Press, 1996.

Thomas Farber for excerpt from *On Water*. Hopewell, N.J.: The Ecco Press, 1994.

Farrar, Straus & Giroux, LLC, for excerpt from "The Pump House Gang" from THE PUMP HOUSE GANG by Tom Wolfe. Copyright © 1968, renewed 1996 by Tom Wolfe.

William Finnegan for excerpt from "Playing Doc's Games—I" from *The New Yorker* (August 22, 1991).

The Hakluyt Society for journal entries by James King, Charles Clerke, and David Samwell from *The Journals of Captain James Cook on his Voyages of Discovery*. 4 vols. Ed. J. C. Beaglehole. London: Hakluyt Society, 1955–1967, and for the journal entry by Peter Puget from George Vancouver's *A Voyage of Discovery to the Northern Pacific Ocean and Round the World, 1791–1795*. 4 vols. Ed. W. Kaye Lamb. London: Hakluyt Society, 1984.

Kimo Hollinger for "An Alternate Viewpoint" from *Surfer* 16, no. 3 (August–September 1975).

Honolulu Star-Bulletin for "Faithless Lover Is Turned to Stone" by Clarice B. Taylor from *Honolulu Star-Bulletin* (Wednesday, November 26, 1958).

Mark Jarman for "Ground Swell" from *Questions for Ecclesiastes*. Brownsville, Ore.: Story Line Press, 1997.

Bruce Jenkins for excerpt from "Laird Hamilton: 20th Century Man" from *The Surfer's Journal* 6, no. 3 (Fall 1997).

Richard Katrovas for "The Surfer" from *The Book of Complaints*. Pittsburgh: Carnegie-Mellon University Press, 1993.

Kevin Naughton, Craig Peterson, and Greg Carpenter for "Centroamerica" from *Surfer* 14, no. 3 (August–September 1973).

Susan Orlean for excerpt from "The Maui Surfer Girls" from *The Bullfighter Checks Her Makeup: My Encounters with Extraordinary People*. New York: Random House, c. 2001.

Penguin Group (USA) for "Chapter 14," "Chapter 15," from GIDGET by Frederick Kohner, copyright © 1957 by Frederick Kohner. Used by permission of Berkeley Publishing Group, a division of Penguin Group (USA) Inc.

Steve Pezman for "The Cat's Ninth Life" from *The Surfer's Journal* 11, no. 2 (Spring 2002).

Richard L. Robbins for "Surfing Accident at Trestles Beach" from *Famous Persons We Have Known: Poems*. Spokane: Eastern Washington University Press, 2000.

Bob Shacochis for "Return of the Prodigal Surfer" from *Outside* 26, no. 6 (June 2001).

C. R. Stecyk III for excerpts from articles in *Skateboarder* magazine: "The Westside Style or Under the SkateTown Influence," August 1976; "Skateboarder Interview Highlights: Stacy Peralta," October 1976; "SkateBoarder Interview Highlights: Tony Alva," February 1977.

Surfer magazine for "We're Number One—Interview: Ian Cairns" by Jack McCoy from *Surfer* 17, no. 1 (April–May 1976); "Mickey on Malibu" by Mickey Dora from *Surfer* 8, no. 6 (January 1968).

Rerioterai Tava and Moses K. Keale Sr. for "Ka Hui Nalu Mele: The Surf Club Song" from *Niihau: The Traditions of a Hawaiian Island*. Honolulu: Mutual, 1989.

University of Hawai'i Press for excerpt from *The Victorian Visitors* by Alfons L. Korn. Honolulu: University of Hawai'i Press, 1958; "Name Chant for Naihe" from *The Echo of Our Song: Chants & Poems of the Hawaiians*. Trans. Mary K. Pukui and Alfons L. Korn. Honolulu: University of Hawai'i Press, 1973.

Matt Warshaw for excerpt, with changes, from "Winterland: Fred Van Dyke and the Blissful, Stressful, Unpredictable Life of the Older Surfer" from *The Surfer's Journal* 14, no. 4 (August–September 2005).

Allan C. Weisbecker for excerpt from *In Search of Captain Zero: A Surfer's Road Trip Beyond the End of the Road*. New York: Jeremy P. Tarcher/ Putnam, 2001.

John Witzig for "We're Tops Now" from *Surfer* 8, no. 2 (May 1967).

Every effort has been made to acquire permissions to reproduce copyrighted material in this anthology. Please notify the editor of any omissions, and he will include appropriate acknowledgments in subsequent editions.

Notes

Introduction

1. For European conceptions of the ocean and water (especially Christian), see Lenek and Bosker, *The Beach*, 38–44.

2. William Bradford, *Of Plymouth Plantation*, ed. Henry Wish (New York: Capricorn Books, 1962), 59.

3. Lamb, ed., *Exploration and Exchange*; see editors' introduction, xix.

4. Ledyard, *John Ledyard's Journal of Captain Cook's Last Voyage*, 103.

5. Hiram Bingham, *A Residence of Twenty-one Years in the Sandwich Islands* (Hartford: Hezekiah Huntington, 1849), 81.

6. Hiram Bingham, "Sandwich Islands," *The Missionary Herald*, 100. Thomas Hopu traveled to the mainland in 1809 along with other Hawaiian boys and was educated at the Foreign Mission School at Cornwall, Connecticut. He returned with the first group of missionaries in 1819.

7. Stewart, *A Visit to the South Seas*, 259–260. Bingham's words appear in a missionary letter appended to Stewart's account.

8. Ellis, *Polynesian Researches*, vol. 1, 310; *Journal of William Ellis: Narrative of a Tour of Hawaii, or Owhyhee* (Rutland, Vt.: Charles E. Tuttle, 1979), 297.

9. Hunter S. Thompson, *Hell's Angels: A Strange and Terrible Saga* (New York: Ballantine, 1996; originally published in 1966), 66.

10. Perkins, *Na Motu; or, Reef-Rovings in the South Seas*, 197.

11. Townsend Jr., *Extract form [sic] the diary of Ebenezer Townsend Jr.*, 76.

12. Harold H. Yost, *The Outrigger: A History of the Outrigger Canoe Club 1908–1971* (Honolulu: Outrigger Canoe Club, 1971), 33.

Part I. Surfriding in Polynesian Culture

1. For the story of Kiha-pi'ilani, see Thrum, *More Hawaiian Folk Tales*, 74. For Hooipo and Hinauu, see *Fornander Collection of Hawaiian Antiquities and Folk-Lore*, vol. 4, pt. 1: 112–125, and Thrum, *More Hawaiian Folk Tales*, 21. Following the scholarship of Mary Kawena Pukui and Martha Beck-

with, names of Hawaiian people and places in this chapter have been translated when possible into English.

2. *Ruling Chiefs of Hawaii*, 53.

3. For several versions of Puna-ai-koae, see Beckwith's *Hawaiian Mythology*, 193–195.

4. For the history of the authorship and Daggett's connection to Mark Twain, who helped publish the collection of myths, see the *Hawaiian National Bibliography*, vol. 4, 294–296, and Weisenburger, *Idol of the West*, 161–164. Most of the words glossed in this text appear in an appendix in the original edition.

5. Martha Beckwith indicates: "The name Laie is probably to be analyzed as La (u)-'ie, 'Leaf of the 'ie vine,' since the equivalent name of a Maui chiefess Laie-lohelohe refers to the 'Drooping 'ie vine.' This red-spiked climbing pandanus (*Freycinetia Arnotti*) which wreaths forest trees of the uplands is sacred to the gods of the wild wood, patrons of the hula dance, of whom Laka is chief. The epithet –i-ka-wai (in the water) belongs also to the food-producing tree Ka-lala-i-ka-wai planted in Paliula's garden" (*Hawaiian Mythology*, 532); the reference to the genre of "romantic fiction" can be found on pp. 489–490. For the common translation of "green cliff," Beckwith indicates that "Pa-liula with reference to the twilight or mirage (liula) . . . would seem to be a more natural original" (72). See also Pukui, *Place Names*, 178.

6. Beckwith, *Hawaiian Mythology*, 403.

7. Kamakau, *Ka Poʻe Kahiko: The People of Old*, 83–84.

8. Ibid., 76–79. See also Beckwith, *Hawaiian Mythology*, 128–135. In his *Ruling Chiefs of Hawaii*, Kamakau offers another dramatic example of the battle between surfers and sharks:

> One day when the waves of Maliu and Ka-pae-lauhala were rolling in magnificently, the cutworm-tearing son of Naʻalehu resolved to show the skill he had got through practice [in surfing] on the bent wave of Kaʻwa, or diving headforemost into the waters of Unahea. He reached for his surfboard and went out to sea beyond Ka-pae-lauhala. He rode in on a wave and landed at Kinaina. Again he went out and, having set himself in the way of a good wave, rode once more to land. As the wave rolled landward, a shark came in with it. It came with open mouth that showed sharp, pointed teeth. Sea water poured between its teeth and through its gills; its skin seemed to bristle; dreadful indeed was the appearance of that rough-skinned one. Six fathoms was its length. Chiefs and commoners fled terrified to the shore, but Nuʻu-anu-paʻahu, the lad who had broken *mamame* branches at Kapapala and torn up *koaiʻe* vines at ʻOhaikea, did

not lose courage. When he saw that the shark was pursuing him, he steered his board for the crest of the wave. The shark saw him on the crest and pursued him there. Nuʻu-anu-paʻahu fled with the speed of an arrow. The shark passed under and turned to slash; Nuʻu-anu-paʻahu struck out with his fists and hit it in the eye. The shark dived downward; Nuʻu-anu-paʻahu turned toward a low surf, and as he rode it the shark passed under him. Again it turned to bite; he sped on and the shark missed. He struck at the shark's gills, his hand found its way in, and he grasped the gills and jerked them out of its head. The shark, wounded, left him. Just as he was about to land, another shark that lurked near a stone appeared with open mouth. Nuʻu-anu-paʻahu struck out at it with his fists, hitting it back of the jaw. The shark turned and gashed him on one side of his buttocks. Then at last Nuʻu-anu-paʻahu reached the shore. Chiefs and commoners shouted applause for his strength and congratulated him upon his escape from death. Sounds of wailing echoed and reechoed. (106–107)

9. Beckwith, *Hawaiian Mythology*, 91.

10. In *Ancient Tahiti,* Teuira Henry translates the following words spoken by a Tahitian canoe maker as he baptizes his craft during the first launching: "If I sail my canoe, / Through the breaking waves, / Let them pass under, / Let my canoe pass over, / O god Tane! / If I sail my canoe, / Through the towering waves, / Let them pass under, / Let my canoe pass over, / O god Tane!" The verses were heard by a great assembly of people gathered on the shoreline and followed initial chants as the workers laid the canoe on rollers and eased the craft into the water. Although canoes played a more central role in Polynesian culture in terms of voyaging and military activity, one can well imagine similar practices and ceremonies established for surfboards built for the ruling chiefs of Tahiti and Hawaiʻi (*Ancient Tahiti* [Honolulu: Bishop Museum, 1928], 109, 181).

11. *Nineteenth Century Hawaiian Chant,* 22–23, 42–43.

12. Pukui and Korn, *The Echo of Our Song: Chants & Poems of the Hawaiians,* 37–38.

13. Mary K. Pukui, "Songs (Meles) of Old Kaʻu, Hawaii," *Journal of American Folklore* 62, no. 245 (1949): 255–256.

14. Part Three was translated by Mary K. Pukui and has never been published; no date is listed on the manuscript for the translation.

15. Beckwith, *Hawaiian Mythology*, 293. See pp. 293–306 for an overview of the Papa and Wākea tradition.

16. Beamer, *Nā Mele Hula: A Collection of Hawaiian Hula Chants,* 1:ix. Most of the Hawaiian words glossed appear in the original publication.

17. For Pukui's articles on the hula, see Barrère, *Hula: Historical Perspectives.*

18. Tava and Keale Sr., *Niihau: The Traditions of a Hawaiian Island,* 39–41.

19. *Hawaiian Proverbs & Poetical Sayings,* vii.

Part II. Explorers, Missionaries, and Travelers (1769–1896)

1. Bates, *Sandwich Island Notes,* 298–299.

2. *Fragments of Hawaiian History,* vii.

3. For the surf contest between Umi and Paiea, see Fornander, *An Account of the Polynesian Race,* 96–97.

4. Tahiti had been opened to the west by George Wallis in 1767, and Cook's mission was to observe the transit of Venus on June 3, 1769; information on the transit, recorded from several locales around the globe, would help scientists determine the size of the solar system. Banks's original journal entry can be found on The South Seas Web site: http://southseas.nla.gov.au/journals/hv23/135.html.

5. Beaglehole, *The Journals of Captain Cook,* vol. 1, cxc–cxcv. Anderson's account appears in vol. II, 150–151 of the 1784 edition.

6. Ellis composed his narrative after having returned from the voyage in 1780; the section in which the description of the surfboards appears precedes a description of Ni'ihau, so it is likely that both Ellis's and Clerke's descriptions are based on their stay at Waimea, Kaua'i, in January 1778. The principal object of Cook's third voyage was to search for a northwest passage from the Pacific to the Atlantic. Cook first landed on Kaua'i on January 19, 1778. After also visiting Ni'ihau, Cook sailed north for the California coast on February 2. The *Resolution* and *Discovery* returned later that year (November 25) to what Cook had dubbed the Sandwich Islands; Cook sighted Maui, and afterward Hawai'i; the ships patrolled the waters for six weeks before anchoring in Kealakekua Bay, on January 17, 1779. The ships left Hawai'i on February 4 to visit other islands, but adverse winds and necessary repairs forced their return to Kealakekua Bay on February 11. After the death of Cook on February 14, the ships visited several more islands (see note 8, below), bartering and resupplying, and finally left the chain on March 15, 1779.

7. In *Captain Cook's Final Voyage: The Journal of Midshipman George Gilbert,* the editor notes that Gilbert's journal was written after his return from the trip (p. 6).

8. In addition to Kealakekua Bay, the ship stopped at Waimea Bay (O'ahu), Waimea (Kaua'i), and Kamalino (Ni'ihau). Because Cook's ships stayed longest at Kealakekua Bay, and due to the number of surfriders mentioned (twenty to thirty), it seems most likely that King's description comes from Kealakekua.

9. Morrison spent over two years on Tahiti: from October 1788 to April

1789 with Captain Bligh, then again between September 1789 and May 1791 after having been put ashore by the mutineers.

10. Eddea (also Itia) Tetuanui (1760–1814) was the sister of great chiefs of Moorea and the wife of Pomare I (1751–1803), first of the powerful Pomare line of chiefs in Tahiti.

11. A footnote in the original article indicates that Kaneo was a queen of the late Kamehameha I.

12. Bingham is referring to John Turnbull's *A Voyage Round the World* (1813). See bibliography.

13. For information on the mission house mentioned by Bingham, see Daws, *Shoal of Time: A History of the Hawaiian Islands*, 66.

14. As noted in the bibliography, Ellis had published an edition of this book in Boston the year before (1825) that omits the description of surf-riding.

15. A convex deck and bottom are usually associated with the longer *olo* boards.

16. See the editor's introduction, 3.

17. The official edition was first published in 1844.

18. Daws, *Shoal of Time*, 104.

19. Cheever, *Life in the Sandwich Islands*, 7.

20. Cheever himself had traveled to the Islands to improve his health.

21. Bishop, *Reminiscences of Old Hawaii*. Horses were introduced on the island of Hawai'i in the 1820s by Captain Richard Cleveland.

22. As noted by the editor of *The Victorian Visitors*, Cracroft's comment about rituals in the "Presbyterian Church" should read "Protestant Church."

23. Twain's description is inserted into a letter dated July 1866; the letter was published in the *Sacramento Weekly Union* on September 29, 1866. See Mark Twain's *Letters from the Sandwich Islands*, introduction by G. Ezra Dane (Stanford, Calif.: Stanford University Press, 1938).

24. The letter was written to his daughter from Hilo, Hawai'i, April 6–7, and appeared in the *Hawaiian Gazette* on April 29, 1868. See Eleanor Harmon Davis, *Abraham Fornander: A Biography* (Honolulu: University Press of Hawai'i, 1979), 177–178.

25. *Honolulu Directory*, 51.

26. The comment about surfriding having "fallen into disuse" appears on p. 55 of the *Honolulu Directory*; the story of Holoua, on p. 51.

27. Charles Nordhoff (1830–1901) arrived in Honolulu in February 1873; a former editor at Harper's Brothers and managing editor at the *New York Evening Post*, Nordhoff published his account of surfriding in *Harper's* in 1873, and later in his book *Northern California, Oregon, and the Sandwich Islands* (1874).

28. According to Kay Chubbuck, the editor of Bird's *Letters to Henrietta*, Bird typically embellished her original letters with borrowed material be-

fore publication, at times including events that she did not witness but wished that she had. In *The Hawaiian Archipelago*, Bird mentions meeting Nordhoff in Hawai'i before her departure. She undoubtedly would have had access to his article in *Harper's* before the publication of her book.

29. Luther Severance Jr. was the son of a retired congressman and U.S. commissioner to the Sandwich Islands who served for three years on O'ahu. He had moved to Hilo from Honolulu in 1867 and was appointed sheriff, postmaster, and customs collector by Kamehameha V (ruled 1863–1872).

30. See Ruth M. Tabrah, *Ni'ihau: The Last Hawaiian Island* (Kailua, Hawai'i: Press Pacifica, 1987), 105, 117; p. 200 indicates a Makahiki-like festival of surfriding for the natives; p. 114 indicates that visitors to the island in the 1860s and 1870s enjoyed surfriding with the Sinclair family.

31. Bolton notes that he presented this article as a lecture with photographs. If the photographs he mentions still exist, they would represent some of the earliest known of surfriding.

32. See Fornander's *Collection of Hawaiian Antiquities and Folk-Lore* in the bibliography for reference to these native legends.

Part III. Surfriding Revival (1907–1954)

1. Harold H. Yost, *The Outrigger: A History of the Outrigger Canoe Club 1908–1971* (Honolulu: Outrigger Canoe Club, 1971), 33.

2. Of interest is Charmian London's description of her wave-riding experience on the same day (from *Our Hawaii*):

> Several times, on my own vociferous way, I was spilled diagonally a down the face of a combing wave, the board whirling as it overturned and slithering up-ended, while I swam to bottom for my very life, in fear of a smash on the cranium. And once I got it, coming up wildly, stars shooting through my brain. And once Jack's board, on which he had lain too far forward, dived, struck bottom, and flung him head over heels in the most ludicrous somersault. His own head was struck in the ensuing mix-up and we were able to compare size and number of stars. Of course, his stars were bigger—because my power of speech was not equal to his. It seems to us both that we were never so *wet* in all our lives, as during those laughing, strenuous, half-drowned hours.
>
> Sometimes, just sometimes, when I want to play the game beyond my known vitality, I almost wish I were a boy. I do my best, as to-day; but when it comes to piloting an enormous weighty plank out where the high surf smokes, above a depth of twelve to fifteen feet, I fear that no vigor of spirit can lend

my scant five-feet-two, short hundred-and-eleven, the needful endurance. Mr. Ford pooh-poohs: "Yes, you can. It's easier than you think—but better let your husband try it out first."

3. *The Outrigger*, 33. Among other contributions to the diffusion of surfriding around the world, Ford may have been the first to take surf films on the road by premiering a motion picture of the sport in Charleston, South Carolina, in 1919. See Noble, *Hawaiian Prophet*, 88.

4. For the beachboy traditions, see Grady Timmons, *Waikiki Beachboy* (Honolulu: Editions, Limited, 1989).

5. Freeth's article was found in the Charles Kenn collection of unpublished papers in the archives of the Bishop Museum. Box 18, folder 7, includes information Kenn had collected on George Freeth, including a typescript of Freeth's article from the *Evening Herald*. Although the original article has not yet been located (internal evidence suggests it appeared between 1917 and 1919), Kenn had either hand-copied or transcribed numerous articles in this collection that have been verified; there is no reason to believe that Freeth's article is inauthentic.

6. See Finney and Houston, *Surfing, The Sport of Hawaiian Kings*, 82, for reference to the three Hawaiian princes in California. For Freeth's legacy as a lifeguard, see Verge, "George Freeth: King of the Surfers and California's Forgotten Hero."

7. See Blake's bibliographical entry for journals where he initially published some of the information in this section.

8. This date should read 1908.

9. Doc Ball's handwritten creed was copied from an exhibit at the California Surf Museum in Oceanside, California.

10. For an account of this crossing, see Gene Smith, "Surfboarding from Molokai to Oahu," *Paradise of the Pacific* 52, no. 8 (August 1940): 21–24.

Part IV. Youth Culture (1957–1979)

1. "Kelea, The Surf-Rider of Maui," in Kalakaua and Daggett's *The Legends and Myths of Hawaii: The Fables and Folk-Lore of a Strange People*, rev. ed. (Rutland, Vt.: Charles E. Tuttle, 1992).

2. For Bob Simmons, see the profile by John Elwell, "The Bob Simmons Enigma," *The Surfer's Journal* 3, no. 1 (Spring 1994): 30–49. Simmons had a bad arm, not leg.

3. Here, and in the sentence ahead, "suction" should probably read "section."

4. Witzig was responding to "The High Performers," an article on the hottest California surfers of the time (*Surfer* 8, no. 1 [March 1967]); see also "The High Performers Answer Australia" (*Surfer* 8, no. 3 [July 1967]).

Part V. Surfing Today

1. Timothy Leary, "The Evolutionary Surfer," interview by Steve Pezman, *Surfer* 18, no. 5 (December–January 1977–1978): 102.

2. See Chapter 22 for correct information on the missionaries' arrival and influence.

3. The expression is probably "full-on."

Part VI. What is Surfing?

1. Timothy Leary, "The Evolutionary Surfer," interview by Steve Pezman, *Surfer* 18, no. 5 (December–January 1977–1978): 101.

Bibliography

General Reference

The following texts are particularly helpful for tracking the history of surf-riding.

DeLaVega, Timothy, comp. *200 Years of Surfing Literature: An Annotated Bibliography.* Hanapepe, Kaua'i, Hawai'i: Timothy T. DeLaVega, 2004. This work is based on Daved Marsh's "The Water Log: A Descriptive Bibliography of Surfing": www.surfwriters.com.

Finney, Ben R., and James D. Houston. *Surfing: The Sport of Hawaiian Kings.* Rutland, Vt.: Charles E. Tuttle, 1966. Reprinted as *Surfing: A History of the Ancient Hawaiian Sport.* San Francisco: Pomegranate Artbooks, 1996.

Forbes, David W. *Hawaiian National Bibliography, 1780–1900.* 4 vols. Honolulu: University of Hawai'i Press, 1998–c. 2003.

Kampion, Drew. *Stoked: A History of Surf Culture.* Santa Monica, Calif.: General Publishing Group, 1997. Rev. ed.: *Stoked! A History of Surf Culture.* Layton, Utah: Gibbs Smith, 2003.

Lueras, Leonard. *Surfing: The Ultimate Pleasure.* Honolulu and New York: Workman, 1984.

Warshaw, Matt. *The Encyclopedia of Surfing.* Orlando: Harcourt, 2003.

Polynesian Myths and Legends

The following sources offer comprehensive (though undoubtedly not complete) information on surfriding in Polynesian history and legend. Page numbers have been noted in certain cases throughout for the reader's convenience.

Amadio, Nadine. *Pacifica: Myth, Magic and Traditional Wisdom from the South Sea Islands.* Sydney: Angus & Robertson, 1993. Hina presents the gift of surfriding to Tahitians.

Beamer, Nona, ed. *Nā Mele Hula: A Collection of Hawaiian Hula Chants.*

Vol. 1. Honolulu: Institute for Polynesian Studies/Brigham Young University, 1987. Surfing chants for Hawaiian Kings William Charles Lunalilo and David Kalākaua.

Beckwith, Martha. *Hawaiian Mythology.* Rev. ed. Honolulu: University of Hawai'i Press, 1987. The classic study of comparative Polynesian mythology first published in 1940. Includes reference to Pamano and Keaka (153), Kalamainu'u and Puna-ai-koae (194), Kelea (385), Umi (392), Kawelo (408–409), and Pikoi (426–427).

———. "The Hawaiian romance of Laieikawai by S.N. Haleole." Bureau of American Ethnology, Report 33, 1919. Martha Beckwith's translation of the Hawaiian myth (see her *Hawaiian Mythology*, 527, for a synopsis); surfriding figures include Hinaikamalama, princess of Hana (94–96), Laieikawai and Hauailiki (164–170), Laieikawai, Halaaniani, and King Kekalukaluokewa (210–234).

Blake, Tom. *Hawaiian Surfriders:1935.* Rev. ed. Redondo Beach, Calif.: Mountain & Sea, 1983. A rich source for Hawaiian myths (with various name misspellings) in Chapter I: "Ancient Hawaiian Legends of Surfriding"; the primary source was undoubtedly Fornander. Blake appears to have written his own myth concerning a love story and surf contest at Waikīkī with characters Nani and Moloa whom I have been unable to authenticate (22–29).

Chickering, William H. *Within the Sound of These Waves.* New York: Harcourt, Brace and Co., 1941. The tale of Umi.

Colum, Padraic. *At the Gateways of the Day.* New Haven: Yale University Press, 1924. "The Story of Ha-le-ma-no and the Princess Kama" from Fornander.

De Vis-Norton, L. W. "Imu O Umi." *Paradise of the Pacific* 34 (August 1921): 9–13. Another version of the Umi story.

Emerson, Nathaniel B. *Unwritten Literature of Hawaii: The Sacred Songs of the Hula.* Washington: Smithsonian Institution, Bulletin 38, 1909. A classic and invaluable study that presents the surfing chant of Naihe (35–37) later treated by Mary K. Pukui.

———. *Pele & Hiiaka: A Myth from Hawaii.* Honolulu: Honolulu Star-Bulletin Limited, 1915. Hiiaka (13) and the story of Lohiau surfriding (152–154).

Faris, John T. *The Paradise of the Pacific.* Garden City, N.Y.: Doubleday, Doran & Co., 1929. References the Kelea story and a version of Kahikilani whom he calls "Kahikilau" (157–159).

Finney, Ben, and James D. Houston. *Surfing: A History of the Ancient Hawaiian Sport.* San Francisco: Pomegranate Art Books, 1996. First published in 1966; Finney and Houston remain the principal source for the history of ancient Hawaiian surfriding. Chapter Three mentions the stories of Mo'ikeha, Mamala, Kahikilani, La'ieikawai, Kelea, Naihe, Pikoi, and Umi.

Fornander, Abraham. *An Account of the Polynesian Race: Its Origins and Migrations*. Rev. ed. Rutland, Vt.: Charles E. Tuttle, 1969. First published in 1879; Fornander references Kelea (83–87) and the surf contest of Umi and Paiea (96–97) (both from Kamakau).

———. *Fornander Collection of Hawaiian Antiquities and Folk-Lore*. 3 vols. Honolulu: Bishop Museum, 1916–1920. The principal written source for many Hawaiian myths, including: "The History of Moikeha" (vol. 4, pt. 1: 112–125) and the two Kauaʻi princesses (Hinauu and Hooipoika-malanai) who fall in love with him while surfriding; "The Legend Of Halemano" (vol. 5, pt. 2: 232) with the princess Kamolalawale listening to the surf at Kauhola, Maliu (242)—she leaves Halemano for Kumoho, who also surfs; "Legend of Kepakailiula" (vol. 4, pt. 3: 510 and vol. 5, pt. 2: 396) details the abduction of Makolea by Keaumiki and Keauka ("gods of the tides") for Kaikipaananea, king of Kauaʻi; "Legend of Halemano" presents two sisters (Laenihi and Pulee) who surf at Makaiwa (vol. 5, pt. 2: 242); "Legend of Pupukea" presents Kings Lonoikamakahiki and Kamalolawolu surfriding together (vol. 5, pt. 2: 436); "Legend of Pamano" details brother and sister lovers Pamano and Keaka who are allowed to surf together but not touch one another (vol. 5, pt. 2: 302); "Kawelo" goes surfing to forget problems with his wife (vol. 5, pt. 3: 706); the famous chant to invoke surf (vol. 6: 206).

Green, Laura C. S., and Mary K. Pukui. *The Legend of Kawelo and other Hawaiian Folktales*. Honolulu: Territory of Hawaii, 1936. "The Stone Face" (124) recounts the legend of Kahikilani and the Bird Maiden above Pau-malu. See also Faris (1929), Raphaelson (1929?), Taylor (1958), and Paki (1972).

Kalakaua, David. *The Legends and Myths of Hawaii: The Fables and Folk-Lore of a Strange People*. Rev. ed. Rutland, Vt.: Charles E. Tuttle, 1992. First published in 1888; this collection offers several myths connected with surfriding: "Kelea, The Surf-Rider of Maui"; "The Story of Laieikawai" (Hinaikamalama surfriding with Aiwohikupua); "Kahalaopuna, The Princess of Manoa" who is bitten in half by a shark (her former fiancé) after she ignores a warning not to go surfriding; "Lohiau, The Lover of a Goddess" recounts the Pele and Hiiaka story.

Kamakau, Samuel Mānaiakalani. *Ka Poʻe Kahiko: the People of Old*. Trans. Mary K. Pukui; ed. Dorothy Barrère. Honolulu: Bernice P. Bishop Museum Special Publication 51, 1964. The story of the shark Ka-ehu who protects Waikīkī surfers (74). See also Westervelt (1913, 1915) and Knudsen (1945).

———. *Ruling Chiefs of Hawaii*. Trans. Mary K. Pukui et al. Honolulu: Kamehameha, 1961. Includes the surf contest of Umi (10–11), the surf-riding lovers Kiha-a-Piʻilani and Kolea-moku (25), and Nuʻu-anu-paʻahu's battle with a shark while surfriding (106–107).

———. *The Works of the People of Old: Na Hana a ka Poʻe Kahiko*. Trans. Mary

K. Pukui; ed. Dorothy B. Barrère. Honolulu: Bernice P. Bishop Museum Special Publication 61, 1976. The *moʻo* woman Kalamainuʻu (aka Kihawahine) leads surfer Puna-ai-koae to her cave (79 and following). See also Westervelt (1915), Thrum (1923), and Beckwith (1987, 125–126, 194–195).

———. *Tales and Traditions of the People of Old: Na Moʻolelo a ka Poʻe Kahiko*. Trans. Mary K. Pukui; ed. Dorothy B. Barrère. Honolulu: Bishop Museum Press, 1991. Kelea (45–49).

———. "Kelea, The Surf Rider." *Hawaiian Almanac and Annual*, 1931, 58–62.

Kanahele, George S. *Waikīkī: 100 B.C. to 1900 A.D.* Honolulu: The Queen Emma Foundation, 1995. Presents several legends (57–58); see also "The End of Heʻe Nalu" (138–139).

Kenn, Charles. Unpublished papers in the Bishop Museum Archives. Kenn organized many notes and references for a project entitled "The Surf Rider" that includes reference to legends and myths.

Knudsen, Erik A. *Teller of Hawaiian Tales*. Honolulu: W. H. Male, 1945. "Little Yellow Shark" (13–15) offers another version of Ka-ehu.

Paki, Pilahi. *Legends of Hawaii: Oahu's Yesterday*. Honolulu: Victorian Pub., 1972. Version of Kahikilani and the Bird Maiden (54–57).

Pukui, Mary Kawena. "Songs (*Meles*) of Old Kaʻu, Hawaii." *Journal of American Folklore* 62, no. 245 (1949): 247–258. The surf chant of Naihe.

———. *Pikoi and Other Legends of the Islands of Hawaii*. Honolulu: Kamehameha, 1949. Tales retold by Caroline Curtis; includes "The Swing," which tells of the surfer Hiku. See also Westervelt (1906).

———, and Alfons L. Korn, eds. and trans. *The Echo of Our Song: Chants & Poems of the Hawaiians*. Honolulu: University of Hawaiʻi Press, 1973. An updated version of the Naihe chant.

———, et al. *Place Names of Hawaii*. Rev. ed. Honolulu: University of Hawaiʻi Press, 1974.

———, trans. *Ōlelo Noʻeau: Hawaiian Proverbs & Poetical Sayings*. Honolulu: Bishop Museum, Special Publication 71, 1983.

———, trans., "He Inoa no Naihe" [Name chant for Naihe]. Bernice P. Bishop Museum Archives. Hawaiian Ethnological Notes (HEN) III (88–122). English translation for Parts I–VI (102–122); Hawaiian text for Part III (87–91).

Raphaelson, Rayna. *The Kamehameha Highway: 80 Miles of Romance*. Honolulu: Pery M. Pond, 1929? "A Lover in Stone" (42–44) offers another version of Kahikilani.

Rice, William Hyde. *Hawaiian Legends*. Honolulu: Bernice P. Bishop Museum, Bulletin 29, 1923. "Paakaa and His Son Ku-a-paakaa." See also Thrum (1923).

Tava, Rerioterai, and Moses K. Keale Sr. *Niihau: The Traditions of a Hawai-*

ian Island. Honolulu: Mutual, 1989. Presents story of the surfer Puuone and "The Surf Club Song" (38–41).

Taylor, Clarice B. "Faithless Lover Is Turned to Stone." *Honolulu Star Bulletin*, Wednesday, November 26, 1958, 20. Story of Kahikalani and the Bird Maiden of Pau-malū.

Thrum, Thomas G. *Hawaiian Almanac and Annual for 1907.* "Kaililauokekoa" (83–92). Tale of the surfrider daughter of Kaua'i chief Moikeha and his wife Hooipoikamalanai.

———. *Hawaiian Folk Tales: A Collection of Native Legends.* Chicago: A. C. McClurg & Co., 1907. Another version of Manoan Princess Kahalaopuna who dies from a shark attack while surfriding (118–132).

———. *More Hawaiian Folk Tales: A Collection of Native Legends and Traditions.* Chicago: A. C. McClurg & Co., 1923. Hooipo and Hinauu fall in love with Moikeha as he surfs (21); surf exploits of Kuanu'uanu (53–54); Koleaamoku falls in love with Waikīkī surfer Kihaapiilani (73–76); Lono and his wife, Kaikilani, surf at Kealakekua (111); the *mo'o* woman Kalamainu lures the O'ahu chief Puna to her cave (185-196); and a longer version of Ka-ehu at Waikīkī (293–306). Thrum notes that the Ka-ehu story is a "Condensed translation" from the Hawaiian-language newspaper *Au Okoa* (November 24, 1870)—this is Kamakau's work.

Twombly, Alexander Stevenson. *Kelea: The Surf Rider.* New York: Fords, Howard, & Hulbert, 1900. Book-length romance of the Kelea story; Chapter two recounts information that appeared in Kalākaua's "Kelea, The Surf-Rider of Maui."

Underhill, Julia Adams. "Pele Claims Her Own—A Dream." *Paradise of the Pacific* 39, no. 10 (October 1926): 5–8. Pele falls in love with a youth as he surfs with his lover, Kealoha.

Westervelt, W. D. "The Bride from the Under World." *Paradise of the Pacific* 19, no. 12 (December 1906): 10–18. Hiku and his sister, Kewalu, surf and fall in love.

———. "Pikoi the Rat-Killer of Manoa." *Paradise of the Pacific* 23 (October 1910): 13–18.

———. "Mamala, The Surf Rider." *The Friend* 68, no. 11 (November 1910): 15–16.

———. "A Shark Punished at Waikiki." *The Friend* 71 (January 1913): 7. Story of Ka-ehu.

———. "A Surfing Legend." *Mid-Pacific Magazine* 6 (September 1913): 249–251. Another version of Mamala.

———. *Legends of Old Honolulu*. Boston, 1915. Separately published tales of Mamala, Ka-ehu, and Pikoi (noted above) reappear in this collection.

———. *Legends of Gods and Ghosts*. Boston: Geo. H. Ellis Co., 1915. "How Milu Became King of the Ghosts" recounts the death of Milu, chief of Waipio, while surfriding (97–98); "Puna and the Dragon" offers another version of Kiha-wahine luring Puna to her cave (152–153); "Ke-au-nini" references the surfriding of Hiilei (170), Kawelo-hea (191), and Lei-ma-kani (200). For Keaunini, see also Beckwith (513).

———. *Hawaiian Historical Legends.* New York: Fleming H. Revell Co., 1923. "The Sons of Kii" presents the Tahitian chief Vai-ta-piha in a surf contest (57–60).

Wichman, Frederick B. *Pele Mā: Legends of Pele from Kauaʻi.* Honolulu: Bamboo Ridge Press, 2001. "Surfing at Wai-lua."

Explorers, Missionaries, and Travelers (1769–1906)

The following primary works (and editions of primary works) that reference surfriding cover the period between Joseph Banks's journal entry in Tahiti (on Captain Cook's first voyage to the Pacific) and the revival of surfriding at Waikīkī. Arrival and departure dates have been noted when appropriate (and possible) to help establish a chronology of surfriding. Several texts by native Hawaiians also appear in this section.

Alexander, Sir James Edward. *Narrative of a Voyage of observation among the colonies of Western Africa, in the flag-ship Thalia; and of a campaign in the Kaffir-land, on the staff of the commander-in-chief in 1835.* London: H. Colburn, 1837. The earliest known reference to surfriding in Africa: "From the beach, meanwhile, might be seen boys swimming into the sea, with light boards under their stomachs. They waited for a surf, and then came rolling in like a cloud on the top of it. But I was told that sharks occasionally dart in behind the rocks, and 'yam' them" (1:192).

Andrews, Lorrin. *A Dictionary of the Hawaiian Language.* Honolulu: Henry M. Whitney, 1865. A seminal dictionary for Hawaiian language that includes two entries for "Hee-na-lu": "To slide down the surf; to play on the surf-board" and "A playing on the surf, a pastime among the ancients; the name of their play on the surf" (154).

Ballantyne, R. M. *The Coral Island: A Tale of the Pacific Ocean.* London: T. Nelson & Sons, 1858. Chapter twenty-five includes a fictionalized account of surfriding likely drawn from Ellis's *Polynesian Researches.*

Bates, G. W. *Sandwich Island Notes. By a Haole.* New York: Harper & Brothers, 1854. Includes Bates's often-cited comment on surfriding "rapidly passing out of existence" and a brief description of the sport (288–289). Bates arrived in the Islands in 1853 working for a San Francisco newspaper.

Beaglehole, J. C., ed. *The Journals of Captain James Cook on his Voyages of Discovery.* 4 vols. Cambridge: Cambridge University Press, 1955–1967. Includes Beaglehole's comments on Anderson (vol. 1: cxc–cxcv), the journal entry of James King (vol. 3, pt. 1: 628), the journal entry of Charles Clerke (vol. 3, pt. 2: 1321), and the journal entry of David Samwell (vol. 3, pt. 2: 1164–1165).

Bennett, C. C. *Honolulu Directory and Historical Sketch of the Hawaiian or Sandwich Islands.* Honolulu: C. C. Bennett, 1869. Includes Fornander's letter regarding Holua and the tidal wave in 1868 (50–51) and a comment on surfriding "long since fallen into disuse" (55).

Bingham, Hiram. "Mission at the Sandwich Islands." *The Missionary Herald* 18, no. 8 (August 1822). The first description of Hawaiian surfriding by a missionary in 1821. Reappears with slight alterations in Bingham's *A Residence of Twenty-one Years in the Sandwich Islands* (New York: Converse, 1847).

———. "Sandwich Islands." *The Missionary Herald* 19, no. 4 (April 1923). Describes Ka'ahumanu "playing in the surf" with attendants on the Sabbath (100).

Bird, Isabella L. *The Hawaiian Archipelago: Six Months among the Palm Groves, Coral Reefs and Volcanoes of the Sandwich Islands.* London: John Murray, 1875. Bird's description of surfriding appears in letter VII (106–109). This letter also appears in the reprint of Bird's original letters collected in *Letters to Henrietta/Isabella Bird* (London: John Murray, 2002) but it does not include the surfriding material. The editor, Kay Chubbuck, indicates in personal correspondence that Bird typically added material to her letters before publication. Either pages from the original letter VII that included the surfriding description have been lost, or (more likely) Bird—like Mark Twain—added the description after having left the Islands.

Bishop, Sereno Edwards. *Reminiscences of Old Hawaii.* Honolulu: Hawaiian Gazette, 1916. Includes "Surf-Riding at Kailua" from Bishop's childhood in the late 1830s (17–18). Beyond missionary influence, Bishop cites another reason for the decline of surfriding: "The natives took to horseback riding with great facility and it is true that as the horses became cheap and everyone had his horse, the people gave up surf riding, as though their idea was to have rapid progress and they abandoned the older method for the newer one. The sport of surf riding was even disappearing when I returned, though some of the outlying islands had a great deal of it" (60–61). His description of surfriding at Kailua first appeared as "Old Memories of Kailua" in *The Friend* 58, no. 12 (December 1900): 102.

Bligh, William. *Log of the Bounty.* Ed. Owen Rutter. London: Golden Cockerel Press, 1937. Bligh's log in Tahiti from November 28, 1788 (1:408–409).

Bloxam, Andrew. *Diary of Andrew Bloxam.* Honolulu: Bernice P. Bishop Museum Special Publication 10, 1925. Bloxam was a naturalist on the *Blonde,* which returned the bodies of Kamehameha II and his queen, Kamamalu, after they had contracted measles while visiting England in 1824. Touring Waikīkī on May 19, 1825, Bloxam noted: "I observed the natives diverting themselves in the heavy surf with their swimming boards, or 'epappa's' as they are called" (46). Bloxam had also noted surfboards hanging inside the walls on one of the dwellings (26).

Bolton, H. Carrington. "Some Hawaiian Pastimes." *The Journal of American Folk-Lore* 4, no. 12 (January–March 1891): 21–26. His experience surf-riding at Niʻihau (23–24).

Byron, George Anson. *Voyage of the H.M.S. Blonde to the Sandwich Islands, in the Years 1824–1825.* London: John Murray, 1826. Byron described the governor of Oʻahu's wife, Liliah, as having been accounted in her youth "one of the best swimmers in the Island, and was particularly dexterous in launching her float-board through the heaviest surf, yet now her sense of modesty, awakened by her residence in a civilized country, induced her to withdraw into her cabin at the sight of her almost naked countrymen" (97).

Campbell, Lord George. *Log Letters from "The Challenger."* London: Macmillan, 1876. The *Challenger* visited the Islands for two weeks in summer, 1875. Campbell noted that a visitor drowned while a group tried surf-riding at Hilo (368–369); also mentioned here is the story of a native (Holua) riding a tidal wave.

Caton, John D. *Miscellanies.* Boston: Houghton, Osgood and Co., 1880. Caton visited the Islands in 1877–1878; observations on "Surf Bathing at Hilo" (242–245).

Chaney, George Leonard. *"Aloha!" A Hawaiian Salutation.* Boston: Roberts Brothers, 1888. A minister, Chaney arrived in Honolulu in January 1876 and departed in April. He described "an exhibition of surf bathing" at Hilo with natives riding "flat upon their faces" and also a man "standing upright on the tottering chip beneath him" (174–178).

Cheever, Henry T. *The Island World of the Pacific.* New York: Harper & Brothers, 1851. Short reference to natives surfriding while Cheever visited the island of Hawaiʻi in 1843 (164).

———. *Life in the Sandwich Islands: or, The Heart of the Pacific, as it was and is.* New York: A. S. Barnes & Co., 1851. Cheever's description of surfriding at Lahaina on Maui in 1843 (66–68); this page also has a plate inserted: "Hawaiian Sport of Surf Playing."

Colton, Walter. *Deck and Port: Incidents of a Cruise in the U.S. Frigate* Congress *to California.* New York: A. S. Barnes, 1850. A chaplain on the U.S. *Congress,* Colton visited Honolulu for two weeks in June 1846, where he noted an experience that would be repeated by the likes of Mark Twain: "Nothing here has amused me more than the surf-sports of the young chiefs . . . A young American, who was among them, not liking to be outdone in a sport which seemed so simple, thought he would try the board and billow. He ventured out a short distance, watched his opportunity, and, as the roller came, jumped upon his plank, was capsized, and hove, half strangled on the beach" (352–353). This is the period (June 1846) when Chester S. Lyman described his surfriding experience at Waikīkī (see Lyman 1924).

Cook, James. *A Voyage to the Pacific Ocean* . . . 3 vols. London: G. Nicholl and

T. Cadell, 1784. The official version of the discovery of the Hawaiian Islands, including William Anderson's observation of Tahitian canoe surfing (vol. 2, 150–151) and the seminal account of Hawaiian surfriding (vol. 3, 145–147).

Dibble, Sheldon. *A History of the Sandwich Islands.* Honolulu: T. G. Thrum, 1909. An important early history for its reliance on native sources, first published in 1843; a short description of "Playing on the surf board" (99).

Ellis, W. *An Authentic Narrative of a Voyage Performed by Captain Cook and Captain Clerke in His Majesty's Ships* Resolution *and* Discovery *During the Years 1776, 1777, 1778, 1779, and 1780.* 2 vols. Amsterdam: N. Israel, 1969. Originally published in 1782; Ellis's account preceded the official account of Cook's voyage by two years. Ellis refers to surfboards as "sharkboards" (178–179).

Ellis, William. *Narrative of a Tour Through Hawaii* . . . . London: Fisher, Son, and P. Jackson, 1826. The most influential description of surfriding in the nineteenth century from Ellis's visit to the island of Hawai'i in 1823 (344–348); an edition appeared in Boston in 1825 that omitted the description of surfriding.

———. *Polynesian Researches during a Residence of Nearly Six Years in the South Sea Islands.* 2 vols. London: Dawsons of Pall Mall, 1967. Originally published in 1829; Ellis added descriptions of *faahee,* or Tahitian surfriding, to his Hawaiian material (304–305).

Emerson, N. B. "Causes of Decline of Ancient Hawaiian Sports." *The Friend* 50, no. 8 (August 1892): 57–60.

Gilbert, George. *Captain Cook's Final Voyage: The Journal of Midshipman George Gilbert.* Ed. Christine Holmes. Honolulu: University of Hawai'i Press, 1982. Gilbert described a surfboard as "nearly in the form of a blade of an oar" (127).

Gordon Cumming, C. F. *Fire Fountains: The Kingdom of Hawaii, its Volcanoes, and the History of its Missions.* 2 vols. Edinburgh and London: William Blackwood and Sons, 1883. A Victorian travel writer, Constance Gordon Cumming visited Hawai'i in October and November 1879; her journal entry for October 20 described surfriding at Hilo.

Hall, Douglas B., and Lord Albert Osborne. *Sunshine and Surf: A Year's Wanderings in the South Seas.* London: Adam and Charles Black, 1901. Brief description of natives surfriding at night at Waikīkī (312–313).

Hawkesworth, John, ed. *An account of the voyages undertaken by the order of His present Majesty for making discoveries in the Southern Hemisphere.* . . . London: Printed for W. Strahan and T. Cadell, 1773. Contains Hawkesworth's edited version of Joseph Banks's journal. Banks's original entry can be accessed at The South Seas Web site: http://southseas.nla. gov.au/journals/hv23/135.html.

Hill, Samuel S. *Travels.* London: Chapman and Hall, 1856. Hill, a gentleman traveler, arrived in the Islands in December 1848 and departed in May of the following year; includes his lengthy description of villagers surf-riding at Keauhua, Hawai'i (196–203).

History of the Otaheitean Islands. Edinburgh: Ogle and Aikman, 1800. Re-prints descriptions of Tahitian surfriding (103–105) from Wilson (1968) and Hawaiian surfriding (232–233) from Cook (1784). The former source derived from information found in the journals of James Morrison (see Morrison 1935).

'Ī'ī, John Papa. *Fragments of Hawaiian History.* Trans. Mary K. Pukui; ed. Dorothy B. Barrère. Honolulu: Bishop Museum Press, 1959. Collected works that appeared originally in the Hawaiian-language newspaper *Kuokoa* from 1866 to 1870; includes the excerpt for this anthology (133–137) and references to surfriding for Kamehameha (6–8) and Ka'ahumanu (51).

Iselin, Isaac. *Journal of a Trading Voyage around the World: 1805–1808.* New York: Press of Mcilroy & Emmet, 1891. In a journal entry for June 13, 1807, Iselin noted seeing natives "amuse themselves in their 'surf boards'" at Kealakekua Bay (71).

Jarves, James Jackson. *History of the Hawaiian Islands.* Honolulu: Charles Edwin Hitchcock, 1847. First published in 1843; short description of surfriding (37) possibly drawn from Ellis.

———. *Kiana: A Tradition of Hawaii.* Boston: James Munroe, 1857. The *Hawaiian National Bibliography* indicates this work is "generally ac-knowledged as the first full-length piece of fiction with a Hawaiian set-ting" (entry for 1857; 2219) and notes that an earlier version appeared in the *Polynesian* in 1841 while Jarves was editor; includes a scene of natives "sporting in the surf" (86–87).

Keauokalani, Kepelino. *Kepelino's Traditions of Hawaii.* Trans. Martha Beck-with. Honolulu: Bernice P. Bishop Museum, 1932. Kepelino (born c. 1830—his mother was a daughter of Kamehameha I) offers an account of traditions from pre-contact Hawai'i (through the lens of an early con-vert to Catholicism) and a well-known observation of surfriding (94).

Korn, Alfons L. *The Victorian Visitors.* Honolulu: University of Hawai'i Press, 1958. Includes Sophia Cracroft's references to surfriding in 1861 at Kailua, Hawai'i (69–70, 73).

Ledyard, John. *John Ledyard's Journal of Captain Cook's Last Voyage.* Ed. James Kenneth Munford. Corvallis: Oregon State University Press, c. 1963. First published in 1783; Ledyard offered the first American ac-count of Cook's final voyage, describing native Hawaiians using "floats" to meet Cook in Kealakekua Bay on January 17, 1779 (102–103).

Lyman, Albert. *Journal of a Voyage to California and Life in the Gold Mines and also a Voyage from California to the Sandwich Islands.* Hartford, Conn.: E. T. Pease, 1852. Lyman spent a month in Hawai'i in early 1850 and recorded a description of surfriding (179–180).

Lyman, Chester S. *Around the Horn to the Sandwich Islands and California, 1845–1850*. Ed. Frederick J. Teggart. New Haven: Yale University Press, 1924. Details Lyman's surfriding at Waikīkī in June 1846 (73).

Malo, David. *Hawaiian Antiquities*. Trans. Nathanial B. Emerson. Honolulu: Bishop Museum Press, 1971. First published in English in 1898; Malo's work appeared originally in *Ka Hae Hawaii* in 1858–1859 and formed an important part of *Ka Mooolelo Hawaii* (1838) and *History of the Sandwich Islands* (1843) published under the direction of Sheldon Dibble, Malo's teacher at Lahainaluna, Maui. Malo described surfboards, competition, and gambling in Chapter 48 (223–224); includes Emerson's footnotes on surfriding. See also Malcolm Naea Chun's new translation of Malo: *Ka moolelo Hawaii: Hawaiian Traditions* (Honolulu: First People's Press, c. 1996); Chun translates a passage that Emerson leaves in the original Hawaiian (282).

Mathison, Gilbert Farquhar, Esq. *Narrative of a Visit to Brazil, Chile, Peru, and the Sandwich Islands, during the years 1821 and 1822. . . .* London: Printed for Charles Knight, 1825. Mathison described his visit to Waikīkī: "Women and children were amusing themselves in the surf, and apparently giving way to unrestrained exuberance of animal spirits" (375). He also described Ka'ahumanu surfriding on the Sabbath, as noted in Bingham's article for the *Missionary Herald* of 1923 (428).

Melville, Herman. *Mardi and a Voyage Thither*. Evanston and Chicago: Northwestern University Press and The Newberry Library: 1970. First published in 1849; the surfriding scene appears in "Rare Sport at Ohonoo" (chapter 90). See editorial appendix for references to Ellis (672); also see additional articles on Melville and the South Seas (680).

Meyen, Dr. F. J. F. *A Botanist's Visit to Oahu in 1831*. Trans. Astrid Jackson; ed. Marty Anne Pultz. Kailua, Hawai'i: Press Pacifica, LTD., 1981. First published in Berlin in 1834; Prussian doctor spent a week on O'ahu and described natives on surfboards at Waikīkī (54).

Moerenhout, J. A. *Travels to the Islands of the Pacific Ocean*. Trans. Arthur R. Borden Jr. Lanham, Md.: University Press of America, 1993. First published in 1837 in French; Moerenhout offered a valuable update on the state of surfriding in Tahiti with natives riding on planks "three to four feet long" (359–360).

Morrison, James. *Journal of James Morrison, Boatswain's Mate of the* Bounty. *. . .* Ed. Owen Rutter. London: Golden Cockerel Press, 1935. First account of Tahitian surfriding from 1778–1779 (226–227). An online version of the journal can be accessed at http://southseas.nla.gov.au/journals/morrison/101.html.

Musick, John R. *Hawaii . . . Our New Possessions*. New York and London: Funk & Wagnalls, 1898. Musick arrived in Honolulu in November 1895 and remained until February 1896. Perhaps influencing Jack London, Musick referred to surfriding as "a royal sport" in a brief description and concluded: "Tho not witnessed so frequently as formerly, surf-riding is still a popular sport on some of the islands" (73); also a drawing: "Native Surf Rider" (72).

Nordhoff, Charles. "Hawaii-Nei" Part I. *Harper's New Monthly Magazine* 47, no. 279-26 (1873): 402. Nordhoff arrived in Honolulu in February 1873 and penned a lengthy description of surfriding at Hilo, Hawai'i; includes a sketch by William Bainbridge. This material was republished in *Northern California, Oregon, and the Sandwich Islands* (New York: Harper & Brothers, 1874), 51–52.

Olmstead, Francis Allyn. *Incidents of a Whaling Voyage.* Rutland, Vt.: Charles E. Tuttle, 1969. First published in 1841; the author described surfriding that he witnessed on the island of Hawai'i in June 1840 (the same year Hiram Bingham left the Islands; Olmstead in fact left for New York on the same ship) and provided an early sketch of surfriders in action: "Sandwich Islanders playing in the surf" (222–223).

Owen, Jean A. *The Story of Hawaii.* London: Harper & Brothers, 1898. References to surfriding include a quotation from an anonymous writer (5–6) and the following comments: "Surf-riding on boards is still much practiced" (81); "The sea being on every hand the boys and girls of Hawaii learn to swim and row, and the island-born foreigners emulate the natives in their surf-board riding, canoeing and fishing by torchlight" (210–211). See entry under A. Tourist (1898) for similar reference to the revival of surfriding during this period.

Perkins, Edward T. *Na Motu: or, Reef-Rovings in the South Seas.* New York: Pudney & Russell, 1854. Perkins arrived in the Islands as a sailor in April 1849 and remained about twenty months. He concluded his trip by surfriding with a group of native children (197).

Ruschenberger, W. S. W. *Narrative of A Voyage Round the World, during the years 1835, 36, and 37.* 2 vols. Folkestone and London: Dawsons of Pall Mall, 1970. First published in 1838; Ruschenberger served as surgeon aboard the U.S. naval ship *Peacock* when it visited Hawai'i in 1837; pp. 373–375 detail his criticism of the Protestant missionaries for suppressing "games" like surfriding.

Smith, J. Tuttle. "The Sandwich Islands" [letter to the editor]. *The Knickerbocker Magazine* 46, no. 2 (August 1855): 151–155. Smith's description of surfriding at Kealakekua Bay included the comment that natives placed "their boards upon the highest wave, and, standing almost erect, they were carried toward the shore with a frightful rapidity, shouting and yelling all the way" (152).

"South Seas: Voyaging and Cross-Cultural Encounters in the Pacific (1760–1800)": http://southseas.nla.gov.au/index.html. An invaluable Web site for the journals of Cook and Banks on Cook's first voyage to the Pacific; includes maps linked to Cook's daily journal entries and many additional resources.

Stewart, C. S. *Journal of a Residence in the Sandwich Islands, during the Years 1823, 1824, and 1825.* . . . Honolulu: University of Hawai'i Press, 1970. Originally published in 1828. A missionary, Stewart was stationed at Lahaina on Maui from 1823 to 1825. In a journal entry for January 24, 1824, Stewart included a lengthy description of surfriding at Lahaina (255–256).

———. *A Visit to the South Seas, in the U.S. Ship* Vincennes, *during the Years 1829 and 1830.* 2 vols. New York: John P. Haven, 1831. This edition included a joint letter from Bingham and other missionaries dated November 22, 1829, that notes: "The slate, the pen, and the needle, have, in many instances, been substituted for the surf-board, the bottle, and the *hula*" (259–260).

Stoddard, C. W. "Kahele." *The Overland Monthly* 10 (July 1873): 238–246. This story was reprinted in *South Sea Idylls* (Boston: James R. Osgood and Company, 1873), 259–282; the English edition of this volume was titled *Summer Cruising in the South Seas* (London: Chatto and Windus, 1874). Stoddard also published *The Island of Tranquil Delights* (Boston: Herbert B. Turner & Co., 1905), where surfriding is briefly referenced (300).

Thrum, Thomas G. *Hawaiian Almanac and Annual for 1882.* Honolulu: Black & Auld, Printers. First published in 1875 and annually thereafter, the *Almanac* provided local information for visitors and inhabitants. Thrum wrote about surfriding in this edition: "Among the various sports and pastimes of the ancient Hawaiians, but few now remain to them, the principal one of which—enjoyed equally, we might say, by spectator and participant—is that of surf-bathing, or more properly speaking, surf-riding. There are a few localities on each of the islands where this sport can be practiced when the weather allows and the surf is at the right height; but of the different locations known to us, Hilo seems to hold the palm. The people of Kauai generally held the credit of excelling in all the sports of the islands. At one time they sent their champion surf-rider to compete with chiefs in the sport at Hawaii, who showed them for the first time man's ability to shoot, or ride, with the surf without a surf-board" (52).

———. *Hawaiian Almanac and Annual for 1896.* Honolulu: Press Publishing, 1896. The anonymous article "Hawaiian Surf Riding" (106–113) along with two sketches.

———. *Hawaiian Almanac and Annual for 1906.* Honolulu: Thos. G. Thrum, 1905. Note on "A surf riding fiesta at Waikiki" being inaugurated (192).

Tourist, A. "Surf Riding." *Paradise of the Pacific* 11, no. 9 (September 1898): 129–130. The author noted: "For years past there has been no place near Honolulu where the conditions were right for surf-board riding, and it became almost a lost art. Up to a few months ago there was only one native known in Honolulu who could ride the surf board standing upon it. But within the past two or three months a sand spit has formed off Waikiki beach right in front of the suburban residence of Colonel George W. Macfarlane, which gives the perfect conditions. Surf-board riding has in consequence been revived, has, in fact, become a fad, and a large number of people, both whites and natives, have become expert in the art" (130). See also *Men of Hawaii*, vol. 4 (Honolulu: The Honolulu Star-Bulletin, 1930), which notes that Clarence William Macfarlane (brother of George W. Macfarlane) is credited "with being the first white man in Honolulu to master the difficult sports of surfboarding and canoeing in outriggers" (333).

Townsend, Ebenezer, Jr./Bruce Cartwright. *Extract form [sic] the diary of Ebenezer Townsend Jr. Supercargo of the Sealing Ship Neptune on her Voyage to the South Pacific & Canton.* Hawaiian Historical Society Reprints (no. 4): 1921/1888. Townsend visited Hawai'i in 1798 and is apparently the first to use the term *surf-board* in print (76).

Turnbull, John. *A Voyage Round the World in the Years 1800, 1801, 1802, 1803, & 1804.* London: A. Maxwell, 1813. Turnbull spent five weeks in Hawai'i in 1802–1803 during a trading voyage; he described natives surfriding on a "thin feather-edged slice of wood" (232).

Turner, George. *Nineteen Years in Polynesia: Missionary Life, Travels, and Researches in the Islands of the Pacific.* London: John Snow, 1861. Turner noted: "Swimming in the surf on a board, and steering little canoes while borne along on the crest of a wave towards the shore, are favourite juvenile sports" among Samoans (217).

Twain, Mark. *Letters from the Sandwich Islands Written for the Sacramento Union by Mark Twain.* Stanford, Calif.: Stanford University Press, 1938. A comparison of Twain's original letters in this volume (composed in 1866) with material later published in *Roughing It* (1872) shows that Twain added his description of surfriding to the latter text before publication. See G. Ezra Dane's introduction in this edition for further information on Twain's editing and additions.

———. *Roughing It.* In *The Works of Mark Twain.* Ed. Paul Baender. Berkeley: University of California Press for The Iowa Center for Textual Studies, 1972. Twain's depiction of his experience surfriding is in Chapter 73 (467–468).

Vancouver, George. *A Voyage of Discovery to the Northern Pacific Ocean and Round the World, 1791–1795.* 4 vols. Ed. W. Kaye Lamb. London: Hakluyt Society, 1984. The reference to Peter Puget's account of Keeaumoku's wife, Namahana, surfriding (January 27, 1794) appears in vol. 3, 1140, n. 1.

Waiamau, J. "Ancient Sports of Hawaii Such As Surfing, Jumping, Sledding, Betting and Boxing." *Kuokoa*, December 23, 1865. The text for this anthology is taken from the English translation (most likely by Mary K.

Pukui) in the Archives of the Bernice P. Bishop Museum (Hawaiian Ethnological Notes Thrum # 49).

Warren, T. Robinson. *Dust and Foam; or Three Oceans and Two Continents.* New York: Charles Scribner, 1859. Arriving in the Islands in 1853, the author described surfriding at Lahaina (245–246) and Honolulu (257), where "Saturday is the grand gala day among the Sandwich Islanders— the missionary sceptre is then sheathed, and the native breathes free again, that the bug-bear taboo is taken off his favorite pastimes. Rushing to the surf, he plunges in, and careless, sports among the mountain combers" (257).

Whitney, Henry A. *The Hawaiian Guide Book.* Rutland, Vt.: Charles E. Tuttle, 1971. First published in 1875; offers a reference to "the daring surf riders" at Lahaina, "many of whom live here and are frequently seen sporting in the breakers" (34).

Wilkes, Charles. *Narrative of the United States Exploring Expedition.* 5 vols. Upper Saddle River, N.J.: Gregg Press, 1970. First published in 1844; vol. 4 (46–47) offers Wilkes's commentary on surfriding and the missionaries. In vol. 5, Wilkes notes for the Kingsmill Islanders: "In swimming in the surf they have a small board like that used by the Sandwich Islanders" (100).

Wilson, James. *A Missionary Voyage to the Southern Pacific Ocean, 1796–1798.* New York: Frederick A. Praeger, 1968. First published in 1799; described the first Protestant mission to the South Pacific and repeated Morris's account of surfriding in Tahiti.

Wise, Henry Augustus. *Los Gringos: or, an Inside View of Mexico and California, with Wanderings in Peru, Chili, and Polynesia.* New York: Baker & Scribner, 1849. Description of Wise's surfriding experience at Lahaina in 1848 (352–324).

Surfriding Revival (1907–1954)

Texts on surfriding have steadily proliferated since the sport's revival in the early twentieth century, especially since the 1960s. Following are the references for texts used in this anthology (Parts III–VI) and other selected works. The most comprehensive bibliography for this period can be found in DeLaVega's *200 Years of Surfing Literature: An Annotated Bibliography* and Daved Marsh's online WaterLog (works cited in the General Reference section, above).

Aeder, Erik. "Indonesia: Just Another Paradise." *Surfer* 20, no. 3 (March 1979): 68–83.

Ball, John H. (Doc). *Early California Surfriders.* Ventura, Calif.: Pacific Publishings, 1995. Reprint of *California Surfriders* (1946). First book devoted to surfriding in California; black-and-white photographs from the 1930s and 1940s.

Barilotti, Steve. "Lost Horizons: Surfer Colonialism in the 21st Century." *The Surfer's Journal* 11, no. 3 (Summer 2002): 88–97.

Blake, Tom. *Hawaiian Surfriders: 1935.* Redondo Beach, Calif.: Mountain and Sea, 1983. First published in 1935 as *Hawaiian Surfboard;* the first comprehensive history of surfriding by one of the sport's preeminent watermen.

Crawford, Leola M. *Seven Weeks in Hawaii.* San Francisco: John J. Newbegin, 1917. Short reference to surfriding at Waikīkī with several photographs (16–19); experiences with Duke Kahanamoku in an outrigger canoe (27–28) and surfriding (63–64); also includes various photographs of Duke.

Dixon, Peter L. *Men and Waves: A Treasury of Surfing.* New York: McCann, Inc., 1966.

Dora, Mickey. "Mickey on Malibu." *Surfer* 8, no. 6 (January 1968): 37–42. For a recent biography of Dora, see C. R. Stecyk III and Drew Kampion, *Dora Lives: The Authorized Story of Miki Dora* (Santa Barbara, Calif.: T. Adler Books, 2005).

Duane, Daniel. *Caught Inside: A Surfer's Year on the California Coast.* New York: North Point Press, 1996.

Farber, Thomas. *On Water.* Hopewell, N.J.: The Ecco Press, 1994. See also thomasfarber.org.

Finnegan, William. "Playing Doc's Games." *The New Yorker,* August 22, Part I: 34–59; August 31, Part II: 39–58 (1992).

Ford, Alexander Hume. "Aquatic Sports." *Paradise of the Pacific* 21, no. 12 (December 1908): 19–20. The first of numerous articles on surfriding by Ford, who helped spark surfriding's revival through his tireless promotions.

———. "Riding the Surf in Hawaii." *Collier's Outdoor America* 42, no. 17 (1909).

———. "Out-Door Allurements." *Hawaiian Almanac and Annual for 1911.* Honolulu: Thos. G. Thrum, 1910, 142–146. Summary of founding of Outrigger Canoe Club at Waikīkī in 1908.

"George Freeth Off To Coast." *The Pacific Commercial Advertiser,* Honolulu, July 3, 1907. Subtitle indicates: "Will Illustrate Hawaiian Surfriding to People in California." Article captures seminal moment in the history of surfriding's revival for California.

Handy, E. S. Craighill, et al. *Ancient Hawaiian Civilization.* Rutland, Vt.: Charles E. Tuttle, 1965. First published in 1933; Kenneth P. Emory's "Sports, Games, and Amusements" appears in Chapter 14; under the section "Surf Riding" the author states: "The art nearly went out of existence between 1860 and 1900" and he cites G. W. Bates's *Sandwich Islands Notes* (1854) about the sport "rapidly passing out of existence." Emory's study became influential for modern histories of the sport.

Hollinger, Kimo. "An Alternate Viewpoint." *Surfer* 16, no. 3 (August–

September 1975): 38–40. See also Hollinger's *Kimo: A Collection of Short Stories*. Honolulu: Anoai Press, 2002.

Houston, James D. *A Native Son of the Golden West*. New York: Dial Press, 1971.

Jarman, Mark. *Questions for Ecclesiastes*. Brownsville, Ore.: Story Line Press, 1997.

Jenkins, Bruce. "Laird Hamilton: 20th Century Man." *The Surfer's Journal* 6, no. 3 (Fall 1997): 84–121.

Katrovas, Richard. *The Book of Complaints*. Pittsburgh: Carnegie-Mellon University Press, 1993. See also Richardkatrovas.com.

Kenn, Charles. Unpublished papers in the Bishop Museum Archives.

Klein, Arthur H., and M. C. Klein, eds. *Surf's Up! An Anthology of Surfing*. Indianapolis: Bobbs-Merrill, 1966.

Kohner, Frederick. *Gidget*. New York: G. P. Putnam's Sons, 1957.

London, Charmian. *Our Hawaii (Islands and Islanders)*. New York: Macmillan, 1922. First published in 1917; reprints Jack London's "My Hawaiian Aloha" (first published in *Cosmopolitan* [September 1916]), which described Alexander Hume Ford's promotion of surfriding (8), Charmian's experience surfriding with Ford and Jack London (93–101) in 1907, and her commentary on differences in surfriding in 1917 ("The newest brood of surf-boarders had learned and put into practice angles never dreamed of a decade earlier") (312). For another reference to surfriding with Jack London in 1907, see Martin Johnson's *Through the South Seas With Jack London*, ed. Ralph D. Harrison (London: T. Werner Laurie, 1913).

London, Jack. "Riding The South Seas Surf." *Woman's Home Companion* 34, no. 10 (October 1907): 9–10. Republished as "A Royal Sport" in *The Cruise of the Snark* (New York: Macmillan, 1911) with minor revisions: London changed the words "black Mercury" to "brown Mercury" (76) and "burnt black by the tropic sun" to "burnt golden and brown by the tropic sun" (77).

———. *The House of Pride and Other Tales of Hawaii*. New York: Grosset & Dunlap, 1914; first published 1912. "Aloha Oe," which includes a fictionalized version of George Freeth, appears in this volume (127–147); it was originally published in *Lady's Realm* (December 1908).

———. *On the Makaloa Mat*. New York: Macmillan, 1919. Reference to surfriding at Waikīkī in "The Kanaka Surf" (194–197).

McCoy, Jack. "'We're Number One'—Interview: Ian Cairns." *Surfer* 17, no. 1 (April–May 1976): 62–65.

Naughton, Kevin, Craig Peterson, and Greg Carpenter. "Centroamerica." *Surfer* 14, no. 3 (August–September 1973): 39–53.

Nicholls, C. P. L. "Lessons in Surfing for Everyman." *Westways* (July 1936): 22–23.

Orlean, Susan. *The Bullfighter Checks Her Makeup: My Encounters with*

Extraordinary People. New York: Random House, c. 2001. "The Maui Surfer Girls" first appeared in *Outside* magazine (1998) as "The Surfer Girls of Maui."

Paoa, Duke. "Riding the Surfboard." *The Mid-Pacific Magazine* 1, no. 1 (January 1911): 2–10. Inaugural issue with lead article attributed to Duke Paoa Kahanamoku but penned by Ford; repeats information found in Thrum's *Hawaiian Almanac and Annual for 1896*, "Hawaiian Surf Riding."

———. "Riding the Surfboard." *The Mid-Pacific Magazine* 1, no. 2 (February 1911): 151–158. Ford recounts his own experience learning to surf at Waikīkī instructed by local children and George Freeth.

Patterson, O. B. *Surf-Riding: Its Thrills and Techniques*. Rutland, Vt.: Charles E. Tuttle, 1960. Part Three presents the stories of Mamala, Kelea, and Umi (119–134) followed by early historical accounts of surfriding (135–146).

Pezman, Steve. "The Cat's Ninth Life." *The Surfer's Journal* 11, no. 2 (Spring 2002): 86–91.

Robbins, Richard L. *Famous Persons We Have Known: Poems*. Spokane: Eastern Washington University Press, 2000. See also english2.mnsu.edu/robbins.

Shacochis, Bob. "Return of the Prodigal Surfer." *Outside* 26, no. 6 (June 2001): 62–63.

Stecyk, C. R., III, and Glen E. Friedman. *Dogtown—The Legend of the Z-Boys*. New York City: Burning Flags Press, 2000. Stecyk's original articles appeared in *Skateboarder* magazine between 1975 and 1979.

"Surf Riding for the Motion Picture Man." *The Mid-Pacific Magazine* 4, no. 3 (September 1912): 276–281. Magazine directed by A. H. Ford; article reviews early filming of surfriding by Thomas Edison's company and a French company, Pathe Frères.

Tabrah, Ruth M. *Niʻihau: The Last Hawaiian Island*. Kailua, Hawaiʻi: Press Pacifica, 1987. Author indicates that visitors to the island of Niʻihau in the 1860s and 1870s enjoyed surfriding with the Sinclair family (115).

Thrum, Thos. G. *Hawaiian Almanac and Annual for 1908*. Honolulu: Thos. G. Thrum, 1907. "Waikiki Surf Riding" gives reference to Alexander Hume Ford, George Freeth, and Jack London's article (112).

Warshaw, Matt, ed. *Zero Break: An Illustrated Collection of Surf Writing, 1777–2004*. Orlando: Harcourt, 2004. See also mattwarshaw.com.

———. "Winterland: Fred Van Dyke and the Blissful, Stressful, Unpredictable Life of the Older Surfer." *The Surfer's Journal* 14, no. 4 (August–September 2005): 46–59.

Weisbecker, Allan C. *In Search of Captain Zero: A Surfer's Road Trip Beyond the End of the Road*. New York: Jeremy P. Tarcher/Putnam, 2001. See also Aweisbecker.com.

Witzig, John. "We're Tops Now." *Surfer* 8, no. 2 (May 1967): 46–52.

Wolfe, Tom. *The Pump House Gang*. New York: Farrar, Straus & Giroux,

1968. First appeared in *New York*, the *World Journal Tribune's* Sunday magazine, as "The Pump House Gang Meets the Black Panthers—or Silver Threads among the Gold in Surf City" (February 13, 1966) and "The Pump House Gang Faces Life" (February 20, 1966).

Zahn, Thomas C. "Surfboarding from Molokai to Waikiki." *Paradise of the Pacific* 66, no. 3 (March 1954): 26–28, 32.

Ancillary Sources

Barr, Pat. *A Curious Life for a Lady: The Story of Isabella Bird.* London: Macmillan, 1970.

Barrère, Dorothy B., et al. *Hula: Historical Perspectives.* Honolulu: Bernice Pauahi Bishop Museum, Pacific Anthropological Records No. 30, 1980.

Bird, Isabella. *Letters to Henrietta.* Ed. Kay Chubbuck. London: John Murray, 2002.

Blair, John. *The Illustrated Discography of Surf Music, 1961–1965.* 3rd ed. Ann Arbor, Mich.: Popular Culture Ink, 1995.

Chun, Malcolm Naea: *Na Kukui Pio 'Ole: The Inextinguishable Torches: The Biographies of Three Early Native Hawaiian Scholars Davida Malo, S.N. Hale'ole and S.M. Kamakau.* Honolulu: First People's Production, 1993.

Colburn, Bolton, et al. *Surf Culture: The Art History of Surfing.* Corte Madera, Calif.: Laguna Art Museum/Gingko Press, 2002.

Daws, Gavan. *Shoal of Time: A History of the Hawaiian Islands.* New York: Macmillan, 1968.

Day, A. Grove. *Books About Hawaii: Fifty Basic Authors.* Honolulu: University of Hawai'i Press, 1977.

Forbes, David W. *Encounters with Paradise: Views of Hawaii and its People, 1778–1941.* Honolulu: Honolulu Academy of Arts, 1992.

Hall, Sandra Kimberly, and Greg Ambrose. *Memories of Duke: The Legend Comes Alive.* Honolulu: The Bess Press, 1995.

Hiroa, Rangi Te (Peter H. Buck). *Explorers of the Pacific: European and American Discoveries in Polynesia.* Honolulu: The Museum, Special Publication 43, 1953.

Kingman, Russ. *Jack London: A Definitive Chronology.* Middletown, Calif.: David Rejt, 1992.

Kirby, David. *Herman Melville.* New York: Continuum, 1993.

Labor, Earle, and Jeanne Campbell Reesman. *Jack London.* Rev. ed. New York: Twayne, 1994.

Lamb, Jonathan, ed., et al. *Exploration & Exchange: A South Seas Anthology, 1680–1900.* Chicago: University of Chicago Press, 2000.

Lears, T. J. *No Place of Grace: Antimodernism and the Transformation of American Culture, 1880–1920.* New York: Pantheon Books, c. 1981.

Leib, Amos P., and A. Grove Day. *Hawaiian Legends in English.* Rev. ed. Honolulu: University of Hawai'i Press, 1979.

Lyncek, Lena, and Gideon Bosker. *The Beach: The History of Paradise on Earth.* New York: Viking, 1998.

Lynch, Gary, and Malcolm Gault-Williams, eds. *Tom Blake: The Uncommon Journey of a Pioneer Waterman.* Corona del Mar: Croul Family Foundation, 2001.

Noble, Valerie. *Hawaiian Prophet: Alexander Hume Ford.* New York: Exposition Press, 1980.

Ragen, Brian Abel. *Tom Wolfe: A Critical Companion.* Westport, Conn.: Greenwood, 2002.

Rutter, Owen, ed. *The Court-Martial of the "Bounty" Mutineers.* Birmingham, Ala.: The Notable Trials Library, 1989.

Scemla, Jean-Jo. *Le Voyage en Polynésie: Anthologie des Voyageurs Occidentaux de Cook à Segalen.* Paris: Robert Laffont, 1994.

Smith, Joel T. "Reinventing The Sport" (Parts I–III). *The Surfer's Journal* 12, nos. 1–3 (2003).

Tatar, Elizabeth. *Nineteenth Century Hawaiian Chant.* Honolulu: Bernice Pauahi Bishop Museum, Pacific Anthropological Records No. 33, 1982.

Timmons, Grady. *Waikiki Beachboy.* Honolulu: Editions Limited, 1989.

Verge, Arthur C. "George Freeth: King of Surfers and California's Forgotten Hero." *California History* (Summer–Fall 2001): 83–105, 153–155.

Weisenburger, Francis P. *Idol of the West: The Fabulous Career of Rollin Mallory Daggett.* Syracuse: Syracuse University Press, 1965.

Young, Nat. *The History of Surfing.* Angourie, N.S.W.: Palm Beach Press, 1983.

About the Editor

PATRICK MOSER received his B.A. from the University of California at Berkeley and his Ph.D. from the University of California at Davis. He is currently Associate Professor of French at Drury University in Springfield, Missouri where he teaches a course on the history and culture of surfing. He has published articles in *Surfer, Surf Life for Women*, and *The Surfer's Journal*. His chapter on the history of surfing appeared in *The Pacific Region* (Greenwood Press, 2005). He collaborated with 1977 world surfing champion Shaun Tomson on *Surfer's Code: 12 Simple Lessons for Riding through Life* (Gibbs Smith, 2006). He most recently received his MFA in fiction writing from the University of Arizona where he completed his first novel, *Surface Lives*. A resource site for instructors is available at: www.drury.edu/pacificpassages.

Production Notes for Moser / *Pacific Passages*

Text design and Composition by Santos Barbasa Jr.
in Galliard Hawaiian with display in Khaki 2.

Printing and binding by Versa Press

Printed on 55# Natural, 360 ppi.